SOME

DESPERATE

GLORY

SOME DESPERATE GLORY

EMILY TESH

TOR PUBLISHING GROUP

NEW YORK

SOME DESPERATE GLORY

Copyright © 2023 by Emily Tesh

All rights reserved.

A Tordotcom Book
Published by Tom Doherty Associates / Tor Publishing Group
120 Broadway
New York, NY 10271

www.tor.com

Tor® is a registered trademark of Macmillan Publishing Group, LLC.

The Library of Congress Cataloging-in-Publication Data
is available upon request.

ISBN 978-1-250-83498-0 (hardcover)
ISBN 978-1-250-83499-7 (ebook)

Our books may be purchased in bulk for promotional, educational,
or business use. Please contact your local bookseller or the
Macmillan Corporate and Premium Sales Department
at 1-800-221-7945, extension 5442, or by email at
MacmillanSpecialMarkets@macmillan.com.

First Edition: 2023

Printed in the United States of America

0 9 8 7 6 5 4 3 2 1

ὡς τρὶς ἂν παρ' ἀσπίδα
στῆναι θέλοιμ' ἂν μᾶλλον ἢ τεκεῖν ἅπαξ.

*I would rather stand three times in the battle line
than give birth to one child.*

—Euripides, *Medea*

PART I

GAEA

Who are the humans?

These misunderstood latecomers to the intergalactic stage have a proud history. It is often forgotten that humanity is one of only three recorded species to discover shadowspace technology entirely without external assistance! No one would accuse the lirem of lacking intelligence, let alone the majo zi, so do not underestimate human intellectual capabilities.

A common misconception is that humans are uncontrollably violent. Humans did evolve as apex predators in a hazardous biosphere and therefore have some remarkable physical capabilities. They are stronger and faster than most people and their adaptable and resilient bodies are capable of surviving devastating injuries. However, the fact that they are capable of violence does not mean that they use it constantly, or for no reason. You should always keep in mind that in the humans' opinion they are being perfectly reasonable when they attack you.

... mostly divided into females and males, though there are substantial minorities which are neither. These categorizations are considered so meaningful that most human languages, including the ubiquitous Terran- or T-standard, embed them constantly in everyday speech. You will find that humans you interact with insist on fitting you into a human sex category, and can be distressed or embarrassed if unable to do so. The fitting is arbitrary: humans tend to regard all lirem as female (using the T-standard pronoun *she*), all zunimmer as male (*he*), and most others as neither (*they* is the commonest pronoun in this case, although others exist). If a human uses a nonsentient pronoun such as *it*, you should assume they are trying to be insulting or even hostile and move on quickly ...

... be aware of local status markers and respectful toward high-status humans. Remember to avoid behavior that reads as threatening, particularly around large young males, who are biologically primed toward overreaction: note that prolonged eye contact is often taken as a challenge. Other humans are usually less volatile, but all are likely to become agitated if they perceive a threat. Whatever you do, do not approach human young without permission from their "family" ...

... will instinctively attempt to defend or to advance the interests of their own tribe by any means possible. Male humans in particular are naturally aggressive and territorial. The popular idea of the violent human maniac is actually a misunderstanding of the way that human physical abilities interact with these instincts. Human histories and media are full of "soldiers" and "heroes"— individuals who perform acts of violence for the sake of their tribe—and astonishingly, these are considered admirable.

—*Humanity*, a popular Majoda guidebook

for the love of whatever god you go for, DO NOT BUY THIS BOOK IF YOU ACTUALLY WANT TO KNOW ANYTHING ABOUT HUMANS. pile of ignorant bioessentialist crap.

—Anonymous review, posted from
a Chrysotheman network

CHAPTER ONE

AGOGE

The sky lit up with green subreal flashes as a Wisdom cruiser dropped out of shadowspace. Kyr took a deep breath, narrowed her eyes to see past the hyperspatial feedback, and watched for the tiny dart coming through in the cruiser's wake, nearly hidden behind its mass and shine. Her battered combat suit wouldn't pick it up yet, but in the visible-light spectrum human eyes were a long-range sensor that the majo always underestimated.

There.

She had two charges of her jump hook left, but using it would set off the majo ship's alarms. Her mask was fractured after the last melee skirmish and held together only by rep gel and hope. If it cracked again, here above the clouds where the battle raged in Earth's outer atmosphere, she would asphyxiate.

A cruiser that size held some seven thousand majo soldiers and countless deadly drones, but it was a distraction. The dart was the real threat. The fist-sized antimatter bomb it carried would go off with enough force to crack the heart of the planet below. The secondary payload would start the crust and core unraveling. If Kyr did not reach the dart first and deactivate it, the living blue curve of the planet below would soon be nothing but a long trail of ice settling into a glittering ring somewhere between Mars and Mercury.

Kyr hesitated, thinking. She had six minutes before the dart's course was irretrievable and the planet was doomed. She could use her jump hook to reach it, alerting the cruiser in the process and leaving herself with majo fightercraft to fend off while she tried to disable the bomb. Or she could attempt stealth. The defense platform she was standing on was littered with the shells of shot-down enemy fighters. Kyr could try to jury-rig one to get it flying again, and sneak past the cruiser toward the deadly sting in its tail. The rest of her unit was gone. The defense platform itself was disabled. If the majo even knew there was still a human soldier here, they would not be paying her the attention due to a threat.

That was their mistake.

While Earth's children live, the enemy shall fear us.

Kyr used her jump hook.

Her suit's built-in alarms screamed at her and the feed in the corner of her vision informed her she was risking permanent neurological damage as she was dragged sideways through shadowspace without any better protection than the cracked combat mask. She gasped, feeling the sensation ghosts of arctic chill and impossible heat blast through her and vanish. Washes of green light flickered around her as she landed on the narrow nose of the dart. She threw herself flat, clinging with her thighs, and started bashing at its covering panel with the hilt of her field knife.

The panel was etched in alien script with a word Kyr knew: *ma-jo*. It was their name for themselves, for their civilization, for their language, and for the source of their power.

It meant "wisdom."

Dark pits opened in the cruiser's underside, and rows of majo fighters buzzed into life in the gloom. The unmanned dart swayed wildly from side to side. Kyr swore triumphantly as the panel came loose and fell away—fifty thousand feet to the ocean below—and used the gun in her free hand to shoot two fighters out of the sky without looking around.

The planet-killing bomb was a coppery sphere. Her breath caught as she stared at it. She didn't have the skills to even open it, let alone disarm it; but the triggering mechanism tucked into its side looked like the diagrams she'd seen. Kyr thought *calm,*

calm, and went to work slowly, using everything she'd been taught about majo engineering.

She almost had it, with forty seconds to spare: and then abruptly a secondary cover panel slammed down over the whole thing, glittering with the greenish light of a shadowspace extrusion, and a voice said, "You act in opposition to the Wisdom. Desist."

"Fuck *you*," said Kyr, getting her knife out again.

"Your actions are unwise," said the dart. "Your actions are unwise. The Wisdom acts for the greater good. Your actions are unwise."

"There's fourteen billion people down there, fuck you," panted Kyr, who had never got this far before, as she bashed at the panel.

But a stabbing pain in her thigh was a shot from a majo fighter that had come up on the blind side of her damaged suit. She lost her grip on the dart and fell and fell and fell, and falling she saw the cruiser pop back out of existence as quickly as it had appeared. The dart aimed itself down toward the blue.

The last thing Kyr saw was the antimatter explosion beginning; the death of her world, just as she had seen it happen hundreds of times before.

The simulation cut out. Kyr sat up slowly on the grey plasteel floor and put her head in her hands. She'd run Doomsday four times today, and now she had the dull headache that happened when you spent too long in the agoge. She worked her jaw a few times as if she could shove the pain out that way, and slowly got to her feet.

"Well done, Valkyr," said Uncle Jole.

He took a halting step toward her. Even with his old war injury slowing him down, Commander Aulus Jole was an impressive-looking man. Like most soldiers of his generation he towered over civilians—he had half a foot on Kyr, who was not short—and was broadly built along with it: evidence of warbreed genetics, of military-grade nanite implants, and of having always had enough to eat as a child. He looked enough like Kyr that he might really have been her uncle. They shared the space-pale skin that was the commonest complexion on Gaea Station, and they both had grey eyes and fair hair—though his was cropped short, while Kyr of course kept hers in a regulation ponytail. On Commander Jole's collar shone twin wing badges: the etched circle of the Earth, for Command, and the lily pin of Hagenen Wing, the elite of the Terran Expeditionary, his old unit.

"Still training in rec hour?" he said. "You're worse than me."

This was a joke: no one was worse than Aulus Jole for spending hours in agoge simulations. Most of these upper-level ones were based on his own experiences from his Hagenen Wing days, when he had been one of the Terran Federation's most successful operatives: infiltrating majo bases, defending civilian installations, commanding troops in open firefights in the final days of the war. And the scenario Kyr had just run, of course. It was Aulus Jole who had stood on a disabled defense platform and watched death come for his world. It was Aulus Jole, newly crippled by majo brightfire, who'd been only a handful of instants too late.

Kyr knew he had tried to kill himself once, because her older sister, Ursa, had been the one who found him. She thought it was probably more than once. She saw the blue planet unraveling in her dreams, and felt it as the void pulling shards of new-forged ice out of her own heart; and she hadn't been there. She hadn't even been born.

"I still failed," Kyr said. "I couldn't do it. I'm sorry."

"We have all failed. But Earth's children endure. And while we live—"

"The enemy shall fear us," finished Kyr along with him.

Jole put his hand on her shoulder, making her startle and look up at him. "I'm proud of you, Kyr," he said. "I don't say that enough. Go find your mess and relax. It's your rec rotation."

Rec rotation was a joke. Kyr knew where the other girls from Sparrow mess were: hand-to-hand practice mats, shooting range, volunteer rotations in Systems or Nursery. Recreation was a waste of time, a luxury that belonged to people who had a planet of their own. For the soldiers of Gaea Station, the last true children of Earth, there was no such thing as rest.

Kyr went anyway, reluctantly. Her head still ached from hours of the agoge. As the chamber closed behind her she saw a glitter in the air as the defense platform reappeared. Jole was running the scenario again.

She had not gone five steps down the grim, ill-lit corridor that led from the agoge rooms back up to Drill when Cleo stepped out of the shadow of one of the other doorways. Here was one of the other Sparrows, probably fresh from running scenarios of her own. Cleo had dark brown skin and tightly curling black hair; since there was no way to make it go into a tidy regulation ponytail, she had special permission to wear it cut short. Like Kyr, she was a warbreed, a child of the genetically enhanced bloodlines of humanity's best soldiers. Her training scores were second only to Kyr's own, and had once been better, before puberty gave Kyr an untouchable advantage in height and strength.

Cleo had been the tallest in their mess when they began their cadet training at age seven, but had never reached the full size her genetics should have given her. She was a brilliant shot and the only girl in their age cohort who could still beat Kyr occasionally in hand-to-hand practice, but she was not up to a Level Twelve agoge scenario like Doomsday—not yet, and probably not ever. They would have their adult assignments before long, and cadet training would no longer be a priority.

She glowered up at Kyr. Her arms were folded. "What did he say to you?"

This again. "Nothing," said Kyr. "He told me *well done*. That's all."

"And what did *you* say?"

"I said thank you," said Kyr.

"What about assignments?"

"What about them?"

"You didn't ask?"

"No, Cleo, I didn't ask," said Kyr, her patience fraying. "He's our commanding officer."

"But he's your uncle, isn't he?" Cleo said. "You could ask. For once you could get something for being special. But you didn't even think of it, did you? You didn't think of the rest of us, because you're the great Valkyr and we're only your mess when it makes you look good."

"Are you *eight*?" Kyr said. "Stop trying to pick a fight with me. Work on yourself if you're jealous. If you want a combat wing assignment, earn it. You could still hit Level Twelve if you tried."

She meant this as encouragement. Cleo took it differently. Her expression went cold, and her dark eyes were full of flat dislike. "You have no clue, Valkyr, do you," she said. "Just no clue at all. Fine. Fuck off, then."

Kyr had nowhere, really, to go. Cadet barracks were for sleeping; no one wasted time in the arcade but weaklings and traitors-in-waiting; and despite everything Kyr had always been taught and everything she knew she owed to her species—as a survivor, as a woman—she always got bored and uncomfortable in Nursery, the one wing that never turned female volunteers away. But Commander Jole's advice to relax had had the edge of a command, and Kyr respected Jole's commands. She walked away from the agoge watching one foot go in front of the other on the chipped plasteel tiling. She put Cleo out of her thoughts—Cleo was increasingly difficult to deal with lately, and Kyr didn't want to think about her—and instead thought of nothing; but that nothing turned again and again into the unraveling death of her planet. She looked up when she heard the tinny music from the arcade. The lights were bright in there. She could see a few people awkwardly hanging around. No one Kyr knew, or wanted to know; no one worth knowing.

Ursa would have told her to be less judgmental, but Ursa's opinion had stopped mattering when Ursa left.

Kyr turned right back around, with sudden decision, and marched herself down through the rock tunnels that riddled the station's heart to Agricole.

Gaea Station was—somehow, just barely—self-sustaining. It was a source of pride and terror to its inhabitants that they lived not on a lifezone planet, where luxuries like *water* and *air* and *food* and *heat* could be relied on, but on and in a rocky planetoid that drifted in four-century sweeps around Persara, their distant blue star. Gaea's water came from an icy asteroid that had been anchored to their little hunk of rock with military-grade cable. Its heat relied on enormous jury-rigged solar reflectors, repurposed from dreadnought-class warships, that Suntracker Wing worked endlessly to defend from debris. Its food and air were the business of Agricole Wing.

Kyr paused when she slipped through the plastic sheeting into the high hall where Gaea's life was sustained. She felt a familiar sting of pride. Gaea might not be beautiful, it might not be rich, but look what humanity could do, even on a dead rock in a worthless system.

Sunlamps poured out yellow-spectrum light on the greedy greenery. Every inch of space was used. Vines were trained around the rungs of the ladders that led from the depths far below to the heights of the rocky ceiling. Condensation dripped down the walls, and mist hung in the air. In among the crammed order of the omnidirectional garden soared great dark shapes that held it all together: the massive trunks of Gaea's private forest, carefully modified trees that processed the station's atmosphere and kept them all from choking to death out here in the depths of dark space.

The trees were precious because they were irreplaceable. The shadow engines at the station core had overloaded fifteen years ago, when Kyr was two years old. Systems had managed to save the station, but sixty-eight humans had died, and the feedback from the interdimensional blast had trashed their delicate gene-tailoring suite. Gaea did not have the resources to repair it. These trees were sterile, and could not now be cloned. They would last a long time. They had to.

Kyr knew what she was looking for here. She went to the nearest ladder and climbed until she reached the shadowy heights of Agricole, where wide green canopies spread. Magnus was there dozing sprawled on a broad branch like a lazy lion. Kyr's twin was even bigger than she was; neither of them was nanite-enhanced, but they had been born before the disaster, back when Nursery was still able to design real warbreeds. They were both based on the same parental cross, the one that had produced Ursa before both their genetic forebears had died. Ursa had already shown signs of being something special, so it had made sense—even though it was against population policy—to create siblings.

And they were something special. Kyr knew this as a fact. They were the best of the best of Earth's warrior children. Kyr was tall and muscular, and to that build Mags had started to add *bulk*, the broad powerful body that frightened the shit out of the majo. Out of the many sentient alien species that made up the so-called majoda, only the spindly zunimmer had a natural height over five and a half feet. Kyr had fought hand-to-hand against eight-foot zunimmer shock troops in the agoge. Their bones were light and brittle, and you could snap their spines easily if you went in at just the right angle. Kyr weighed more than one of them. Mags probably weighed more than *two* of them.

But then Mags was a living propaganda poster for both sides. In the old days you could have slapped a *Strong Together* slogan over him—massive, blond, square-shouldered—and made a recruitment still for the Interstellar Terran Expeditionary. Since Doomsday, human actors who looked like him played villains in majo dramas. Collaborators. Kyr felt disgusted just thinking about it.

It made her voice come out sharp when she said, "What are you doing?"

Mags opened his eyes. "Hi, Kyr."

"Why are you asleep?" demanded Kyr.

"It's rec rotation," said Mags. "Sleep is recreational."

"We can't afford to sleep."

"What's the point of being alive if you can't sleep?"

Something in Kyr bubbled and burst. "The *point*," she snapped, "is that we're *at war* and we're *dying*, that they've taken everything from us and *you* just—"

"Oh, hey, hey, Vallie, hey," said Mags, sitting up from his enormous slouch and before Kyr's eyes transforming back from the unconquerable giant to the soft idiot who'd been a natural victim for bullies when they were still in Nursery. "Don't cry. Why are you crying?"

"I'm not," said Kyr. She sat on the broad branch beside him. The air smelled thick and sweet, and condensation was beading on her arms and face. Agricole felt more alive than anywhere else on Gaea. Mags put his arm round her shoulders. "I nearly beat it," Kyr said. "Uncle Jole's scenario. Doomsday. I nearly beat it. I couldn't do it."

"Oh," said Mags.

"Don't *oh*. It matters. You know it matters. And it's all right for you. You have beaten it."

"Once," said Mags. "And I think he went in and made it harder afterward. You get that it's meant to be unbeatable, right?"

"It was the Wisdom," said Kyr. "I got as far as the dart and then the Wisdom put an extra shield on the bomb and then—"

"Yeah," said Mags. "That's what I mean. It's supposed to be unbeatable because of the Wisdom. Because *they're* unbeatable, with the Wisdom."

"How did you do it?" Kyr demanded. She had never asked. She'd wanted to do it herself first. But she'd been so close. "How did you win?"

Mags took his arm away from around her shoulders, and lay back down on the great branch staring up into the patterns made by sprays of foliage hanging down from above. He said, "Do you know Avi?"

"Who?"

"Avi," said Mags. "Otter mess, cohort above us. Assigned Systems Wing."

Kyr said, "Oh, the queer one?" She had only a vague mental picture of the person Mags was talking about. Short, red hair, a squint. Not a warbreed. Gaea had been founded by survivors of the Terran Expeditionary, but armies were more than just soldiers, and there were the genes of technicians, cleaners, medical staff, administrators in the cadet messes too. Kyr knew how important they were. Genetic variety was vital for a species to survive, and there were already so few true humans left. Without people like—oh, like Lisabel, in her mess, who was a guaranteed Nursery Wing assignment if Kyr had ever seen one, humanity had no future.

"Sure," Mags said. "The queer one."

"What?" said Kyr.

Mags didn't answer.

"What about him?" Kyr said. "How do you know him?"

"Met him in the arcade in rec rotation."

"What were you doing in the arcade?"

"Rest and relaxation?" said Mags. "I find losing really badly at video games relaxing."

"You lose?"

"Everyone loses at something, Vallie."

Kyr, who didn't, gave him a narrow look. Mags was only gazing peacefully up at the tangled plants. There was something coming into flower directly above them, big purple clusters of waxy blossoms. Kyr didn't know the name of the plant. She had no expectation of ever being assigned to Agricole. "So what about Avi, then?"

"Avi," said Magnus, "does not lose at video games. He was beating me. We got talking."

"What is there to talk to someone like that about?" said Kyr. "He's leaving, isn't he?" It was amazing how selfish people could be. Nearly everyone like that she had ever heard about had ended up refusing assignment and leaving Gaea Station, taking themselves over to the majo side, as if having sex that achieved nothing mattered more than saving your entire species or taking vengeance for a murdered world.

Mags said, "I don't know if he's leaving. We'd be sorry to lose him. He's beyond good at what he does."

"Systems?" said Kyr. "It's important, sure—"

"Games," said Mags.

"Oh, come on."

"I'm serious," said Mags. "That's how I beat Doomsday. Avi talked me through it."

"I don't remember ever hearing about him beating a Level Twelve simulation." Kyr would have heard: she tracked the training rankings constantly, for the boys as well as the girls. It was how she knew that there were only a handful of boys (five, exactly five) with better scores than her in her entire age cohort: six of them altogether who regularly trained on Level Twelve, the hardest. There were, obviously, no girls as good as Kyr. Boys had a natural advantage. Mags, the perfect soldier, was one of the five. His scores since his last growth spurt were the best in Gaea's short history.

"Well, we were a team," Mags said. "I went in with an earpiece. He talked to me the whole time. He's not even an agoge designer—" Kyr snorted; of course a nearsighted nineteen-year-old who'd never even cracked the top thirty wasn't allowed anywhere near military training, the heart of Gaea's strength. "No, Vallie, it was incredible. He's the smartest person I've ever met. He watched me run it and fail a few times, and then he said we'd do a serious run while he called the shots, and doing it with him in my ear made Doomsday feel like—I don't know, like having fun. He knew everything that was coming and he knew exactly what I had to do about it. I just followed along. It was magic."

"So you cheated," said Kyr.

"It wasn't official," Mags said. "It was a rec hour thing. It didn't go in my scores." Mags knew how serious training scores were.

"It was all over the station," said Kyr. "Everyone knew you'd beaten Doomsday." *Magnus could have saved our world* was how people had said it. *Magnus* could. Kyr had put every free minute into the Doomsday scenario since she'd heard. And now it turned out the whole thing was just fake, some arcade-haunting nobody taking advantage of Mags the way people always seemed to, treating the agoge like a game.

"It was just a thing," Mags said. "Avi wanted to see if we could do it." He propped himself up on his elbow to meet Kyr's eyes and said more urgently, "But you see what I mean, right? We shouldn't want to lose someone like him."

"Because he's a cheat?" said Kyr.

"*They* cheat, don't they?" Mags said. "The Wisdom cheats. Why shouldn't we have cheats of our own? And anyway it's not cheating to have someone else giving orders in agoge, we do that in tactical exercises, that's normal. Avi's just really smart. I think they ought to tap him for Command."

"Of course you do," said Kyr, but she couldn't help it, she smiled. Mags was just like this, he had this absurd soft spot for lost causes. "Okay, fine, it's nice that you're being friendly. Someone like that probably doesn't have a lot of friends, right? Just don't get too upset when he leaves."

Mags lay back down. A purple flower had come loose from the waxy tangle above and drifted down onto the branch. He picked it up and with great care balanced it on his forehead, not looking at Kyr the whole time. "I don't want him to leave," he said.

"People leave," said Kyr. "When they're not tough enough or committed enough or honorable enough. Ursa left."

Mags made the same pinched face he always made whenever someone mentioned their older sister. "Yeah," he said. "I guess she did."

CHAPTER TWO

SPARROW

Kyr was so used to living by the rhythm of Gaea Station's eight-hour shifts that she was never late for anything. Ten minutes before the shift bells she had already swung herself down from the hidden treetops of Agricole. Mags refused to move. "I'll go when the bell goes," he said. "Rec rotation's a full shift. Five-minute rule."

Five minutes was how long you had between rotation change and a black mark. Kyr had received exactly two black marks in her life, both when she was seven, her first year out of Nursery: the best record in her mess. Mags's record was nearly as good despite his cavalier attitude. Kyr knew he and some of the other boys in Coyote mess had an ongoing competition to see how close they could get to four minutes fifty-nine exactly at rotation change. It was hardest going from Suntracker to Drill, but you could do it by cutting through the station core with a grapple.

Kyr could do it in four fifty-five.

Not that she would. She'd just wanted to prove to herself that she was as fast as any of the Coyotes.

Kyr's mess, Sparrow, had had Drill before rec, so they'd be eating and then into an Oikos quarter-shift before lights-out. Kyr jogged through the rock tunnels around Agricole and dropped down two levels past Drill in order to reach the plasteel-tiled corridors of the Oikos level at the bottom of the station. This rotation was normally dull—repairs, cleaning, sewing. When Kyr arrived at the kitchens the mess before her was just going off duty: they were Blackbird, a gaggle of twelve-year-old girls who were giggling and splashing each other with water from their mop bucket. Kyr could see that they hadn't finished cleaning. The black dust of the planetoid that got everywhere on Gaea, even tiled areas like this, was drawn in soggy lines across the floor. Kyr walked up to the juniors and folded her arms.

The giggling stopped.

"Tell me why we need water," said Kyr. She was not angry, exactly. There was no point getting angry with idiots. She was annoyed, because cadets as old as the Blackbirds should know better. And she was enjoying, as she usually did, being in the right.

Silence.

"You," Kyr said, picking out the small one who'd been giggling loudest. "Tell me."

"Um, to drink, Valkyr," said the girl. Kyr felt a sting of gratification that the girl knew her name. "And to wash, and to cook, and to clean."

"To live," Kyr said. She raised her eyebrows. The people of Gaea should know their duty. It was Kyr's duty—and her pleasure—to make sure that juniors like these behaved themselves.

"To live," the Blackbirds echoed in ragged chorus.

"So why were you playing with it?" Kyr said. She pointed at a damp patch underfoot. The precious wetness was already seeping away between the tiles. Whoever had worked on these kitchens had done their best, probably, with materials never meant to build a space station; there were wide gaps between the tiles, grout flaking, bare black rock underneath. "Drink that."

"It's got soap in—"

"*Drink it.*"

The girl looked at her mess for support, but they all drew away. Then she looked up at Kyr pathetically, wet-eyed. Kyr frowned. Few things annoyed her more than someone trying to play on other people's feelings. Feelings were not important; using them to manipulate your way out of a deserved dressing-down was shameful. "Do you think crying would save you from the majo?" she said. "I'm waiting."

The Blackbird's tears spilled over, but she had the sense not to wail. She got down on her knees and licked the damp patch of tiles. It was mostly damp black dust now. She looked up at Kyr with a black smear across her chin. Kyr could see her trying not to grimace at the taste.

Kyr waited grimly.

The Blackbird bent and licked the floor again.

"Is it good to drink?" Kyr said.

"No, Valkyr," said the girl. The black smear was over half her face now.

"Is it going to *rain* here tomorrow?"

"No, Valkyr."

Kyr said, "Take a black mark." Seniors had the right to hand them out to younger messes. "And finish putting all this away."

The shift bells rang as she was speaking. Blackbird all looked at each other. They had five minutes. Kyr watched them without pity. If they were smart, they would leave one person to clean up for all of them; that way their mess would get fewer punctuality black marks. The person who was *really* late would work a punishment shift instead of their next rec rotation, but their mess wouldn't suffer. And next time they'd all know not to waste water doing something as stupid as playing.

"Go on," said the little one Kyr had forced to lick the dust. She was still in tears, but her voice was steady. Kyr respected her for it. "I'll do it."

The rest of Blackbird scattered and fled past the tall figures of Sparrow, who were coming in as the last shift bells died away. Lisabel—the only one of Kyr's messmates who would pity idiot juniors—gave the remaining one a sympathetic look. Kyr pretended not to see it, because she was very fond of Lisabel.

There were seven of them in Sparrow: Cleo and Jeanne, Zenobia and Victoria and Artemisia, Lisabel—whose proper name was Isabella, after a warrior queen from history—and Kyr. They were the only girls' mess in their age cohort. There were Coyote and Cat for the boys. Sparrow's scores were better than Cat's, largely because of Kyr. Kyr was proud of that. There was no beating Coyote, who were all warbreeds. Only Kyr and Jeanne and Cleo came from warbreed bloodlines in Sparrow. Cleo despite being undersized was a mean, focused, aggressive fighter. Jeanne was six foot one, red-haired and freckled, lean and deadly, utterly and unflappably calm. In the last two months she had moved up to running occasional Level Twelve scenarios along with Kyr, who had been working on them for nearly a year.

The three of them, Kyr thought, were near-certainties for combat wing assignments, despite being girls. Of the other Sparrows—she had worked hard with them, pushing them to their limits, making them the best they could be. They were better than any other girls' mess. She thought that Arti—not a warbreed, but tough and hardworking and surprisingly broad-shouldered for a baseline human woman—had a decent chance of making combat too.

Cleo's worrying about assignments made no sense to Kyr. Command had their training scores, their aptitudes, their ten years as cadets. Command knew what they were worth. Vic was small and jumpy, but she was clever; she and her great obsession with solar sails belonged in Suntracker. Lisabel—who was beautiful, with blue eyes and lustrous dark hair, and who was also enormously softhearted—should go to Nursery. And Zenobia with her sharp features and bland expression and placid practicality was meant for Oikos. It was all obvious.

And they were all of them Kyr's.

"Where's Jeanne?" she said, when they'd finished cooking together and sat down to eat. The five-minute grace period was long past.

The others exchanged looks.

"She got assigned," said Cleo at last. "Halfway through rec." She seemed to have forgotten their weird little confrontation outside the agoge. Her eyes were focused on Kyr's face, very intent, as if she was looking for something, or perhaps trying to tell her something. Kyr wished she wouldn't be so weird.

And then she registered what had actually been said. "Really?" she asked. Suddenly Commander Jole in the agoge telling her he was proud felt like it had another meaning. He would have just come from the Command meeting. Ten years of training for *this*. All Kyr wanted from her life was the chance to serve humanity. "What wing?"

"Ferox," said Cleo, in that same intent way. The other Sparrows were silent.

Kyr said, *"Yes."* She couldn't control her grin. The combat wings were where you got respect and luxury allowances and the chance to advance in rank. It was a fantastic assignment, worthy of Jeanne's training scores. It was a good sign for Cleo, too. And for Kyr herself, but Kyr had never had any doubts about herself. She jumped to her feet, abandoning her half-eaten potato stew, and went back into the kitchen to take down a canister of clear triple-brewed spirits from a top shelf. She scooped up some battered tin cups between her fingers. "Lisabel!" she called.

Lisabel came and took the cups so Kyr could manage the canister. Kyr poured everyone a measure of the liquor and then dropped back into her seat, still smiling uncontrollably. She'd spent the whole year they were thirteen running Jeanne through the hand-to-hand sections of the Level Five agoge final over and over again, *forcing* her to do it properly, to pick up the bright-fire grenades, to grab the majo noncombatants and use them as shields. It had all been worth it.

"Fortune favors the bold!" she said, lifting her cup. It was the Ferox toast. Every wing had its own. The other Sparrows echoed her, and Arti and Vic touched their cups together before they knocked back their gulps of mouth-burning vodka. Kyr pretended not to notice; they seemed to think Kyr didn't know they were kissing in secret. Kyr actually just knew it didn't matter. Genetic variety threw up dead ends, everyone knew that, and what counted was that you did your duty.

Kyr grinned at them too. "Maybe you'll be next," she said. "What do you want, Arti? Ferox as well?"

There was a pause. Finally: "Scythica," said Arti. "I like the little horsey badge."

Vic nudged her, affectionate. "I want Suntracker," she said. "I'm *sure* the topside array could be reangled. If I'm assigned there then they'll have to listen to me."

Cleo said, "Amazing, Victoria, we had no idea. Tell us more." But she was smiling, no longer flat and intent now that she'd been distracted from whatever that was all about. Cleo in a good mood loved to tease. It was a while, actually, since Kyr had seen her in anything approaching a good mood. She was surprised by what a relief it was, being able to relax and leave Cleo to dominate the conversation without fear of getting snapped at over nothing. Kyr herself was not chatty at mealtimes. Instead she shoveled down mouthfuls of lumpy potato stew as the others talked. It wasn't the best food—cadets didn't *get* the best food—but Kyr's warbreed body, which had run Doomsday four times that day, was greedy for fuel.

The Sparrows, warmed by the toast, were debating assignments. The best were the four combat wings: Ferox, Scythica, Augusta, Victrix. They got the smart navy uniform out of the old Terran Expeditionary stores; they got the best quarters, and first pick of off-station supplies, and luxury allowances to reward them for the dangers they faced. Without them the station would not survive. The majo hated that there were still humans in the universe they didn't control. The combat wings engaged enemy incursions, chased off spies, and corrected the majo long-haul traders brazen enough to cut across Gaean territory as if human sovereignty was beneath their notice. Only the cadets with the best Drill and agoge scores made the cut for combat. And of course that meant more from the boys' messes than the girls'.

Next after the four combat wings came the ones that kept the station alive: Systems, Suntracker, Agricole. They were vital in their own way. Kyr had done her shifts willingly, though she'd never understood Vic's Suntracker obsession; it seemed strange to her to care that much about solar arrays. But that was why Vic would make a good Suntracker and Kyr wouldn't. Then the last two official wings were Nursery and Oikos: both necessary. Without Oikos, none of the dull work of maintenance and repair and shift organization would get done. Without the women of Nursery Wing, humanity had no future.

At least two of the Sparrows would have to be assigned to Nursery to hit the population targets. Kyr had worked it out at some point. Lisabel was obvious, but it was hard to say the other. Maybe Zen, instead of Oikos. Maybe Arti: humanity would lose a soldier now but gain every child she bore them in the future.

"We'll find out soon enough," Kyr said, when the conversation had gone from excited to circular. "Command knows best."

"Oh, of course, how stupid of us. What about you, Kyr?" said Cleo. "Straight to Command?"

Kyr frowned. Command Wing wasn't an official assignment. You had to be the best of the best. Kyr wouldn't be ready for years. "Don't be ridiculous. Not yet. Scythica or Victrix."

Cleo's flat look was back. What now? "Not yet, right. How humble you are. An example to us all."

The words were teasing, but the tone was off. Kyr said, "Cleo, what's wrong?"

"What's *wrong*?" Cleo repeated.

Kyr genuinely couldn't think of anything. "Did you get some rec time in?"

There was a pause. Kyr became aware of the rest of the Sparrows looking silently between them: four pairs of eyes, because Jeanne was missing. Lisabel's worried expression. Vic looking guilty because she'd somehow started this, and Arti shifting to take her hand under the table. Zen expressionless—Zen never seemed to react much to anything.

A thread of the conversation had slipped out of Kyr's grasp somewhere. She couldn't understand it.

"Rec time," Cleo said at last, with enormous scorn. "Sure. I went and did a volunteer Nursery shift. Taught a dozen brats their times tables and gave a blow job to every admiral in quick succession. I felt so uplifted!"

"Cleo," said Lisabel.

Cleo stood up. "We've got a quarter-shift to get to," she said, "unless we want to sit around toasting Jeanne until we all get kicked off the station for having too much fun. Or does our fearless leader have a better idea?"

"I'm not your leader, Cleo," Kyr said. "I'm your messmate."

"Oh, right, my mistake," Cleo said. "How could I forget you're one of us?"

"Jeanne made Ferox," Lisabel said quietly. She had her hand on Cleo's wrist. "You'll be combat too. Don't be scared."

Cleo drew in a deep breath, and then sighed and shook Lisabel off. "Well. Command knows best. I don't care really."

"You don't?" said Kyr.

"Sure," Cleo said. "Anything but Strike. I just want to live."

"There's no such thing as Strike," said Kyr. *Strike* was enemy propaganda: as if Gaea had nothing better to do with its precious people than send them out to die in showy bombings and assassinations. The humans elsewhere who sacrificed themselves were worthy of respect: they were Earth's children, even if they lived among collaborators. But Strike Wing wasn't an assignment, because it wasn't real.

Cleo laughed a hard little laugh and said, "Where's the lecture? Sweet and meet, right? Shouldn't I be longing to die for a dead world?"

It is sweet and meet to die for your fatherland: old Earth poetry, which they'd all learned by heart in Nursery. "It's all right to be afraid," said Kyr.

"Are you afraid?"

Kyr didn't answer. She wasn't. She hadn't realized Cleo was. "There are different ways to serve," she said at last. "As long as you serve. That's all that matters."

"You should be Strike," Cleo said. "Go blow yourself up to teach the majo a lesson. You'd do it in a heartbeat."

"Thank you," said Kyr. "But there's no such thing."

They had their Oikos quarter-shift to get to. They washed up quickly. Kyr noticed out of the corner of her eye Lisabel taking a moment to wipe down a spot the little Blackbird had missed earlier.

Well, as long as the work got done.

A runner from Tiger, the youngest boys' mess, dashed in just as they were putting away the plates. He hopped from one foot to the other in nervous impatience until Kyr turned to acknowledge him and then said, "Sergeant Harriman requests Sparrow in Victrix Hangar, please!"

Sergeant was a courtesy rank for the chief of Oikos. "We'll be right there," said Kyr. "Dismissed."

Harriman, a big bald old soldier with a fringe of greying hair and the glint of long-ago visual enhancement visible in his eyes, was waiting when they jogged up to the giant metal doors that opened into the Victrix hangar. "There you are," he said. He passed Kyr a keycard and a clipboard with a blank storage log on it. "Storeroom sixteen," he said. "Strip, catalogue, and pack. Off you go, kids."

Kyr saluted. "Sergeant."

The other Sparrows were nudging each other and whispering. Strip, catalogue, and pack was the order for captured enemy spacecraft. A Victrix patrol had run into a majo incursion and won a victory. What would it be? A fat stupid merchant ship carrying luxuries was the most likely, but two years ago Scythica had brought in a real fightercraft still whining to itself about the orders of the Wisdom, a sleek murderous machine that Kyr had glimpsed only once before Systems took it apart.

"—or *chocolate*," she heard Vic whisper to Arti, and rolled her eyes a little.

They ducked into the hangar through the service hatch. There was a squadron of Victrix on guard: Kyr saluted again, and they nodded slightly and waved the Sparrows through. One of them was smoking a cigarette. He took it away from his lips to smile at them—no, at Lisabel specifically. She was too small to be useful in combat, but she was pretty. The tobacco was a luxury, so these men had probably been in the engagement and survived. No wonder they were cheerful.

The Victrix hangar, one of four, was a long cavern that dove deep into Gaea Station's native planetoid. Down below them, at the base of a long spiraling stone ramp, lay the massive metal hulk of a dead ship. The *Victrix* had once carried thousands through the void to conquer strange worlds. Chunks of her hull were gone, repurposed to build the station. What was left was buckled and distorted under the lash of gravity weapons. The dreadnought's complement of light nukes and Isaac slugs now formed the basis of the main defensive battery just outside the hangar's atmospheric seal. Fightercraft in lovingly polished cradles filled most of the hangar. They were one- or two-man machines, short-range, state of the art before Kyr was born: they'd once filled the belly of the ravaged dreadnought.

Near the top of the hangar was something alien.

Kyr felt the rest of Sparrow slowing to a halt around her.

The captured majo ship wasn't a merchantman, though they'd had to use one of their tiny handful of big merchant cradles to hold it. It had the sleek dangerous lines of a fightercraft, but it was more than twice the size. The Victrix guards keeping watch were dwarfed beside it. Kyr narrowed her eyes as she took it in. She had never seen anything so mad-looking: the entire hull was painted in extravagant, wasteful swirls of bright color, reds and blues and golds.

Handcuffed to the struts of the cradle under the alien ship was a majo. Both its hands were cuffed above its head. Kyr did not recognize the species. She had never seen anything like it in the agoge. Its crest, made of fine white flukes, was flat to its skull in what looked like a fear gesture. Its too-large eyes were a very pale silver color. Kyr stared at it.

The Victrix soldiers were both trying to guard it without looking at it. Kyr couldn't blame them. "Why is that thing still alive?" she demanded.

The majo lifted its head, and its crest came up a little. In clear if oddly accented T-standard, it said, "Because if you kill me my very nice ship will explode before whatever passes for a scientist in this tragic place can learn anything useful from it."

"Shut up," said a guard, and backhanded the thing across the side of its face.

"Please remember that I am not nearly as durable as a human," said the majo after breathing hard for a second. A purple bruise was blooming around its left eye like a gigantic flower.

"Shut up!"

"Gag it," said Kyr practically.

The Victrix guard scowled, presumably wishing he'd thought of that first. Kyr nodded to Lisabel, who donated her belt. The majo did not resist having its mouth stuffed full. It let the guard manhandle it like a doll. Kyr tore her eyes away when the thing was properly silenced. It felt like trying to ignore a live grenade, but she refused to be afraid.

"We're here to strip and pack the ship," she told the Victrix guards, and showed them the clipboard.

"Mnf," said the majo. It wiggled the hands cuffed to the cradle struts, like a child trying to get attention in a Nursery lesson. It had three long thin fingers and a short thumb. When they all ignored it—Kyr with determined insouciance, the guards sullenly, the other Sparrows nervous—it said "Mnf" again, more urgently.

"What if it matters?" said Lisabel.

Kyr rolled her eyes. She went to the painted ship's hatch and reached for the handle.

There was a flash of green light, a moment of screaming heat and terrible cold, and Kyr was suddenly on the floor ten feet away. One of the guards sniggered. Kyr jumped up, coldly furious. Who put dimensional trapping on a civilian vessel?

The majo finished spitting out its mouthful of Lisabel's belt. "I was going to say," it said mildly, "the keys are in my pocket."

The ship's inside was as ridiculous as its outside. There was nothing useful, just a stupid jumble: fancy glassware in the cupboards, ornamental carvings in alien biomatter stuck on the walls, a whole compartment that turned out to be a *wardrobe*, practically overflowing. Some of the clothes were made from rare fabrics. Kyr, tossing garments over her shoulder one after another, stopped when she felt the familiar-strange texture of wool. Ursa had once had a wool scarf. She'd said it was their mother's. This wool was a white robe thing with something silvery knitted into it. It had a tag inside. Kyr puzzled out the Majodai. *Made on Chrysothemis from Genuine Terran Biomatter!* and then *All Sales Go to the Home for Humanity Refugee Resettlement Fund.*

Kyr knotted the thing up into a white and silver ball and tossed it out into the hangar as hard as she could. Disgusting.

The clothing all went under "luxury fabrics" in their log. They sorted it into boxes in front of the handcuffed majo. They hadn't gagged it again, but it seemed to have enough sense not to chatter. It watched its clothes being ripped up along the seams without much reaction. Kyr couldn't read its expressions very well but she thought it was resigned. That made her angry. She'd wanted it to be *hurt*.

She faked a stumble and gave it a kick in the side as she hauled herself back up the cradle into the ship. The guards ignored it. One of them grinned a little, but in the other direction.

Half an hour in they were interrupted by another runner from Tiger. "Sparrow!" he gulped, and saluted. He held out a flimsy in Kyr's direction. The others paused what they were doing. Cleo was halfway through hoisting a box of glassware onto her hip. "Wing assignment!" said the runner. Kyr took the flimsy, glanced at the name scribbled on the outside, and passed it to Lisabel.

They all watched her unfold it and read it, even though they knew what it said. Even the Victrix guards were paying attention. Wing assignments didn't happen every day.

Lisabel read it, folded it up again, and lifted her head to smile at them all. "Nursery."

"Congratulations," said Zen, after a moment when no one said anything.

Kyr turned to the nearest guard and said, "Soldier, your flask?"

He passed it over. Cleo had caught the idea and was unpacking the top row of glasses from the storage box. They'd toasted Jeanne. Kyr glanced up from pouring out vodka when she felt eyes on her. It was Vic who was staring. "You can't live by the rules all the time," said Kyr. "Mess is mess."

Vic paused, and then said, "Mess is mess," and smiled at Kyr, a little uncertain, almost surprised. Arti silently came up and slung an arm around her waist—silly of her, thought Kyr, but she wasn't going to say anything. She just handed them their vodka, and Arti and Vic clinked the glasses together. Zen snorted a little when she got her glass, and took a preliminary sip and made a face. Cleo was smirking, her sharp smile like the edge of a knife, her posture ramrod perfect as ever. She took her glass and lifted it to Kyr, a wordless half toast, as if the two of them had been carrying on a conversation the whole time since they'd clashed outside the agoge, and Kyr had now somehow settled it.

Kyr turned to Lisabel last, and caught hold of her hand and clasped it in both of hers as she passed the glass over. Lisabel's eyes were deep blue; the glass sparkled between her hands. Kyr paused for an instant longer.

She became aware of the majo looking at them. The majo probably thought that they lived lives of dreary misery on Gaea Station. It had its shipful of luxuries, its easy life, its precious fabrics made from the plundered remains of Earth's biological glories. But it did not have, and could never have, the things Kyr had: her mess and her cause.

It nodded at the glass—crystal clear, embellished with traceries of silver—and said, "Those are *very* valuable, you know."

Kyr let go of Lisabel's hands. She stepped away one pace, and picked up the last glass, her own. She held it up to Lisabel and said, "I would rather stand three times in the battle line than give birth to one child."

It was the Nursery toast: another line of ancient Earth poetry, an acknowledgment that what Nursery had to do was also an act of courage. Lisabel watched Kyr's face for a silent moment. Finally she smiled, just a quirk of her lips. "Thank you," she said.

"Three times," said Cleo abruptly, lifting her glass.

"Three times," echoed Vic, and then they all said it, all except Jeanne, who should have been there too. Even after assignment, your mess was your mess.

"Maybe we'll be lucky enough to visit you soon," said the guard who'd shared his flask. Lisabel turned pink and looked away. Kyr grinned. She gave him his flask back, and paused for a moment, looking at the majo.

"Very valuable, you said?"

It blinked large silvery eyes. "That's right. Also of some sentimental value, if you care."

"Oh, well, in that case," said Kyr.

She drained the last gulp of liquor, held up the little shining glass so it caught the light and its silver traceries sent strange shadow-patterns spiraling across the floor.

Then she tossed it into the air, caught it, and smashed it against the pleasure ship's painted hull. "Cleo!"

Cleo let out a sharp crack of laughter and threw hers too. Then the others joined in, first Vic, then Arti, then Zen; little tinkling smashes one after the other as the tiny shiny glasses broke and shards of glass and silver went everywhere. Zen shouted something Kyr didn't catch as she threw hers, and for a moment her usually placid expression was alight. Only Lisabel was left holding a glass. Kyr said, "Don't be shy!"

Lisabel threw the last glass against the floor, so hard that the shattered pieces went everywhere in a shining spray.

"That's what we think of your *very valuable*," said Kyr to the majo.

It didn't say anything. Its pale crest was flat to its skull again. They'd frightened it.

CHAPTER THREE

FAMILY

Two more of Kyr's messmates were assigned in the next three days: first Arti to Augusta and then Vic to her heart's desire in Suntracker. Arti got scramble orders at the same time as her assignment: majo drones in the Mousa system, which in galactic terms was next door. Kyr felt unworthy envy squeezing at her chest as she watched her run for the Augusta hangar.

Vic called Arti's name after her, but she didn't look back.

Kyr took Vic down to Level Seven in the agoge that day after watching her stumble and make a fool of herself in her usual Eight. She had never understood why anyone would let a sex thing distract them so much. It worried her a little that Vic was being so visibly stupid about it. She was already so jumpy and fluttery so much of the time. It would be embarrassing for all of them if she got herself gossiped about.

There was news later that Augusta had been victorious but would remain on patrol in Mousa until they were sure it was clear—four or five weeks. Kyr was relieved when Vic got her Suntracker assignment that same evening, because she'd looked like she was going to cry herself to sleep. Without Lisabel in their narrow cadet dormitory it was probably on Kyr to say things to crying people, and she didn't have the patience.

Three unassigned Sparrows were left: Cleo, Kyr, Zenobia. They were given Oikos rotations, cooking and cleaning and reorganizing storerooms. They spent the third day after Augusta went out in Textiles, a long dim chamber tucked away near the back of Oikos, the opposite end from the stairs up to Drill. They took over from the mess before them—Starling, which was seven fifteen-year-old girls—and sat on folding metal chairs among repurposed plasteel shelving heaped with fabric, carefully sewing up bloodstained tears in old uniforms and putting reinforced patches on knees and elbows. Kyr recognized the fabric they were using, soft and hard to rip, dyed slightly the wrong shade of navy blue. It came from the wardrobe of the captured majo. Kyr wondered if they'd executed it yet.

Cleo took Textiles badly. "If they're just hemming and hawing about assigning us, they might as well give us rec rotations while we wait," she said. "Since we're not going to have any for months once we're in wing training. Ugh!" She'd stabbed herself with a needle. "Do you think majo use the Wisdom for this? O mighty and beneficial master of reality, turn these rags back into clothes!"

"Cleo," said Kyr. Cleo rolled her eyes but subsided.

Zen said nothing. She was always quiet. Now that there were only three of them it stood out more.

Kyr wouldn't have minded a rec rotation. She hadn't seen Mags since that day in Agricole. She wanted to know if her brother had been assigned. She wanted to know where.

Maybe it was Augusta, and he was out on patrol with Arti. Kyr felt her shoulders tighten at the thought. If Mags was already in combat, and she was stuck here in Oikos *sewing*—

She never finished the thought. A runner darted in with a flimsy for Zen. Zen waited for him to leave before she opened it, very slowly. Kyr and Cleo watched in strange, tense silence. Oikos or Nursery, Kyr thought. Predictable either way. Why do we feel so frightened?

"Oh," said Zen finally.

"What?" said Kyr.

Zen paused. Then she held the flimsy out in Kyr's direction. Kyr took it from her hand. *Sparrow / Zenobia: OIKOS*, she read. The signature was a *J* and a squiggle for *Jole*. Cleo crowded in at Kyr's shoulder, read it too, and let out a harsh breath.

"What?" said Kyr.

Zen looked at her, frowned, kept looking, and finally said, "The population targets."

"What about them?"

Then for the first time Kyr felt the cold burn of uncertainty. One of them had to go to Nursery. And there were only two left: two warbreed girls, with the best training scores in their mess. She'd even thought of it, that maybe it would be Arti, because her sons would be good soldiers. But Command didn't want just *good*, did they. They wanted—Cleo's sons, surely. It had to be Cleo. It couldn't be Kyr. But the cold and logical part of Kyr's mind said: *Cleo never got her full height and strength, so if they want the best—*

No.

Zen took her assignment back out of Kyr's hand. She looked from Kyr to Cleo, expressionless.

Finally she said, "I never liked either of you. But I'm sorry."

And she left.

Kyr and Cleo sat on the rickety metal chairs with a new space between them. The room felt very empty with five Sparrows missing. They both still had sewing on their laps. For the sake of breaking the awful silence Kyr said at last, "What did she mean, she never liked us?"

"Pretty unambiguous, Kyr," said Cleo. "At least, I thought so." She picked up a needle and drove it through some cloth, apparently at random. Then she dropped the whole navy-blue mess of fabric on the floor and looked at Kyr and said, "You know Commander Jole. He's your uncle. You must know. Is it going to be you or me?"

"What?"

"Nursery," Cleo said. "You or me, Valkyr? Or both of us, ha, wouldn't that be a surprise. Ten years fighting you to be the best and as a reward we *both* get to spend the next two decades pregnant. Well? Don't you know?" Her expression did something complicated and unfamiliar. Kyr would have said she knew all the Sparrows like she knew herself, but she'd never seen Cleo like this. In a small hard voice she said, "Only I'd rather know now. I'd rather just know. I don't know why they spin it out. Maybe there's someone in Command who likes knowing we'll squirm."

"No," Kyr said, on firmer ground. Command were humanity's leaders and its servants. They weren't like that. Her uncle Jole wasn't like that.

"You really believe that," Cleo said. "I wish I was you. I wish I could just not *notice* things like you do." Her eyes were on Kyr's, deep brown and strikingly luminous. Kyr was oddly reminded of Lisabel, holding up the shining glass next to the majo ship. "So you don't know."

"No," Kyr said again. She swallowed around a sudden inexplicable lump in her throat. "Nursery's not a bad assignment," she said. "It's . . . a sacrifice. A noble sacrifice. And you get things. Luxuries. Chocolate. You could grow your hair."

Cleo leaned back in the metal chair—it creaked alarmingly—and closed her eyes. She ran her hand over the close-knit curls of her cropped scalp. "Wouldn't *that* be nice," she said, without expression. "And as much sex as you want."

"Yes?" said Kyr, who had never really thought about this, but it was also true.

"What fun," Cleo said. She opened her eyes and scooped up her sewing from the floor. "We've got work to do, Valkyr. Come on."

Kyr and Cleo were alone in the Sparrow dormitory that night. Kyr slept poorly. She was surrounded by empty bunks that no longer had even the single blanket cadets got given on them. Heating was saved for important parts of the station. Without five other human bodies in here, it was very cold.

It had to be Cleo. They couldn't give Kyr Nursery. They *couldn't*. Nursery was for girls like Lisabel. After all, someone had to do it, and Lisabel would never have made a warrior. Kyr had tried and failed to teach her, and if she couldn't do it, no one could.

It wasn't that Nursery was hard. Kyr wasn't afraid of hard, she wasn't afraid of work, she wasn't afraid to *serve*. Nursery was a necessary service. Before the war people had just had children, or not had children, whichever way they wanted: with fourteen billion humans on Earth and another eight billion scattered across the colony worlds, it hadn't mattered. Now it did. With such a tiny gene pool, and no genetic tailoring available, everything had to be planned. No one could afford to take years away from real work to raise one or two random offspring in whatever stupid way occurred to them. Earth's children were Earth's future and Earth's only hope of vengeance.

The women of Nursery Wing bore the children: one every two years, in carefully planned crosses that preserved as much as possible of the genetically enhanced military lineages of Earth's warbreed bloodlines. They also reared them, up to the age of seven. To avoid unfair favoritism, no one in Nursery had responsibility for a child she had carried. Kyr had been drilled in hand-eye coordination, taught to read, beaten for misbehavior, and tucked into bed by Corporal Ekker, who had died a couple of years ago. She had not recognized the face of the figure in the recyclable coffin at the funeral. Ekker had gone skinny, flesh sloughing off her bones, hair grey and thin.

Mags had cried a little.

Kyr knew her actual lineage, of course. Commander Jole had explained: why he had an interest in her and Mags, why there were two of them, why they were allowed to call him *uncle*. Their father had served with Jole in Hagenen Wing. Their mother had been a junior officer of the dreadnought *Victrix*. Ursa had been produced the old-fashioned way, before the end of the world. But Kyr and Mags were born after both their genetic parents were dead, an attempt to preserve a valuable cross.

She'd had nothing but respect for Corporal Ekker. She even respected Lisabel, sort of. Lisabel would do well at tucking children into bunks, teaching them to read and write, keeping them healthy until they were old enough for their real lives, the mess and the agoge. But Kyr *herself*—

Her thoughts went in circles. She fell asleep at last counting Cleo's even breaths. Her shoulders and spine were stiff with cold and tension. They couldn't give her Nursery. She was a warrior, a soldier of humanity. It would be a waste.

There was no assignment for Kyr or Cleo in the morning, and there was no rotation for Sparrow on the noticeboard in the hall outside the female cadet barracks. There was nothing. The two of them stood there as the younger girls' messes moved around them. Finch, the sixteen-year-olds, were the senior mess on the board now. Starling below them. None of them said anything to Kyr. She'd never bothered learning the names of younger girls. A Finch paused like she was about to speak to Cleo, but Cleo gave her a withering glare—Kyr felt the force of it even standing to one side—and the girl changed her mind.

"Well," said Cleo at last, when the hall was empty, everyone showered and scattered to their rotations. "Are we supposed to just guess?"

"It's rec," said Kyr. "We've got a rec rotation."

There was a little pause.

"All right, why not," said Cleo. "Rec time. Possibly our last rec for months. Or years, depending. You don't get time off from—"

"Stop it," said Kyr.

"Do you still believe it's not about making us squirm?" Cleo said. "What else would it be about?"

"We're not that important," Kyr said. "Command have better things to do. They just didn't get to us yet."

"Wonder if the boys are all assigned too," Cleo said.

Without exactly discussing it, the two of them made their way through the technically off-limits fault in the rock of the station walls which led to the hallway outside the male cadet barracks.

This was a much bigger space—there were almost twice as many male cadets—and a more formal one, too; there were benches laid out in rows, even, because sometimes the boys got briefings and lectures. The female cadets could crowd in at the back to hear if their rotations allowed it, which they usually did.

The rotation noticeboard here was bigger as well, because there were two male cadet messes for every age cohort. Coyote and Cat were missing from the board just like Sparrow.

Cleo said, "You don't have to worry about Mags, at least. He'll be combat for sure." When Kyr said nothing she went on, with the air of someone making a peace offering, "We could go and look for him?"

"No," said Kyr. Newly assigned adults went straight into wing training. Mags would be busy. "We should do something useful."

Cleo laughed. "Like *what*?"

They went to Drill. There were no free agoge rooms—all of them were full of rotations from the combat wings or cadets working on their training—so they couldn't run Doomsday, or another scenario. They went to the mats instead.

Kyr had learned to fight in the dim and cavernous main hall of Drill. She had fought countless legions of majo in the agoge, she had fought Mags when their rec time overlapped, and other Coyotes too when they'd seen her against Mags, because no sensible cadet wasted a chance to work on themselves. But more than any of them she had fought the Sparrows: with them, against them. She knew their bodies intimately, their strengths and weaknesses, their injuries—the broken fingers, the permanent aches, the ankle that Jeanne had twisted when they were twelve and that still bothered her if she hadn't warmed up properly.

And above all she knew Cleo, because Cleo had always been the messmate Kyr measured herself against. At seven Kyr had not been able to beat her. At twelve, as Cleo's childhood advantage in height began to disintegrate, it had been an even contest. At seventeen, Kyr won two rounds out of three when they sparred—but even now she could not relax when it was Cleo on the mats against her. Cleo knew Kyr's habits and weaknesses just as well as Kyr knew hers, and Cleo in combat was aggressive, merciless, and warbreed fast.

They fought. Kyr won. Again; Kyr won again, but only just. Cleo took the third bout. Quietly the instructor on duty led his current charges—the seven-year-old warbreed boys of Tiger mess—across the hall to watch. Kyr tuned out the background staccato of his comments and criticisms; they were not for her. She and Cleo only watched each other, attacked, defended, struck again, fell back, circled, breathing hard—and oh, it was good. Cleo took another win off Kyr. Kyr took her down hard in retaliation in the following bout, pinning her facedown on the mat, arm twisted up behind her back. "Fuck *you*," Cleo said when Kyr let her up. Her teeth were bared in a glittering grin.

We might never do this again, Kyr heard herself think. She pushed the thought away as hard as she could.

Shift-change bells came and went. The Tigers ran off to their next rotation, and were replaced as an audience by a squadron of Scythica Wing, adult men in navy-blue uniforms with the silver horse badge of Scythica on their collars. Kyr still did not pay attention to them, but she caught a glimpse of a familiar, young-looking face. Last time she'd seen him he'd been a Coyote, one of Mags's messmates, and he was probably the one telling the others their names—*Cleopatra, Valkyr*—because Kyr heard the men calling them aloud, cheering whenever one of them landed a hit. She ignored them like she'd ignored the Tigers, even when they got louder, more insistent. Only this exchange of blows mattered, and the next one, and the next—

Cleo slammed Kyr down hard. There was a burst of cheering and, strangely, a shout of laughter. Kyr looked up. Cleo held out her hand. Her expression had gone cold and flat again, but it didn't seem to be aimed at Kyr. "We're done," she said, and pulled Kyr onto her feet. "Let's go."

She said nothing else until they were out of Drill. They were both covered in sweat, but Cleo marched past the showers like they weren't there. Kyr discovered her ponytail had fallen apart, and fixed it. "Fuckers, fuckers, fuckers," Cleo said. "I'm going back to barracks to wash up. Come on."

Kyr sat showered and shivering in the cold of the unheated bunkroom with her ponytail dripping cold water down the back of her neck. Cleo said, "Still no assignments."

Kyr said nothing.

"Did you hear them?" Cleo said. "Did you hear what they were saying?"

"It doesn't matter," said Kyr. "It wasn't important. Just soldiers being soldiers. It's hard service. They're allowed to—"

She stopped, because she still wasn't sure what, exactly, the soldiers watching them had been doing; or why it felt so crawlingly unpleasant to think about it.

"It doesn't matter," she said.

Cleo sat on her bunk, and put her face in her hands, and said, "I wish I was dead."

Kyr didn't understand the words at first. Then she said, "You don't mean that."

"You don't know what I mean, Kyr, you don't know anything," snapped Cleo. "What! Are they! Waiting for! Just *tell* me, just *do it* already." She was silent for a moment. Then she said, "It's going to be me. It's going to be me in Nursery, isn't it. Me and Lisabel."

"I don't know," said Kyr.

"It wouldn't be you," said Cleo. "You're the best of us. Our fearless leader. Jole's favorite. It wouldn't be you, so it's going to be me." She rolled over and lay flat on her back. "I just want it over with. I can't take this."

Kyr stood up.

"What?"

"I'll ask," Kyr said. "He's my uncle, like you said." She swallowed. "I'll go and ask Commander Jole."

Jole's quarters were tucked among the Command suites, close to Agricole. There was a shortcut through Nursery, but Kyr took the long way around past the Augusta hangar instead. Jole's suite was only two rooms, a modest sitting room and a monk's cell of a bedchamber. He was entitled to more. Kyr respected him—loved him—all the more because he took none of it. Jole was totally unselfish. Everything he did was for humanity. He didn't even take the minimum luxury allowance that any serving soldier had a right to.

Kyr pressed her hand to the door and it slid aside. That made her feel warm inside. Last time she had come here she'd been seven and crying over her first punctuality black mark. Back then she had not understood that running away to her uncle Jole to complain about her punishment was not fair on her messmates. He'd wiped her tears for her with an ancient patterned handkerchief and explained it carefully. It was true that Kyr and Mags were dear to him. It was true that they were family, and special. But all true humans were family, were special: all of Gaea served the cause. Sparrow were Kyr's sisters. Kyr had left with the memory of Uncle Jole's serious expression spurring a new determination inside her. It meant so much to be taken seriously by someone like him. He was a hero. Kyr had decided then to become a hero too.

He'd told her not to come back, and she hadn't. But she was still on the priority permissions for his rooms. They were still family.

Jole was not there. The sitting room was as plain as she remembered it. There was an ancient photograph of Kyr's genetic mother in a frame on the desk, a big smiling blond woman with her name written in the corner: *Elora*. Next to it there was a Systems terminal that Kyr did not even think of touching—Command had all sorts of permissions which were far above her level. She did not go over to look at the photograph either. She sat down on the hard chair nearest the door to wait.

When she was small, there had been a trundle bed in this room. It had been their sister Ursa's. Ursa had her own mess, of course, but she'd slept here. Looking after her was a promise Jole had made to their mother before the world ended, and Uncle Jole never forgot his promises. The great treat of Kyr's childhood had been getting summoned away from Nursery and conducted to these plain rooms in Command to see her big sister and her uncle. No one else had a big sister the way Kyr and Mags did. No one else had an uncle. Ursa, eight years older, had liked to sit Kyr on her lap and show her the picture of their mother. Mags had craned over her shoulder, but Kyr had been Ursa's favorite.

Maybe it was the special treatment that had made Ursa go wrong.

Kyr didn't mean to doze, but the long sleepless night in the Sparrow dormitory, followed by hours in Drill, told on her. Her eyes kept drifting shut. She wasn't asleep, she was just waiting. She could wait with her eyes shut. There was nothing to be alert for here. These rooms were the safest place in the universe.

She was woken by a thud and a shout. She startled so hard that she nearly fell off the chair. Jole was framed in the doorway, his chest rising and falling fast as he pointed his sidearm into the room. Kyr stared at him. The thud must have been the door slamming open.

"*Valkyr*," said Jole after a long second. He took a deep breath and lowered his weapon. "Forgive me. I saw an unexpected entrance on the log."

"Sir?" said Kyr.

"It wouldn't be the first time someone with evil intentions made it as far as Command, sweetheart. I wasn't expecting you."

Kyr's body went tight with outraged alarm. "They send people to hurt you?"

"Traitors and fifth columnists," said Jole. "And the misguided, and the stupid, and the weak. It has happened."

Kyr could hardly wrap her head around it. Assassins? *Here?* "But—and you don't even have a bodyguard!"

"I am not afraid," said Jole. He smiled. "Though if humanity's enemies had ever managed to recruit anyone as good as you, Valkyr, I might be."

"I would *never—*"

"Of course. I know." Jole limped further into the room and closed the door behind him. He groaned faintly as he lowered himself into the desk chair. His hand went to his side, above his bad leg, and he dug in his thumb there for a moment. Then he looked up at Kyr. His grey eyes were kind. "I'm glad you came," he said. "It's been a busy week, but I was planning to send for you tomorrow. I'm sure the last few days haven't been easy."

"We haven't got assignments," said Kyr. "Me and Cleo. This morning we didn't have a *rotation.*" She swallowed. "Sir. I came to ask. For both of us. I know I shouldn't. But Cleo is," and she stopped, because there didn't seem to be a way to explain how Cleo was, not without calling her weak in front of a commanding officer, which Kyr didn't think was true. "Please," she said instead.

"You do have assignments, Valkyr. I signed off on them myself." Jole dug into a pocket and pulled out a pair of flimsies. "Here. A day early."

Two notes: one with her name on the front, and one with *Cleopatra.* Kyr carefully put Cleo's in her pocket. She unfolded hers.

She nearly dropped the scrap while she was smoothing it out flat.

Sparrow / Valkyr: NURSERY. And the J, and the squiggle.

Kyr breathed out. And breathed in, and breathed out again. When she thought she had her expression under control she looked up. Jole watched her gravely.

"*Why?*" said Kyr. Her voice cracked.

"Do I need to talk you through the population targets?"

"No, I—I meant—" and then Kyr stopped, because she was arguing with a senior officer—with her *commander*—which she would never normally have dreamed of doing.

"You meant, why you?" said Jole.

Cleo's assignment in her pocket. It wasn't Nursery. It would be something else, because Kyr was the one getting sent to Nursery. She said nothing.

"We must serve, Valkyr. You know that."

"I know," said Kyr. Her voice still didn't sound quite right.

"I can see what you want to say," Jole said. "You want to tell me your training scores, and your aptitudes, and how hard you've worked. This isn't the service you wanted. I understand."

"I can fight," said Kyr.

"You can," said Jole. "And you can train others to do so, which you proved through your work with your mess. And you are in outstanding physical condition. And your sons, Valkyr, will be everything you are and more. You might become a great soldier, but you would only be one. We need many more. Gaea is asking you to be the mother of Earth's children. Are you afraid?"

"It's not fair," said Kyr, and was immediately ashamed of herself. Was she an infant? Even the stupid little Blackbird who'd spilled the water hadn't embarrassed herself by complaining.

"Are you refusing assignment, Valkyr?" said Jole sternly. There was no trace of Kyr's uncle in his face now. He was entirely the commander. Kyr stared at him and remembered with humiliation and horror the rumors that had accompanied Ursa's disappearance from the station.

Kyr was not her traitor sister.

"I will serve, sir," she said. She could not say it steadily, but she tried anyway.

There was a pause.

"Is there anything else, Valkyr?" said Jole.

What about Mags. Kyr couldn't say it. Why should it matter? She had her duty. "No, sir," she said.

"You may as well treat the rest of the day as recreation. Sergeant Sif in Nursery isn't expecting you till tomorrow morning."

"Yes, sir."

"Dismissed," said Jole.

Kyr nodded. Then she remembered too late to salute. Then she made blindly for the door.

"Kyr," said her uncle behind her.

Kyr hesitated.

Jole was smiling when she looked back at him, but his expression was still somehow sad. "I'm proud of you," he said. "I don't say that enough."

CHAPTER FOUR

NURSERY

Kyr stumbled away from the Command suites with a hand on the wall to keep herself upright. Her feet didn't seem to go where she wanted to put them. Her stomach was churning. Even her vision blurred. Shock, this was shock. She was shocked. That was allowed. There was nothing wrong with being shocked.

But Kyr's body was the thing she understood best, and she could not bear for it to be misbehaving like this. Once she was well away from her uncle's rooms she ducked into a side passage— dim lights, bare black rock walls, no one ever came here—and ran through breathing exercises to calm down.

And breathe out.

Kyr stood up straight. She wiggled her toes. She shook out her shoulders. She interlocked her fingers and stretched her hands above her head, then out in front, then behind her back, feeling her spine unlock. She was acting as if she was about to run through a top-level agoge scenario. She'd stretched like this right before the last time she'd attempted Doomsday. Which she hadn't beaten, because it was impossible. That was the point.

And breathe out.

This isn't the service you wanted, Jole had said. But Nursery was the service the murdered Earth needed from Kyr. It was meaningful. It was important. She could do valuable work, work that someone like Lisabel couldn't do. Physical training. Preparation. Command had noticed Kyr working with the weaker Sparrows to improve their scores and they'd seen something useful. Kyr should be proud.

She felt like she'd been stabbed from behind.

Be *proud*. Her uncle Jole was proud of her. Did that mean nothing? But if he was proud of her, why—

Breathe out. Don't finish the thought.

Kyr lifted her head, shifted her weight from foot to foot. The flimsy with Cleo's assignment was still in her pocket. Shame beat down hard on her thoughts as she pulled it out and unfolded it. This wasn't for her. She had no right.

Sparrow / Cleopatra: VICTRIX. Commander Jole's signature, and underneath it Admiral Russell, the commander of Victrix Wing.

Well.

Kyr refolded the flimsy and put it back in her pocket.

She thought about going back to the agoge. She had a free day—not just a shift but a whole day of recreation. She could do whatever she wanted. She could run Doomsday for hours. Maybe *today* she'd beat it. Maybe if she beat it—

Kyr already knew that beating Doomsday would change nothing. Proving you were capable of saving the world didn't mean you could, or that anyone would let you.

She was still standing in that dim silent rock passage. At some point she'd put her back against the wall. The stone of Gaea's native planetoid was so cold she could feel it through her grey cadet's uniform. Breathe in, breathe out: and she might as well spend the day on Doomsday anyway. When she was pregnant no one would let her run a Level Twelve scenario.

They might not let her train at all. People made jokes about how Nursery got coddled. Medical on call all day long. All the best food. Luxury allowances higher than anyone except actual soldiers, allowed to request anything except alcohol. And they got alcohol anyway, because soldiers would offer up *their* allowances for a chance to pass the time with you, to get some comfort, maybe to start a love affair and so know for a fact that they had children, a stake, a genetic future, when they went out to patrol the bleak scrap of space that was all that remained of humanity's glories. No one expected Nursery women to stay fighting fit, or even to put in anything above the bare minimum certification for small arms—the same standard as a *ten-year-old*—because, after all, when did they have time?

Kyr would not have time to train. She would not have anything. Even her body would not be hers. The Corporal Ekker in her thoughts was distorted, swollen, always complaining about her aching feet and back and head, constantly in need of somewhere to sit down. The highest rank anyone in Nursery achieved was sergeant, the wing chief, and even that was only a courtesy rank.

No one took Nursery women seriously. That was not what they were for.

"Breathe," Kyr said, aloud, and did not recognize her own voice.

She went back to barracks.

"Well?" said Cleo, sitting up fast from her miserable sprawl on her bunk. "How much trouble are you in?"

"I'm not," said Kyr. "It was fine." She pulled the flimsy out of her pocket and threw it at Cleo. It did not lend itself to being thrown, and wafted sideways. Cleo snatched it out of the air with her characteristic eye for motion in space. *Is it because she's a better shot?* thought Kyr. But projectile weapons were a secondary discipline. You couldn't use them in spacebound environments unless you wanted to risk death by asphyxiation. Kyr was infinitely better at *real* combat. Kyr had won more than two out of three of their bouts that morning, while first the Tigers and then the soldiers of Scythica watched.

Cleo unfolded the flimsy with quick, jerky movements. Then she went still.

"Victrix?" she said quietly.

Kyr said nothing.

Cleo looked up. Her dark eyes were sharp. "What about you?"

And Kyr lied.

"Don't know," she said. "They haven't decided yet, apparently. I still have rec."

She was expecting Cleo to challenge it. To herself she sounded absurdly transparent. But Cleo didn't. She just shook her head once and then looked back at the assignment in her hands as if she was expecting it to say something different. "Victrix," she said again. "A combat wing. I *did it*."

"Congratulations," said Kyr. They didn't have anything to toast with in here. She mimed lifting a glass and then felt stupid. But she gave Cleo the Victrix toast anyway: "*Victory or death*."

"Victory or death," Cleo whispered.

She stood up, and put the flimsy in her pocket, and turned to Kyr. "I have something I've always wanted to say to you," she said. "And I might not get another chance."

"Go on, then," said Kyr.

The corner of Cleo's mouth lifted. "All right. So," she said. "You're a horrible bitch, Valkyr, and everyone hates you. I hope they give you Strike and you die."

Kyr swallowed. Weirdly she wanted to cry. *Strike*: the vengeance of humanity. The wing that didn't exist.

Cleo breathed out. "That didn't feel as good as I thought it would," she said. "I meant every word, though. Promise."

"I know," said Kyr.

"Maybe not every word," said Cleo. "I'd better report in."

"They'll be expecting you," said Kyr.

"Right. So . . . bye."

Cleo's hand connected with Kyr's shoulder as she walked past her and out of the Sparrow dormitory for the last time. Kyr turned to watch her go. Cleo didn't look back. None of the Sparrows had looked back.

Kyr was alone.

She wanted someone to talk to. She wanted her mess, her sisters—as Jole had told her so long ago—her family. But they were scattered all over the station, each assigned a new dormitory within her own wing, a new sisterhood. And—it wasn't Cleo that

Kyr thought of right then, saying *everyone hates you*. Cleo was dramatic. You didn't have to take her seriously.

But Zen, before she left, had spoken calmly. Zen was always calm. And she had said, as simply as if she was asking someone to pass her a mop, *I never liked either of you*.

It was not possible that Sparrow really hated Kyr. They were her mess. They were *hers*. But crawling at the back of her skull was a three-year-old memory of Jeanne and Arti and Cleo (the three bravest, though Kyr had never thought about it that way before) confronting Kyr over the extra drills she was forcing on Lisabel. They'd asked her to stop, so she'd stopped.

She'd been considering it anyway. Lisabel just wasn't any good at the things that mattered. The minuscule improvements Kyr was getting out of her were not worth the time she was taking away from her own training, or the awkwardness of Lisabel's fits of exhausted, hopeless crying. Besides, by the time they were fourteen it had already been obvious that Lisabel would get Nursery.

Your mess was yours, and you were responsible for everyone in it. Kyr had done the right thing to try, and she'd done the right thing to stop. She'd never second-guessed anything about the whole episode before.

I never liked you. Zen had said it as if it was obvious. As if Kyr should already have known.

Where was she supposed to go now? Not to the agoge, to wallow in everything she was about to lose. Not to her mess, who weren't hers any longer. Not to her brother. Kyr didn't even know where her brother was. It wasn't her business to know. It was her business to serve.

Really there was only one place Kyr could go.

She went to Nursery.

"Kyr!" said Lisabel.

She looked different. Nursery uniform standards were relaxed, so although Lisabel was wearing a neat grey uniform jacket, she had a *skirt* on. And she hadn't tied up her dark hair; it was loose on her shoulders. But her smile crinkled the corners of her eyes. She was happy to see Kyr. "What are you doing here?" she said.

Kyr said, "I'm not officially assigned till tomorrow. I have a day of rec."

Two true things, but not the truth. She hadn't known she was going to do that until she'd done it. She wasn't in the habit of telling lies; they were beneath her. But she didn't let herself think about it, too caught up in the staggering relief of Lisabel's smile. *There*, her heart said. If anyone in Sparrow had any right at all to bear a grudge against Kyr, it was Lisabel, and Lisabel didn't. So that was all right.

"And you came to see me?" said Lisabel. Her smile grew. "I can see you at the next bell. Wait for me?"

"Okay," said Kyr.

It wasn't in Kyr's nature to sit around doing nothing, so she helped with a mealtime while she waited. Tired women were serving up measured portions of protein slop and vegetables to the children old enough to feed themselves, from age two to seven. Senior members of the wing stalked among the tables watching eagle-eyed for misbehavior. Kyr spotted Sergeant Sif, a tall dark-skinned woman, her future commander, lecturing a chatty group. Sergeant Sif had never come through the agoge. She was an outsider, one of the adults who had left behind collaboration and submission and sought out Gaea Station, taking on a new name and a higher duty of her own free will. You could respect that, couldn't you?

Kyr watched her for a moment or two. She was heavily pregnant. She kept putting one hand on the small of her back.

Mealtimes in Nursery were grim, serious affairs. Food wastage was the worst crime, but so were silliness and chatter and not finishing your meal. Volunteers on their own rec hours, members of the junior girls' messes, were on cleanup duty. At the other end of Nursery's one long hall, women were overseeing the feeding of the toddlers. Anyone currently breastfeeding would be excused, because she would be in with the babies.

Kyr took a place by the bins, taking bowls from the small hands of nervous-looking children and hauling off stacks to be washed. It was boring, but at least no one expected her to talk to the children. She could see Lisabel out of the corner of her eye patiently spoonfeeding a toddler who clearly had no desire to be fed.

When the shift bells went, the wing moved smoothly into Lessons, a rotation that didn't exist anywhere else on the station. Kyr didn't miss it. Ten years later she still remembered how bored she had been, sitting in silence through hour after hour of human history. She'd had the unfair advantage of knowing that their teacher was bad: because Uncle Jole had taught her history, and Ursa too, and the way they told it had been *real*.

Lisabel came and found her by the food bins. "We can use the kitchen," she said. "This way."

"You have . . ." said Kyr, pointing.

Lisabel tried to wipe the spatter of protein slop off her uniform jacket. It left a greasy brownish stain. "Oh well," she said. "Have a seat."

The Nursery kitchens were smaller than the Oikos ones, which were used on an ad-hoc basis by most of the station as well as being the place where the cadet messes got their meals. Three worn-looking women were just finishing the washing up. Kyr helped dry and put away dishes, automatically. She was very aware of Lisabel right at her elbow. They didn't talk.

Maybe this was what she would be doing every day, now.

When the kitchen was clean and the other women were gone, Kyr sat on an ancient metal folding chair. Lisabel went to a cupboard and pulled out two glasses. Kyr said, "I recognize those."

They were from the majo pleasure ship, the same pattern as the ones Sparrow had broken. "Oh," said Lisabel. "Yes. I think they got sent up by one of the Victrix officers." She looked at them in her hands a moment, grimaced a little, and then said, "Well. Water? Or . . . we have tea."

"Nursery really does get all the luxuries," said Kyr.

"Tea," said Lisabel, as if her question had been answered, and she made it for them while Kyr sat and watched her. Was she already carrying a child for humanity? It had only been a few days. But there were those population targets to think of.

The tea turned the glasses a shimmering amber color. Kyr drank quietly from hers, and Lisabel sat down on a wobbly white stool opposite and did the same. Kyr was in uniform, the plain grey trousers and shirt of a cadet mess, her fair hair pulled back into a tight ponytail, as if she was going to head off to Drill again soon. But it was not really possible to pretend things were the same as always. Lisabel looked so different. None of the others were here.

It was not possible, but Kyr tried anyway, for as long as she was drinking the tea. The glass was warm in her hands but not painfully hot the way she'd half wanted. She did not say anything because she could not imagine a way to start a conversation without talking about the other Sparrows, and if she said *Cleo to Victrix, Zenobia to Oikos* then Lisabel would know. She would know at once, just as Cleo had generously pretended *not* to know, and then it would be real.

Kyr couldn't put it off forever. She wasn't a coward. She wasn't going to be afraid, not of anything; not even of Lisabel looking at her differently.

She put down her empty glass—it made a solid bright *clink* against the table, the sound of quality—and took a breath.

Lisabel said, "I'm glad you came. Are you all right?"

Kyr said, "I—"

"When I heard about Magnus, I was worried about you."

"I—What?" said Kyr. "What about Mags?" Her pulse kicked up. "Do you know his assignment?"

Lisabel stared at her. After a second she put her hand over her mouth. "I thought you knew," she breathed. "I thought—when I saw you—"

"*Where is my brother?*" said Kyr.

Lisabel stood up and took Kyr's hands in hers and held them. "I only know what I heard," she said. Of course Lisabel always heard everything. She'd been the first to know about Mags beating Doomsday. Kyr could feel the tension that had slowly unwound while she drank the amber tea reclenching its tight fingers around her shoulders.

"His assignment," said Kyr. Had it happened to both of them? Had Mags been given something all wrong just like Kyr? Had— They wouldn't put a boy into Nursery, men were never assigned here, there was no point—but if at least what was happening to Kyr was *fair*—

"Ferox," said Lisabel, cutting off that line of thought completely. "But he turned it down."

"What?"

"Magnus refused assignment," said Lisabel. "He's left the station. He's gone."

Kyr snatched her hands out of Lisabel's. "No."

"It's what I heard," said Lisabel. "Maybe I'm wrong."

"You're wrong."

Lisabel reached out again. Kyr knocked over the metal chair with a clatter as she jumped up and backed away. It made no sense. Mags wasn't a traitor. Mags had run Doomsday nearly as many times as Kyr had, he had *seen* what the majo had done to their world. He had spent those childhood evenings listening to Uncle Jole tell them the story of humanity just as Kyr had. And he was Kyr's brother.

"He wouldn't," said Kyr, and then, "He would have told me."

"I'm sure you're right."

"He would have told me," Kyr repeated.

But if Gaea Station had lost Mags, lost him now, then the decision to assign Kyr to Nursery made a terrible sense. Kyr was fifth best in their age cohort: Mags was the best. His scores since his last growth spurt were unmatched in the station's short history. If Gaea's gene pool did not have him, it needed Kyr. It needed another chance at him. Kyr's brother was too valuable to lose.

And he *knew* that. "He wouldn't just *go*," Kyr said. It made no sense. There was no reason. There was no *why*.

"You must be right," Lisabel said.

Kyr glared at her. "Tell me what they're saying." Lisabel kept looking sympathetic. Kyr hated it. "Tell me!"

"He said no to Ferox," said Lisabel. "So Command offered him his pick of the combat wings. And he said no again. And they're saying it's to do with your—with Ursa." If Lisabel had said *your sister* just then, Kyr would have hit her. "That he was under her influence all along."

"Under her influence?" said Kyr. "*How?*" There was no communication between Gaea Station and the rest of the universe. What did they care for what the majo had to say? Once Ursa left, she had been *gone*. If Mags had not mentioned her now and then, it would have been like she never existed.

Did Mags mentioning Ursa's name make him a traitor? No. It was Mags: he was sentimental to a fault, but Kyr knew, she *knew*, that Kyr herself mattered more to him than the so-called sister who'd abandoned them and their home and their whole species.

"It's just what they're saying, Kyr," said Lisabel. "I'm sorry."

Kyr said nothing.

"I'm sure he's all right."

Rumors went around the cadet messes about what happened to people who refused assignment. Some said they were executed. That was nonsense. Jole had explained it once: humanity could not afford for a single member of their species to be lost, not even the traitors, and so those who were not worthy to serve were simply sent away. Gaea was a beacon, a place of hope. It was not a prison. "Don't be ridiculous," said Kyr.

Lisabel's expression was sympathetic, which was only another way to say *pity*. Impossible to bear the thought of being pitied by Lisabel. Lisabel was lovely, she was sweet and softhearted, Kyr was *glad* they'd been cadets together even if it *had* dragged their mess's collective training scores down, but she could not be pitied by someone like her. "I need to . . ."

To what? For the first time in her life Kyr had no idea at all what she was supposed to do next.

Something said quietly in the back of her mind: *You could refuse.*

Kyr could refuse to serve, like Mags had. She could say no to Nursery, no to her species, no to her future: turn her back on her duty and her murdered world, and skulk away to . . . to do what? Sell her services to the rich majo who liked human bodyguards because they were more fearsome? Drag out years of her life in dreary shame, knowing what she'd betrayed?

She could not, and would not. If Mags had really left—and Kyr was more and more horribly sure that he had, because it was the only thing that made her assignment make sense—then Kyr alone would bear the burden of the service that should have belonged to both of them. It was her honor as well as her duty.

She felt a warm hand slip into hers and glanced down at Lisabel, who looked like she was going to cry. Kyr frowned. Why would *Lisabel* cry? "Well. I'll see you later," she said. She summoned up a smile. "Thanks for the tea. Don't make such a fuss."

Kyr let Lisabel accompany her to the entrance to Nursery. She was clearly only just restraining the urge to fuss enormously, and it was funny: the more Lisabel looked sad and tried to say brave things, the less inclined Kyr felt to any kind of outburst at all. She was smiling by the time they reached the double doors. Lisabel stared up at her with huge eyes and then abruptly flung her arms around Kyr, and Kyr actually laughed, and patted Lisabel on the back before she pushed her off. "You're as bad as the babies."

"Take care of yourself," said Lisabel.

She obviously thought that Kyr would be going off to a combat assignment soon. Kyr didn't let herself feel the little stab that wanted to lance through her at the idea. There were too many things in her mind at once: Commander Jole, who was proud of her, and Lisabel whose tears always made Kyr feel obscurely guilty, and Zen and *I never liked you*, and Mags lounging under the purple flowers in Agricole.

It was not possible that he was a traitor. There was something else happening here. Kyr was *sure*.

As she pulled away from Lisabel there was a cough from the doorway. They both turned. Kyr saluted. Lisabel followed her a beat late.

Admiral Russell smiled indulgently at them under his luxuriant white mustache. The winged sigil of Victrix shone on his lapel next to his Command badge. He was the second-highest-ranked member of Command, deferring only to Uncle Jole. He had won battles for humanity, and conquered worlds. Kyr had always respected him, because she knew Jole did.

"Sorry to interrupt, girls," he said. "I thought I'd pay the brave ladies of Nursery Wing a visit."

"Sir," said Kyr, since Lisabel seemed to be paralyzed. Lisabel had probably never spoken to an admiral before. Kyr had, but only because of Uncle Jole.

Admiral Russell was not offended. He came over and took Lisabel's hand and patted it before he tucked it through his own arm. "You look very pretty in that skirt, my dear," he said. "We must have Textiles send you up more treats. I'll see to it myself. I haven't seen you here before, have I? Congratulations on your assignment, young lady. I am sure you'll do humanity proud."

"Thank you, sir," said Lisabel.

Kyr stepped away politely. It was obvious the admiral did not want her there. Lisabel turned her face up to him and smiled a little. The admiral clucked his tongue. "Have you been crying?" he asked. "We can't have that."

"No, sir."

"What's your name?"

"Isabella, sir. Lisabel."

"Very pretty," said Admiral Russell, with another indulgent smile. "A pretty name for a pretty girl. And this is—ah, Valkyr."

"Yes, sir."

"You were just leaving, I see?"

"Yes, sir."

"Dismissed," Admiral Russell said.

He turned back to Lisabel, but not right away. His gaze lingered on Kyr a moment longer.

It occurred to Kyr, suddenly and forcefully, that Admiral Russell had not needed to ask Lisabel's name. The wing assignments were determined by Command, and the admiral's signature had been on Cleo's assignment under Commander Jole's. There was no way, none at all, that he had not been in the meeting room looking at training scores and personnel records. It was not as if there were *many* cadets. Only seven girls.

He had not needed to ask Lisabel's name, but he still had his heavy-knuckled hand tucked over Lisabel's small one through his arm. There was a silver ring on his third finger. He was a warbreed soldier of the old school, enhanced at every stage. Even now, closer to seventy than sixty, he had a soldier's powerful and dangerous body.

He knew Kyr's assignment. Kyr felt his knowledge in that moment while he looked at her. She looked back at his knowing eyes, and she thought—not as a decision, not as a realization, just as a simple and obvious fact—*if you ever put a hand on me, I will break your wrist.*

Admiral Russell looked away.

Kyr was astounded by the wave of contempt she felt. He was a leader of humanity, a hero, a great man. She despised him.

"Come along, dear," the admiral said abruptly. He did not look back as he steered Lisabel away. Neither did she. Kyr watched them go and forced her hands to relax out of fists.

She had been assigned to Nursery. She knew her duty.

She could not be a traitor.

She could not obey.

There had to be another way. There *had* to.

Kyr wanted Mags, wanted him desperately. She was feeling too much, and Mags was a safe place to feel things: like the agoge on the easiest level, where you could take every risk, make every mistake, and still come out victorious. No matter what Lisabel said, no matter what station gossip was saying, Kyr could not—she *could not*—believe that her brother would turn against humanity.

Nothing fit together. Trying to think felt like running through Doomsday. There was no solution that worked. There was no way for Kyr to win.

How had Mags done the impossible?

"Oh," said Kyr aloud, remembering.

He'd cheated.

CHAPTER FIVE

AVICENNA

Kyr tried Systems first. Systems and Suntracker were the two top levels of the station, with power feeding down into Systems from Suntracker's solar sails to supplement the trickle that came up from the shadow engines at the station core. The main work-space of the wing was a maze of consoles arrayed on several levels in one of the planetoid's natural rocky caverns. Kyr did not know it well. She had no talent for Systems work. When Sparrow had a rotation in the wing she usually found herself shunted off to try out agoge simulations for scenario designers. She hesitated just inside the entrance. She could not exactly go wandering through the wing asking if anyone knew Mags's queer friend.

While she was hovering a woman with iron-grey hair and a corporal's patch on her sleeve looked up from behind her array of consoles. "Need something, cadet?"

Kyr found herself tongue-tied. "Corporal," she said, to buy time.

The woman raised her eyebrows, and after a long pause finished, ". . . Lin. Corporal Lin, Valkyr. Your mess has rotated through here once a week since you were ten. After Victoria? She'll be up in Suntracker."

"No," said Kyr.

"Spit it out," said Lin. "What's the matter?"

"Nothing," said Kyr quickly.

Lin gave her a long look. Kyr pressed her lips tightly together. Once again she had a horrible suspicion she was being *pitied*.

"Avi," she snapped. "I'm looking for Avi."

Lin's eyebrows went up. "Avicenna, really?" she said.

Kyr didn't say *what*, because that would have been speaking out of order to someone who was technically her superior.

Corporal Lin said, "Try the arcade."

Once, each of the four dreadnoughts that had been stripped to build Gaea Station had had an arcade of its own. Now, *there* was proof of how rich humanity had been: even active-service warships had spared space for entertainment. The consoles and media libraries from all four had been combined into one entertainment space for Gaea. It was a long low room with booths and chairs set out around game stations and flickering displays. The lights were kept dim. Old music played on a loop. Kyr winced as she walked in. It wasn't loud, but it was *constant*, and she disliked the wastefulness of it: power that Suntracker risked their lives for, thrown away on meaningless noise.

There was almost no one in the long dim room apart from a junior mess on rec. Kyr glanced at them as she walked past. It was just Blackbird. They were playing a game where you had to dance to the music—tinny from the machine speakers, clashing with the background hum—and catch at lights as they flashed in the air. Kyr saw one of them spot her and falter, missing her jump for a darting yellow sparkle that appeared and disappeared in time with the thumping beat.

But her gaze slid past and kept going.

She missed the young man at first. He was slumped alone in a booth at the far end of the room, his shoulders almost horizontal, his feet propped against the edge of the seat opposite. From that angle it was hard to get a sense of him except that he was undersized.

Kyr hadn't expected him to be alone. The way Mags had talked about *Avi* had made him sound like someone who could be impressive. She'd supposed there would be a ring of similar types, the worst of Systems and Oikos: not friends, but weaklings clustering together for safety.

Avi was ostentatiously by himself. He was watching some

media or other loaded up on the screen. It wasn't even a game. If you had to be in the arcade, the least you could do was laze around with something worthwhile. The Blackbirds were working on their group bond and improving their coordination while they jumped around grabbing at sparkles.

Kyr tried to relax, told herself it would be stupid to start by antagonizing him, and marched over to the booth.

"Avi?" she said.

The young man said nothing.

"*Excuse* me," snapped Kyr.

"Shh," he said. The flicker of the screen illuminated his face in unpleasant flashes. He had squinting eyes under an untidy mess of red hair. "I'm watching this." He waved a dismissive hand in her direction without looking round.

Kyr's patience ran out.

She reached over the back of the booth, grabbed him by the scruff of the neck, and dragged him upright. He let out a squawk of surprise. He really was scrawny. Lifting him was practically effortless.

"Turn that off," she said.

He didn't. Kyr reached over to the controls and did it for him. The screen went dark.

Avi stood up. He only came up to Kyr's chin. He stepped further back into the newly dimmed booth and folded his arms. Kyr didn't miss how he'd kept the back of the booth between them like a shield. He looked her over, and his face did a fair impression of boredom, but she could tell he was afraid.

"What do you want?" he said.

Kyr made herself breathe out. This was *not* how she'd meant to do this. "You're Avi," she said. "You're friends with my brother."

"I wonder who," Avi said. "I don't have many friends built like tanks. Let me guess, you must be *Vallie*."

"Valkyr," Kyr corrected.

Avi smiled unpleasantly. "Then it's Avicenna," he said. "Lovely to meet you. What do you want?"

"I want to know where Mags is," Kyr said.

"So?"

"So," said Kyr, "you're going to find out for me."

Avi was Systems, so he had access to information. Avi was supposedly the smartest person Mags had ever met. And Avi was already a cheat. That had to mean something.

"Or what?" he said.

Kyr narrowed her eyes.

Avi sneered. "Yes, I know, there's a huge range of *or what* you could do to me, Valkyr. I'm just wondering which part exactly of the no-doubt-merciless bruising you're offering would be worse than getting exiled or executed for digging into files I'm not supposed to touch."

Kyr shifted her weight, and had the satisfaction of watching him flinch away even though the back of the booth was still between them.

"I *have* been beaten up before, you know," he said, but the tight stillness of his body didn't match his bored voice.

"Do you care if you're exiled?" said Kyr. "People like you leave anyway."

"Let's ignore *people like you* for now because, actually, it was the *executed* part that concerned me," Avi said. "Crazy, I know, but I want to keep living."

With honest confusion Kyr said, "Why does he *like* you?"

"Must be my winning personality," said Avi. But he unfolded his arms and sighed. Kyr didn't understand what had changed his mind, but she didn't care, because he stepped out of the booth— still giving her a wide berth—and said, "Damn. All right, all right," in a defeated way. "Come on."

Avi took Kyr down to Drill. "What are we doing here?" said Kyr. "I want—"

"I know what you want," said Avi. "Go on." He swiped the key for an agoge room. "In you go. Take this." He passed her an earpiece.

"What?" said Kyr.

"Do you want my help or not?" Avi said.

Kyr stumbled into the agoge. The plasteel floor gleamed green with shadowspace sublight as the room hummed, warming up. Kyr put the earpiece in. "What do you think you're doing?"

"Well, I'm going to use the agoge as a jumping-off point to get myself into some places I'm not supposed to be," said Avi. "Which happens to be one of my hobbies anyway, luckily for you. And you're going to pretend to be testing some simulations."

"Why can't you just do it in Systems?"

"One, boring. Two, the odds of getting anything past Yingli Lin from there are slim to negative."

"Her? She's just a corporal."

"And of course you're one of those people who thinks rank correlates directly with ability."

"You realize people look at the agoge logs," Kyr said. "They can watch what I'm doing in here."

"No, I'm not an expert and I had no idea. Thank you so much for telling me. Fine."

"Fine what?"

"I was going to spoof something but you're clearly going to be unbearable if you haven't got something to do," Avi said. "Here."

The green flickers disappeared as the agoge room brightened to a clear shadowless white. Ghostly shapes began to trace themselves on the air.

"That should keep you busy," Avi said. "Have fun."

The simulation resolved into a narrow street. Kyr had seen streets before—had drilled in simulated urban environments since she was twelve—but this was no majo city. The walls were primitive, smooth blocks of white stone rising to her left and right. An arch marked the end of the street. Somewhere far overhead was a very blue sky.

Kyr did not have time to take in more, because the shadows slowly taking form beneath the arch resolved into three—no, five—no, *eight* separate hostiles, like nothing she'd ever seen.

They weren't a majo species. The shortest was six and a half feet tall, with a broad heavy build underneath its armor. Kyr didn't recognize the style of armor either: dark organic material with plates of actual metal sewn to it. The hostile looked at Kyr and gave a low unpleasant rattle of sound, like a laugh.

The leader was nearly eight feet high, with sharp tusks in its mouth that would be dangerous weapons in their own right, and it was gripping a solid length of steel. The agoge could give you a good jolt of pain to teach you the lessons of war, and Kyr could tell that thing was going to be agony.

She had no weapons. She'd trained for years in snatching majo weapons from simulated enemies and turning them on their makers, but the *weight* of that mace made the prospect absurd. She doubted she could even lift it.

"What are these?" she demanded.

Avi answered, *"Orcs."*

That meant nothing. Kyr eyed the things again. They were hanging back under the arch. In the Level Twelve runs Kyr was used to, you didn't get this moment to think.

At least none of them seemed to have anything ranged.

As she thought it, the short one lifted a length of organic material and began to swing it around its head. Kyr's body moved faster than her brain. Eight hostiles and she was unarmed: when the missile zipped from the slingshot through the space where her head had been, she was already running.

Kyr ran between walls of smooth white stone and under gleaming white arches, and the hostiles ran behind her. It didn't matter how fast she moved, they stayed the same distance back: far enough that their heavy weapons wouldn't touch her, close enough that if she stopped moving that slingshot was going to be a problem. Occasional missiles cracked the stone walls around her as she ran, but the thing's aim didn't seem to be much good with a moving target. "What the hell is this *for?*" she yelled at the air.

"Do you mind? I'm working," said Avi. *"On something you asked me for, if you remember."*

"I need a weapon!"

"*So find one. You're not very good at this, are you?*"

Kyr snapped her mouth shut on the words she *wanted* to say and glanced around as she ran. Urban-combat scenarios were normally full of civilians, but there was nothing in the white city but Kyr, and Avi's absurd monsters.

And walls. Primitive white stone walls, with mortar crumbling from the cracks. Kyr could make it from Suntracker at the top of Gaea Station to Drill at the bottom in under five minutes. She skidded around a corner to give herself a few extra seconds out of the sight line of the monsters and flung herself up.

The stone was cold under her hands as she scrambled for handholds. She was grimly aware of that slingshot—she was a much easier target heaving herself up the vertical than she had been as a running figure at the far end of a street. She heard the orcs come round the corner below and start talking. They spoke in grunts, but the confused tone was clear.

They spotted her when she was nearly at the top. A slung stone smashed into the wall next to Kyr's hand as she pulled herself up to a parapet and rolled over the edge. She crouched against the other side, breathing hard.

Overhead the sky was still deep unending blue. Kyr tilted her head back and looked for a moment as her lungs strained for air.

She was on a flat rooftop with a kind of garden on it. There were tubs of earth with vegetables growing in them, and a stack of wooden crates next to a door that led into whatever this building was supposed to be. Residential, maybe. Kyr stayed crouched against the parapet, better cover than nothing. Could those things climb up after her? She could still hear them grunting down in the street, so maybe not.

"Why would you make this?" she demanded when she had enough breath to speak. "This is a waste of station resources."

"*Hardly. The agoge drains power constantly regardless of what you use it for.*"

"*You're* a station resource."

"Rec time is your own time, those are the rules. Aren't you the rules type? You seem like a rules type." Avi sounded amused. *"You're on the roof, huh? I set it to easy so they're too stupid to climb, but the bad news for you is that eventually they're going to find the stairs. Got a weapon yet?"*

"I get it, you're good at this. You could make something meaningful," said Kyr. "You could be building things our soldiers actually need."

"You don't think our soldiers need to know what it feels like to be hunted by a gang of merciless war monsters twice your size?"

"Majo are small," Kyr reminded him.

The voice in her ear didn't answer. Kyr walked between the vegetable planters toward those wooden crates, keeping an eye on that door. The grunted conversation from the street had gone quiet. Probably a bad sign.

Propped up in the shadow of the crates was a staff, capped and weighted at either end with gleaming silver. Well, it would give her some reach, and against that eight-footer she would need all the reach she could get. Kyr picked it up.

There was a thud. The door shuddered on its hinges. Kyr went to wait in front of it. The doorway was human-sized. It wasn't big enough for more than one of Avi's monsters to get through at a time.

Another thud. Then the door smashed into pieces around a massive armored shoulder.

Kyr attacked.

It was the eight-footer with the mace. Kyr hadn't got a close look at the primitive body armor when the simulation started, but since she was using a fairly basic weapon herself she doubted she could achieve much by going straight at it. She went for the face instead, smashing the weighted base of the staff into the tusked jaw so the thing's head snapped sideways, and then went in with a low sweep and knocked the monster's feet out from underneath. She came up turning and kicked it hard in the chest, feeling the blow rattle through her knee. The orc went stumbling backward through the doorway windmilling its arms and knocked down the three behind it when it fell.

"Stupid, huh," Kyr said.

The orc got to its feet, snarling and shaking its head hard. The rest of them were piling up confusedly behind it, except for one on the ground which had taken the spike of its ally's ax in the thigh as it tripped. Kyr bounced on her feet, waited for her moment, and then as the giant advanced she smashed it in the face again—going for its nose this time, snapping its head backward.

The orc howled and fell.

Avi said, "*Huh.*"

"I *am* good at this," said Kyr. The big one wasn't getting up. Two behind it tried to squeeze past it through the doorframe at the same time. "Are these human? They move like humans." It was more like mat practice than agoge work. The agoge was where you fought majo. Mat practice against Coyote, maybe—though even the warbreed boys of Mags's mess weren't *this* much bigger than Kyr.

Avi's orcs really were stupid. The only tactic they seemed to be able to think of was rushing her. It would work if they were out in the open. If even one of these giants had her pinned, Kyr would not be able to get loose again. But as long as she could control how they came at her, the problem of their size stopped mattering.

"*Well, I had to base them on something,*" Avi said, sounding irritated. "*Are you actually having fun?*"

"This is still stupid," said Kyr.

"*That's supposed to be a wizard's staff,*" Avi said. "*You're hitting them in the face with it when you could literally just set them all on fire.*"

"What would be the point of that?" said Kyr, knocking another orc down and stamping hard on its fingers. Its grip on its wicked-looking serrated knife relaxed a fraction. Kyr snatched it up and cut the thing's throat. Black blood sprayed everywhere.

"*Not everything has to have a point!*" said Avi. "*Are you sure you're Magnus's sister?*"

"*Yes,*" said Kyr. "I am."

As she said it she killed the last of the stupid orcs. The rooftop shimmered and dissolved around her. Kyr was left standing in the middle of the grey plasteel floor in an empty room. She felt a sudden sharp tug of loss—for that primitive stone city, where the steps and doorways were all the right size for a person, and the sky blazed blue.

"Was that a real place?" she said.

"No," said Avi's voice in her ear after a moment. "*I got it out of a book.*"

Kyr for no particular reason felt angry. So that was what this *very smart* person did with all his hours in the arcade: dragged up old media to read books about things that never existed. "Is that what you did with my brother? Wasted his time treating the agoge like a game?"

"*The agoge is a game,*" said Avi.

"The agoge is training for war."

"*If you say so.*"

"Did you find him yet?" demanded Kyr.

"No," said Avi. "*It would help if you shut up.*"

Kyr clenched her hands into fists. She couldn't remember ever wanting to hit someone quite as much as she wanted to hit Avi now. It wasn't the cold simplicity of how she'd known she would break Admiral Russell's wrist. She wanted to punch him right in the *face*, to feel the crunch of cartilage against her knuckles when his nose broke. Mags was gone, and he was supposed to be Mags's friend, and all he did was sneer.

The grey room was too cold. Kyr missed the sky.

"Give me another scenario," she demanded. "Something you built for my brother."

"*Maybe I build these for me,*" Avi said.

"You think I can't handle it? I'm as good as he is. I'll fight your monsters. Show me."

"*Fine.*"

The space dissolved. Kyr looked around, and then up, at the reappearing sky.

She was standing in a semicircular courtyard. There was a building behind her made of more white stone, reaching high into the sky. At its upper levels the stone gave way to glass that shone in the sunlight. A fountain was set against the wall, water bubbling up and splashing over a basin. Climbing plants were trained along its edges, and the water dripped down dark green leaves, leaving a wet sheen.

More plants were laid out in the rest of the courtyard, in beds that followed the curved shapes of the semicircle. All of them seemed to be in bloom. Kyr saw nothing she recognized from Agricole—nothing useful, nothing edible. Just color, almost more color than she had known existed in the world: white and cream and red and pink and blue and yellow and riotous purple. Small winged invertebrates moved between blossoms, making low buzzing sounds.

The courtyard was on the lip of a cliff. A carved balustrade marked its edge, and beyond that the world dropped away. Kyr went to the edge and looked over.

There were birds nesting down there. Kyr knew what birds were from Nursery, from Ursa's stories, from the names of the girls' cadet messes. The birds had their nests tucked in crevices where dull greenness spread, clinging stubbornly to the stone. Far below, at the base of the cliff, there was a white stone city. Tiny human figures moved through the streets. Kyr thought that if she looked long enough she might be able to see the rooftop where she had been killing monsters moments ago.

"What is this?" she said.

"*Something I made for Magnus,*" said Avi. "*You asked.*"

Kyr looked up into the sky. She had to shield her eyes against the light with her hand. There was nothing descending on her out of the shining expanse. "Where are the hostiles?"

"*I guess we didn't get around to those yet.*"

Kyr said nothing.

"*Let me know when it all gets too pointless for you,*" Avi said, but Kyr found she could ignore him.

After a while longer looking out from the cliffside at the city below, she went to the fountain. When she put her hands into the water it felt real. The scents of the flowers mixed in the air to create a chaotic kind of perfume. It was a little like being in Agricole, but Agricole did not have a sky.

Kyr took her hands out of the fountain and sat down. Drops of water ran past her wrists. There was a deep green leaf at the edge of the basin with water dripping steadily from its tip. Kyr put her hand underneath it.

Slowly the light changed. The sun was dropping down the sky. Some of the flowers closed. Kyr heard sounds she couldn't make sense of coming from the cliffside, until she realized it was the birds calling to each other. She stayed where she was, watching the water bubble and splash in the stone basin and drip through green leaves to sink away into the ground.

Eventually a voice in her ear said, *"Found him."*

CHAPTER SIX

STRIKE

The garden on the cliffside flickered and dissolved back into the plasteel box of the agoge. Kyr scrambled to her feet. After a second Avi came in. His expression was flat. His unruly red hair was even more tangled than before, as if he'd been running his hands through it.

"Where?" said Kyr, taking out the earpiece.

"Hold on," said Avi. He double-checked that the door was locked, then made a one-handed gesture. The agoge materialized controls out of nothing.

Kyr was startled. "How—"

"They all have this," Avi said. "No one tells you how to use it. You're not meant to understand what's going on, you just fight. I got six black marks when they realized I'd figured this out. Then they dumped me in Systems, where they specifically banned me from working on anything interesting. Lucky me."

"What were you using it for?"

"Cheating," Avi said. "The Drill supervisors checking the feeds saw me running comfortable Level Sevens. I used the time to try building things. Don't look so scandalized. The fact that I actually understand the agoge is the reason I could find your precious brother. There." His hands had been moving across the controls as he spoke; now he gave her a narrow smile. "Privacy. If anyone looks, they'll see you running through a drill while I take notes."

"Great. Where's Mags?"

Instead of answering, Avi said, "Did you know all this is based on majo technology? Same as the jump hooks, or the dimensional trapping around the hangar exits. Anytime you get into this kind of fine-tuned reality bending, serious shadowspace stuff, you're working off the majo. They know more about it than we ever have. Or ever will, probably, given that we don't talk to them and Command hates fun."

"I suppose you admire them," said Kyr.

Avi's hands paused on the controls. "They killed our world."

Kyr hadn't expected him to say that.

She hadn't expected him to obviously *mean* it.

"Well?" she managed after a moment. "I thought you said you'd found him."

"I have," said Avi. "Look."

One wall of the agoge melted away. It was replaced with a life-sized image of Kyr's brother, broad shoulders and blond hair. COYOTE / MAGNUS hung in the air over his head. Blocks of text flashed up, appearing and disappearing too fast for Kyr to read as Avi narrowed his eyes and made skimming gestures at them.

Kyr ignored them. She had not seen Mags in days. The ghostly image looked through her rather than at her, but it had his slight slouch, his expression of endlessly neutral patience. Did his eyes always look that hollow?

"Is this his *Command file*?" she said.

"Of course."

Kyr wasn't meant to be looking at this. At least she wasn't reading anything. Avi was. He read very fast, if the speed at which boxes of text appeared and were coolly dismissed meant anything.

"There you go," Avi said at last. White text that said FEROX (REF) was floating in the air next to Magnus's name. "Assigned to Ferox. Refused assignment. Dismissed from service. Left the station two days ago."

"No," said Kyr. Her stomach felt like it was collapsing on itself. "No, he wouldn't."

There was a pause. She became aware of Avi looking at her. She refused to look back at him. She made herself stand straight.

Everything in her hurt. She wouldn't let this nasty little nothing of a person, this *cheat*, see it.

"No," said Avi at last. "He wouldn't, would he?"

Kyr rounded on him. Maybe she *would* break his nose. "If you think you can make fun of me—"

"I'm not," Avi said. "He was my friend, you know."

"Why was my brother ever friends with someone like you?"

"I guess we have some things in common," Avi said. He was still looking at her in that odd way. "I'm saying you're right, Valkyr. Magnus wouldn't have just left."

"He would never turn his back on humanity—"

"Oh, to hell with that. He just wouldn't have left you."

Kyr froze.

"Sorry," Avi added, and averted his gaze. "Didn't mean to make you cry."

"I am *not*—"

"Something's weird here, that's all." He turned back to the controls. "I wonder if I can—Huh. Yes, I can." He paused. "Are you sure you want to know?"

"Of course I want to know!"

"I'm asking because we're going to get caught," said Avi. "Not right away, but what I'm about to do will get picked up next time Corporal Lin does the security sweep. Probably first thing tomorrow. And then we're both going to get into a lot of trouble. I live in trouble anyway, but *you*—"

"Do it," said Kyr.

"Last chance."

"*Do it.*"

Avi nodded. He turned back to the controls. A second later the ghostly image of Magnus dissolved. Kyr nearly asked him to bring it back. But Avi was frowning. "Okay," he murmured softly to the agoge, "okay, okay . . . oh, beautiful, there you go."

The wall opposite turned into a flat screen showing a picture of a human Kyr had never seen before. The person had long thick hair and was wearing a buttoned sleeveless jacket and something a little like Lisabel's red skirt—or, well, it *was* a skirt, definitely, but it was fitted to the person's body the way Command uniforms fitted, and it draped and shone. Kyr had never seen a human wearing such expensive textiles. The person also had tight jeweled bands wrapped around—his? her?—thick biceps, and the shape of his-or-her jacket showed he-or-she was flat-chested. A banner across the bottom of the image said ARI SHAH, GALACTIC CORRESPONDENT. "Is that a man or a woman?" Kyr asked.

Avi rolled his eyes. "They're a journalist," he said. "Are you ready to commit an exile-or-execution offense?" He cast a sharp grin at her over his shoulder. "We're about to watch some foreign propaganda."

He snapped his fingers showily. The picture started moving. The—man, Kyr decided, based on the arms and not much else—said, "—development," and flashed a toothy smile at his invisible audience. "There has been huge excitement across Chrysothemis since the announcement of the Prince of the Wisdom's visit. We'll go live to an expert at the Xenia Institute—Professor Hussain. Professor." The screen split and showed an elderly brown-skinned woman sitting in a chair in front of a panel that had a circular design of green diamond shapes on a white background. She too was wearing expensive cloth, a purple headscarf and a heavily draped purple shawl. "Who—or what—is the Prince of the Wisdom?"

"First you have to understand that the Wisdom is an enormously complicated technology," said the woman in a deep strong voice. "It's not just that *we* don't understand it. Even the majo don't fully comprehend how it works."

"How does anyone build a machine they don't understand?" asked the journalist. Kyr was starting to think the person was a woman after all, but her perception kept shifting back and forth again. The journalist stayed good-looking whichever gender Kyr's brain settled on. It made her uncomfortable, and it was hard to concentrate on what the professor was talking about.

"It's likely the majo *did* understand it when they built it," said Professor Hussain, "but that was thousands of years ago. The

Wisdom, remarkably, is able to improve and refine itself, in order to pursue its ultimate goal of peace and happiness for all sentient beings."

That got Kyr's attention. She heard herself hiss involuntarily. She had known that human collaborators existed; but there was something singularly horrifying about watching this handsome old woman talk about the Wisdom and peace in the same sentence.

The journalist was just nodding. "So tell us how a Prince of the Wisdom fits into the picture. Is it true that they rule the majoda?"

"That's a common misconception," said Professor Hussain. "The majoda is not a single state. It's barely even a federation. It's more a loose association, made up of many thousands of independent worlds—and so it doesn't really have a ruler as such."

"But the Wisdom unites those independent worlds," said the journalist.

"That much is true. The Wisdom is a technology meant to steer the whole majoda toward the greater good—whatever that may be."

"Then what exactly is a Prince of the Wisdom, if not a ruler?"

"Well," said Professor Hussain, "in many ways, the answer is *we don't know.* The Wisdom custom-designs these individuals to its own specifications and produces them in artificial reproductive environments. They themselves don't seem to know what they're for. Many have gone down in the history of the majoda as great scientists, philosophers, or even leaders—but a lot of people don't realize that many more have just lived out unremarkable everyday lives. The most commonly accepted theory is that the Wisdom sees its creations—the Princes of the Wisdom—as case studies. Though that of course gets into arguments about just how sentient the Wisdom *is.* The answer to that is we don't know either."

"So how about our visitor, Professor?"

"Leru Ihenni Tan Yi," said Professor Hussain, and the screen split and put up a portrait of an alien. Kyr stiffened, for a moment.

Slim build, huge eyes, a crest of stiff slender flukes: at first she thought it was the majo that had been captured by Victrix. But no: just another alien of the same type. "Don't be surprised if you don't recognize the species," said the professor. "The majo zi are usually thought of as the founders of the majoda—notice that their word for 'sentient' is *majo*. But their numbers are few, and they are reclusive. Prince Leru, in their capacity as a diplomat, is possibly the best-known representative these days—"

"Is it true they were one of the generals of the majoda during the Terran War?" interrupted the journalist.

Professor Hussain wore a microexpression of dismay, there and gone again. "Well, that's in the past, and I'm not a historian," she said. "I'm sure Prince Leru is looking forward to coming to Chrysothemis and enjoying the hospitality of humanity ahead of the activation of our first Wisdom node, and I know we all hope this is the next step toward lasting peace and friendship between humankind and the rest of the universe."

Avi snapped his fingers and the image froze on the journalist—the *man*, Kyr told herself firmly—opening his mouth to say something else. "So," he said. "That's it, then."

"Peace and friendship," said Kyr. "They're sick."

"Chrysothemis is the only majority-human world left," said Avi. "Former colony. Surrendered early during the war. It's got a population of something like two million."

"*How* many?" Kyr had not known there were that many humans left in the universe.

"Not counting all the aliens," Avi said. "Do you not know this?"

"Why should I know anything about a planet of traitors?"

"Your sister lives there," said Avi. "Magnus asked me to find out."

Kyr felt the usual stab of bitter disquiet at the thought of Ursa. But it wasn't all anger driving it this time. There was also dread. They were bringing the Wisdom to that traitor human world. Ursa would be living in its power.

"So," she said, "you think Magnus somehow knew they were

going to install a node of the Wisdom on Chrysothemis, and he went to save Ursa?"

It made sense. Mags still loved Ursa, even after what she'd done; even after she'd abandoned them and Gaea.

"No," Avi said. "This clip was cross-referenced to his file. I think *Command* knew. And they sent him there."

"To do what?"

Avi took a deep breath. "Here's the bit that's definitely going to get us caught," he said, and he brought up Mags's file again, that larger-than-life image surrounded by every record Command had about Kyr's brother. And then he did something at the agoge controls that made all the floating bits of text dissolve except for COYOTE / MAGNUS—FEROX (REF).

Avi frowned at it. He flicked his fingers at the control panel and the text changed color. Now it was red. It said: COYOTE / MAGNUS—STRIKE.

"They sent him there to kill," said Avi. "And to die."

Kyr stared.

"But," she said, "but Strike's not real. It's not a real assignment."

"Looks pretty real to me," said Avi. He was bringing up more red text now, and pictures of human-sized streets under a clouded sky. "There's the mission. Dates, times, contacts, targets. Maps. Don't you think it's funny? The rest of the universe is throwing information at us day and night, and no one's allowed to look at any of it except Command. The sad part is most of them just use all that high-level access to watch porn. Of course, some of them take things seriously." Avi pointed at the signature underneath a set of bullet-pointed instructions: *J*, and a squiggle. "Aulus Jole. You know, I always thought Strike had to be his baby. He's the only person in Command without his own wing."

"Because he's a war hero," said Kyr. "Because he stands for us all, because—"

But it made sense. Kyr knew Uncle Jole. Everyone knew about the hours he spent in the agoge, refighting their lost war. He'd built the Doomsday scenario, based on what he'd seen and suffered. He'd been there the day the majo murdered Earth. Did she really believe that he didn't fight anymore, didn't even take an interest in Gaea's warrior heart? He made a point of not interfering with the combat wings.

Because he had a wing of his own.

And he'd claimed Magnus for it.

"Why else do you think they let people leave?" Avi said. "All that hot air about the sanctity of human lives and no one *having* to serve. You think they really want defectors out there telling the majo what our defenses are like?" He smiled nastily. "No. But they let it happen, because every once in a while they want to remind the rest of the universe that we're still here and we're still angry, and every once in a while there's a defector who's not really a defector at all."

Kyr went closer to the place where Jole's name hung in the air. She started reading through what was written above it. It read like a scenario briefing for the agoge. Goals. Obstacles. Warnings. Kyr pressed her lips tight together and breathed through her nose as she read.

While she was still reading Avi waved his hand over the agoge controls and everything he'd summoned up disappeared: the Chrysothemis journalist still smiling out from one wall, the larger-than-life image of Mags, the blocks of instructions and photographs and maps. "I was reading that," said Kyr.

"Don't make things worse for yourself," Avi said. "When Lin picks it up tomorrow, you'll want to be able to say you were a good girl once you realized the stuff was confidential. Blame me, if you like."

"This was all my idea," said Kyr. "I told you to do it."

"You're saying you *wouldn't* blame me?"

"No."

"Huh."

Without the agoge filling the space with uncoiling information the two of them were left just standing in a cold plasteel room with a high ceiling and a dull hum in the air. Avi pushed his ugly tangle of red hair away from his face and said, "So. Your brother's gone off to be a hero. Happy now?"

Kyr barely heard him. Her head was full of what she had managed to read. Mags's training scores were better than hers, because he was bigger, stronger, faster. All the Coyotes were bigger and stronger and faster than Kyr. She was made for war, but so were they: she had realized early in adolescence that the absolute limits of her body's abilities would still never beat the boys. She'd had to succeed a different way. Mags had needed Avi to talk him through beating Doomsday. But Kyr had nearly beaten it alone less than a week ago—*after* Jole had made it harder. She was good at thinking her way through an impossible fight. It was the one thing she was better at than Mags.

"I'm not happy," she said.

Mags's Strike mission focused on a specific moment: the arrival of Prince Leru on Chrysothemis, and the crowd that was expected to gather to watch traitorous human diplomats greet the alien. Jole had given an overview of expected security: aliens and humans, top-of-the-line majoda weaponry—majo were weak, but their drones were frightening—and the unknown quantity of the Wisdom, which was capable of all sorts of reality-twisting cheats.

"He'll die," said Kyr.

"What do you think Strike is for?" said Avi. "Yeah, he'll die. They're supposed to die."

Kyr didn't think his casual tone was honest. There was a flat look in his squinty eyes. He was Mags's friend. "He'll die and it won't even do anything," she said. "He's going for the crowd. He's not supposed to try to get near the majo. He won't change anything, he won't stop anything, he'll just die killing humans and it won't matter and—it's the wrong mission!"

She could not believe her own voice was saying it. But it was true. Command had got it wrong. Uncle Jole had got it wrong. They'd sent Kyr's brother away to a meaningless death. It was their duty to obey, but this was wasteful, pointless, *stupid*.

Kyr tried not to let herself think all the way to the end of the idea she was having, but the possibility had so much weight it distorted everything around it. If Command could be this wrong about Mags—then maybe that wasn't the only mistake they'd made. Maybe they were wrong about Kyr. Maybe they'd misjudged the way humanity needed her service.

She could change everything.

She could show Command what she was really capable of. She could save her brother from a pointless death. She could say to the universe, to the Wisdom's universe which the majo thought they owned: *You killed our world, but we are still here. We have not forgotten. We will not forgive.*

Earth's children live.

And while we live, the enemy shall fear us.

Kyr pressed her hand to her chest as if she could feel the bright ball of clarity expanding there like a star. She turned to Avi, who was eyeing her uncertainly. Time, there was no time. How long before she had to report to Sergeant Sif in Nursery? Refusing the assignment would mean answering questions and Kyr did not think she could keep the shining decision inside her from showing. It wouldn't be enough just to tell Commander Jole he was wrong. She had to prove it. "I need your help," she said.

"You've had my help," Avi said. "Now what do you want?"

"I'm going after him."

Avi's jaw worked. "Okay, I take it back," he said at last. "You're not the rules type. You're *insane.* What do you think you're going to do?"

Kyr told the truth. "I'm going to save my brother's life. You *are* going to help me."

"Why would I do that?"

"You're in love with him," Kyr said confidently. "Aren't you?"

It made sense of their weird friendship. It was the only thing that could. Oh, Mags's soft spot for lost causes didn't need explaining, but the *other* half of the equation was Avi, who was clearly an asshole. Still, Kyr and Mags belonged to the same carefully planned warbreed lineage: the whole point was to embody human physical excellence. So when Mags—big, beautiful, the perfect soldier—had noticed Avi and started talking to him, got interested in his games and his daydreams, his imaginary cities and his clifftop garden, why wouldn't Avi, bitter sharp-tongued friendless little queer that he was, have fallen in love with him?

Kyr almost felt sorry for him.

Avi was wearing the same arrested look he'd had when Kyr said she wouldn't blame him for digging into confidential files. "That wouldn't bother you?"

"I don't care. Help me save him."

"Gaea has no midrange ships," Avi said. "We still have the dreadnought shadow engines, but without something the size of a dreadnought to absorb the shock of the jump they're pretty much useless. They get defectors off the station by dropping them on a neutral-zone asteroid with three days of air and a distress beacon. But that only works as a way to get away if they're not trying to keep you. And they *will* try to keep you, Valkyr."

Kyr said nothing.

"It's Nursery, right?" Avi said. "They want another ten Magnuses, and you're how they're getting them."

"It doesn't matter," Kyr said. "I'm bringing him home."

Avi said, "I have a condition."

"What?"

"You take me with you."

Kyr considered him. He was scrawny and too short and he'd spent his cadet years skipping drills. Since he'd been assigned to Systems odds were good he hadn't bothered keeping up with more than the very minimum fitness requirement. The squint suggested vision issues on top of everything else. He was going to be completely useless: a chain around Kyr's neck every moment she was trying to reshape her destiny and the destiny of the last human planet and at the same time save her brother's life.

"Why haven't you defected already?" she said.

"They killed our world," Avi said. "The agoge's here." He ticked the answers off on his fingers, one, two. Then he tapped a third finger and said, "And—Command doesn't know how *much* I know about how Gaea actually manages to function, but they know I know more than I should. You defect by refusing assignment, you know. They let you go because it's before you've got anything of value to tell the majo: unassigned kids don't know anything. Except I knew too much by the time I was fourteen."

"They wouldn't let you leave," Kyr said. It was a reasonable precaution.

"It was made very clear to me on the day I got my assignment that if I tried," Avi said, "they'd just shoot me."

"Why didn't they shoot you anyway?"

"Probably because I'm a genius," Avi said. "Gaea's got plenty of people like you. Good soldiers prepared to die for humanity. It doesn't have anyone else like me." He folded his arms. "Well? You heard me. If you want my help, that's the price. Take me with you. And you can try bringing Magnus home if you want—but I'm not coming back."

So Kyr's plan would cost Gaea an asset that humanity could use. She could see, grudgingly, that Avi could be useful, provided you kept him well away from any actual fighting. He was clever. The agoge scenario he'd created had had more depth and detail in it than anything else Kyr had ever run except the scenarios Jole had built himself. Maybe Command was hoping to scrape the sharp edges off him with the dull Systems work he obviously hated until he understood his place, and then finally put him to work making Gaea stronger.

It didn't matter. At the end of the day, Mags and Kyr together were worth more to the future of humanity than someone like Avi ever could be. The trade-off was worth it. It had to be.

"Fine," she said. "I'll take you with me."

CHAPTER SEVEN

DREADNOUGHT

There had never been spare resources to build a prison on Gaea. Besides, they didn't need one. Each of the four dreadnoughts at the station's heart had a brig. All that was required, on the rare occasions it was necessary to waste resources keeping someone alive but useless, was for Systems to bring a corridor's worth of ship security back to life.

Kyr had never been inside the empty hulk of the *Victrix* before.

She left Avi in the shadowed caves under Suntracker with a grapple. He looked at it like she'd handed him a poisonous vine. "It's not going to bite you," Kyr said.

"Is this really necessary?" Avi said. "Wouldn't it make more sense if I waited somewhere around the Oikos storerooms—"

"Look," said Kyr, "do you want me to take you with me or not?"

"I'm just saying—"

"Sergeant Harriman would send a patrol to scoop you up in the first ten minutes," Kyr said. Avi even knew that, she could tell by his face: he was just a coward. "No one's going to come through here till rotation change. Wait till I give the word, then jump. You'll have six minutes."

Avi looked sick. "I never went in for this stupid challenge—are you sure that's enough time—"

"I can make it from here to Drill in under five," Kyr said, "and that's twice the distance."

"You're a genetically enhanced killing machine," Avi muttered. "Fine. Fine."

"Unless we take a dart instead," said Kyr. She'd argued for it. She did not like Avi's plan.

"No," said Avi. "Trust me, we would just die. The only person who's ever pulled off an escape that way was your sister, and she took a hostage."

A *hostage?* Kyr had never heard that before. But she did not care about anything Ursa had done. She was nothing like Ursa, and this was nothing to do with Ursa. "All right," she said.

She didn't have her own grapple. You couldn't sign out too much at once from Drill storage. She'd thought carefully and in the end taken nothing. A gun would have been good, but you had to actually talk to someone, and then you were supposed to go straight to the range. It would be too easy to get caught. Every adult on Gaea was supposed to carry a field knife, but Kyr, unassigned, didn't count as an adult yet, and Avi said he'd traded his to someone for more food.

"Okay," she said, standing at the crack that ran down the middle of the cave. Gaea's core was pitted with tunnels. She knew them well. She'd spent a long time practicing her five-minute run. She could do this.

Kyr jumped.

The first ledge was six feet down. Kyr landed hard and swung herself over the edge, reaching for handholds automatically. She normally did this part with a synthfiber rope, but that didn't mean she *needed* one. The tunnel walls were rough natural rock. She had no gloves and her hands were quickly scraped and stinging. She had to hang by her fingertips and then let go in order to get past a tunnel entrance that would take you through a sidelong route to Systems.

Now it got harder.

The closer you got to the shadow engines pulsing at the heart of Gaea's native planetoid, the less meaningful directions like *up* and *down* were. Kyr scrambled onward as fast as she dared, clinging to the wall even when she could have stood up and called it *floor*, ignoring the dizzy swoop of her stomach when her mind felt certain she was upside down. Sometimes it was easier to just close your eyes as you moved. All of it was a lot easier with a rope. Kyr gritted her teeth. Avi couldn't do this without a grapple, and she could, so she was doing it.

She opened her eyes when she heard the hum. It was a little like the hum in the air in the agoge, but louder, with an edge that made her teeth ache. People said that if you stayed here too long your teeth would fall out. They said you would start bleeding from your eyes. There were rumors about a cadet who'd misjudged a jump and died smeared across fifteen dimensions.

Kyr crouched on a ledge just below the lip of the tunnel she'd climbed through. Her confused inner ear had settled on *up,* so she was looking up rather than down into Gaea's central chamber. Over her head, hanging suspended in massive jury-rigged cradles, hooked together with thick exposed cables that were deadly to touch, and shimmering with green ghost flickers as they shifted in and out of reality, were the four great shadow engines that maintained Gaea's gravity.

They didn't do much more than that. Vic had got interested once and not shut up about it for weeks: Gaea *had* a power source capable of giving them at least four hundred times what Suntracker eked out with its aging array of solar sails. But powering the shadow engines up to full was deadly without the elaborate shells and layers of protection that had been stripped from the dreadnoughts before human patriots managed to rescue what was left. No one tried to bring them up past five percent, not since the explosive disaster that had wiped out the gene-tailoring suites fifteen years ago.

The unshielded engines, running at five percent of their real power, hummed soft and deadly over Kyr's head. She looked at them for a moment too long. It was a stupid thought, but sometimes they seemed almost alive.

Dragging them from the ships they'd once been mounted in had not been easy. The dreadnoughts had used their close-combat gravity cannons to blast openings in the rock, then crashed themselves inside. The cavernous hangars of Ferox, Augusta, Scythica, and Victrix all ended in tunnels that led down here, each with a dreadnought's corpse forming a seal on the core. Kyr narrowed her eyes against the green subreal glow and looked for it: the stenciled shape of a stylized *V* made from the body of a winged woman. That was the *Victrix*'s shadow engine. It was near the top of the cavern. The dark hollow above it was the only unsecured entrance to the Victrix hangar.

Unsecured was relative. There was a live shadow engine in the way. Even running at a mere five percent, it could definitely smear Kyr across fifteen dimensions if she touched it. And time and space distorted once you got in range, so not touching it wasn't just a question of being careful.

This was the part Kyr knew for a fact Avi *couldn't* do, the reason she'd had to leave him to catch up later.

She'd never done this before either. The Suntracker-to-Drill run took you straight down the middle of this cavern at top speed with a grapple, well away from the shadow engines. You had to lean *into* the gravity distortions to speed yourself up. You'd be halfway to Drill before the world inverted and you were falling *up* and for a glorious instant it felt like flying.

Kyr had trained with jump hooks in the agoge. By the time you hit Level Eleven you needed them. They were just miniaturized shadow engines with a directional boost, but you had to know how to feel your way through the invisible currents of spacetime, or you'd end up hurled disastrously in a random direction like you'd stepped in a dimensional trap. River rapids, Uncle Jole had called it once; and then he'd looked older for a moment, and impossibly sad.

The four humming engines were a lot bigger than a single jump hook.

The shiver that went through Kyr felt more like joy than fear. She leapt.

Gravity meant next to nothing in the space between the four engines. Avi had tried to tell Kyr what to do, talking about feedback loops and distortion wells. Kyr had said, "You need to have seen it at least once to be sure, don't you?" Mags had said that about running Doomsday: *He had me run it a few times, and then—*

Avi looked grim, and then he said, "Yes."

"Don't worry about it. Leave it to me."

"If you die—"

"I won't," Kyr said. "I can't."

Ferox was the closest. Kyr fell into the engine's pull and let it drag her sideways. It flickered in and out of reality in a pulse pattern like a heartbeat, and Kyr felt the pulses rush over her with pinpoints of ghost sensation, green light and prickling temperature changes and finally a ring of soundless noise. The human body couldn't really process what was happening during a pass through shadowspace, but it tried.

Beat. Beat. Beat. *There.*

Kyr pushed away from a springy belt of nothingness that existed for just a fraction of a second before it collapsed into a sucking well that would have spat her straight into the Ferox engine's maw. Her vision flickered and she saw herself fall-flying across the echoing chamber, her own lean long-legged body visible from two angles at once as her selves dove past each other: a time split, mirrored. She caught her breath as she touched the wall of the cavern at an angle from where she'd started, out of the worst of the distortion field for an instant, but she didn't wait: she was round by Augusta's engine now, and she needed to be under Victrix. She let herself fall backward and into the current of Augusta's quick one-two-three pulses, a different pattern from Ferox's and a different chain of distortions, and let it carry her to the center of the cavern. Her whole body was alight with the motion. She felt the moment when the great slow wave of the Scythica engine tried to take hold of her from the other direction, and she twisted and jackknifed and—

flew—

—almost directly into one of the live cables that kept the power output of the four engines yoked together. Kyr shouted and snatched her hand back from where it instinctively tried to grab the strut of the Victrix engine cradle to avoid the danger, which would have *killed her.* The cable passed over her face with inches to spare.

She landed in a heap on the cavern floor under the Victrix engine and burst into laughter.

Like flying; like the jolt of joy from smashing Avi's orc warrior in the face. River rapids. Kyr's heart was thumping. She felt magnificent.

The entrance she'd climbed up through was a shaft in the ceiling now. Kyr tapped the earpiece Avi had given her. "I'm through," she said. "It's easy from here."

After a moment Avi's voice said in her ear, *"You really are insane."*

Kyr couldn't even find him annoying. She had to swallow laughter to answer, "Six minutes, remember. I'll tell you when to move."

The dead warship was naked. Its armor plating had been stripped before Kyr was born. But the patriots of Gaea had not been able to bring themselves to dismantle the strip of forward armor marked with the name: TE-66 VICTRIX, in letters twice as tall as Kyr. Underneath them a jagged patch of metal had been left hanging on the ship's frame, stenciled with Victrix's sigil, the winged woman. Her gigantic face looked down at Kyr from the shadows, stern and silent. The only light came from the flickers of green in the tunnel behind Kyr, leading down to the shadow engines in the station core.

Kyr did not let herself pause. She scrambled over the remains of forward weapons casings and outlying shield generators and solar-sail mounts until she found a cracked airlock. Avi had dug up a schematic to show her: this was the way to the bridge.

Kyr heaved open the inner hatch with her legs pressed against one wing of the lock and her back against the other. She fell through it when it popped apart, and a scrap of metal clattered to the deck beside her. The sound felt very loud. Kyr froze.

Nothing happened. Dim emergency lights began to glow around her with an uncertain reddish hue. Kyr pictured what she'd seen from outside: the *Victrix* tilted nose-first toward the heart of the station. The way she needed to go was technically up, but right now it felt like down.

She followed the slope of the corridor till it turned. The emergency lighting followed her. Kyr wished it wouldn't, though it was unthinkable that anyone would be in this part of the empty dreadnought. Red glimmers kept catching her attention. Even her breathing felt too loud.

"I'm here," she whispered when she reached the bridge. "What do I do?"

"*Auxiliary power,*" said Avi in her ear. "*On your left—smash the glass, hand on the plate.*"

The glass was already smashed. There were shards on the floor around Kyr's feet as she put her hand onto the black handprint shape on the wall behind where it had been. She heard—half felt—an answering hum when she touched the spot. The red emergency lighting seemed to be shining a little brighter. "Now what?"

"*Engineering bridge console. Directly ahead of you. Under the admiral's nose.*"

Kyr saw what he meant. The dreadnought's bridge was laid out so that someone sitting in the chair on the rear platform could instantly see everything that was going on and make eye contact with anyone they needed to speak to. The console Avi meant was directly below it. When she touched it a bank of lights came to life. One of them was flashing in a familiar urgent pattern: *distress.* Kyr frowned and touched it.

"*What are you doing!*"

"—ston. I repeat, this is Admiral Elora Marston, TE-66 *Victrix.*" A woman's voice. Kyr stood still. Elora. Wasn't that a name she knew?

The name on the photograph in Jole's office: Kyr's genetic mother, right. But she'd been just a junior officer. Uncle Jole had told them so. This Elora was an admiral in the Terran Expeditionary. There were no women ranked higher than sergeant in Gaea's command structure. There were only a few of those, and one of them was Sergeant Sif in Nursery, a courtesy rank.

The voice cut out in a screech and then started again: "—*ix*. The hijackers have taken control of aft weapons and the dart hangar. My 2IC and systems chief have been suborned. Officers Nguyen and Villeneuve are dead. I have sealed the bridge. I will attempt to—"

Another screech of damage on the recording.

"—shadow engine," panted Admiral Marston. "If these stupid fucks want to restart the war *now* they're going to have to go *through* me." More screeching. Then the distress signal started to play from the beginning again.

Kyr cut it off just as Admiral Marston finished identifying herself. She looked up from the console to the admiral's platform. There was a long dark smear up the white plasteel wall.

She didn't know why she'd listened for so long. A female admiral, but a traitor. She'd tried to stand in the way of patriots claiming the *Victrix* for Gaea Station. She was nothing to Kyr.

Anyway obviously she'd failed, and got what she deserved.

"Why was that still there?" she asked.

Avi said quietly, "*I don't know.*" Kyr pictured him standing alone in the caves under Systems, at the top of the tunnel that led down here, clinging to the grapple she'd handed him. He really would be hopeless without her.

He directed Kyr to the console input he'd actually wanted and had her put in a bunch of commands she didn't understand. "*All right,*" he said at last. "*It's up to you now. I can set all that off remotely when you give the word. It'll buy us some time.*"

"And then you jump," said Kyr. "If you're coming with me."

"*If I'm not coming with you after this then I'm dead, genius or no genius,*" Avi said. "*Fuck, what I could do with these beautiful engines if we actually had the resources. All right. You're on your own."* He added grudgingly, *"Good luck."*

Kyr said, "Thanks."

Her voice echoed through the dreadnought's silent bridge. Kyr had never been here before. She looked around one last time. There were drifts of black Gaean dust starting to form in the corners. That was strange, because it meant someone *had* been here, and touched nothing, as if this place were a kind of shrine. Kyr did not look too directly at the smeared bloodstain up the wall behind the admiral's platform. Most of the easy ways to kill a human enemy were less messy than that. You'd have to do it on purpose, to leave that much splatter. You'd have to mean it.

She thought for some reason of Avi's orcs, their massive tusked forms bearing down on her, eight hostiles all twice her size. The blood smear went onto the floor as well. There were footprints in it. Maybe not eight sets of footprints.

Kyr was wasting time.

There was only one guard in the brig. The problem with prisoners was that it wasted at least two sets of resources: whatever it took to keep the prisoner alive, and then the waste of time that was having people stand around doing nothing but watch. Kyr had expected two guards, though. She crept along girders that had once supported a ceiling to get a better look, but her first assessment had been right.

She didn't recognize the soldier. He was old enough to have some grey hair, and he kept yawning. He didn't look up once. Kyr almost wanted him to. She could see it in her head: he'd look up, gasp, she'd leap down and land on his shoulders and overbalance him before he could react—

He didn't look up. Kyr wriggled back along the girder until she was round the corner out of sight, then dropped softly to the floor, ran her fingers through her ponytail to get rid of the gritty black dust, and walked smartly round the corner. "Message for you, sir," she said, and saluted.

Sir was flattery: he had no rank insignia.

The soldier, surprised, held out his hand for a flimsy. Kyr handed him the only one she had, her assignment: *Sparrow / Valkyr: NURSERY*. It was still crumpled where she'd clutched it.

While he was unfolding it Kyr knocked him sideways and then got her arms around his throat and hung on, choking him. He barely had enough time to yell.

He made some stifled noises before he finally sagged unconscious. Kyr went still, waiting. In her ear Avi said, *"He had a comm, but it's one of the shitty ones. Transmission down. Systems didn't catch anything."*

"Okay," said Kyr.

The soldier was breathing all right, kind of raspy. It would be safer to kill him. In the agoge, if it was an alien, Kyr would kill it. If she'd gone with her first impulse and jumped him from overhead, she would probably have had to kill him.

But he was a human being, a real person.

She took the flimsy back out of his nerveless fingers, and then she took his field knife and his gun. He didn't have any other weapons. If all you were doing was standing in front of a prison cell, you probably weren't going to need them. Kyr frowned at him anyway. Serving soldiers were meant to have full kit whenever they were on duty, in case of majo attack.

She picked up his Victrix insignia too. It was an old one: the winged woman was carefully inscribed on it, down to the details of her stern face and the individual feathers rising from her shoulders. Kyr had thought she would be wearing something like this by now.

She slipped it into her pocket along with the flimsy. The knife and gun went on her belt.

She turned to the cell. "Brig power now," she murmured to Avi.

A second later the shimmer of light over the lock went off. It was only a flicker, but it was enough time for Kyr to shoulder the door open.

The majo was sitting on the bare floor of the cell, near the back. For a moment Kyr thought it didn't have any arms, and then she saw that its hands were tied behind its back. Someone had put it in people clothes, the patched grey uniform of a cadet. It still had a purple discoloration across the side of its face, and there were more visible where the shirt collar gapped around its neck. Its silvery eyes were fixed on the door, probably, though without a pupil it was hard to tell. Its crest was flat against its skull, and its long narrow ears were still. There was no light in the cell except a low reddish glimmer around the door. Kyr could see the red box shape reflected in the alien's eyes.

She looked at the alien, and the alien looked at her. It didn't react at first, and then its ears twitched and its crest flicked up a little.

"Haven't we met?" it said softly.

Kyr said nothing.

The alien's head tilted. It was looking at Kyr's hand, which had drifted onto the hilt of her stolen field knife.

"Why are *you* afraid of *me*?" it asked.

Kyr drew the knife. She went into the cell, bent down, and cut the rope tying the majo's hands together. There was a lot of rope. Someone had been really determined to make sure it couldn't move. And one of its weird long fingers was swollen and pointing the wrong way. Broken, maybe.

It was hard to do the job without touching the alien. It kept trying to turn its head to see what Kyr was doing. One of its long flexible ears brushed her arm. Kyr worked to control her flinch. She wasn't afraid of *one majo*.

"Get up," she said, when it was loose.

The majo didn't move. "I don't understand. Are you here to kill me?"

"Be quiet. Get *up*."

"I don't want to die," it said. "I'm a person. A sentient. I don't want to die. Can you understand that?"

"I don't have time for this," said Kyr. She got her hands under its arms and dragged it upright. It made a whimpering sound. Its flailing hand brushed Kyr's. Its skin was cool, and it had regular patterns of short fine hair—fur—whatever—extending back in darkening diagonal lines from its wrist. "Can you walk?" Kyr demanded, letting it go in a hurry.

"Maybe," said the majo.

"Can you *run*?"

"Almost certainly not as fast as you, and that was before you all started kicking me. I think I would rather be killed here, honestly."

It started trying to sit down again. Kyr grabbed its wrist and hauled it upright. The majo cried out. And then there was a moment of weirdness. Kyr's vision blurred. She felt briefly sure she *had* killed the soldier outside, that she'd broken his neck and seen him fall; she remembered the awful crunching sound of it.

The majo snatched its hand away as if it found touching Kyr almost as weird as Kyr found touching it. "What was that?" snapped Kyr.

"What?" said the majo. "Nothing. I don't know what you're talking about."

"*For fuck's sake, be nice to it,*" Avi said in her ear. "*Have you heard of nice? Do you need me to talk you through it? Pretend you're Magnus.*"

Kyr stiffened. The majo's long ears flexed. "Who was that?" it said. "Who are *you*? I *know* I've seen you before."

Kyr couldn't be Mags. She wasn't nice. She never had been. Maybe Mags could have found something to like in this beaten-up enemy with inhuman silver eyes.

"I'm the person who's rescuing you," she told the majo. "Come with me."

On the floor outside the cell, the soldier she'd knocked out was still unconscious. His breathing was fine. Kyr shouldn't have stopped to check. She didn't have time. But it was a relief all the same.

CHAPTER EIGHT

YISO

Kyr was on edge the entire time she was leading the majo up through the bowels of the dead ship. It kept trying to talk to her. "I do know you. I remember you," it said. "We've met before. Then you broke some glassware. I think? Was that you? I'm afraid you all look quite similar."

"Shut up," Kyr muttered.

"My name is Yiso."

"Shut up, shut *up*."

"It was you, wasn't it? I think you also might have kicked me. Quite a lot of you have done that, though. I'm losing track. Will you tell me your name?"

Kyr rounded on it. Its ears went flat against its skull and it stared up at her, very still. Kyr didn't need Avi snapping at her to know that scaring the thing any worse than it already was wouldn't help her get what she wanted. How was she supposed to be nice to it? Who knew what majo even thought was *nice*?

"I'm Valkyr," she said. "If you're not quiet we're going to get caught. *Please* be quiet."

Please, it mouthed. Kyr wished she could read its expressions better. "I'm sorry," it said. "I'm in quite a lot of pain. It's making it harder for me to control my behavior. That's normal for me."

"I don't care what's normal for you," Kyr said.

"I'm getting the impression that's normal for you," it said. "Humans. Not humans. Gaeans. I'm sorry I ever came here. Oh, no, you wanted me to be quiet." It opened and closed its mouth. Kyr caught a glimpse of a dark tongue. "Please," it murmured, and its long ears flicked, and it finally stopped talking.

Kyr was relieved. They reached the reinforced gap that had been cut in *Victrix*'s hull long ago to drag the fighter cradles out. She held out her arm to halt the majo. It stumbled into Kyr's side. "Sorry," it said in a small voice that was probably meant to be a whisper, and pushed itself upright again by placing one of its cool hands on Kyr's forearm. Kyr forced herself not to flinch and gave it a glare. "Quiet," the majo repeated, staring up at her with its big silver eyes, and then its crest shivered and it touched its unbroken hand to its thin chest in a gesture Kyr guessed was supposed to be apologetic.

She was having a hard time thinking *it* while the alien kept talking to her. But what else was she supposed to think? It was an *alien*.

The Victrix hangar opened out in a spiral overhead, empty. Wing barracks were close by, but no one would be in here casually: unless a rotation had been scheduled, there was always a risk of the atmospheric seal going down during a Systems rebalance or one of Suntracker's dark spots. The majo ship in its big cradle stood out against the dimness, all its painted swirls of color glowing. Kyr watched for a long time, looking for movement. Avi had said they'd taken the guard off the ship once they'd worked out how to keep it from blowing itself up the minute its majo was out of range. Systems would be in charge of trying to make use of it, so he had reason to know. But Kyr waited anyway, because she wanted to be sure; and because once she began, there would be no going back.

The cavernous hangar was empty. There was no guard. This wasn't even going to be *hard*.

"Avi," Kyr said softly.

She heard him catch his breath.

"Jump."

Without waiting to hear him move she took the majo's wrist and dragged it out into the hangar. In the same instant there was a series of gigantic echoing clangs as entrances slammed shut and locked themselves, obedient to the commands Avi had routed through the *Victrix*. Warning lights flashed and an alarm started bleating as the atmospheric seal went into its shutdown sequence. Kyr quickly realized that the majo couldn't keep up with her, even being dragged. "Come on," she said, "come *on*," what had it said its name was? "*Yiso, come on.*"

"I can't," the majo whined. "I can't do it. I'm sorry. I can't."

The minute Kyr let go of it, it fell over. Kyr went down to one knee and scooped it up in her arms—it was heavier than it looked, a surprisingly solid weight—and then because she couldn't run like this she threw it over her shoulder. There was a Level Ten scenario where you had to do this with an unconscious teammate during a fire. Lisabel had let Kyr use her for practice during rec rotations, though she'd always failed at being unconscious, she'd laughed too much—

Kyr kept the whimpering majo in place with her arm across its pelvis and aimed herself at the ramp and *ran*.

There were bangs and shouts coming from the hangar entrances she ran past, so Victrix Wing had realized something was happening. "Avi," she gasped.

"*Busy!*" he yelled in her ear. "*I hate this!*"

Kyr hit the last turn of the ramp, just below the level where the majo ship sat, at the moment when the station seemed to lurch. It hadn't—even Avi couldn't do that—it just felt that way because the Victrix shadow engine had gone offline, temporarily taking the other three down with it. There'd been no choice, to get Avi through that cavern of reality distortions: *he'd* never used a jump hook. The fighter darts shifted and clanged in their cradles. Metal screamed. Kyr stumbled, shifted the majo over her shoulder so it didn't bash its head into the wall as she went down, scrambled upright again, and kept moving. There were sirens squealing now over and above the blare of the atmospheric seal alarm. Kyr knew the meaning of the new rise-and-fall sequence without thinking about it: *enemy action.*

She skidded to a halt underneath the majo ship's cradle and the majo toppled off her shoulder. "Come *on!*" Kyr shouted. The majo's ears went flat against its skull and it cringed away, but it let her help it scramble up through the hatch. The nearest steel door to the hangar was only yards away, and Kyr could see dents appearing in it from the other side. How much of the six minutes she'd given Avi had passed? She didn't have a combat mask feeding her information, but her mental sense of the movement of things told her about three. He should be through the shadow engines now and coming down fast along the corridors of the hulk. Kyr had a new definition of *slow* now she'd seen the majo try to run, so she tried not to be impatient. He might have a hard time with the ramps in the hangar: she hadn't thought of that. If he'd kept the grapple—*please* let him have been smart enough to keep the grapple—Kyr could haul him up. Two minutes. Where *was* he?

The majo leaned out of the painted ship's hatch and said, "Valkyr?"

"We're waiting for someone." The whole hangar was still shuddering and lurching, but not as badly as it had been. Systems must have restarted and stabilized the shadow engines fast, as Avi had predicted. They hadn't managed to do anything about the atmospheric-seal shutdown, though. Not *yet*. Avi had muttered something about Corporal Lin. Kyr looked up. If the seal went down before Kyr was in the ship, she'd asphyxiate. If Systems prevented it from shutting down, there was no way out of the hangar and they'd have all of Victrix Wing to deal with in a moment. If, if, if—

If she died here, Mags would die on Chrysothemis.

Kyr couldn't fail now.

"*Avi!*" she screamed over the bleating seal alarm and the *enemy action* siren.

No sneering voice answered in her ear. There was movement below. A figure emerged from the shadow of the dreadnought.

It had its hands on its head.

There was another person behind it.

Two guards, Kyr thought suddenly. The majo in its cell with just one man to watch it, when there should have been two guards. She'd been *relieved.*

Stupid. Appallingly stupid. A child's mistake. Kyr would have ripped a verbal hole through any Sparrow who made that assumption in the agoge.

There was a buzzing sound in her ear as someone fumbled with the earpiece. Then the Victrix guard spoke. Her voice was perfectly clear despite all the alarms, as close as if she'd been standing at Kyr's shoulder.

"*Valkyr,*" she said. "*Stop.*"

It was Cleo.

Kyr went still. Down below she saw the figure behind force the one in front to get on its knees. Avi's hands were behind his head. His head was bowed. Then Cleo turned her face up. Her eyes locked with Kyr's across the hangar.

"*Kyr,*" said Cleo again in Kyr's ear. She was holding the comm she'd taken from Avi by her lips. "*I'm warning you.*"

Kyr stared down at her messmate's familiar figure, her dark skin and sharp cheekbones and close-cropped soldierly curls. She couldn't move. Alarms wailed, hissing sparks sprang from around the edges of the nearest steel door as Victrix soldiers worked on it, and the painted majo ship behind her came alive suddenly and rose an inch or two in its cradle with a faint hum. The majo leaned out of the ship's hatch again.

"Are you coming?" it said.

There was nothing stopping Kyr from turning around and saying *yes, let's go.* The six minutes were all but gone, and Systems *would* catch up with whatever Avi had done to the seal before long. And who was Avi, anyway? No one. Twenty-four hours ago Kyr had never even spoken to him. A week ago she'd never thought twice about him—had known his name, because Lisabel picked up all the station gossip including *did you hear they assigned the queer from Otter mess to Systems and he's still here?*, but would never have dreamed of striking up a conversation.

"Kyr," repeated Cleo softly, and without looking away from Kyr's face she jammed her gun more firmly into the back of Avi's bent head.

They would execute him.

They might spare Kyr, even after everything she'd just done. Uncle Jole might say something. Command might decide that they needed her, to be the mother of Earth's children. It wouldn't matter then what she'd done or who she'd betrayed, as long as they got another dozen Magnuses out of her body, boys they'd send out to die just like Mags himself would die without Kyr to help him.

They might spare Kyr. But if she left Avi now, a friendless no-body on top of being a proven traitor capable of shutting down the shadow engines on a whim, he wouldn't survive to the end of the day.

She stood there staring down at Cleo for just a few more seconds. It only *felt* like hours.

The struggling shadow engines gave another hiccup, and a wave of distorted gravity rolled up from below flickering with sub-real light. It was too beautiful an opportunity. It was like those moments in the agoge when certainties locked together and Kyr knew she could win, coincidence tapping her on the shoulder with an encouraging whisper: *Jump.*

"Yiso," Kyr said. "Don't you dare leave without us."

She jumped.

Cleo was a better shot than Kyr was. She misjudged the shape of the distortion by only a fraction, but her first bullet sang by Kyr's ear and didn't touch her. Then Kyr was on the ground in the well of the hangar with the dark hulk of *Victrix* looming. She hurled herself forward. She didn't even bother going for the hand-gun she'd nabbed from the other guard: it wasn't going to help. Kyr *knew* Cleo, she'd measured herself against Cleo for years, in the agoge, on the mats, right up to this morning in Drill. Kyr and Cleo were the best of Sparrow. Kyr knew she was brilliant, knew she was fast and aggressive and clever and skilled. It was only on brute force that she fell short.

So it was brute force Kyr needed.

She went in low and fast. Her shoulder collided with Cleo's rib cage, slamming her backward. Kyr grabbed at her arm and bent it back, digging her short nails into the soft skin of Cleo's wrist. Cleo grunted. The gun went skittering out of her hand and Kyr kicked it away. "Get up! Run!" she shouted without looking around. "Avi*cenna*—"

Cleo swept her legs out from under her. Kyr wasn't ready and went down hard, taking Cleo with her. Now they were grappling, but on the ground Kyr's extra size and strength gave her an advantage, and Cleo couldn't get her pinned. They both had field knives that neither of them had reached for yet. Kyr wasn't going to be the first if she didn't have to. Cleo was Sparrow. Cleo was *hers*.

Cleo's face was twisted, a mask of furious grief that Kyr didn't understand. They rolled—Kyr was over her, under, over—and Cleo grabbed a handful of Kyr's ponytail and pulled so hard that hanks of hair came out at the roots. Kyr bit her. They broke apart and scrambled up and Cleo remembered her knife.

It shone dully in her hand. The Victrix badge gleamed at her collar. It was a newer one, only a stylized V instead of the winged woman. Kyr had her stolen knife in hand as well, and both of them watched each other, silent, breathing hard, turned sideways to present less of a target. The thing about a knife fight was that it didn't matter so much now that Kyr's reach was better. It didn't matter that Cleo was properly uniformed, the base layer of body armor under Terran navy blue. Kyr's blade could thrust straight through that. Cleo's would take her low in the ribs when she did.

"I knew it," Cleo spat. Her eyes were glittering.

"Cleo—"

"After all that. After everything. I *knew* you couldn't be real."

"You don't understand," said Kyr.

"You always acted like you were better than everyone," Cleo said. "You were always so special. With your precious brother and your traitor sister and your *uncle*. We are Gaea! We don't have any family but Earth's children. But not you." She feinted left. Kyr ducked away from it, had to go backward. Cleo was between her and the ramp up to the majo ship. At least Avi seemed to have been smart enough to run. "So here's the truth," Cleo said. "Our fearless leader. When it comes down to it you're as scared as anyone. You're worse than anyone. No one said service would be easy, but even Lisabel didn't—try—to run!"

Three wild slashes, only the last of which touched Kyr, leaving a long jagged tear through her sleeve and a shallow cut in her off arm. It wasn't the way she'd seen Cleo fight majo in the agoge. It wasn't the way they had clashed on the mats in Drill, the way they had been taught to fight since they were children.

Far overhead the lights blazing around the atmospheric seal came up to full power, shining in all directions, sending flaring shadows through the hangar among the cradles of the fighter darts and throwing dazzling angled beams out into the endless night of deep space to mark the pathways among the dimensional traps. Kyr was out of time. "Cleo," she said. "You're my messmate. My friend. *You're* my sister."

"I'm no sister to a traitor." Cleo was crying now, tears and snot on her twisted face, but the hand that held the knife was steady. "You always made me so angry! But you were supposed to be the perfect one!"

"It's Mags," said Kyr. "He's going to die, please—"

Cleo yelled and attacked again, and Kyr had to fight back, she had to, she was defending herself.

"Valkyr!" yelled someone overhead. Avi. He'd made it to the majo ship. "Vallie, dammit, *Kyr*, come on! We're out of time!"

He didn't know what he was asking.

He was asking Kyr to kill Cleo.

She'd never killed a real person, a human being. She could do it, probably. She *was* better than Cleo. She was stronger, faster. And if she failed here—if she failed now—

She hesitated a fraction too long. Cleo gave a hoarse shout of triumph and her knife went into Kyr's thigh.

Kyr felt it slide through her trousers and her skin in the same easy motion. Her leg gave way, and the knife twisted as she fell. *Artery*, she thought. No. Wrong side for that. Too deep, though. Everything around her looked suddenly very still and bright and clear: the dizzy angles of spotlights, the hollow shadows of the dreadnought's corpse, the nearest set of steel hangar doors finally giving way, the faceless shapes of Victrix soldiers advancing through it, and Cleo's face closer than she'd thought, tearstains on her cheeks, eyes wide, lips moving: *Kyr, I'm—*

The world shifted. Kyr felt blazing cold, bitter heat, the ghost sensation of something soft wrapped around her midriff and squeezing. Her strange clear vision persisted, but she was seeing things that weren't true: a cliff's edge, wheeling birds.

Then she was sprawled on a familiar glittering floor, the bare inside of the majo ship a lot bigger now that all its furniture had been carted off to Oikos. "And now we go! Go!" Avi was yelling.

"Um, they're leaking—bleeding—quite a lot," someone else said a few moments later. "Do you know what to do? What do I do?" The voice was musical, strangely accented, a little bit panicky.

"You *show me the controls* and then once we're past the dimensional traps and out of range of the Isaac slugs we'll worry about first aid!"

Good. Smart. Good prioritization. The floor seemed to be swinging about wildly. Maybe the whole ship was.

Kyr a little later tried to force her eyes open. There wasn't time to lie about. There was—there was Mags. The alien, the majo, was crouched over her. It, he, she, whatever, looked even weirder upside down. It reached out and touched her face with its cool hand.

"Thank you for saving me, Valkyr," it said solemnly.

I didn't do it for you, Kyr thought.

She blacked out.

PART II

CHRYSOTHEMIS

The signing of the Zi Sin Accords only ratified what the universe already knew: the war was over, and the humans had lost. Earth, the human homeworld and capital, accounted for over eighty percent of the Terran Federation's financial resources and the majority of its population. With its destruction, humanity was left leaderless, devastated, and extraordinarily poor.

The Zi Sin agreement laid down provisions for dismantling the Terran Expeditionary. This vast military machine represented a substantial fraction of what humanity had left: the world-conquering dreadnoughts that formed its core remain unmatched in majoda history as machines of war, and the human forces numbered in the millions. A buy-back agreement was reached with the sinnet free worlds which had borne the brunt of the fighting . . .

. . . four dreadnoughts refused to stand down and broke away from the fleet. In retrospect, it is plain that this audacious theft was carefully planned. Skeleton crews whose access should have been revoked were ready and waiting aboard *Victrix, Ferox, Augusta,* and *Scythica*. Key communications frequencies were jammed at exactly the right moment. The only clue we have as to what exactly happened comes from a distress call placed by Admiral Elora Marston of the *Victrix*. From this we can see that not all those aboard the four guilty ships were involved in the plot . . .

. . . broke away toward the Persara system under the command of Admiral Isamy Russell. Russell had been until this moment a model Terran officer, popular with his troops, famously generous toward defeated nonhuman forces and especially toward civilians. Russell was the officer who gave the order for the Gyssono-IV rescue, diverting a human combat wing toward a risky and ultimately successful evacuation effort for a badly damaged majo space station. His decision to throw in his lot with the radicals speaks volumes for the depths of rage and agony suffered by human survivors after "Doomsday" . . .

. . . became clear that Russell, although nominally in command, was neither the instigator nor the real leader of the Gaean separatists. The shadowy figure of Commander Aulus Jole is hard to separate from the misleading impressions given by popular depictions. We know very little of his personal history, and the records which might tell us more were destroyed with Earth. He was certainly at one point a member of the legendary "Hagenen Wing," an elite force of the TE created in response to human perceptions of majoda military capabilities, intended to "hit 'em where we're strong." Hagenen commandos, drawn primarily from the controversial "warbreed" genetic enhancement program, received training emphasizing the extremes of human physical abilities—strength, speed, spatial awareness, and tolerance for injury. It perhaps says enough that the patently insane "jump hook" technology—permitting a single soldier to travel alone and nearly unprotected through subreal space over short distances—was a standard part of Hagenen kit.

That Jole was a Hagenen commando is certain, though his rank of commander may be spurious. Those who knew him in his youth describe him as a serious and thoughtful young man with "great potential." The sinister charisma and obvious mania of popular media are both conspicuous by their absence.

—F. R. Levy, *The War in Heaven*

HABITABLE PLANETS ("WORLDS") BY TYPE

BARREN WORLD: A "barren world" may not be literally barren, but it does not have a native biosphere and requires extensive development to become habitable. See also FREE WORLD.

CAPITAL WORLD: Inhabited for millennia, characterized by high settlement intensity (>90% planetary surface urban), these planets usually form the core of larger political and economic units, and often house several nodes of the Wisdom. See also HOMEWORLD.

CITIZEN WORLD: Less intensely developed than capital worlds, these planets are nevertheless characterized by primarily urban settlement and an advanced economy, as well as at least one Wisdom node.

ENCLAVE WORLD: A planet inhabited by a primitive sentient civilization, which in time will become a candidate for the majoda. These worlds are protected by the Wisdom from interference; trespassers face severe penalties. See TERRAN WAR, THE.

FREE WORLD: These newly settled planets are not yet secure politically or economically. Settlement types vary (corporate venture, religious commitment, etc.) but usually require heavy external investment to offset the difficulty of biospheric design and development. Free worlds are intended to mature into citizen worlds with their own Wisdom nodes in the future, although not all succeed.

GARDEN WORLD: A planet with its own advanced biosphere capable of producing new life-forms is a garden world. All homeworlds are garden worlds by definition, although many have had their native biology damaged by poorly planned early development. Most known garden worlds are home to sentient life in some form and have been for a long time (see CAPITAL WORLD, CITIZEN WORLD, ENCLAVE WORLD); new free world settlements must seek out barren (hence "free") worlds.

HOMEWORLD: The originating planet of a sentient species. See also CAPITAL WORLD.

MUSEUM WORLD: Sometimes confused with enclave worlds. A museum world planet is capable of supporting life, but settlement has been interdicted by the Wisdom or by other appropriate authority. Usually only applies to planets formerly inhabited by advanced sentients. Interdiction is sometimes controversial but has been overturned only on one recorded occasion—see HFA (CHRYSOTHEMIS) and TERRAN WAR, THE.

CHAPTER NINE

RAINGOLD

"Found him," Avi said.

It was their twelfth morning on Chrysothemis. The twelfth morning of bleary wakefulness after a too-silent night. Kyr found it hard to sleep without the breathing of her messmates in their bunks and the comforting hum of shadow engines at the edge of her awareness.

The shack on the outskirts of the city of Raingold had just enough room for the three of them. They'd traded away the painted ship to an illegal scavenger outfit Avi had led them to, in exchange for entry papers, identity chips. Kyr hadn't even thought about those things. Avi's ironic look had said he knew she hadn't.

The pirates had offered to buy Yiso too. "Majo zi are rare," the leader had said. "We'll find a buyer. We're used to moving Gaean product." He'd grinned, showing off even white teeth.

Kyr had said no, before Avi could say anything.

She didn't know why. The stupid alien was just a majo. She didn't like the pirate either, though. A criminal; a person without honor.

Avi's look had stayed ironically amused, and he'd gone off and fucked the pirate, and then they'd had entry papers and identity chips and money to pay rent, which was another thing Kyr hadn't known about. She had the feeling she was an interruption into a scenario Avi had been over in his head hundreds of times, all the variables accounted for except the critical one of getting off Gaea Station in the first place.

That feeling had lasted through eleven days on Chrysothemis: through Avi finding them a rental where the owner didn't care that they had no references and no history, a tiny corrugated tin shack to keep off the endlessly drumming rain; through the days where Kyr, injured, fuming, had stayed in the shack with the alien while Avi went out on mysterious errands he refused to explain—*you wanted it, you keep an eye on it*, he'd said, as if Yiso was Kyr's now, just because she hadn't liked the pirate; through Avi spending half their rent money on a personal device and a network access key—*hey, if you want your own pocket money, go whore yourself for it like I did*, he'd sneered. Yiso slept for long hours in a pile of sheets in the corner of the shack while Chrysothemis's cold rain echoed on the tin roof, the bruises on its face shrinking more slowly than the cleaned and stitched stab wound on Kyr's thigh was healing. When it woke up at last, ten days since they'd fled from Gaea, it turned to Kyr with its huge silvery eyes shining with something Kyr refused to understand.

Once it was awake she made a splint and fixed up its broken finger, just because looking at its obviously wrong sideways bend was annoying her. Yiso whimpered while she bandaged it and eventually passed out again. Kyr didn't know whether majo zi healed properly. Aliens weren't as tough as people.

She also didn't care, obviously. But Yiso was hard to take seriously as a threat or a monster. It was so clearly young. Maybe it hadn't even been born when the Earth and its fourteen billion people were murdered.

Kyr thought of that when it passed out with its hand bandaged, and felt obscurely justified. It wasn't fair that Kyr didn't have a world, because she hadn't been born; so it made sense that she wasn't bothered by this particular majo, because it probably hadn't been born either. On Gaea things were different, because on Gaea things had to be useful, and an enemy prisoner might be useful; but since Yiso was now completely useless to anyone, it was all right to treat it like it was just . . .

Well, not a *person*.

An animal, Kyr decided eventually. She did not know much about animals. She had learned the list in Nursery: *ape, bear, cat, dog,* all the way to *zebra.* And the cadet messes had their signs. They'd hidden their Gaean uniforms, exchanged them for the brightly colored T-shirts and trousers that would make them look normal on Chrysothemis, but Kyr missed her Sparrow patch. She'd sewn it herself when she was seven, carefully copying the picture Corporal Ekker had found in archives. Only Zen had managed to get hers looking anything like an actual sparrow.

Humans had once shared their world with animals, and they were lesser species but they still felt pain, so if you didn't *hate* a majo, because it had been mostly unconscious for ten days and basically not scary, and you'd carried it in your arms and felt how small and terrified it was, and it reminded you a little of someone—

Well. Then maybe it was like an animal, and you weren't a traitor for not being bothered by it. Maybe it was okay to find yourself thinking *him* instead of *it* sometimes.

Unfortunately then Yiso woke up again and turned out to be *chatty,* so Kyr hated him after all. Not the way you were supposed to hate majo, with the cold implacable fury of the living hand of vengeance. She hated him roughly the same way she hated doing Nursery rotations, supervising six-year-olds who just *never stopped talking.*

Things Yiso wanted to talk about:

Kyr's stab wound, if Kyr was going to die from a stab wound, how it was possible for Kyr not to die from the stab wound after losing so much fluid—blood!—how scary the human who stabbed Kyr was, wasn't Kyr brave, and—oh really?

Warbreed genetics, what Kyr meant by warbreed genetics, his opinions about the punishing physical costs of accelerated healing, his opinions about something he called eugenics—

Nursery; babies; how exactly human reproduction worked, which Kyr found too embarrassing to explain so she snapped at Yiso which made him cringe; then later he asked Avi about it instead, and Avi gave a concise smirking explanation which made *Kyr* cringe—

His own species' sex habits, which Kyr didn't want to know about but Avi was having fun and kept encouraging him; apparently majo zi didn't have males and females; *I think in T-standard I'm meant to use the gender-neutral sentient pronoun.* Yiso insisted it was *they*, which was obviously wrong, so Kyr told him *he*, and then Avi somehow turned it into an argument where he was gleefully supporting both sides at once. They ended up going back and forth for most of a rainy night, after which Kyr finally slept well for once—

Chrysothemis and its wealth, which Kyr hadn't known about at all, but Yiso did. Out in this system's asteroid belt people mined a substance that Yiso called *irris*, which was key to shadow-engine shielding; but the planet, Yiso said, was under interdiction, no one was supposed to settle it, that was how the war began—

Gaea Station. What Yiso thought about Gaea Station. Kyr didn't care that Yiso hadn't liked her home. He was an alien; she came from the last fortress of the patriots; he wasn't *supposed* to like her home. But he said other things, niggling things that stuck in Kyr's head: he asked about how luxury allowances worked, and how Nursery access for Command and combat wings and then the other wings worked, and as she was explaining it Kyr found herself wondering things she'd never really wondered before— why *was* it, exactly, that Command deserved more of a stake in the genetic future of humanity than serving soldiers? Why could Admiral Russell put his hands all over Lisabel, and why couldn't Kyr stop him?

And then Yiso asked how often combat wing patrols went out, and what they actually grew in Agricole. Kyr finally realized she was being manipulated and refused to give away any more information, so Avi told him. Yiso promptly came out with a whole flood of statistics about the intergalactic black market, and illegal drugs, and pirates and scavengers and slavers, all of which was obviously majo propaganda and lies—except Kyr couldn't help remembering the scavenger outfit Avi had known how to find, which meant that the information had already been somewhere in Systems; the pirate who'd smirked at them without surprise, offered to buy Yiso, and said *we're used to moving Gaean product*.

It was all this thinking. Kyr had had nothing to do but *think* for twelve days. First she couldn't move around too much because her leg was still healing, and then it was okay and she would have been glad to get out of the tin shack, but Avi insisted it was too dangerous. Kyr was inclined to trust his ability to assess a situation now, uncomfortably aware of that neatly arranged escape plan she'd burst in on for Mags's sake. So she did push-ups and crunches when she felt edgy from not training, and gulped down the tasteless food that Avi brought back for them—she was ravenous after burning through her body's reserves healing a stab wound.

And she thought. She kept thinking thoughts she didn't like, and she told herself it was because Avi was a dissident and Yiso was an alien and both of them were getting to her somehow, except that Kyr had too much confidence in herself to really believe they *could*. Avi was still a whining weakling when it really counted, and Yiso was just a majo. Kyr kept thinking things anyway.

Maybe it was because they both talked so much. It made her brain start talking to itself.

Through all of this a low anxiety was beating somewhere in her chest. There was so much she hadn't thought of when she abandoned her home and her species, made herself a traitor in Cleo's eyes and in her uncle Jole's eyes, and one of the things she hadn't thought of was: on a planet with two million people on it, Mags didn't stand out the way he did on Gaea Station.

On Chrysothemis there was nothing special about Kyr's brother. On Chrysothemis, she didn't know how to find him.

And then on the twelfth day it turned out Avi did.

"Found who?" said Yiso, looking between them with his ears flicking up and out, which Kyr had learned was curiosity. Yiso was curious about everything.

"None of your business," said Kyr and Avi at the same time. Kyr exchanged a glance of understanding with him. One of the things she'd thought about—in a desperate attempt to avoid thinking about Yiso's eugenics opinions, which were irritatingly logical but led to conclusions so unspeakable they had to be lies—was Avi. Avi's thing, feelings, whatever, about Mags. Someone who could build that garden on the cliffside was someone who understood Kyr's brother at least a little. Kyr felt disquieted by it, and protective in a way she hadn't needed to be since Mags finally started putting on weight and height, but also oddly comforted. It meant Avi had to be as serious as she was about not letting her brother die.

"Here," Avi said, and handed Kyr the personal device he'd spent half his fucked-the-pirate money on. "The key is *magnolia*."

"Magnolia," Kyr repeated, and the corner of her vision lit up with a bare-bones feed—a weather report and a map. It was like being in the agoge, though without the valuable combat intel Kyr was used to. "Yeah, you don't need to kill anyone here, so," Avi said. "The map'll give you directions. It's apartment five. Say hi for me."

"You're giving me this?" said Kyr—he'd been clinging to it like it was a precious human child since he'd first brought it back—and then, "You're not coming with me?"

"Someone's got to look after our little friend," Avi said. He smiled a thin little smile. "Yeah. Anyway, I have things to do."

Kyr set out alone into the city of Raingold. It was a dim misty morning. The planet's atmosphere was thick with precipitation, not quite resolved into rain. Sunlight from its cheerful little star penetrated in angled rays that were filled with brilliantly gleaming dewdrops. It wasn't cold, but it was very damp. There was a bell ringing somewhere, not the familiar shrilling command of the shift-change bells but a slow echoing resonance that was singing out into the morning air from some faraway tower. It seemed to have no purpose at all.

Kyr hadn't been outside for more than a few moments since they arrived at the planet's one spaceport, and she'd still been disoriented with exhaustion after her injury then. She hadn't had time to think about the enormous fact of the sky. She had run plenty of agoge scenarios set on planets. She'd thought she knew what skies were like.

It turned out it was quite different when the clouded curve of a living atmosphere was over your head all the time, huge and bright and totally uninterested in you. She felt dizzy, like she might fall upward into it.

She started walking.

As if the sky wasn't disturbing enough, Chrysothemis was also *wet*. Kyr's ratty ponytail stuck to the back of her neck. Water beaded on her face. Her colorful T-shirt and trousers *were* normal, she saw, glancing at the people making their way through the narrow streets around her, but it would have looked *more* normal if she'd also had a waterproof. She passed a group of cadet-age children, maybe eleven or twelve, all of them wearing waterproof overalls. They had found a large puddle and were splashing each other by playing some complicated ball game while running around in it. Their orange ball sent up a plume of water into the damp air every time someone dropped it, which was constantly. One of them fumbled a throw and sent the ball straight at Kyr.

She caught it one-handed—it was heavier and slicker than it looked—and threw it back. They called out to her. Kyr didn't understand the words.

She'd known that there had once been human languages other than T-standard. She'd thought they were all dead with Earth.

She went on, determinedly not shivering in the damp, following the map at the corner of her vision. It took her through the winding streets of outer Raingold, where most of the buildings were like the one Avi had rented for them, oblong prefabricates with tin roofs and water rolling down their sides. Then there were streets of shops, where more people than Kyr had ever seen in her life wandered in and out of brightly lit buildings, or gathered in friendly little knots to chatter like children.

A person who was either a very masculine-looking woman or a very feminine-looking man (*or neither, Valkyr, they is for neither, get used to it*—Avi had an irritating way of sticking in your head) chased Kyr along the street near the shops. She tensed up, but she—he—they, *fine*, thought Kyr, irritated—only wanted to say, "Hello! Here, please take this."

They gave her a package of waxy cloth. Kyr shook it out and it was a bright yellow waterproof.

"Recent arrival?" they said, looking sympathetic. "Raingold mornings can be a bit of a shock. Put it on! And listen, if you've found yourself here alone, if you need any help, or support, there's a charity—Homes for Humanity—"

"I don't need help," said Kyr.

The person stepped back and held up their hands. "All right," they said. "All right."

Kyr did put the waterproof on. She didn't bother with the hood, because her hair and face were wet anyway. So much *water*. The Blackbirds at home, playing with the bucket of soapy water melted with terrible care off a chunk of space ice, had never seen riches like this.

And then Kyr left the shopping street behind, and was suddenly standing on a broad promenade, looking out at what the map at the corner of her vision told her was Raingold Bay.

The mist broke over the sea, and the sunlight shone boldly down on the water, glittering in the foam caps where small waves tossed. Little boats with white sails moved swiftly across the blue. Kyr saw the bright splashes of red and green and yellow that were people in waterproofs sailing them. A gleaming white building, smooth and shining like the buildings in Avi's dream-city in the agoge, rose almost out of the water on a spar of land on the far side of the bay. Bell-song was still ringing out across the water, coming from that direction somewhere.

This was real. All the time Kyr had been working, training, giving everything she had inside her to the service of humanity, there had been a place like this. Kyr's thoughts rattled around in her head in bizarre directions. Lisabel. The Blackbirds. Avi's weird little smiles. Uncle Jole. *I'm proud of you.* Homes for Humanity. Yiso's lies, his—their—stupid *statistics.*

A colossal statue of a woman stood on the promenade gazing out to sea. She looked a little like the figure on the Victrix sigil that was hidden in their shack along with Kyr's gun and knife, inside the bundle of her cadet uniform. The statue was dressed in falling folds of white that Kyr could not quite believe were made of stone. She had one arm stretched out toward the water.

Kyr went a little closer. There was a plaque by the statue's feet. IN MEMORY & IN HOPE, it said.

Kyr looked at it for a while.

Rage rose inside her slow and hot, like the burn of taking a toast for your messmate's assignment. The hand that was not extended toward the water was held at the colossal figure's breast. A dim blue sphere hovered over it, suspended by nothing, flickering in and out of existence: the familiar image of the murdered Earth.

That's it, Kyr thought. *Fourteen billion people, and that's it.*

She didn't hang around any longer. She didn't stop to gawk at the broad ocean, the yellow tint it took on far out beyond the bay where Chrysothemis's native swaths of minute ocean-drifting organisms gave the water its color and the city its name. She bulled past the rich happy spoiled humans who lived in this city and never thought about the cost of their collaboration, their *submission:* she broke into a run, eventually, and as her long strides ate up the shining white flagstones of Raingold's ocean promenade the damp air became a spray of water she was running into. It tasted of salt.

CHAPTER TEN

ALLY

Avi's map led Kyr to a cluster of apartment blocks, all yellow brick and shimmering wet glass, right in the shadow of the gigantic white building she'd seen from across the bay. Her footsteps slowed as she got closer. She'd expected—she didn't know what she'd expected. A Strike base, whatever that was like. But the people hurrying through the streets here had umbrellas as well as hooded waterproofs, and tall gleaming boots to keep off the damp. This place felt rich.

Rich by Chrysothemis standards was decadent by Kyr's.

The building took a while to find even with the map in the corner of Kyr's vision. The entrance was set back from the street: you had to go through an arch to find a little courtyard where tall spikes of green plants had been planted in big tubs. Kyr loitered next to one. It had a plaque on the front, explaining that this plant was called *Cordyline australis* or cabbage tree, that on Earth it had been native to somewhere called New Zealand, and that the cutting that was the ancestor of this specimen had been kindly donated to the Terran Biohistory Project of the Xenia Institute by a sinnet oligarch named Asal Mlur. Kyr looked at that for a while.

Two men in striped waterproofs came out of the building and one of them gave her an odd look. "Just an ordinary treehugger," his friend said to him as they turned the corner.

"There's botanical enthusiasm and then there's wallowing. When it's kids, Jac, I just don't know," Kyr heard the other one reply.

She looked at the entrance. There was a double glass door. On the other side she could make out the sturdy shape of a security guard. This didn't feel right. Now that she was thinking about the yellow brick building like a secured location to crack, she noticed cameras too, one at the entrance to the courtyard, one covering the door. Probably more inside. Maybe if she came back when the planet went into night cycle—into *night*—and went up over the walls. The yellow brick looked soft enough to give her some handholds, and she could see open windows farther up.

"Hello."

Kyr startled. Her damp shoe caught on the slick edge of a paving stone. She only just recovered her balance in time to avoid an embarrassing fall.

The speaker was a child. He was small, pale, and swathed in a bright pink waterproof, though like Kyr he had the hood down. The drizzle had plastered his hair flat; it could have been any color between brown and blond. His nose and cheeks were pink. His eyes were hidden behind a pair of misted-up glasses.

Kyr had seen glasses before. Commander Jole had some for reading flimsies. But most of the handful of unfortunates on Gaea with inferior vision just squinted, like Avi. The child was watching her through the lenses with solemn curiosity. He said, "I'm Ally. Are you okay?"

"I'm fine," Kyr said. "Go away. Go and—" She swallowed *get back to work*. What did children even do here? She plumped for "—play."

"I'm not a *baby*," said Ally, with enormous disdain. "I'm eight. Are you really okay? You look sad. And you're all wet."

"So are you."

"Are you crying? Are you crying about a tree?"

"No!" said Kyr.

"My mum cries about trees sometimes," Ally informed her. "It's okay to feel sad about things if that's how you feel."

Kyr gave him her best glare. It had no effect.

"Do you know about invasive flora?" Ally said. "We did it in school last year. It's when Terran plants start taking over and all the native plants die out. It's because Earth stuff is really tough, especially Earth stuff that made it out to space so we have samples of it. I think it's actually really bad? Because Chrysothemis is its own planet and it has its own things and we can't just kill them all before they've had a chance to evolve how they want when we're not even from here. That's my opinion."

". . . What?" said Kyr.

"So I think we shouldn't have Earth trees in the university planters," Ally said. "I think they should be native, actually. I wrote to the chancellor about it. My mum said I could." He took off his glasses, wiped them on his waterproof, which made them smearier, and then put them back on. "Anyway if you're sad about trees maybe that helps? It helped my mom. She said she felt lots better after I explained."

"Leave me alone."

"Okay," said Ally, sounding injured. "I was just trying to help." He turned and trudged away toward the double glass doors, a small pink balloon deflated by random injustice.

"Wait!" Kyr called after him.

Ally turned around.

"Maybe you can help me," Kyr said. "I'm—um, I'm visiting someone who lives here."

"Who?" Ally said. "I probably know them. I know everybody in the whole building."

He said this with some self-importance. He was just a child, Kyr thought, scrambling for a lie. It couldn't be that hard to fool a child. But what she ended up saying was "My . . . my brother."

Ally frowned at her. "Who's your brother? Are you Jac's sister? You don't look like Jac. Are you Jac's boyfriend's sister? You don't look like him either."

"It's complicated," Kyr said. She didn't even know what name Mags was using. "He—Listen, I have the number of the apartment. Five."

"Oh!" said Ally.

"What?"

"You're *Magnus's* sister."

"You've met him?" Kyr said. "You've *seen* him?"

"Obviously. That's my apartment," Ally said. "He lives in our spare room."

"But—what—" Whatever Kyr had imagined a Strike base looking like, it definitely hadn't involved chatty eight-year-olds in pink waterproofs.

"He's my secret uncle," explained Ally. "Wait, are you my secret aunt?"

"*What?*"

"Mom's still at work," Ally said. "Do you want to come in? It's going to rain more soon. And I can make you a sandwich."

There was a plaque on the wall next to the door of apartment 5. It said MARSTON in shining letters. Kyr stared at it. *Admiral Elora Marston, TE-66* Victrix, she thought, and then pushed the thought away. It was nothing to do with Kyr. Marston had probably been a common name before the end of the world.

Ally unlocked the door with two different keys, and then stood still and looked at a security camera above the door for a moment, and then said, "Ally Marston, and *guest*," before the apartment would let them in. "Mom's really paranoid," Ally said. "What kinds of sandwiches do you like?"

He showed Kyr a hook for her yellow waterproof, and hung up his pink one underneath it. He was wearing something a bit like a uniform underneath, a red jacket cut with almost military formality. Then he led Kyr through the apartment—she got an impression of blues and greys and soft furniture—and into a room that she just about recognized as the same species as the mess kitchens she'd grown up with. There was a stove, and there were pots and pans. But everything was too small: sized to cook for two, not a dozen at a time.

This was a kind of home Kyr hadn't known existed anymore,

a place for a family. No mess, no Command—just Ally and his mother, whose faces appeared together over and over in the pictures stuck up on the walls in shiny white frames.

Kyr let her eyes skim over them, intentionally not seeing. She let Ally make her a sandwich and prattle about whatever he wanted to talk about. She didn't know what she'd done to deserve a life suddenly full of talkative people; Avi, Yiso, now an actual child. She ate the sandwich. The bread was soft and fluffy and the protein strips *tasted* of something, and on top of that Ally had put in some sharp-tasting sauce that made Kyr's body light up with the information that she was ravenous, actually. She'd taken a serious injury when they were leaving Gaea Station and she'd been living on scraps ever since.

Ally gave Kyr a second sandwich. He was regarding her with admiration. "You've got sweet chili sauce on your chin," he said. "You ate that really fast. I bet you eat almost as much as Magnus. He ate an entire cake in one go and he was still hungry. I didn't even get any."

"What's cake?" said Kyr.

Ally gave her a look of sorrow and horror. "You don't know what *cake* is?"

Cake was like the bread but sweeter. There was chocolate on it. Kyr had tasted chocolate before, of course. It was a reward for doing well; for training well, for working hard, for being the best. She would have said she didn't like it that much.

The stuff on the cake was nice.

Ally watched her eat four slices and then told her you were only supposed to have one. "But it's okay!" he said quickly. "Because you're a guest."

Kyr pushed the plate away. Her eyes caught on another one of those pictures, this one stuck onto a metal surface with a magnet shaped like a tree. She tore her gaze away and stared determinedly in the first random safe direction she could find, out of the window where the Chrysotheman day was brightening out of drizzle into glittering sunshine. She could see the yellow shimmer of the sea.

If she didn't look at the pictures then it wasn't real yet, and she didn't have to think about it, or about *Marston* on the door, or about anything at all.

Yet part of her *was* thinking, and she couldn't make it stop. It was this stupid planet. Kyr had always been able to stop thinking, before. She'd been busy. Even in her handful of rec hours she'd been able to run scenarios in the agoge, or wipe herself out on the mats against Cleo or Jeanne or one of the Coyotes, or force Lisabel through two hours at the range until she was hitting the target three times in four, enough to pass her next assessment. If all else failed, she could go and find Mags. She never worried when she was with him. She'd never suspected herself of being one of those stupid people who couldn't stop thinking.

But Mags had been sent to Strike, and he was here. He was here in this rich and comfortable home, where an eight-year-old with bad eyesight and sandy hair lived with a mother whose face seemed to be looking at Kyr out of every single one of those stupid pictures.

Ally did not look like his mother: because the woman in the pictures looked like Kyr, and he did not look like Kyr.

It was more obvious in profile. Head-on he was plump-faced and serious and just a child. But when he clambered up on a stool to reach a high cupboard where there was a tin of more chocolate things—cookies, these were called—Kyr got a good look at the straight line of his nose and the sharp jaw under the childish softness of his face. The freckles didn't hide it; the glasses barely obscured it. As his hair dried fair out of its rain-darkened mess, the conclusion became inescapable.

She'd been ten years old when Ursa turned traitor. Ten years old, when the older sister who had told them stories and saved them chocolates from her luxury allowance had abandoned her home and her duty to the human race. Ursa had been an adult, in her wing assignment already. She'd been Command. Kyr had never heard of anyone else getting assigned straight to Command. She hadn't dreamed of it for herself. She hadn't wanted to. It was the special treatment, everyone said, that had made Ursa fail.

She'd run away. She'd stolen an Augusta dart, and she'd used her Command codes to disable the station defenses, and she'd sent a message to Systems as she left full of dissident ranting so shocking that no one dared to repeat what she'd actually said. She'd gone, and she hadn't told Mags she was going, and she hadn't told Kyr.

Mags had cried. Kyr hadn't. Mags had tried to talk to Kyr about it. Kyr hadn't let him. She'd been too angry. It had been years before she would even let Mags say Ursa's name to her.

Avi had said, hadn't he, that Ursa had taken a hostage. Kyr hadn't asked at the time. Now it was all she could think about. She sat silently in her runaway sister's pleasant light-filled kitchen, eating cookies, thinking about it. And when the child who was plainly Aulus Jole's son offered her a glass of fruit juice to go with them, she said yes.

It started raining outside and stopped again, and the light in the kitchen changed. While Kyr drank her juice, Ally gave her a small and forceful lecture about ocean bioclearance for Terran fish stocks, of which she understood mainly that there were fish in Raingold Bay, and people fished for them, and Ally disapproved for some reason. She didn't care. She was still thinking, and trying *not* to think. Everything in the little kitchen was so clean and neatly put together that Kyr herself felt lumbering, dirty, strange. She put her hands one on top of the other, and carefully dug her fingernails into the thin skin by her wrist. They were short and blunt but she got a sting of pain out of it. It made her vision clear a little.

"Is that yours? Can I see?" Ally was saying. "Why do you have your visual feeds up all the time? That's really bad for you." He did something to Avi's device and the map and weather and temperature readout disappeared from the corner of Kyr's eye. She had the sense of being unmoored, like one of the little sailing boats scudding across the bay before the drizzling wind, set loose on the surface of something huge and unknowable.

"Are you crying? Are you sad?" Ally said. "Are you sad about fish?"

And then Ursa was there.

The last time Kyr had seen her sister, Ursa had been in full uniform: smart navy trousers creased neatly along the sides, gleaming black boots, a white shirt buttoned to the throat, navy tunic belted at the waist, long navy coat with gold detailing at the collar, the hems, the shoulders, and her Command sigil at her throat. Kyr had known the wing badges all her life—horse, hound, crown, winged figure for the four combat wings; star and tree, lightning bolt and keys for Suntracker, Agricole, Systems, Oikos; the covered cradle of Nursery. Command was different. The flat disc of Ursa's badge was a twin to Uncle Jole's, and it had engraved on it the familiar lines of disappeared continents.

Command carried the Earth with them.

Ursa had worn her hair long, neatly tied back into a low blond ponytail under her navy cap. Kyr had long since grown out of grabbing at it, of course. She was ten, and *assigned*, a Sparrow. But Ursa always acted like she was going to do it anyway, and laughed at her, which was annoying.

She'd come down to Drill to watch them run a Level Five. Kyr remembered the agoge cutting out to reveal her sister standing next to Sergeant Marius, the instructor, who'd looked dour. It hadn't gone well. Kyr had been furious. She didn't remember now what had gone wrong: Lisabel's fault, probably, though, because it usually was.

It had been the first time Kyr had seen her sister in almost a year, because when you were assigned, your mess were your sisters. She remembered that Ursa had looked different, though she didn't remember how or why. She'd given Sergeant Marius a thinned-out variation of one of her normal humorous smiles, and she'd said, "Not quite there yet, ladies," to all the Sparrows, her eyes not lingering on Kyr.

Then five days later she'd been a traitor, a traitor and an exile and *gone*.

She hadn't grown shorter. It was just that Kyr was tall now.

Her hair was gone, the blond ponytail cropped to chin length. Women were supposed to wear their hair long enough to tie back neatly, unless it was too curly to stay tidy that way. Ursa's ponytail had been longer than was standard. More special treatment, Kyr had thought later. Only Nursery women wore their hair past their shoulders.

She was up to Kyr's chin; five foot seven or eight. She'd lost muscle and put on fat; there was softness around her face and arms. She was wearing a sleeveless smock with a pink pattern on it, and white trousers. Her eyes were unchanged under straight brows, hard grey Gaean eyes, the eyes of a woman who'd been promoted to commanding rank of a spaceborne fortress before she was eighteen years old. Kyr had once been so proud of her brilliant sister.

The light coming through the kitchen window was distorted by waterdrops on the glass. It threw shadows across the room that made the pink pattern on Ursa's smock look uneven and alien. Kyr stood up. She wiped her face with the back of her hand, and a smudge of chocolate came away. Ursa stood in the doorway, lit by that translucently strange Chrysotheman light, looking at her, and Kyr looked back.

"Hi Mom!" chirped Ally. "This is—Oh, I forgot to ask," he said to Kyr. "What's your name?"

"Alexander," said Ursa evenly, "what have I told you about strangers?"

"Mo-om," Ally said. "It's not a *stranger*. She's—"

"Your auntie Valkyr," said Ursa, not looking away from Kyr once. Kyr knew that look, the assessing weight of it. Ursa said, "If she wasn't at least partly a stranger, Ally, she would have told you her name. Come over here."

Ally looked uncertain and then crossed the room to her side. Ursa's hard stare the whole time said as plainly as words: *I think you might hurt him, and if you do I will stop you.* Kyr, with her own version of that weighted look, noted the bulge at the waist under the smock that was either a gun or a stunstick. She hadn't seen a single person carrying a weapon today. Raingold sat damp and cheerful at the edge of its alien ocean as if it had never heard of a war.

Ursa put her arm around Ally's shoulders when he got close, which he accepted with an air of confused tolerance. "I was just being friendly," he said.

"You're not in trouble, Alexander. I'd like you to go to your room, please. Your auntie and I need to have a chat."

"Don't be mean to her," said Ally. "She got upset about trees. And she ate *so much cake*. Mom, did you know some people don't know about cake?"

"Yes," Ursa said. "I did know that. Go on, Ally, please."

"Don't be mean," Ally said.

"I'm not going to be mean to my baby sister," said Ursa, and for the first time she looked away from Kyr, so she could look at the child and give him a smile. Kyr knew that smile, full and humorous and promising. It was a smile that said, *You can trust me. I understand. I love you.*

"Go," Ursa said, and Ally went.

Then it was just two of them in that bright little kitchen. Kyr looked at her sister, and Ursa looked back at her. The assessing stare changed: the straight brows drew together, and crumpled a little, as Ursa took in all six feet of Kyr.

"Vallie," she said.

It had been her name for Kyr first. Mags was the only one who was still allowed to use it. Avi had started doing it anyway because he was a jerk. Kyr said nothing.

"You got so big," Ursa said.

What a stupid fucking thing to say. Kyr folded her arms.

"I'm," Ursa said, "I'm *so sorry*."

She flung herself across the room and wrapped her arms tight around Kyr, up around her neck like she thought Kyr was still ten and smaller than she was. Kyr froze. Her folded arms were an awkward lump between them. People didn't touch her very often. Kyr didn't permit it. The last person she'd touched was—Yiso, to fix his, their, whatever, that broken finger. Not a person, though, Yiso wasn't a—

She had to tell herself to unfreeze. By the time she'd done it Ursa had already backed off, shaking her cropped blond head. She gave Kyr a half smile. She had a slight gap between her front teeth, like Mags did.

Kyr's skin was crawling.

"I can't believe you're really here," Ursa said. "Both of you came here."

"Mags," said Kyr.

Ursa smiled, a dizzying, devastating, gloriously familiar smile, and said, "He's at school. He's at *school*. When he found me—but I thought *you* were still—"

She stretched out a hand toward Kyr again, and said, "I'm sorry." She was smiling, but those eyes which Kyr had thought she recognized were full of tears. Kyr didn't know this woman, didn't know her at all. She swallowed hard.

"So," she said. "It was all lies, then?"

"Yes, of course," Ursa said. "Everything was a lie. I had no choice, and you were too young so I couldn't explain—"

Kyr swallowed again around the lump in her throat. "You weren't really a traitor."

It was where all her thinking pointed to. Ursa was here, and Mags was here, and Ally was obviously the son of the commander in chief of Gaea Station, his genetic legacy and his stake in humanity's future.

"You didn't really want to leave us. You did it for humanity. You came here and you—established a cover, didn't you, and it was about Ally because he's not as strong as he should be," it was obvious and that made Uncle Jole a hypocrite, which Kyr hated, but she *understood*, it was *different* when someone was yours. She knew that. She'd watched Arti and Vic fall in love, breaking all the rules, and she'd never said a word to anyone. She never would have. They were Sparrow and Sparrow belonged to Kyr so Kyr loved them.

"You didn't turn your back on humanity," she said to her sister, to the person whose betrayal had hurt her more deeply than anything else ever had, worse even than getting assigned to Nursery because at least that had eventually almost made sense. "It wasn't because of anything we did, it wasn't me or Mags, you're still one of us, we're Earth's children, you're—you're *Command*, aren't you, you command Strike here." The *relief* in Kyr as she said this, the shudder that went through her body. If Ursa was in command she would understand instantly that Mags's mission was wrong. Ursa was brilliant, Ursa was smart, Ursa's training scores—Kyr had looked them up once, and never told anyone, but only one other female cadet had beaten them since and that was Kyr herself.

The glory of it, the freedom of it: where everything had seemed to be narrowing down and growing heavy, all Avi's snide insinuations and Yiso's earnest explanations, the despicable pirate, the distress signal on the *Victrix*, the physical fact of Ally Marston who had his father's nose—Kyr had started to feel like all the thoughts she was trying not to think were tearing a hole through the fabric of the universe by their sheer weight. But having a superior you trusted took all the weight away. You only had to obey.

"*I'm* sorry," she said to her sister. "I hated you so much. I should have believed in you instead. I'm here. I'm strong. I'm not as tough as Mags, but I'm smarter. I'll do whatever you need me to do."

And then she took in Ursa's expression.

"No," she said.

"Valkyr," Ursa said.

"*No.*"

"Vallie," Ursa said quietly, "everything was a lie."

Very slowly, telegraphing every movement, she reached under her smock and pulled out the weapon. It was a stunstick after all. She laid it down on the floor and kicked it across the room toward Kyr. "There," she said. There was lingering dampness on her face but her eyes were hard Gaean eyes after all, calculating, merciless. Kyr ignored the stunstick. She didn't need it. There were six kitchen knives within easy reach, Ursa disarming herself meant nothing.

"Everything was always lies," Ursa said. "You have been lied to all your life."

"That's what a traitor would say."

"They were the traitors!" Ursa snapped. She visibly collected herself, straightening her back like a soldier on inspection parade, and she said, "Valkyr. On the day that the Zi Sin Accords were signed, a mutiny began in the old Charon dockyards. The instigators were—"

"—a *hero*—" Kyr knew this story, this beginning.

"—a pair of ex-Hagenen commandos who had already been dishonorably discharged following court-martial and were lucky to escape worse punishment," Ursa said over her. "Under their leadership four dreadnoughts were hijacked, their orderly crews given the choice to join the mutineers or die, their commanding officers murdered. Additional mutineers joined them as they fled. Their intention was almost certainly to assault the mid-industrial civilization on Mousa III, a protected—"

"—primitive—"

"—enclave world, in order to obtain resources and weapons. But the mutineers' lack of discipline worked against them, and their progress was slow and chaotic; it wasn't until one of the original pair of instigators killed the other and took ruthless control of the whole enterprise that they were able to make real progress, by which point a Wisdom cruiser had taken up a station on the edge of Mousa—"

"Are you a majo?" Kyr spat. "It's lies. It's *lies*. Can't you hear yourself! Don't you know? You're supposed to be one of us. You're one of Earth's children—"

"I am a *historian*," Ursa snapped back. "And I know, Valkyr, I do know, because I have seen the footage, because I have read the reports, and most of all because I was a child but I was *there*. Aulus Jole is not your uncle. He is a criminal. My name is Ursula Marston and that man murdered my mother on the bridge of her own command, he murdered your other genetic contributor, your father if you like, in order to take control of the Charon mutineers, he runs Gaea Station as his own petty kingdom for no other purpose than to feel himself worshipped and to send children out to die—"

"—to serve humanity—"

"—just like thousands of despots before him," Ursa went on, her voice rising, "because our species has been producing Jole's type of human for as long as we've existed, and he damn well knows it, too, he knows what he's doing and he knows what he is, and he does it anyway because—"

"Because they killed our world!" yelled Kyr.

Ursa stopped talking.

"Was that a lie?" Kyr demanded. "Was it? *Was it?*" She gasped for breath. "Did the majo kill our world?"

Ursa didn't look away. But she didn't answer either.

"How can you think about anything else?" Kyr said. "How can you not see? It's all for humanity. Not *these* people, not the traitors and collaborators who just gave in, but for them, for the dead"— she was crying, embarrassingly, outrageously—"*in memory and in hope*, I saw that stupid statue."

"What hope, Vallie?" said Ursa softly. "What will change what happened to the Earth? Nothing, now."

"But while we live—"

"—the enemy shall fear us?" Ursa shook her head. "Or maybe, while we live, we're alive, and that's all."

Desperately Kyr flung out, "If you hate him so much, why are you playing Nursery for his son?"

Ursa's expression flattened. "Ally is mine."

"He's obviously—"

"He's my son. He's mine."

CHAPTER ELEVEN

MAGNUS

There was nothing else to say, after that. Kyr wanted to walk out and hit something, hurt something, burn this whole bright city down. But where was she going to go? Back to what she now knew was the very worst of Raingold's slums, back to Avi and his sneering, back to Yiso and his—their—its—*facts*?

Or else home, where she'd abandoned her duty for the sake of a mission she'd given herself. Kyr felt a crawling shame. She didn't want to go home. She didn't want to take the only honorable course and give herself up for the court-martial, to accept whatever Command felt she deserved, whether it was the execution that was the proper fate of a traitor or a merciful return to her proper place in Nursery.

It would probably be the second one. Gaea needed Kyr's sons for humanity's soldiers. Kyr tried to imagine it: going home, being punished. Living in Nursery Wing with Lisabel. Looking Cleo in the eyes again, after Cleo called her a traitor.

No.

Kyr just wanted her *brother*.

She wanted to scramble up the rungs of an Agricole ladder and find him hidden in the upper reaches of Gaea's secret forest, gigantic and lazy, probably asleep, too big to hurt, too good to fail, and the only person Kyr had ever permitted to see her looking weak.

"Vallie," said Ursa. "Sweetheart." The endearment fell off her tongue like it was a word from an alien language she'd only recently learned. Kyr sat down. She put her hands over her face and stared down between her fingers. The table was covered in brown cake crumbs. That stunstick was still on the floor. When Ursa tried to put her hand on Kyr's shoulder, Kyr flinched so violently that Ursa took two steps back.

"Traitor," said Kyr. "You're a traitor, you left, don't touch me."

Ursa let out a hard breath. "I'm going to help you," she said. "I want to help you."

"You don't."

"All humans have citizenship on Chrysothemis if they want it," Ursa said. "Even Gaean refugees. Everyone can live here."

"I'm not a refugee."

"You can live here. You can go to school. You don't have to do anything you don't want to do. You're free, Vallie. You can stay here, with us, with me and Ally, and Magnus too, and I'll never let Gaea touch any of you again. You'll get help, sweetheart, there are people to talk to for what you're going through, deradicalization specialists, and—and we'll be a family. Vallie, I love you. I thought of you every day. I'm so proud of you both for running away. You've been so brave. We'll be a family again."

Kyr lifted her head. Ursa was on her knees next to the kitchen chair. There was the smile Kyr remembered from long ago, the same smile she'd given to Ally. Kyr swallowed hard.

I'm so proud of you both for running away.

Ursa thought Magnus had done the same thing Kyr had. Ursa thought Magnus had run away.

Ursa didn't know he was Strike.

Kyr hadn't come to this planet expecting to find people to trust. She didn't need people to trust. So Ursa was a traitor: Ursa had always been a traitor. Nothing had changed. Kyr just needed to get to her brother, and work out what the right mission was for them: be her own Strike commander, since no one else would do it for her, and then—

Then they'd go home.

She swiped the back of her hand across her eyes. Ursa held out her hands.

Kyr let herself take one of them, just for a moment. She said, "I just . . . I just wanted to find Mags."

"He's safe," Ursa said at once. "He's safe, he'll be home soon."

"Okay," Kyr said. "Then . . . fine."

"What's fine?"

"All of it," Kyr said. "Staying here, school"—did they really send people Kyr's age to school here?—"and de-whatever, the talking thing, fine. *Fine*. If Mags is here as well, then fine."

Ursa called Ally back down and told him, and Ally said scornfully, "I *guessed* she was staying. Wait, is she going to have my room? Do I share with Magnus? I don't want to share my room. It's my room."

"No, sweetheart, she'll have my room for now," Ursa said. "I'll sleep in the study. And I'll put in an application to the Institute and we'll get a bigger place. Now can you and Vallie keep each other company in the sitting room for a little while? I need to make some calls."

"I have to do homework," Ally said. He gave Kyr a considering look. "She can help if she wants."

Kyr was stuck with the child again, this time in the blue and grey room that was the biggest in the apartment, while Ursa locked herself in the study. She was edgy all over. Lying was beneath her, so she didn't have much practice at it. She was uncomfortably aware that Ally was obviously smart. Of course he was: whatever Ursa said, he was Jole's son.

Luckily Ally didn't seem all that interested in Kyr apart from her ability to eat a lot of cake and pay attention to him. He gave her two more lectures on Chrysotheman biology, and showed her his schoolwork, with the air of someone offering a gift. It was all incomprehensible. Kyr refused to ask any questions about it, which seemed to disappoint him, but he sat down and got to work. After a while he got out some stiff paper and pencils and started drawing stupid pictures, wasting valuable resources. "You're supposed to be working," Kyr said automatically.

"This is my art homework," Ally said. "Do you want to draw? You can use my pencils."

Kyr hadn't done anything so pointless since she was a child half Ally's age in Nursery. They obviously spoiled children here. "No."

Ursa did not reappear. Kyr could make out her voice rising and falling through the study door. Ally lost himself in his stupid drawings. Kyr sat around and did nothing, and hated every second of it. She hated it even more than she'd hated sitting around doing nothing in the shack with Yiso and Avi, because there at least she'd had a goal, and there hadn't been pictures of Ursa and her stolen son on the walls everywhere.

She had a goal now too, she reminded herself. No need to worry. No need to think. She knew what she needed to do.

She had to suffer through nearly an hour of patience before there were male voices in the courtyard outside, drifting up through the big room's open window. Kyr jumped to her feet.

It was the two men who also lived in the building—*Jac and Jac's boyfriend*—back from wherever it was they'd gone, both with their striped waterproofs over their arms now that the sun had come out.

With them was Mags.

He was there. He was alive. He was shifting from foot to foot as the two men chatted to him, but he didn't look unhappy or afraid: just shy. Not a lot of people knew Mags was shy. Kyr knew.

He was a foot taller than either of the men, almost a foot *wider* than the skinnier one, and there was something strangely familiar about the sight of him, big and blond and wearing a red school uniform jacket as he stood in that pretty courtyard where Terran trees donated by aliens grew in painted tubs. Kyr's mind went back to Avi's dream-city in the agoge: seeing the massive monsters called orcs appear at the corner of a white street. Mags in Raingold looked, somehow, like that.

Kyr clutched the window frame so tightly her fingers hurt.

She didn't make a sound. Maybe it was the weight of her stare. Her brother looked up.

The other two both looked as well to see what he was staring at, but Kyr didn't care about them.

Mags broke her gaze, and looked around in a faintly lost way. Kyr saw him pause and stare at the building's glass doors with their security cameras as if he had no idea what to do about them. He had a small satchel slung over his shoulder. He turned to the man standing nearest to him and said, "Excuse me"—Kyr could hear it perfectly clearly—and handed him the strap of the satchel. He looked back up at Kyr.

With a sudden wild delight Kyr knew what he was going to do next. She burst into laughter as Mags threw himself at the soft yellow bricks of the wall, a short run-up for one big jump—Mags's vertical leap was substantially better than Kyr's, easily seventy inches—and catch and scramble up on the doorframe, foot braced on the security-camera bracket for another jump to the frame of a first-floor window, handholds between the bricks and swing sideways and up. Kyr was laughing almost too hard to get the window the rest of the way open and reach out to catch him as he threw himself up to the second-floor window of apartment 5.

She braced a foot against the wall under the window to haul him in. Once he had a knee on the frame they overbalanced and toppled back together into the room. Mags turned it into a pivot and caught them both upright, clinging to each other. They got one good look at each other's faces. *This* was family, not the strange mirror experience of looking into Ursa's hard grey eyes; this was what it was like to see yourself in someone else. Then they both dragged each other at once into a crushing hug, and unlike being grabbed by Ursa, unlike making herself fix Yiso's irritatingly broken finger, nothing about this touch made Kyr's skin crawl.

"You're here," Mags said.

Ally had migrated over to the window and was peering out in

a dubious way. "How did you get in the window?" he said. It was background noise.

"I'm here," Kyr said.

"*It's two stories.*"

"*How* are you here?"

"*That's really high.*"

"I had a free rec rotation."

"*There are stairs inside.*"

"So you just decided to—"

"*You could have come up the stairs.*"

"—take a little break, you always say I'm doing rec wrong—"

"You're here."

"*You're* here."

Somewhere unimportant a bell rang and Ally went to the door to get Mags's satchel, from Jac, who said some things. Someone was laughing in the background. Ursa rushed out from the study, took a moment to understand what was going on, and then started talking too, and all the time Kyr and Mags grinned at each other. For the first time since Uncle Jole had handed her the flimsy with her Nursery assignment, Kyr felt the universe settle back into its proper alignment.

Everything was under control now. They were Earth's children, and they were together, and there was nothing the two of them couldn't do.

Their enemies would fear them.

That evening Ursa made them dinner, flaky white protein stuff and potatoes and then slices of a big red-fleshed fruit Kyr didn't know the name of. It was the best-tasting meal Kyr had ever had. Afterward she told Ursa that she and Magnus would share a room, thanks. They hadn't had a moment yet to strategize.

Magnus's bed was made up with green sheets with sharp military corners. Ursa insisted on helping Kyr set up a second folding bed on the floor, though Kyr would have been fine on just the soft carpet. It took Ursa forever to leave. She acted like the room was too small and apologized, which made Kyr give her a confused look because Ursa *knew* what size cadet dormitories were. A room this big could fit ten bunks, easily, with a narrow gap down the middle. Kyr did not let herself think about the Sparrows' barracks.

Ally came in, bored of being left out, and Mags picked him up and turned him upside down. He shrieked wildly when dropped on Mags's neat little bed. Kyr caught Ursa wiping at her eyes for some reason. She wished her traitor sister and the child she'd kidnapped would both just *leave*.

And then, finally, they did.

Kyr and Mags both started talking at once. Kyr halted herself. "You first."

"I don't believe you," Mags said. "Vallie, how the hell. You're incredible. You got out?"

"Who says this isn't my assignment?" Kyr said, and looked at his face, and got it. "They told you my assignment."

"I knew you'd hate it. But—"

"What?"

Magnus sat down on the edge of his little green bed. Kyr sat next to him. "I don't know," he said. "I thought, if you weren't a combat wing, you probably wouldn't die. I thought you'd be safe."

"I'm not a coward," said Kyr sharply.

"Obviously. I don't know. It was stupid."

After an incredulous moment of something halfway between furious insult and feeling rather touched, Kyr said, "'I'd rather stand three times in the battle line than give birth to one child.' The Nursery toast? You know why, right?"

Mags frowned. "Because it's giving up the glory—look, I know how much combat matters to you, but—"

"No, idiot, because it's *dangerous*," said Kyr. "You're not safe in Nursery. Don't you know how many of them die?"

"What?" Mags said.

They'd never talked about Nursery, Kyr realized. Not since

they'd left it. And boys didn't get Nursery rotations. Not ever. Kyr had a vague idea it was something about . . . not trusting the older ones, or something, with the children? The women? Except she'd never even seen one of the younger boys' messes in there: not even messes like Cat or Weasel, where most of them weren't from warbreed stock, weren't meant to make soldiers.

"Yeah, they die," she said. "One in three."

"But—aren't women's bodies meant to be *for* children? Why would they die?"

"I don't know," Kyr said. "It just happens. Didn't you know?" Except come to think of it she wasn't sure how she knew, exactly: who had told her why it was that sometimes, when women who were heavily pregnant disappeared from the noisy main hall of Nursery, they never came back again. It was just something you knew.

"But they—they're for children. And they get to be around them, and play with them, and"—Mags was staring at Kyr now—"and to—touch people and have, you know. Love affairs. In Coyote we made jokes, but it was because—we thought it wasn't fair."

"Not fair is one in three," Kyr said. "And I'm not for children. I'm for *Earth*."

There was a moment of quiet.

Then Mags took Kyr's hand and squeezed it. Kyr understood the apology. She squeezed back.

Mags said, "I still don't understand how you're here."

"You know your good friend Avi?"

Mags grinned suddenly. "He didn't. He *did*. Of course he did." And then his expression changed. "But if he gets caught—"

"Oh, they know it was him all right," Kyr said. "He knocked out a shadow engine for twenty minutes."

Mags went ashen. "They'll kill him."

"What? No. I brought him with me. He says hi, actually." She was making it sound like Avi was the accessory to *her* plan. Well, it wasn't like Avi could have made it off Gaea Station without Kyr. She'd done the work. She'd even gone back for him, when

Cleo had a gun to his head and Kyr could have got clean away. Thinking of it like that cheered her up immensely. "I saved his life," she said. "He's *really* annoying, though. I can sort of see why you like him, but seriously."

Mags was still ashy, staring at her. "He's on Chrysothemis? He's—and did he tell you about—"

"What?" Kyr said. She couldn't think of anything that justified Mags's dreadful expression. "You mean that he's queer? I already knew, everyone knows, you know that sort of thing doesn't matter. It's just sex stuff." She paused. Mags wasn't looking any better. "Do you mean his thing about you? No, he didn't tell me. I worked it out myself. It was obvious."

"He doesn't," Mags said. "He doesn't have a thing about me."

Kyr rolled her eyes. "He's less of an ass about it than he is about most things, so I don't see why you care."

"He *doesn't*," Mags said.

Kyr stopped and looked at him. He wasn't acting like the Mags she knew. Mags was calm all the time—calm even when he shouldn't be. Mags didn't get upset. "What's the matter?" she said.

Mags took a deep breath. "I was going to say—did he tell you about—but he didn't, did he. He wouldn't. So I guess he just let you think—"

"What are you talking about?"

"Me," Mags said. "Did he tell you about me."

"What?" said Kyr. "What about you?" She felt insulted by the idea that Avi might know something about Mags that she didn't. Of course not. "Oh, I saw that garden he made you—but I already knew you can be soft about trees and things, Mags, come on. That's not a secret."

"You're so hard to talk to," Mags said. The way he said it shook something in Kyr for a moment. It chimed with a memory. Mags in Agricole, staring up through the branches—avoiding Kyr's eyes. Mags turning away, the last time she'd spoken to him on Gaea Station. *You're so hard to talk to*, he'd said. And then, oddly, that made her think of something else—of Zen folding up the flimsy with her Oikos assignment on it, saying as if Kyr should already know: *I never liked either of you.*

"What?" she said. It came out sharp.

"Don't you know why I'm friends with Avi?"

"Does it matter?" Kyr said.

"I went looking for him," Mags said, "because he was the only person I'd heard of who was—I went looking for him. And he was playing some old game where you build stuff. And I said hi. And he looked at me and he said, *Oh joy, another one.*"

"Another what?"

"Another *queer*, Vallie," Mags spat. "I'm *queer*, okay?"

He gasped after he said it, like he'd just broken the surface of deep water, like he hadn't been expecting air. Kyr stared at him.

Mags said, "I want—I feel—I'm just like him, all right?"

Kyr didn't say anything. She saw Mags's expression start to crumple and thought—*if he cries, I will*—she didn't know. She said the first thing she thought of. Her voice came out quiet and flat. "Is that what he meant? Another one?"

Mags's breath hissed between his teeth. "No, he meant he gets someone like me turning up to bother him every six months, all right?" he said. "And to him I'm just another one, *all right*? He doesn't—about me. Well?"

"Well what?"

"Well, why don't you say anything?"

There was a silence. It went on for a long time.

"I don't care," said Kyr. "It doesn't matter. Why would it matter?"

"Because—"

"It's just sex stuff," Kyr said. "It's not important unless you let it be important. Who cares? It's just a distraction, it gets in people's heads and takes their focus away from the real problems, the meaningful things, the war. We're Earth's children. We're the last humans. Feelings aren't important. It's what we do that matters." She made a face at Mags, trying to be comforting though it didn't come naturally. He was obviously worked up about this. "Avi's," she couldn't make herself say either *nice* or *handsome*, because he definitely wasn't the first and Kyr wasn't any judge of the second, "well, I suppose he was fun to play his stupid games with, and you won Doomsday, fine, but you know it doesn't count for anything in the end, right? So it's all just . . . fine. I don't care, you shouldn't either."

Mags jumped up, walked across the room, wrapped his arms around himself and squeezed for a moment. Kyr thought how mismatched he looked: the broad shoulders of a perfect warrior, the body language of an unhappy child. "And that's it," he said. "That's all you're going to say."

"What's wrong?"

"It matters. Why don't you see that it matters?"

"It just doesn't, though."

"Haven't you ever liked someone, or cared about them?"

"I care about you," Kyr said.

"Not like that!" Mags rounded on her. "Haven't you ever *wanted* someone?" Kyr got to her feet, not liking the look on his face, but before she could say anything he barreled on. This was the most she had heard him talk at once in years, the most expression she'd seen him show since the awful months after Ursa had left. "Forget the queer thing," he snarled, "just—don't you ever want to touch anyone? Don't you ever want to be with someone, to *love* someone—"

He broke off, gasping again.

Kyr's body moved before she realized that she knew what to do. Kyr's body was always the best of her. She went to Mags and put her arms around him, and he shuddered like it hurt and then collapsed into the hug. Kyr could feel dampness where he had his hot face against her temple. "It's okay," she said. "It's okay." He was shaking. Kyr found that her hand was rubbing soothing circles on his shoulder. "I'm sorry," she said. "I'm sorry. It's okay."

Do you really think it doesn't count, that I care about you? she wanted to say. *Do you think it doesn't count, when I refused my assignment, when I left home, when Cleo called me a traitor—I got stabbed, did you know—when I came to this stupid collaborator planet and lived in a shack with a majo for two weeks and then had to see Ursa again—all of that—just because it's nothing to do with sex stuff, do you really think it doesn't count?*

She wanted to say it, but Mags was still making faint snuffling noises into her hair, and even Kyr with her limited tolerance for crying people could tell it wasn't the time.

They stayed like that for a little while.

Kyr hadn't known this, or even suspected it. She felt strange. Avi *had* known something about her brother that she didn't. And Avi and Mags had been doing their weird little friendship for months, messing around in the agoge, building up to Mags beating Doomsday. Kyr's understanding of it was all backward now. She'd thought she'd made sense of things when she assumed Avi wanted him. But now she remembered Avi's grimace when she'd said so.

It had been the other way round all along. Which meant for months at least Mags had kept this from her. Maybe longer. How long had he known? When did you know you were queer? Kyr had no idea. The only other point of reference she had was Arti and Vic, who'd been kissing for at least three years.

Had Kyr's brother been keeping a secret from her for three years?

When Mags pulled away from Kyr at last, he looked ashamed. "Sorry," he said. "Thanks. I didn't think you'd—Thanks."

"You didn't think I'd what?"

"Take it this well," Mags said. "A couple of guys in my mess figured it out, and they made me give them half my rations not to report me. I was bumming a lot from Agricole for a while, until Avi figured out a workaround for some of the storeroom locks for me."

"*Who,*" snarled Kyr, stiff with fury. Food was vital; for someone Mags's size, spending as much time as Coyote did in combat drills, missing half his meals was *dangerous.* And the thought of some pathetic lesser Coyote daring to blackmail Kyr's brother—

But Mags just said, "It doesn't matter." He sat on the green bed.

His hands clenched into fists and then opened, relaxed, empty. "We don't have to go back. I'm never going to see them again."

"What about your mission?"

"My mission?"

"You don't have to lie. I know you're Strike."

"Oh," Mags said. "That."

"Yes, the reason we're here, *that*!"

"I'm not."

"What?"

"I'm not Strike," Mags said. "I'm not doing it. I was never going to do it, Vallie. They wanted me to kill people."

"Right, it was the wrong mission," Kyr agreed. "The correct target has to be the Prince of the Wisdom."

"No."

"It's a short timetable but we can—What do you mean, no?"

"I mean *no*. I'm not doing it. I'm not Strike," Mags said. "Not for them and not for you either. I'm not killing anyone. I don't want to."

"You don't have a choice," Kyr told him. "We're Earth's children. We're the soldiers of humanity."

"You can be if you want. I'm not," Mags said. "I'm done. I'm *free*. Earth's gone, and Gaea's a shithole."

Kyr stared at him. Mags didn't look sorry.

"I don't want to be a soldier," he said. "No one ever asked if I wanted to be a soldier. And now I'm not. I quit."

CHAPTER TWELVE

WATER

Kyr slept, because it was stupid not to sleep.

She woke in the yellow dimness before the planet's day cycle— *day*—began. Mags was breathing steadily in the little bed with green sheets.

She looked at his big quiet form for a little longer. He'd been unhappy. He'd lied to her for years, and he'd been unhappy. Kyr hadn't known.

Maybe he'd be happy here.

Kyr took care to be quiet when she got up, because even if Mags wanted to end up like Ursa with all his edges gone, it wouldn't have happened yet. His hearing was as good as hers. He was as strong and well-trained and fearsome as she was. He could stop her.

She got dressed in the bathroom, in the cheap colorful T-shirt and trousers that Avi had secured from the pirate. She picked up the yellow waterproof from the hook by the door. There were pencils and paper—*paper*, of all the luxuries—left out on the table in the main room where Ally had been doing his art homework. What a weird happy little life he had. What a weird happy little life all of them had. Maybe lives like this had been normal for humans before the end of the world. Kyr sat down at the table and picked up a pencil and then stared into space. She'd done what she'd set out to do. She'd wanted to be sure Mags wouldn't die, and he wouldn't. He'd never been in any danger of dying. He wouldn't fight, he wouldn't risk anything for humanity, he wasn't Strike after all.

And Ursa was here, and she seemed happy. Here, alone in the dim dawn-lit room, Kyr could admit that she was glad. Mags would be all right. Ursa was all right. She was even glad about Ally, whom she'd met yesterday. He'd be all right too. Whatever delusions Ursa had about Commander Jole, he was family to Kyr—*I'm proud of you*—so his son was family too.

Kyr even tried, for a moment, to picture herself staying. She could do all the things Ursa had said. Be part of this life, this family. Go to school and learn whatever it was schools were for here.

All it would cost her was her war. All it would cost was the memory of the dead, and the service she'd been born for, and the knowledge that out in deep space, clinging to a cold rock orbiting an unfriendly star, the last soldiers of humanity were still refusing to surrender, and Kyr was not among them. Cleo and Jeanne and Arti, Vic and Zen and Lisabel: Kyr's mess, her sisters, the Sparrows. Earth's children.

Kyr bowed her head.

Never.

Kyr knew her cause and she knew her duty. She owed no explanation to traitors. She put down the pencil she was holding and let out a breath.

"What are you doing?" asked Ally behind her.

Kyr turned. Ally was wearing striped blue trousers and a matching shirt that buttoned up the front. He was holding a glass of water. There were three ice cubes in the glass.

Kyr should have heard him. She'd let herself get distracted.

"Just thinking," she said.

"Are you going out?"

Kyr said nothing. Ally was looking at the waterproof on the table next to her. There was a faint pattering of raindrops against the big window.

"Are you going for a run?" Ally said, and then he frowned. "Are you running away?"

"I don't run away," said Kyr.

"Maybe I should wake Mom."

Kyr was on her feet. "Don't even think about it."

Ally blinked owlishly up at her from behind his glasses. He wasn't afraid. Kyr was twice his size. She could break his arms and legs. She could slam him into the nearest hard surface and knock him senseless. She could kill him.

Just like she could have killed the alien Yiso if she'd wanted to, just like she could have killed the Blackbird child she'd found playing with the bucket of water, was it only a few weeks ago?— and she could have killed any one of the Raingold children she'd seen playing in the street yesterday, and she could have, she could have killed Ursa, picked up a kitchen knife and executed a traitor, she could have killed Mags in his sleep just now, because—she forced herself to think it—because he was just as much a traitor as Ursa was. A whole rainbow array of violence and power and possibility unfolded in Kyr's head, and Ally only looked confused. He wasn't afraid. It would never occur to him to be afraid. He lived a life that didn't have fear in it.

It wasn't fair.

Kyr forced herself to unclench her fists. He was a human child. "Please," she said. "Please don't wake anyone."

Please, she meant, because then she would have to stop him, and she did not want to.

Ally frowned. "You really are leaving."

"Yes," Kyr said.

"Promise to come back."

"What?"

"Promise," Ally said, "and I won't tell Mom."

"Why?"

"She's my *mom*. I don't like it when she's upset."

"I will," said Kyr, "if you promise not to tell her you saw me."

Ally considered this. "Okay," he said, and then recited solemnly, "I promise not to tell Mom."

"Fine," Kyr said. "I promise I'll come back." She was lying, but there was no harm in lying to a child. She tugged the yellow waterproof over her head. "And now I'm going."

"Okay," Ally said. "Bye. But don't forget you promised!"

Raingold's streets were thick with morning mist. Visibility over the water from the great promenade was almost nil. Kyr walked past the giant memorial statue of the woman with the Earth cradled at her breast, and avoided looking at it.

The streets weren't empty. She saw cleaners in uniform green waterproofs picking up trash with long poles. One majo, a four-armed lirem, ambled along with some sort of animal on a string. Kyr crossed the road to avoid it. A group of yawning young women sauntered past her with arms around each other. They were skimpily dressed, hair flat with sweat, some barefoot and dangling what looked like very impractical shoes from their fingertips. Kyr kept moving. As the sky brightened she passed a building with a tower. From the top of it someone began singing an unfamiliar up-and-down song. The echoes hung in the damp golden air as Kyr made her way through the last human city.

The tin-roofed shack in the slums was just as she'd left it. Kyr used her ID chip on what Avi had said was a shitty cheap lock.

It didn't work.

She tried again.

Nothing.

Kyr gritted her teeth. She'd been locked out. She eyed the door disdainfully, then set her shoulder against it and gave it one good shove. It gave way instantly, and she stumbled as she entered the shack's cramped main room.

The place was empty.

Kyr checked the only other room—the bathroom—just to be sure. Nothing was there, not even the clippers Avi had insisted on wasting rent money on to shave off half of his red curls. The corner of the main room where Yiso had created a kind of nest of scarves and sheets was empty. There was no food in the cupboards. Kyr got on her knees and yanked out the board that blocked access to the space under the sink. Wrapped in the bloody rags of her cadet uniform had been the field knife and handgun she'd taken from the guard in the brig of the *Victrix*. There'd been a wing badge, too. Kyr had kept it even though Avi had hinted the pirates would pay for what he called "Gaean memorabilia."

All gone.

Kyr had been counting on those weapons.

She jumped to her feet when she heard a sound at the door. "Squatters," came the voice of the landlord. Avi had done most of the talking to him. Kyr didn't know his name. "Typical. Listen, you, I don't run a charity here—"

Kyr turned to look at him. He was old—older than anyone ever really looked on Gaea, a fringe of white hair left around his tan face, saggy wrinkles on his cheeks. He wore a shapeless brown coat with a wet shine to the material. Badges were pinned to the lapel. "Where are they," she said.

The landlord took a step back. "Don't know anything about that," he said.

The kaleidoscope of violent possibility in Kyr's thoughts co-alesced into simplicity and motion. She grabbed the man's wrists. She spun him round and pinned him against the wall. Rain drummed on the tin roof. "Where *are* they," Kyr growled.

"Never wanted a filthy majo in one of my properties anyway!" the landlord yelped. "I don't know—I don't know—"

Kyr gripped his wrist tighter and twisted.

The landlord let out a little wail. "Left," he whimpered. "Paid off next week and gone. Don't know where. I *don't* know. I'm a patriot. You wouldn't hurt a human."

Kyr let go and backed off a step. He stayed where he was, cringing against the wall. "You know something about me," Kyr said.

"Don't know, don't know anything—"

Kyr looked at him in disgust. Among the badges and pins on the lapel of his old brown coat she saw a silver circle with the figure of a winged woman on it. Kyr reached out, ignoring his terrified flinch, and tore it away. "Hey!" the landlord protested.

"The gun," said Kyr. "The knife. Where are they."

"I don't know what you're talking about," he said. "I never broke the law—"

Kyr grabbed him by the collar.

"Gone! They were already gone!" he yelped. "I sold the uniform, I can tell you the name—I told them it was a girl's, they paid me more for it—the weapons were gone—I kept the badge—I'm a patriot! A true human! I could have called the police on you the day you showed up here, couldn't I? I know what warbreed kids look like—I served—the *size* of you—the fucking majo was a prisoner, right? I'm on your side!"

Kyr shoved him to the floor. "You don't know anything about where he's gone," she said. "The human. I don't care about the majo." Maybe Avi had gone off to sell Yiso to a slaver to buy himself another device. That seemed like something Avi would do. He was so *selfish*. Who disappeared like this? What did he think he was doing? Kyr was furious because she had been counting on Avi, as much as she had been counting on the gun and the knife. She knew she could make him do what she wanted. He was a coward.

So was the landlord. Kyr smelled something sour. He'd pissed himself in fear.

"You never served," she told him scornfully as he gibbered at her feet. "You're nothing." She paused, thinking. "If you call the police now," she added, "or anyone else, I'll find you and I'll kill you."

The old man's eyes showed white all around. "I don't know," he said again. "I don't know where they went."

Kyr looked around once more. She took the Victrix Wing sigil and she carefully pinned it to the inside of her pants pocket. It was clear that some locals at least knew what Gaean insignia looked like, so having it was a risk, but she could not bring herself not to wear it. It was hers. It should have been hers all along. Even if no one else could see it, *Kyr* would know it was there.

And when they found her body it would be there, and Chryso-themis would know, and the majo would know, who she was and why she had done what she had to do.

Kyr had not realized until that moment how sure she was that it would be her body, afterward, and not her. But of course it would have to be. If it had been her and Mags together, that would be something different. If she'd had Avi on hand to scheme and suggest and murmur instructions through an earpiece, that would be different. But Kyr was going to be alone. Part of strategizing for victory was acknowledging the costs. Kyr alone was no different to Mags alone.

Except weaker, of course. She'd always known the gap between their training scores.

She left the tin-roofed shack walking briskly, though she did not know yet where she was going.

"Fucking bitch!" the landlord yelled behind her, with sudden courage. "Fucking whore! Who do you think you are?"

Kyr ignored it and kept walking, serene and powerful in the knowledge that she *could* turn around and kill him. She could do anything she wanted. She could do her duty, alone, if she had to.

"What about my door?" howled the old man. "Who's going to pay for my door?"

Kyr was planning as she walked. Leru Ihenni Tan Yi: that was the name of the majo zi, the Prince of the Wisdom, who was coming to Chrysothemis. She wished she'd read the briefing that Avi had found in Mags's Command files more closely. She'd hoped Avi would remember more of it. She only had a rough picture in her head. Mags had been supposed to get up high during the alien's arrival and open fire on the human crowd.

Kyr wasn't interested in hurting humans. Not even these humans.

Chrysothemis already had a node of the Wisdom, dormant: the planet had been inhabited by some dead alien species once upon a time. Kyr had a good memory for maps. If she struck out following a light railway line east from Raingold, it would bring her to the small archaeological settlement of Hfa, just a few miles from a star that on Gaea's maps had been labeled w (INACTIVE—SECURED).

In order to bring the Wisdom back to life on this world, sooner or later Prince Leru would have to go there too.

It was not the whole of a plan. But it couldn't be, not yet. Kyr had faith in her own ability to improvise.

She would find the dormant Wisdom node, she would get in position, she would *wait*, and when the Prince of the Wisdom showed up, she would kill it. With luck she would be able to do some damage to the machine as well. Assassination of a majo leader, sabotage of a Wisdom installation; these were goals worth dying for.

Kyr had no doubt she would die. She felt light as air. She had spent nearly two weeks on Chrysothemis, and between Yiso and Avi, between Ursa and Ally and Mags, something had almost shaken loose in the foundation of her world. But Kyr was stronger than that. Let others preach and smile and argue and lie; she was still a soldier of humanity. Her family was her station. Her family was her cause. Her family was fourteen billion dead, and her mother was a murdered world.

She'd arrived back at the promenade again. This time she kept walking, ignoring the statue, the people, the friendly cry of a woman who was selling hot food from a stall. She walked all the way to the strip of dark sand at the water's edge.

A tracery of gold was just visible where wavelets broke on the sand. Kyr kicked at the algal bloom and it fell apart.

Then she stood there for a moment, looking out at all that water, and imagined what it might have been like to be, oh, to be Ally; to be taken from Gaea as an infant and grow up in a nice apartment on a world that was two-thirds ocean, a world where it rained all the time.

It was all worthless, though. All the riches and beauty of Chrysothemis were a distraction, a seductive and treacherous lie.

Kyr slipped her hand into her pocket and fingered the Victrix insignia. The pad of her finger picked out the fine lines of the winged woman's stern face, and the delicate traceries of her tiny feathers.

PART III

WISDOM

Every traveler who has found themselves among humans has experienced the problem. Imagine: a friendly conversation is in progress. The verbal communication is in T-standard, a robust standardized language easily understood by almost all translator technologies. (Humans have not yet achieved a linguistic technology of this kind compatible with their biology; language acquisition for adults is a laborious process, hence their difficulties with Majodai, Sinneltha, and other common linguae francae.) The more subtle communicative elements given informally through bodily expression are sometimes hard to decode, but the basic "smile" and "laugh" are straightforward and readily understood.

But slowly over the course of this friendly conversation something changes. It is impossible for the visitor to pinpoint the transition. The humans do not realize that there is a problem, and continue to smile and laugh; while the bewildered majo finds themselves surrounded by aliens speaking purest gibberish, with a snatch of coherent meaning here and there but no continuous sense.

What has happened?

The answer is simple. You will almost never meet a human whose language of choice is T-standard. Nearly all can use it—though there are groups of linguistic purists who cut themselves off by choice from galactic communication for the sake of preserving traditional speech forms—but it is in fact a simplified "translatorbot-ese" based on a much older Earth language. The humans did not intend to exclude you. It is simply that as they grew comfortable, they forgot you were there, and so slipped into one of the many hundreds of dialects of Classical English.

These dialects range from the unusually pronounced but largely comprehensible (International Business English and its ancestor "US" or "American" English) to the utterly strange (this author once found themselves at a gathering of individuals who spoke principally in an ancient dialect called "Scots").

This is not even taking into account the equally strong possibility that the preferred language of your human companions is not an ancestor or even a distant relative of T-standard. Nearly all modern human settlements have at least one official language which bears no relationship whatsoever to the humans' galactic tongue. The commonest "native" (first-learned) languages of modern humans are IB English, New Swahili, and Galactic Chinese.

There is only one human community where T-standard is the language of choice. Ironically, in claiming a position as the sole "true" humans, the extremists of Gaea Station have made themselves an enclave of galactic-language speakers. This twist of fate is unsurprising to students of human history. Since language and identity are closely intertwined in human culture, a society seeking to eradicate individual cultural identities and histories in favor of a fictitious pan-Terran "cause" must begin by robbing its people of their languages.

—S. Lopor, *Communication: A Human History*

The "warrior code" or "code of honor" so often used to explain human behavior to other sentient peoples is in fact more often honored in the breach. Humans may claim to be honorable, but they will cheerfully lie, betray, and exploit every available weakness in the pursuit of their goals. Actions which at other times would be considered even by humans themselves to be hideous crimes are justified in warfare as the price of victory. It is perhaps best to understand honor as operating optionally and on the individual level, while the authoritative driving forces of human military design work perpetually on the most ruthless calculus of cost and benefit.

A useful case study is the Gyssono-IV incident. The Gyssono binary system contains no habitable worlds but in its quadruple asteroid belt are some of the largest known natural deposits of irris, a scioactive substance vital to the construction of the gigantic shadow engines which power human dreadnoughts. Early in the Terran War (known to humans as the Majo War) the Terran Expeditionary moved to secure the system. The inhabitants of Gyssono—miners and technicians, mostly settlers from the sinnet citizen worlds of nearby systems—occupied a chain of space stations numbered I through VIII. In the course of the conflict Station IV was repurposed as a hospital. Given the precarious nature of the Gyssono settlements, it was also decided to concentrate the system's small civilian population on Station IV, simplifying the difficulties of defense.

It was predicted that the TE would attempt to bombard the station, which they did; the Wisdom cruisers patrolling around it succeeded in preventing any serious damage. However no one predicted the accident which actually took place. The overloaded station, removed from its usual safe orbit to a harder-to-approach position at the center of an asteroid belt, collided with an asteroid which contained a gigantic unsuspected irris deposit. Irris in its unprocessed form is highly volatile, particularly in the subreal dimensions which Wisdom systems rely on. The explosion left the Wisdom cruisers paralyzed and blind. It also sent Station IV into a doomed fast-collapsing orbit around Gyssono's twin stars.

At this point ordinary analysis fails. The Terran Expeditionary, by a stroke of chance, needed only to destroy the damaged and defenseless cruisers to win total control of Gyssono at no cost to themselves. But instead the humans, under the command of Admiral Isamy Russell of the dreadnought *Temeraria,* launched a dangerous rescue operation for the population of Station IV, including the injured enemy combatants aboard. Human soldiers risked their own lives to evacuate enemy aliens. Several died in the final stage of the evacuation, when, as the station fell toward the binary star, the humans abandoned useless attempts at employing combat darts as shuttles, and volunteers instead continued to pull evacuees out one or two at a time using shadowspace jump hooks—at this time a barely tested technology, and one which often failed.

It was only when every possible effort had been made to save the people of Gyssono-IV that Admiral Russell turned his attention to the Wisdom cruisers and attacked. By this time they had recovered from the effects of the irris explosion, and what followed was a close and brutal battle in which the human forces only narrowly achieved a decisive victory.

The rescue of innocents over the defeat of the enemy: this, humans say, is honor. But to quote Russell himself on the whole affair: "If I hadn't won the battle after, I would've been taken out and shot."

Honor is a personal choice, and one which humans will admire—up to a point. But only Russell's subsequent victory saved his military career from oblivion. Instead he was acquitted of wrongdoing by a court-martial, and feted by media both human and majo. He was later awarded a medal by the people of

Gyssono, who had carefully researched this appropriate human custom. Moving accounts exist of the whole affair: it is, as one evacuee remarked, an extraordinary feeling to see the gigantic form of a human soldier rushing toward you and experience *relief*.

To this day all humans have honorary citizenship of the Gyssono system; and in the aftermath of the destruction of Earth, the primarily-sinnet population of the eight space stations voted symbolically to secede from the majoda. The eight stations of Gyssono are now home to the second-largest human population in the universe, approximately seven hundred thousand individuals, who live in remarkably well-integrated harmony with the earlier sinnet inhabitants. For those human refugees who reject the militant extremism of an enclave like Gaea Station, but cannot bear to live under the shadow of the Wisdom, there is nowhere else to go.

—Isia Mlo-Samar, *Reflections on the Human Question*

CHAPTER THIRTEEN

ALONE

Kyr had never once in all her life been truly alone.

Gaea was too compact and too well-ordered for minor concerns like privacy. She had been grouped with others, constantly watched and assessed against them, from the very first moments of her life. She had always slept in dormitories, first with a mixture of little ones under Corporal Ekker's supervision and then with her mess. Even after she came to Chrysothemis she had not been alone. Avi had shared that one-room shack with her, and Yiso too, if that counted. And then there had been a single night in Ursa's apartment listening to Magnus's breathing before she crept away. It was not the first time she had been there while Mags slept. He had napped away every rec rotation he could get away with.

Now she looked back at it there was something strange about the way Mags had always insisted on sleeping as much as possible—as if he didn't like to be awake. Some of Kyr's memories were resettling in the light of her new knowledge, that Mags had been unhappy all that time: not lazy confidence, but shirking; not teasing, but real dissident muttering; not boredom, but fear. Her brother shrank in her regard the longer she thought about it, and there was a kind of satisfaction in that. Mags had always been so *much* better than Kyr, in every way that counted. But at least she was loyal. At least she was true.

This gave her something to think about as she lay wakeful under an overhang of brownish rock on the outskirts of the tiny human settlement at the Hfa Research Outpost, unable to sleep because it was too bright and too quiet.

It was not that there were no sounds. It turned out a living world made all sorts of noise. The wind blew, disturbing the shadowy fronds of the native vegetation and the leaves of the handful of Earth trees. Rain stop-started with pattering sounds, which had different qualities depending on whether the droplets hit the trees, or the soil, or the rock overhang Kyr was sheltering under, or the surface of the stream that ran nearby. Whenever the rain stopped, bugs appeared, seeming to sprout out of the moist air. There were several different kinds, but all of them glowed with some inner luminescence, creating little trails of light when they flew into the shadow under the overhang; and they made whining and whirring sounds as they flew, almost but not quite like the distant whines and whirs Kyr was used to, the hum of a working space fortress.

It was hard to sleep on the dry ground, not because it was uncomfortable but because it was unfamiliar. It was hard to sleep without the distant deep song of the shadow engines at the back of her awareness. It was hard to sleep when you were quite alone, and could not hear anyone else's breathing.

Kyr made herself lie still, and tried not to start at every sound the waking planet made. She turned over and put her hands under her head. This was how she discovered that a puddle had formed in a sunken corner of her sheltered nook. She'd meant to get some rest and wait for darkness before she tried to break into the Wisdom node installation. If the mental map Kyr had was right, then it should be just over the next ridge.

Rest wasn't happening. She might as well get on with it.

Kyr climbed over the ridge, picking her way past the yellow-gold fronds of Chrysothemis's native vegetation and the blaring green of the handful of Terran weeds. *Invasive flora*, said Ally in her head. Kyr shoved the thought away. Stupid. Pointless.

At the top of the ridge she found herself looking down into a circular depression in the landscape. The rain had stopped, and the light of Chrysothemis's yellow afternoon sun was blazing reflected in the lake at the bottom. It gleamed too on the metallic roofs of a collection of low buildings on the lakeshore. Kyr waited. The Strike files hadn't said anything about security for this place. Mags's mission had been to bring death and pain to the crowds of Raingold he hadn't been expected to come anywhere near here. But there had to be something.

A tiny movement near the buildings. A guard? No, not a person: just an oversized insect. Kyr narrowed her eyes. It didn't move like the insects that had been annoying her earlier. Its lazy circlings were more like . . .

A patrol pattern, barely disguised. Not an animal. A majo drone. Probably not the only one. The sky was beginning to dim, but Kyr's vision was extremely good. She sat down to watch and wait, and by the time the sun was a sliver on the hilly horizon she had picked out a dozen more drones. No way to know their weapons capabilities.

No sign of any human guards. Nor any aliens. Strange.

She remembered her mistake in the brig of the *Victrix*, when she'd forgotten to account for a second guard; when she hadn't expected Cleo, and Cleo had appeared out of the shadows. But as she watched, and Chrysothemis's small oblong moon climbed swiftly up the sky, she became certain. There really was no one here to guard the Wisdom. There was nothing but the drones.

Get inside, Kyr thought. *Sabotage it first, or work out how. Then wait for the target.*

There wasn't a convenient gap in the drones' patrol pattern. That sort of thing only happened in scenarios meant for babies. This was real, realer than a Level Twelve. Realer than Doomsday. Mags had never won anything except a game, and Kyr was here, in this very real place, getting bitten by insects as she circled the valley. She got as close as she dared to the low collection of buildings. She'd thought at first they were ordinary prefab shacks, like the slums of Raingold, but the closer she got the stranger they looked. The metallic roofs glimmered under a coating of atmospheric moisture, but the walls were crumbling stone with blotched patterns of pale native moss crawling up their sides. They looked old.

Humans had not made this place.

Kyr's stomach growled as she lay flat in the scant and scrubby cover around the lake with her elbows in the mud, reminding her that she needed fuel eventually. And still the patrolling drones looped and looped in their efficient circles. This wasn't fair.

Life wasn't fair.

She risked crawling closer. Still no guards. She picked up a stone and threw it. It bounced loudly off the roof of the closest building, still a good distance away. The *clunk* sound echoed across the water. One of the drones broke its patrol loop to investigate, and the others slid smoothly into place to cover the gap. Great.

The machines didn't look sturdy. They *did* have an organic look about them, so Kyr's first guess of insects hadn't been completely stupid: little yellow and black bodies, less than a foot long, studded all over with hexagon sensors that shifted like eyes, supported on fast-moving transparent wings.

Kyr mentally named them Bees, after a picture from Nursery. After a long while spent watching from her muddy, uncomfortable spot on the ground—*Patience*, Commander Jole had said once, *is as vital a weapon as strength*—she was almost sure they were unarmed. Chrysothemis's yellow moon was fully up now, and a mist had sprung up. She could no longer see the whole patrol pattern at once; only two or three Bees at a time, those closest to her. Still no sign of humans, no figures in the mist, no voices. Kyr's stomach rumbled again.

She drew herself slowly up from flat in the mud to crouched. There was no opening. There was no special chance. She waited until the nearest Bee came out to the farthest extent of its busy little pattern, and she pounced.

It was lighter than she expected when she grabbed hold of it. Her fingers punched holes through its gauzy wings. It made no sound, but moved frantically in her hands, twisting against her grip. Maybe it *was* organic, at least in part. Kyr threw it on the ground and stamped on it as hard as she could.

There was a crunch. The Bee did not move again.

As Kyr had expected, its fellows emerged from the mist on gauzy wings to investigate their fallen comrade. But she was already past them, in among the rain-slick walls of the old stone buildings on the lakeshore. There was writing on them, in human letters and in the symbols Kyr knew were Majodai.

The human letters said SECURE SITE—KEEP OUT—DANGER OF DEATH.

The majo words were much the same, but there was another symbol with them. Kyr had seen it before: in the Doomsday scenario, repeated over and over until it became a kind of decoration, adorning the dart that had brought death to her world. She knew it meant "wisdom."

The largest stone building had a small dark gap at one end, not even a door. Kyr had to duck her head to get through it. She didn't know what she was expecting inside. A fancier version of the Systems hub room, all displays and rows of lights. Or something Chrysothemis-ish, tidy and shiny. Or maybe just some crumbling alien remains.

Inside the building, where there should have been floor, there was a hole in the ground. Its lip came so close to the doorway that Kyr nearly fell into it. It went from wall to wall.

It wasn't that Kyr had never seen a tunnel before. Gaea's planetoid was riddled with them. She knew their ins and outs perfectly. She could get from Drill to Suntracker in under five minutes.

She stared down into the hole. It was lined with a shiny pearlescent material that was pitted and scarred with age. The faint moonlight coming through the door behind Kyr illuminated the upper reaches, showing the cracks and the shine in its walls. As with the Bees, Kyr had an unpleasant sense that she was looking at something organic.

Shadows possessed the depths. Below the uncertain circle of moonlight there was no way to tell how far down the tunnel went.

There was no stair, or ladder, or rope. And Kyr was used to tunnels, but she was also used to knowing where they led, or at the very least knowing there was only a handful of places that they *could* lead.

This was no time to stand around thinking about how big and unknowable a planet could be. Kyr had plenty of experience with clambering along dangerous surfaces. She was in the right place: the glyph of the Wisdom proved it. Time to move.

The pearly material of the tunnel walls was full of hidden sharpness; it was slick-smooth where it shone, but every place it cracked seemed to fracture into needle points that dug in only just short of breaking Kyr's skin as she climbed down into the dark. It did not take long for the entrance to become only a pale illuminated circle above her head. Her eyes adjusted fast, but she still had to find the handholds by feel. She expected the bottom after twenty feet or so, then after forty. It did not come. Her hands were growing damp with sweat. She came to a point where she could not find the next handhold, and felt an inexplicable dizziness.

Hard on its heels came self-disgust: weak, weak, *weak.* For a moment she had a vision of herself not as the strong soldier of humanity she had always known herself to be, but as a tiny scrap of life clinging blindly to an impossible vertical, with safety too far above and an immeasurable fall below.

"While we live," she said aloud, and the smooth circle of wall around her caught the words and made them echo.

Don't think. Don't fear. Find the next thing to do, and the next. Kyr worked her way crabwise along the wall. The circle of moonlight from the surface was a very long way over her head. The next thing, and the next. She found herself standing on a ledge, clinging to the wall, and then she tested the length of the ledge with her heel and discovered it was a floor.

Kyr turned her back to the wall and leaned against it and breathed out hard. Her hands were scraped raw; her arms and legs felt heavy with effort. Even when she'd been working her way through Gaea's heart without a rope she'd had the comm in her ear so Avi could call her insane. If she'd had her mess—if she'd had her mess, and a grapple—

How strange, that the agoge didn't prepare you for being on your own, when Earth's children needed to be prepared for anything. Kyr would have to say something when she went home.

Oh, she remembered. She would never go home. She was Strike now. She was the hidden blade of humanity's lasting defiance, and she was here to kill and to die.

As if in answer to the thought, there was a change in the quality of the darkness. Something was moving. Kyr turned toward the sound. She caught a glimpse of a double circular shine and thought, *Eyes?*

That was all the warning she had, and then it was on her.

It was impossible to tell what it looked like in the dark. It was big, heavy, rank-smelling. It had a mouth full of teeth and its breath blasted hot and disgusting over Kyr's face as she twisted away from it. She was on her back on the floor underneath the thing—the *animal?*—and it was all she could do to thrash and struggle against it. Now and then she got another glimpse of its shining eyes. The fight was almost silent on Kyr's part; she let out small grunts and groans. The animal made low rumbling growls as it tried to subdue her. It kept going for her neck with its huge jaws. She was not strong enough to stop it. It was fast on top of everything else. *Nothing the majo can throw at you is scarier than you are,* a Drill sergeant had shouted at them once. *We are the biggest and the strongest and the baddest species out there. They get you without weapons, they're still the ones who should be scared. Fight 'em! Bite 'em! Even little girls like you! Nothing is mean like a human's mean!*

Kyr's nails and teeth were pathetic blunt scrabblings on the shadow-thing's furred hide. No, she told herself furiously. No, she *wouldn't* die like this, alone in the dark, not even for a reason.

Its drool kept falling on her face, hot and foul. "No," panted Kyr, "no—get—*off*—"

And then the beast in the dark fell backward off her—no—

was *pulled* backward off her. Another great dark shape that had landed across its back. Kyr gasped for breath. She was bleeding from long scratches all across her arms and torso. Two massive bodies were struggling in the gloom. Kyr couldn't make sense of the shape of them, intertwined in the shadows; there were arms and legs and was that a tail? It was uncertainty that held her back; she was on the floor, shuddering, in pain, she had never been so sure she was about to die and she had never missed more the things she had taken for granted in the agoge, the comm in her ear, the combat feeds at the corner of her vision, knowing what she was *doing*—

The struggling pair slammed into a wall with a thud and lights came on, flickering and faintly green, shining out of the pearlescent walls. The thing that had jumped on Kyr was a cat—Kyr had seen pictures of cats—well, it was the same shape as a cat, though it was several times the size. The massive figure with its gigantic arms locked tightly around its muscular neck from behind—

"Mags!" cried Kyr.

Mags didn't answer with anything but a grunt. He was occupied in squeezing. The oversized cat thrashed and clawed, but the angle was wrong for its sharp claws, its toothy mouth. There was a crack as a bone gave way under the force of Mags's killing embrace. The beast twitched a few more times and then stilled.

Mags slumped on top of it a moment, and then forced himself back up on his feet. He was swaying; injured. They stared at each other across the animal's corpse.

Kyr recovered first. "What are you doing here?"

"Ally talked to me," said Mags. He was wearing Chrysothemis clothes, a blue T-shirt and loose trousers with zipped pockets. The T-shirt was bloodstained. His blond hair was dark with damp; he'd been caught in the rain. There was another streak of blood up his arm; the giant cat had managed a deep scratch there.

Kyr felt a flash of rage. "He promised—"

—not to tell *Ursa*, she remembered how solemnly and emphatically he'd said it. Little sneak! He'd left himself a loophole. Kyr's anger was with herself too. *Did you think Aulus Jole's son would be* stupid?

"It was my mission," Mags said. "I guessed where you'd be. I didn't tell Ursa."

"You shouldn't be here," said Kyr.

"No one should be here," Mags said. "No one knows. Nothing's happened yet. Come home, Vallie. Don't do this."

"You're the one who walks away," Kyr said. "Not me."

"I just saved your life," said Mags.

Silence.

"Thanks," said Kyr. "Now go away."

"What is wrong with you?" Mags said, and then, "Oh, I know what this is about."

"Honor," said Kyr. "That's what it's about. You wouldn't understand."

"Honor, right. As in *winning*. You're jealous, aren't you," Mags said. "You're jealous they made me Strike. You're jealous that Jole didn't pick you out for a suicide mission. That's it?" His expression tightened. "That's really it, isn't it? That's all you care about."

"I'm not that small," said Kyr. "I'm not *petty*."

"Yeah? But you can tell me all my monthly training scores for the last four years," Mags said. "And the rest of my mess. And the rest of your mess, even though you haven't thought about Sparrow for more than two minutes since you left, have you? No one's people to you. Everyone's an enemy or else they're competition. You didn't even care when Ursa left."

"I cared that she betrayed us!"

"You didn't care that she was your sister! You never tried to find out what really happened. You wouldn't let me talk about it. I cared. I found out."

"Right," Kyr said. "You snuck off to the arcade—you shirked your duty—it was all about Ursa, obviously, it wasn't that you had a crush on your nasty little dissident—"

"Fuck you!" Mags said. "You've never taken me seriously, have you?"

"You're the best in our age cohort, of course I take you seriously—"

"As a person, I'm a person. I told you I didn't want to be a soldier!"

"No one gets a choice," said Kyr, "about being a soldier."

"I'm not a killer."

"Tell it to the cat."

Mags flinched. He looked down at the massive corpse of the animal he'd strangled. "I thought they were smaller," he said.

"You're being selfish, Mags," Kyr said. "It's no use whining about *I want this*, or *I don't want that*. Earth had fourteen billion people on it, do you think they wanted to die?"

"Who cares? They're dead!" Mags said. "What are you even going to do?"

"I was also wondering about that," said another voice.

Both of them startled. Kyr was furious with herself. She should have noticed.

"Also, seriously, Valkyr, what the hell," Avi said, stepping out of the gloom. "I handed you a normal life with a bow tied around it, why did that not get rid of you? Hi, Magnus."

"Avi," said Mags.

Avi looked . . . different. He'd shaved off some of his mess of red curls back in the shack, leaving only the top, but that wasn't it. He'd found some glasses for his bad vision somewhere. He was wearing Chrysothemis clothes that looked more natural on him than they did on Kyr or Magnus, tight black trousers and a yellow shirt with symbols on it Kyr didn't recognize. But that wasn't it either. It was in the way he stood. It was in the way he smiled. Until now Avi had always looked as if he were cringing slightly. Kyr had thought it was natural to him. But down here in the dark of the Wisdom installation he looked confident. Like he belonged.

"I can't believe you killed my tiger," he said. "I worked hard on that tiger."

"What are you doing here?" said Kyr.

"Same to you," Avi said. He leaned against the wall—no, that was a doorframe, right behind him. He folded his arms. "*I* engaged in several days of subtle and complex network espionage—Gaea's systems really are twenty years behind the times, by the way, I had to teach myself almost everything—and eventually figured out how to break into the location of Chrysothemis's Wisdom node, though I had to steal a bunch of technically imaginary money from some sinnet oligarchs to do it. I can't tell you how difficult it was convincing the place I belonged: or, I mean, I *can*, but you wouldn't understand a word of it. And apparently that was a huge waste of my time anyway, because it turns out the knuckleheads I grew up with were right all along and the real best of humanity is some oversized moron blundering around the wilderness and killing things until they end up in the right place by accident."

"I'm not here by *accident*," said Kyr.

"I followed her," said Mags.

"I didn't ask, but cool, great, now I've got two of you." Avi sighed. "And no tiger. Fine, I'll explain. This way. What's wrong with you?"

"It'll heal," Mags said.

Avi led them through the gloom with perfect confidence. Kyr and Mags weren't on the strand of warbreed bloodlines with enhanced low-light vision—that had been only Cleo, in Kyr's mess—but she had a sense of close walls, narrow spaces. This place hadn't been built with humans in mind. In a couple of places her head brushed the ceiling. Mags hit his head once and grunted in pain.

She couldn't keep track of the route, and she was trying. A hand trailed against the wall let her know that it was made of that same smooth-and-sharp stuff as the tunnel she'd climbed down, and that there were openings and turnings. Some they passed. Others they turned in to. Once Avi said, "Wait, shit," and made them backtrack until they found the archway he wanted. This place was a labyrinth, down in the dark, deep below the surface of this living world. "Where are we?" she said.

"Shh," said Avi, and did not speak again.

Finally they emerged. Kyr could hear the change in the way three sets of breathing sounded in the air. She could smell, too, something rich and sweet. Avi said, "Don't move."

"Mags," said Kyr, because his breaths did not sound right to her.

"I'm fine," said Mags.

"*Mags.*"

"I'm—"

"Got it," Avi said, and the cavern flooded with light.

It *was* a cavern, smooth walls high on every side and arching into a pearlescent vault, like climbing into one of the delicate shells on the shores of Raingold Bay.

It was also a paradise. The rich sweet perfume of the air was the mingling of a hundred kinds of—flowers? Flowers, they must be, though barely any conformed to flower-shapes Kyr knew. Their foliage was yellow and gold and shimmering blue. Drones like the Bees she'd seen outside swooped among them, as high as the distant ceiling, their gauze wings casting peachy reflections of the apparently sourceless light. Some of the glimmer of the pale walls was water, reflecting as well; an endless gossamer waterfall, and the soft whisper of its sound as it fell. It was like Agricole, with its profusion of life, the way the shapes of trunk and stem and extending tendrils led one to another and confused the eye so it was impossible to quite know where anything began or ended. Yet it was also not like Agricole, because nothing here seemed to be meant for any useful purpose.

"What do you think?" Avi said. "Magnus?" And he turned with a look of self-delight: *look at this, how clever am I.*

Mags said, "Sorry," and fell over.

Kyr caught him on the way down; his massive weight, warbreed weight, *no one is scary like a human's scary* weight. She couldn't hold him upright but she went to her knees as he sagged and he didn't hit his head on the hard pearlescent ground. He was conscious. "Sorry," he said again, and Kyr saw that the bloodstain on his T-shirt had spread. Now it was a broad dark blotch, red only at the edges, closer to black in a set of three jagged lines across his stomach.

"*Shit*," said Avi.

Kyr was pulling away the soaked fabric of the blue T-shirt. The gashes were claw marks. Mags hadn't said a word.

Gut wounds were a bad way to die. Kyr knew that. Her medical training had been: *If you can get hold of this, and this, and this, if the enemy supplies have this, if, if, if—otherwise here's what you can do, and if you're from a warbreed bloodline you'll probably survive, and if you're not, who knows.*

Mags had the good genes. Accelerated healing. *The problem with eugenics*, Yiso had said, because they knew nothing, nothing, about what it was like to be human. Kyr shook the thought away, let her mind go hard and cold and clear. "Alcohol," she said. "Spirits." *Clean it up before it closes, all the fast knitting in the world won't do you any good if it's infected.* She didn't have a knife. Not even a—"Give me my knife," she said, holding out her hand, and Avi put into it the knife she'd nearly killed Cleo with. Kyr started cutting away the T-shirt. *Perforated bowel, don't waste your time*, said a Medical sergeant from Augusta in her head: an old man with tired eyes. *The old days, we'd do intravenous antibiotics, cut them open and patch it up, and you supersoldiers would be back in the field in a week. Now*, and he made a harrumphing sound, *cut his throat. Faster death. How do you know? Feed him something that stinks, see if you can smell it.*

"Alcohol," Avi said. Kyr took the bottle, irregular clouded glass, and poured some over a pad made from the clean part of the ruined shirt. "Why didn't he say something?"

"Don't show weakness," Kyr said. "*Your* tiger, was it."

"I made it," Avi said. "I didn't think—" and then he stopped, and Kyr didn't care. She cleaned the wound. Mags moaned and then at some point he lost consciousness and went quiet. A Bee came to investigate, circled Kyr's head, hovered over Mags's face and swiveled all its hexagonal drone eyes to examine him. Kyr pinched the edges of the claw gashes together with both hands. She didn't have a needle; all those shifts in Textiles, and she'd never stolen a needle. *Clean the wound, apply pressure,* intoned the Medical sergeant in her memory. *It used to be eight years of training to know what I know. You get four rotations. Remember them.*

CHAPTER FOURTEEN

THE DEPTHS

When the edges of the claw marks in Mags's stomach were visibly knitting, Kyr took up the clouded glass bottle of quote-unquote *alcohol* and took a gulp. It burned, but not worse than the potato vodka for a toast. All around them, the paradise cavern was blue and gold and glorious. The smell of Mags's blood was thick in her nostrils.

"I was trying for whiskey," Avi said. He'd gone back to being cringe-shaped. "I don't know if the Wisdom didn't do it right or if I just don't like whiskey. Is he comfortable? Can we move him?"

"*You* can't," said Kyr.

Neither could she. Mags was too big. He'd be fine. He'd be fine unless the cat had clawed him deeply enough for *perforated bowel*, in which case he was already dead, still breathing but dead, and there was nothing she could do.

Such a stupid way to die. So pointless. Kyr had come to Chrysothemis to save her brother's life. If Mags died saving Kyr from a *cat*, what was she supposed to do?

What she'd been doing anyway was the answer. Serve humanity. Defy the majo. Make it mean something, that someone thought you were worth saving.

"You took my knife," she said. "My gun."

"Neither of those were technically yours," Avi said, but he curled in on himself under her gaze, and then he sat down on the hard pearlescent floor. "Yeah. Okay. I didn't think you were going to need them. I hoped that you weren't going to need them. I sent you home."

"You sent me to a traitor," Kyr said.

Avi said nothing for a moment, and then he said, "Nothing stops you, does it."

"No."

"It's almost impressive," Avi said. "I'm almost impressed."

"What did you need my weapons for?"

He shrugged one-shouldered. "Yiso," he said. "Not that scared of me. Is he okay?"

Avi hadn't paid attention to Medical rotations, Kyr saw. He'd been busy designing a dream-city in his head, or planning an escape he couldn't get away with until she came along. She didn't explain the perforated bowel question. "It's knitting," she said. "He'll be unconscious for a while."

"Like you with that stab wound," Avi said. "And I know I did a shit job stitching it, but you're still fine."

Cleo's knife deep into her thigh, and not a scar, not a twinge, by the time Kyr could hold on to wakefulness again. She nodded.

"I guess that teaches me," Avi said, "not to bother with pangs of conscience. I knew where Magnus was on the second day."

"We were in Raingold for *almost two weeks*."

"I thought I might need you," Avi said. "You're big, you're tough. Useful. But then I thought—no. You got me off Gaea. Fair's fair. I got you where you wanted to go. And for big and tough, I made a tiger."

"You *made* a tiger," Kyr repeated.

"There are a few left. Menageries on majo worlds. The Wisdom pulled the genetic sequence out of some oligarch's records." He looked at Mags again and winced. "Blood makes me feel sick," he said, fast, like he didn't want to admit it. "Always has. Otter—my mess was Otter—you better believe they loved that. Should he be in a hospital? There's a hospital in Raingold."

Yes, Kyr wanted to say at once, *yes, of course*, get Mags to a hospital, with a dozen men like the old Medical sergeant with tired eyes and eight years of training, antibiotics and surgery and back in the field in a week. But something about the way Avi said it made her pause and say, "Or?"

Avi said nothing.

"Why did you think you might need me?"

"Oh, insurance," Avi said. "But I didn't. Did I? I got myself here."

"Why *are* you here?"

Avi grimaced. "Same reason you are, I think. The only reason. To fight for humanity."

"So you came here—*you*—to sabotage the Wisdom node," said Kyr. Avi as a hero? Avi—the weakling who had skipped training, who couldn't bear the sight of blood—*Avi* as the hand of humanity?

"No," said Avi. "To take control of it."

It took a moment to register. Then Kyr stared at him.

"Don't you know what it can do? It can do *anything*. Want whiskey? Want a pet tiger? Or do you want to kill a planet, fuck, do you want to rule the universe?" Avi's grey eyes were bright, sharp, dangerous. "It's here, the power for all of that. It's everywhere the Wisdom is. Do you know why Earth lost the war?"

"Because the majo cheated," Kyr said.

"No," Avi said. "Of course they cheated. Everyone cheats. We were cheating too. For half a century before the war even started, military intelligence was working on their own version of the Wisdom. Technology to take control of reality; technology to take control of the future."

"But the Wisdom is evil," said Kyr.

"Not if it's ours," Avi said. "Nothing's evil if it's on our side, Valkyr. What do you think the agoge is?"

"Training—"

"A failed attempt," said Avi. "It's not a coincidence, you know— *Victrix, Ferox, Augusta, Scythica*, it wasn't *random* that those were the ships the Gaean mutiny took. They were warships, sure, dreadnoughts, but we had lots of warships, we had a thousand dreadnoughts. But they were the ships with the reality-building prototypes aboard. Giant shadow engines to power them. We were so close to cracking it. We didn't lose because the majo cheated. We lost because we didn't cheat fast enough."

". . . So?" said Kyr.

"I'll let you decide," Avi said. "We can call the emergency services in from Raingold. I'm in all the planetary networks here. You can't move him, I can't move him, we should absolutely not be where we are, they'll come with doctors to help him and police to arrest us." His eyes darted down to Mags and away again, fast. "And that'll be it, Valkyr. For whatever you were planning here, which I'm guessing was random and fairly stupid, and for what *I* was planning, which was brilliant. But prison on Chrysothemis isn't worse than Gaea Station." He made a stifled little noise: a laugh. "So we can do that. Or . . . the Prince of the Wisdom gets here in five days. I meant to have full control of this node before then, and with *you* here I might still actually do it."

"Right. And then you strike a blow for humanity," said Kyr. "*You.*"

"To hell with that," Avi said. "I'm not planning to make a point or sacrifice myself or whatever it is you saints of the cause think is worth dying for. I'm here to win the war."

"*What?*" said Kyr.

Avi said, "You heard me."

But you can't, Kyr found herself wanting to say. *But no one can. But we're not* supposed *to—*

"Yeah. No one talks about winning," Avi said. "No one even imagines it. And just in case anyone starts to harbor delusions of victory, Jole sends the best of the best through a Doomsday scenario he's set up to be impossible. That always annoyed me. What's it *for*, except to break you down?" He looked at Mags again. This time he managed to keep looking, and his mouth twisted, and he said, "I was trying to make a point, when we beat it. No one listened. Do you need help, doing that?"

"Don't touch him," said Kyr. She was still holding the edges of the claw marks pinched together. Mags's skin was hot around them, his body burning itself up to heal. If it could heal. If.

Avi held up his hands. "Okay. Sorry. Okay. I'm fucking . . . sorry, okay, I made a tiger, I always wanted to see a real one, I got through the first layer and I was having fun. So. Hospital?"

"What did you mean, with me here?"

"What?"

"You said, with me here," Kyr said. "You thought you could take control of the Wisdom node."

"I've got the basics," Avi said. "Replication, generation." He held up the whiskey bottle. "But I can't get through to where the real power is. It keeps blocking me. It's throwing up miniaturized dimensional riftspace paradigms." He saw Kyr's blank look and rephrased. "It's creating random scenarios. Like the agoge, but bigger."

"You want me to run scenarios for you," Kyr said.

"I thought we were calling emergency services," said Avi.

Kyr looked down at Mags. His eyes were closed. When she let go of the edges of the claw marks they stayed in the position she'd pinched them in. How deep had the wounds been? Already she wasn't sure. If it wasn't too deep, Mags would live anyway. He'd be fine.

And otherwise—if Mags died because Kyr hadn't said *yes, all right, we get him to a hospital and we let them arrest us for it*—

But the thought became its own dark mirror; what if Avi was right and there was a chance here not just to strike at the majo but to defeat them? She had never even dreamed of victory—elusive, impossible, unimaginable victory! But it hadn't always been impossible. Victrix Wing was named after the winged figure who brought triumph. There was a Victrix insignia pinned to the inside of Kyr's pocket. Her hand dipped down to touch the ridges of the metal, warm from her body heat.

We didn't cheat fast enough.

Imagine cheating fast enough, *being* fast enough, seizing an opportunity. Imagine turning to Uncle Jole, to Ursa, to the whole universe right down to the majo Yiso and saying: *Look what I have done.*

What if they could have claimed victory for humanity, and Kyr in selfish concern for her brother let it slip from her grasp?

"Valkyr?" Avi said.

"He'll be fine," said Kyr: forcing herself to believe it, ordering the universe to comply. "I'll run your scenarios. How long did you say we had?"

"Five more days," said Avi. "Till the Prince of the Wisdom shows up. I can't hold on to the node with one of those here. They're born for this. I'm just hijacking it."

"When the alien shows up," said Kyr, "I'm killing it."

"Oh. Good," Avi said. "That will definitely help."

There was no question of moving Mags, but Avi called over one of the Bees and murmured a string of nonsense to it—not human language, but nothing like what Kyr understood of Majodai either. Then the drones started building a bower around Mags's still form, out of woven foliage and that pearly substance which the whole system of tunnels and caverns seemed to be made from. It appeared behind them in a faintly green shimmer as they darted industriously back and forth. "If you want to wait till he wakes up," Avi said.

"Five days," said Kyr.

Avi looked relieved. "Come on, then."

He didn't glance back once. Kyr did. A small cloud of Bees was clustered around the spot where Mags had fallen. Their gauzy wings were in constant motion; their yellow bodies shifted in air. "I'll get an alert if something changes," Avi said. "They're eager to please. I repaired one and now they all love me."

"What are they?"

"Maintenance, I think," Avi said. "This place has been quiescent for a long time, ever since the Hfa—the last sentients to live here—managed to wipe themselves out somehow. I wonder what went wrong there." He laughed. "I bet you don't care. Maybe I'll ask the node once I'm in control."

Another tunnel, going even deeper; a spiral ramp around a central trunk of pearl-stuff that was pitted like the bark of a tree. "How did you get down the main shaft?" Avi asked.

"Climbed."

"Fuck me. Magnus too, I suppose."

"I don't know. Probably."

"Fuck me," said Avi again, and then nothing else. They descended in silence for a few minutes, and then there was a shivering crash of non-sound out of the darkness. All of Kyr's hair stood on end. It took her a second to place the familiar sensation. That was a shadow engine—a live one.

"What the *fuck*," Avi said, and took off at a run.

Kyr followed him. She didn't recognize the cavern they finally entered—Avi panting for breath, Kyr a little warm from the jog—as a control room. The walls were shiny-slick and dripping with condensation. Broken ripples of green light were reflected here and there, without it being quite clear where they were coming from. There was more of the foliage from the paradise cavern, blue-gold and flourishing. Kyr pushed through the branches.

The room sloped down to a central pool of clear shining water. The shape of it matched precisely the shape of the valley on the surface where the Bees patrolled. Above the pool, hanging down from the ceiling, loomed the glittering contours of a shadow engine's cradle. The throb of power from within was so strong that Kyr had to wait for the instants of stillness in between pulses to advance. The engine must have been properly shielded, the way Gaea's weren't, because it should have been distorting the planet's gravity, and Kyr's feet were planted firmly on the floor.

It didn't *feel* shielded. It was like being in a room with another tiger.

"Stop, stop, stop that," Avi was chanting to himself, and this *was* a control room, because he was working on a misty bank of controls. They were half present and shaded with the pale green-ish light of unreality, and they looked exactly like the controls that Avi had called into being in the agoge when Kyr made him find Mags for her. "Stop it," Avi said, "don't *make* me—" and then he threw up his hands, a furious gesture, and the control hub evaporated as if it really had been just mist. Avi turned to Kyr. "Knife," he demanded, and Kyr obeyed that snap of command without thinking.

Avi turned and spoke—to the shadow engine? To the water? "Behave," he said. "I'm *warning* you."

It's a machine, Kyr nearly said, not understanding. Avi strode across the room, setting his thin shoulders square against the shivering pulses of the shadow engine, and something that Kyr had only registered as more foliage, a bundle of twigs or some-thing, suddenly took shape in her vision as a curled-up figure bound hand and foot. Avi grabbed it by the crest and stuck the knife under its chin.

Kyr could have told him that he had the angle wrong. The throat was a vulnerability for most majo species—nearly all the bipeds, in fact—but she was pretty sure Yiso had a subdermal car-apace there. A cut would glance away without hitting anything vital.

The alien's large pale eyes were fluttering. It was hard to tell if they were conscious.

Avi screamed at the cave, "Don't make me!"

The shadow engine went silent. The ripples of light reflect-ing off the walls vanished, leaving only the faint clear light that seemed to be coming from the pool. The absence of the engine's thrum of power was almost as overwhelming as its presence. It was as if the air had been solid earth and had now become void. Kyr stumbled.

"*Your actions are unwise,*" said a soft voice. It sounded like it was standing right behind her. Kyr turned sharply, but there was nothing: shadows, branches, stillness. It didn't come from anywhere. "*Your actions are unwise,*" repeated the voice of the

Wisdom. She knew it. She'd heard it before, in the Doomsday scenario.

"Your error message is *boring*," Avi spat.

"*Consider being less unwise*," the Wisdom said, and then it did not say anything else.

"I really hate that thing," Avi said. He was probably aiming for his usual cynical detachment, but it was not working. He sounded too sincere. "Come over here and make yourself useful." He passed her the knife.

Yiso looked bad, almost as bad as they had in a cell on Gaea Station. Their skin was yellow-grey, the angular patterns of hairs on their arms stark and discolored. The finger that Kyr had patched up for no real reason—irritation, nothing more—was broken again, bent at a terrible angle. That whole three-fingered hand was a mass of purple bruises, extending up Yiso's narrow arm.

"Keep the knife close enough that the Wisdom knows better than to try anything while I get a leash on it again," Avi said. "It might take me a while. The fucking thing *learns*. But so do I."

Kyr crouched. She put the knife against the edge of one of Yiso's long ears. It was notched, she saw, a little triangle cut from the flesh, only part healed. That was new. "But you were going to sell him," Kyr said. "Them. It. To the pirates."

"Under no circumstances was I going to do that," Avi said. "I was a little stuck trying to think of a way to say *no* without that asshole working out just how valuable Yiso actually is. Lucky for me you had that attack of principles, huh. They were scared of you."

"They were?"

"Valkyr," Avi said, "everyone who meets you is scared of you."

Kyr sat with the unconscious majo and watched Avi work on his mist-controls. "Why would the Wisdom care what happens to him?" she said. "It."

"Shh," said Avi.

Kyr thought about Mags, unconscious, maybe dying, in the

paradise cave far above their heads. How deep in the earth were they now? Kyr shouldn't have been missing Chrysothemis's sky. She hadn't had that long to get used to it. Would Mags wake up, if he was dying? Would he know Kyr wasn't there?

Yiso was making soft rasping noises. Not healthy-sounding, she thought, though Medical didn't cover first aid for aliens. "You could have held back," she said, "if this is all the leverage you've got."

Avi looked up and fixed her with a poisonous stare. "Let me be really clear," he said. "You are not here because I need to hear your opinions."

Please remember that I am not nearly as durable as a human, Yiso had said. It seemed like a thousand years ago. *I'm a person. A sentient. I don't want to die.* Who had taught majo to say human words? It shouldn't be allowed. Kyr tested the edge of the knife on her thumb and found it blunt. She didn't have anything to sharpen it with.

"*Ah,*" Avi said. "Got you."

The shadow engine was waking up again, but with a soft obedient hum, not the dreadful pulses from before. The pool underneath its cradle changed color and then disappeared under a sudden curtain of pale fog, which resolved itself into a shape Kyr understood: the heavy reinforced rectangle of the doors to the agoge rooms.

"What?" Avi said. "Thought you'd like to feel at home."

"Objective," said Kyr, getting up. She didn't have a sheath for the knife, so she kept it in her hand.

"Excuse me?"

"A scenario has an objective," Kyr said. "Tell me what I need to do."

"I don't know."

"What do you mean, you don't know?"

"I didn't design this one," said Avi. "The Wisdom did. I can try to pull you out if you call for me. Otherwise . . ." He shrugged. "Why do you think I'm not going in?"

"You're a coward," Kyr said.

"If you like. If I had to guess . . . there's a door somewhere, and a key. Get to the door and unlock it. I should be able to get through from there."

"A door, a key," Kyr repeated. She resisted the urge to glance down at Yiso's still figure. They were just an alien. They didn't matter. "Okay. I'm going in."

CHAPTER FIFTEEN

A DOOR, A KEY

The empty hall was made of a pale shining substance like the inside of a shell. It reminded Kyr of—

She didn't know.

There were no cracks, no openings. This place belonged to a world whose atmosphere had been peeled from it like the shell from an egg long ago. Kyr knew this like she knew her own name, which was—

Valkyr, she thought, fierce and clear, and on the edge of hearing a note sounded like a deep distant bell.

Very well. She was Valkyr. A fitting name. (Why? She knew the word *valkyrie* somehow; she knew a thousand thousand histories, all the thinking peoples on their little worlds like the manifold leaves of an infinite tree—no, it was gone.) She was also—

Late! She was late!

Kyr took off at a run. The tightness in her chest was shame, not shortness of breath; she could run as far as she liked, she was a fit healthy animal. But she *couldn't* keep being late like this—

I'm never late, Kyr thought. Two black marks when I was seven. None since.

She stopped running. She looked at her hands.

Nothing was in them. Why had she been expecting a knife?

Urgency snapped at her like a whip. Late, late, shame on you! Kyr said, "Stop that." She was furious. She'd never heard of a scenario that tried to *think* for you. She hated it. "I'm not late for anything. This is fake."

There was a door in the shell-wall. It had not been there before.

Kyr folded her arms and glared at it. She had an objective, she thought. She was not entirely sure what it was. Something made her try the door.

Locked.

"All right," she said. "Let's see what you've got for me, then. But I'm not late."

Nothing answered. Kyr walked the way her feet wanted to go, stubbornly forcing herself to dawdle, to look around at the dull shell-colored sameness like a tourist on the streets of—

—some city. She couldn't think of the name just now. She had been in a city recently, though. A brief memory of shining towers and dreadful pursuit flickered through her thoughts and was gone.

"Oh!"

A figure at the end of the hallway. Stopped, shocked, staring. It was wrapped in layers of fabric, all the same russet color but a half-dozen textures, shining over smooth over crinkled and soft. "Hello," Kyr said. It was an alien, but not a threat. Why was she looking for threats? Obviously nothing was a threat, here, in this place she would remember the name of any moment.

"Where did you come from?" said the alien.

"I just got here," Kyr said. "I'm Valkyr."

"Yiso," the alien said. "Are you speaking my language or am I speaking yours?"

Kyr paused. "I think you're speaking mine," she ventured. "But—"

"I hear it too," Yiso said: a susurrus every time either of them spoke. "Are you a human?"

"Of course I'm human."

"I've never seen one before," Yiso said. "I always wanted to. I think we're both speaking our own language and the Wisdom is translating. What if I spoke like this?"

They had an accent now; musical, oddly pitched. For some reason it sounded right. "That's better," Kyr said.

"T-standard," Yiso said. "If the Wisdom is messing with my

language perception this is probably just another scenario. Are you real?"

"I'm *real*," Kyr said.

Yiso's ears twitched downward. "That's what everyone says, though. I bet it's the Wisdom again. Wait, I know an idiom." The crest dipped, the ears moved: flick, flick. "*Playing silly buggers*," announced Yiso, with satisfaction.

"I've never heard that," said Kyr. "You made that up."

"I didn't!"

"Why do I think I'm late?" asked Kyr.

"Oh," said Yiso. Ears down again, gloomy. "That's probably for me. I should be doing exercise."

Kyr looked them over. The tawny layers of fabric were beautiful and profoundly inconvenient, a series of trips and catches waiting to happen. "Well, you'd better get changed."

"Is *that* why you're here," Yiso said. "To make me do exercise."

"Sure, why not," said Kyr. It sounded right. At some point in her life her purpose had been—"Training," she said. "I trained with my mess." Even if someone didn't want to work, Kyr could make them, she could help. "You can't be worse than Lisabel."

"Who's that?"

"I don't know," said Kyr, and her shoulders were tight for some reason, and her head ached. "I don't know."

The shell-palace seemed to be a maze of storerooms. Yiso knew them all and said things like "Traditional lirem stonecarving," "Cosmetics, gendered," "Cosmetics, ungendered," "Gemstones of minor religious significance," and "Furniture suitable for quadrupeds" as they walked through each one. Their contents were stacked high on either side, unusable. It all felt familiar to Kyr.

"Like Oikos," she said.

"Whatever that is, we've probably got a storeroom full of it," said Yiso. "This corridor is all clothing."

"What *is* this place?" Kyr asked, as Yiso opened up a chamber of red and yellow fabrics, swathes of which had been taken down and crumpled up and scattered on the floor. As Yiso started taking off their layers, Kyr saw that they were not really clothes as such, just a dress-up game played with an assortment of things made to fit other bodies, some bigger and some smaller, all differently configured. Underneath Yiso wore all white.

"The Halls of the Wise. It used to be a palace," Yiso said. "And then it was a holy place. And now it's just a place where a lot of things no one uses are."

"Are you here alone?"

"That depends if you're real, doesn't it?" Yiso said. "And also if I'm real, but I don't think I can cope with that question *and* exercise on the same day."

"Show me what you're supposed to do for exercise," Kyr said.

They went to a room with a rubbery white floor. Yiso, with exaggerated crest-flattenings and ear-twitchings meant to indicate boredom and inability, picked up a stick and did a silly dance with it.

"That's it?" said Kyr.

"Why, what do you do?" said Yiso.

Kyr started to recite an upper-level Drill workout.

"All at *once?*" interrupted Yiso, before she was halfway through.

Kyr looked at them, really looked: at their narrow arms and legs, the flukes of their crest and the flexible tips of their ears, the strange shape of their long three-fingered hands which was matched by the even longer and bonier three-toed splay of their bare feet. *How does your body work?* she nearly asked. It was not a question she had ever asked before; what answer was there, unless it was *like mine but better,* or *like mine but worse?*

"Show me the stick dance again," she said.

"Um," Yiso said, alarmed. "Okay?"

A few movements in Kyr said, "Slower," and then, "Stop."

"What?"

"Again," said Kyr, and then, after watching, "You're doing it wrong."

"Excuse you," Yiso said. "This happens to be a traditional performance of great ritual significance, and you are a very large representative of a barbaric warrior culture—are humans *really* as big as you?"

"Some are bigger," Kyr said. "Men. Males."

"You're a female?"

"Give me the stick. You're doing it wrong." She took the stick out of Yiso's unresisting hands and demonstrated what she meant. Her elbow would not bend through the whole shape she wanted, but the rest was pretty clear, she thought. "See? Now you."

"You did that so beautifully," Yiso said. "Won't you show me again?"

"Nice try," said Kyr, and handed them the stick. "Okay. Go. No, slower. Go slow till you get it right, then do it right every time."

"Are all humans as stressful as you?"

"How should I know? Are all majo as lazy as you?"

"I don't know," Yiso said.

"Is it?"

"What?"

"Ritually significant whatever," Kyr said.

"Yes," Yiso said. "Probably. Everything I do is significant. I can't *sneeze* without significance. That's not the right word." They did the steps Kyr had demonstrated again, slower, as Kyr had told them. "What's a word for a minor embarrassing autonomic function?"

"*Fart.*"

"I can't do that without significance either."

Kyr laughed.

"Bless you!" Yiso said.

"What?"

"Isn't that what you say for a sneeze?"

"No," Kyr said. "I was laughing."

"How is that different?"

How does your body work; Kyr saw that Yiso was looking at her in just that same way, with as much curiosity, uncertainty, interest.

She did not know how to explain a sneeze. "You laugh when something is funny," she said, and then, to get away from that look, she asked, "Do you have another stick?"

Yiso taught Kyr the silly stick dance. It had a name, which they told her several times, but each time the trilling syllables fell apart on Kyr's tongue. Kyr was sure that neither of them was doing it right; herself because her body was the wrong shape and size, and Yiso because they weren't any good. She still enjoyed herself. "Is there more?" she asked, when Yiso was making small wheezing noises of exhaustion.

"I've decided you're not real," Yiso said. "Even humans couldn't keep going this long. You're a phantasm sent by the Wisdom to torment me."

"Why would the Wisdom send anything to torment you?"

"I often ask myself this question," Yiso said.

"I'm real," said Kyr. "I'm looking for something."

"What are you looking for?"

"A door," Kyr said. "A key."

"Why?"

"To . . . strike a blow," Kyr said.

"That sounds violent," said Yiso.

It wasn't the right answer anyway. Why were Kyr's thoughts so foggy? Who had given her these objectives? "Does the Wisdom think for you?" she asked.

"It tries," Yiso said. "I'm winning. Where would your door and key be?"

"I saw a locked door earlier," said Kyr.

But when they retraced their steps through the maze of store-rooms, the door was gone.

"Oh, then it is a scenario," said Yiso glumly. "It does that. Moves things when you're not looking."

"How do you know so much about it?"

"Isn't it obvious?" Yiso said. "I live here." An enormous flat-eared sigh. "It's the *worst*."

"It doesn't seem so bad," said Kyr.

"Can you imagine, for your whole life, knowing your purpose? Everything mapped out for you, everything always the same," Yiso said. "Don't ask questions. Don't argue. Do your exercise, do your assignments, read every improving book in existence—they're *always* dull—and never go anywhere, and never see anyone new, and spend half your time observing outcomes in stupid little sub-realities that never happened and never will, and change nothing and help no one—Oh, what's the use? You're fake. It saw me get interested in something and decided to ruin it."

"What am I ruining?" Kyr said, offended.

"Humans," said Yiso. "I always wanted to meet one."

"Am I *disappointing* you?"

"You're basically just another person," Yiso said. "I thought you'd be . . ."

"What?"

"Scary."

"Everyone who meets me is scared of me," said Kyr.

"Why? In case you make them do exercise?"

"I can hurt people," Kyr said. "I can hurt anyone I want. I could kill you." She knew this as an absolute truth.

Yiso turned and considered her, silver-eyed, thoughtful, crest high. "But you don't want to, do you?" they said. "So it's fine."

"Wanting doesn't come into it."

"If you don't want to do something, then don't," said Yiso. "You're not like me. *You're* not stuck."

"There aren't even guards here," Kyr said. "Leave if you hate it so much."

"Leave and go where?" said Yiso. "Where do you go, if you don't want the Wisdom to find you?"

"You don't like it?"

"It's an all-powerful god machine," Yiso said. "It has good intentions, probably."

"You don't like it."

"I hate it," Yiso said. "And I belong to it, that's what a Prince of the Wisdom *is*, it's what I'm for." They frowned. "I've said this before," they said. "To someone else. This is a rehash, those are the worst. I'm going to wake up with a headache and not know what day it is."

"You're a Prince of the Wisdom?" said Kyr.

"T-standard makes it sound so impressive," Yiso said. "I'm a servant. Also a test subject. What's the matter?"

Kyr shook her head. She didn't know.

"I need to find the door," she said. "And the key."

"Well, I'm tired of this anyway," Yiso said. "It's all stupid. Maybe one day I'll run away."

"And go somewhere the Wisdom can't find you," said Kyr.

"It can always find me," said Yiso. "It's in my head. Fine, you want a door and a key?" They held out their long thin hand. Kyr noticed, as if for the first time, the pattern of diagonal hairs on the back of their arm. "Door," said Yiso, peremptory. The locked door came into being in front of them; not set into any wall, but standing alone in the shell-like corridor. "Key," said the majo. Green light shimmered over their fingers and resolved into a keycard.

Yiso frowned at it. "That's not what I think a key looks like," they said. "Where did—" They looked up at Kyr again. "Are you real?" they asked.

"No, sorry," said Kyr quickly, and snatched the key out of the alien's hand. "Bye."

The scenario dissolved into mist. Kyr was ankle-deep in the pool of water in the underground control room. The pearly substance of the walls *was* the same as the place called the Halls of the Wise; though there had been no profusion of blue and gold vegetation growing there.

"*Finally*," said Avi, rapidly adjusting something on his vaporous control board. The faint hum of the shadow engine changed pitch, and Kyr smelled ozone in the air. "Took you long enough. We're down to four days."

"Did you know?" said Kyr.

"What?"

"Yiso," she said. "Did you know they were a Prince of the Wisdom?"

"You're pretty slow, huh," Avi said. "Of course I knew. I told you. Valuable. What did you think was going on when I threatened it to make the Wisdom behave? You think the god machine is *squeamish*?"

"How?"

"Hm?"

"*How* did you know?" Kyr said. Yiso had seemed almost like a person, during those days in the Raingold slums. Chattering constantly. She'd fixed that broken finger. And all along it had been a servant of the thing that killed the Earth.

Avi said, "I think Systems would have figured it out, if they'd had a bit longer to look at that ship. I wasn't the only smart person on Gaea. Corporal Lin would have gotten it."

"So it was the ship?" Kyr said. She'd unloaded that ship, pulled out luxury fabrics and glassware—*cosmetics, ungendered; gemstones of minor religious significance*, she thought—and it had not seemed any more sinister than any majo pleasure cutter.

"Miniaturized shadow engine and long-haul subreal jump capacity on something barely bigger than a fighter dart," Avi said. "The majo are ahead of us, but not *that* far ahead—with one exception."

"And there was no other way to know," Kyr said. That made sense. The majo were liars. They did not fight fairly. They did not show their true colors until it was too late.

"Well, except the obvious," Avi said.

"What?"

"It's a majo zi," he said. "The founding species of the majoda.

Did you even know that? No, you didn't, because they don't come up in combat scenarios and *you* never went digging in the archives."

Kyr didn't like being patronized. "What's that got to do with anything?"

"There are exactly four majo zi," Avi said, "that anyone ever sees. The Princes of the Wisdom. The rest supposedly live on their extremely closed-off and private homeworld, and no one knows where it is, blah blah, very mysterious."

"So Yiso had to be one of the four—"

"No, moron, Yiso's obviously *young*," Avi said. "Those four zi, they've been around for centuries. Millennia, even. But this one's new. And the galactic gossip, which is of course *totally* irrelevant to Earth's children, is that there isn't a zi homeworld. It's dead."

"Dead how?"

"Who knows? The point is, the world's gone, the species is gone," Avi said. "They're extinct, unless the Wisdom decides to build one from scratch. Which it clearly did."

"But you were *nice* to Yiso," Kyr said, and then, realizing, "and you're never nice to anyone."

"Not unless there's something in it for me," Avi agreed, mouth twisted at the corner. "Take a break. I can already tell I'm going to need you to go back in later."

"No," Kyr said. She did not look at the crumpled shape in the corner that was a Prince of the Wisdom bound and bruised with a notch in one of its long ears and a finger bent the wrong way. She was holding the knife; she'd come out of the scenario holding it, though it had vanished in the place Yiso called the Halls of the Wise. She put the weapon through her belt. "I'm going to check on Mags."

The paradise in the upper cavern had not changed. A balmy scent filled the vaulted expanse. The bower the Bees had built around Mags's unconscious form was empty.

Kyr stood very still, refusing to acknowledge the kick of fear against her pulse.

"Over here!" came her brother's voice. She bit her lip hard.

Mags had crawled into the bushes. A couple of Bees had followed, and were hovering over the spot where he lay: flat on his back under a blue-gold tangle, with a couple of blue fronds dropped into his fair hair. It was oddly familiar, like Agricole.

Mags was alive. Clearly conscious. Kyr's vision blurred.

"Oh—hey, hey, Vallie," Mags said.

"I'm fine," Kyr said. "Let me see."

She wiped her face hard several times while she examined the wounds. Three thin scars, where there had been three jagged tears. They might tear open again if Mags moved around too much. "You should have stayed still," she said.

"I was bored. Where did you go?"

"There's a time limit," Kyr said. "Avi said," and then she stopped. She turned her face away. "Sorry."

"You're not going to stop, are you," Mags said. He sat up slowly. Kyr put an arm around his shoulder to support him.

"I can't," she said. "I can't."

Mags sighed. "If I said you owe me?" he said after a while. "For the tiger."

"Avi thinks we can win the war."

"*Win?*"

"Yeah."

Neither of them said anything for a while.

Eventually Mags said, "It's weird, but I never thought of that."

"No," Kyr said. "Neither did I."

"You're still upset," Mags said. "Is it me? I'm going to be fine. I'm tough."

"I know," Kyr said. "It's not you."

"Is it—home?" Mags said. "Your mess?"

The Sparrows. Kyr had been trying so hard not to think about them. They were fine. They were all safely assigned, sorted into their proper places. Arti and Jeanne in their combat wings.

Vic in Suntracker like she'd always wanted—hadn't she always wanted that? Zen in Oikos being practical. And Cleo in Victrix, and Lisabel in Nursery. Kyr didn't need to think about it. She didn't need to think about any of it. But she was.

Cleo had failed to stop Kyr leaving—would they punish her for that? Admiral Russell had put his hand through Lisabel's arm, and she had smiled up at him, her nice smile, which she did for everyone, whether she actually liked them or not, because Lisabel was a person who knew how to survive.

I'm not upset. But it was impossible, with Mags, to pretend that she did not have feelings, that she was untouchable.

"There was a majo captured," she said. "Right before assignment." Assignment felt like it had happened to someone else about a million years ago. Kyr could not remember now how she felt about being assigned to Nursery. "Avi got me to break it out, when we left. We needed it to steal the ship. So we brought it with us. Him. Them." She took a breath. "It."

"A majo," Mags said. "Was it . . . What was it like?"

"Like a person," Kyr let herself say. "No one said they were *people.*"

"Avi said they probably were," Mags said. "He'd read all sorts of things, he showed me, he said—"

"Avi, Avi, Avi," Kyr said, and she laughed weakly. "You really are gone on him, aren't you?"

Mags said, "Yeah," and then, "He said I'd get over it."

"Will you?"

"No," Mags said, with certainty. "I don't think so."

Kyr *understood* certainty, how it anchored you and overbore you all at once. She felt obscurely that something of equal weight needed to be said in return. What came out of her mouth was "I like them."

"Who?"

"Yiso," Kyr said. "The majo. They're a person, and I like them."

"Vallie," Mags said, "you don't like *anyone.*"

"You," Kyr said. "My mess—" but *did* she like the Sparrows, or were they only another certainty she'd always had? *I never liked you*, Zen had said. Kyr swallowed. "Lisabel," she corrected, feeling sure of that, at least. "Cleo, I think. And, I guess, one majo."

"Ursa?" said Mags. "Ally?"

Kyr shook her head. No. Not a traitor sister. Not a stranger child. She felt *something*, about both of them, but not liking.

"Ursa's probably worried about us," Mags said.

Kyr bit her tongue on *she wasn't worried when she left*, because it would not help; and besides, that was another thing that had happened a million years ago. This was the trouble with feeling things. It tangled you up; it distracted you. It was a distraction to think about Ursa being worried, and it was a distraction to think about Yiso, both the silent bruised alien that Avi had tied up downstairs and the person in the Wisdom's scenario, which was probably *fake* anyway, Kyr told herself. The Wisdom did that, it cheated, told you lies, probably the real Yiso had never played dress-up in a storeroom, or done a silly stick dance.

"Do you think you can walk?" she said.

"Can't hurt to try," said Mags, and laughed. "Can't hurt *worse* to try."

CHAPTER SIXTEEN

CURSED

Avi didn't look up when Kyr brought Mags into the control room. The water under the shadow engine was churning as if a hard wind was blowing across it. Avi stood at his misty control board, scowling, working.

Kyr sat Mags down and checked the wound again. One of the cuts had reopened. She fetched the bottle of whiskey and cleaned it. Mags winced and made small pained noises. Then he passed out, or went to sleep so fast and hard that it looked like passing out.

Accelerated healing took it out of you. Kyr had slept a lot, after Cleo stabbed her. It was fine.

He was fine.

Kyr went to sleep too, curled into a comma beside her brother. Nothing had changed when she woke up. Avi was hunched over, muttering to himself, wrestling with the Wisdom. He looked demonic. Kyr got up, and since she could hardly help, she went to look at Yiso.

Well, they were alive.

"Did you have to hurt them?" she asked.

"I'm going to make a list of people who don't get to judge me," Avi said, without looking up. "You're going to be at the top of it." A pause that had the sound of fast-moving water in it, and he added, "I didn't like it."

Kyr didn't answer. She was looking at the bruises, the notched ear, the broken finger. Yiso's eyes weren't quite closed, but they did not look conscious. Their breathing was rapid. "The Wisdom cares about them," she said. "They're leverage."

"*Cares* might not be the word," Avi said. "It would help if anyone, literally anyone in the entire universe, understood how the Wisdom really works."

"Can you control it if you don't understand it?"

"The majo seem to make it work," Avi said.

"I'm going to patch them up," Kyr said. "In case you need leverage again."

"Whatever helps you sleep at night, sure. Be my guest."

So Kyr tried to do first aid. Medical had never taught them about aliens. Drill had, but only in reverse: how to hurt them, how to kill them. She started with the broken finger, because she'd already done that once. She used whiskey as disinfectant, and the rags of Mags's T-shirt for bandages. She cleaned the notch in Yiso's ear, and did her best with the other small cuts she found. She was not sure what to do about the bruising, or even what it meant. Internal bleeding? She didn't know what Yiso's insides looked like. *How does your body work?*

When she looked up, Avi was standing over her. He might have been there a while. Kyr had been concentrating.

"I didn't have a choice," he said abruptly. "How's Magnus?"

"He walked down here," Kyr said. "He'll live."

"We could still call for doctors," said Avi. "There's probably a doctor somewhere on Chrysothemis that knows what to do for majo."

"If you torture a prisoner, you torture a prisoner," said Kyr. She finished tying Yiso's wrists back together. She didn't bother with the ankles. Yiso couldn't run faster than Kyr. "Feeling weird about it afterward doesn't change anything."

"Remember my list?" Avi said.

"I'd do it too," Kyr said. "If I had to. To win the war." Though she could not quite imagine it, putting a knife against Yiso's ear and cutting out a neat triangle. Why couldn't she imagine it? She'd kicked Yiso in the side, when they were chained up in the Victrix hangar; the guards had sniggered. It hadn't bothered her then. What had changed? Yiso hadn't. Yiso might as well not have been taken off Gaea at all, for all the good it had done them.

"I wonder what it's like to be you," Avi said. "In a weird way, I think it must be restful."

"Restful?"

"I'd like to be as sure about anything as you are."

"You think too much," said Kyr.

"You are not the first person to say so."

"Why aren't you working?"

"I need a break."

"Four days—"

"Three, now," said Avi. "But I'm not made of stone. I have to sleep. It keeps trying to generate another scenario anyway. I'm going to send you back in soon."

"While you're asleep?"

"No," Avi said. "I'll stay awake for that."

Kyr looked down at Yiso again. She thought about the stick dance, the Halls of the Wise, the thousands of storerooms. She said, "Are the scenarios real?"

"They're exactly as real as the agoge ever was," Avi said.

"I meant—"

"I know what you meant," Avi said. "That's the answer. The Wisdom runs on shadowspace. Subrealities, miniaturized universes. Which is what the agoge scenarios are too."

"I thought they were virtual realities," said Kyr. "Pretend."

"Nope," Avi said. "The agoge's the real thing. Fourteen billion people die every time someone fails Doomsday."

Kyr went still. For a vivid instant she could almost taste the stale air of her combat mask as she stood on the defense platform and watched the blue planet begin to unravel.

"If it's any comfort," Avi said, with a nasty little smile, "it's the same fourteen billion, and by this point they're probably used to it."

"You're joking," Kyr said.

"True. They're not used to it. They don't know," Avi said, and Kyr saw that he was serious, that it was true. "Fucked up, but not more fucked up than anything else that happens on Gaea. Anyway, that's how real the Wisdom's little variations are. They're pocket realities, subuniverses, time jumps. Shadowspace stuff, which I could explain but you'd just keep giving me that blank look. Why? Anything interesting going on in there?"

"No," Kyr said. She licked her lips. "It was just some old holy place. The Halls of the Wise."

"Never heard of it," Avi said. "Did you talk to anyone?"

"No, it was empty," said Kyr.

"Oh, you're back," said Yiso, or the version of them that the Wisdom had generated. That translating susurrus was in the air. Yiso was sitting sideways on what Kyr was pretty sure was a piece of *furniture suitable for quadrupeds*, short legs in white leggings swinging. They looked glum. Kyr could read it in the code of crest and ears.

"You remember me?" said Kyr.

"I still haven't decided if you're real," said Yiso. "Probably not. I wonder what's taking so long? Usually it reaches a decision pretty quick. Must be a tough one. Maybe we're obliterating another species."

"What?"

"Leru said," said Yiso, "with the human question, the Wisdom took months working through it. The longest they'd ever seen."

Kyr knew that name. Leru Ihenni Tan Yi was the Prince of the Wisdom who was coming to Chrysothemis, the alien she'd set herself to kill.

"You know Leru?"

"They named me," Yiso said, and when Kyr looked blank, said, "Oh, right, you're supposed to be a human. I don't know the equivalent relationship. Maybe," and the susurrus vanished as they switched into T-standard, "*uncle?* I've always wondered, is there a difference between a maternal uncle and a paternal one? Does it matter which part of you your genetic connections belong to?"

"I don't know," Kyr said. "I never had parents."

"Do you have uncles?"

"One. But it's not—genetic."

"Oh," Yiso said. They kicked listlessly at their complicated chair. "I didn't *know* that. I don't know anything. It's not the same just reading, or watching records, or when it's all scenarios, and—I'll never get off this stupid rock," they said. "I'll never meet a normal person, let alone a human. Leru probably won't even let me on the same planet as a human."

"Why not?"

"Because you're so dangerous," Yiso said. "I bet you're not, though, are you. Have you ever actually killed anyone?"

"No," said Kyr.

"There you go," said Yiso, as if this proved something.

"I *am* dangerous," Kyr said. "I could kill you." And, when Yiso did not seem impressed, "I'm going to kill your uncle."

"I'll believe it when it happens," Yiso said.

"You think I won't do it?"

"Well, if you're *real*," sarcastic ear-flick, "you can *try*."

"Why don't you think I'm real?" Kyr said. "This is a pocket universe, isn't it?"

"Or a time loop, or a side step, or something," Yiso said.

"Don't I have to be real, then? How can I be fake?"

"Oh, not *fake* fake. Randomly generated. A mask persona. Why are you asking?"

It's the same fourteen billion, so they're probably used to it by now. "I want to know how it works," said Kyr.

"How the *Wisdom* works?"

"If you're its servant, shouldn't you know?"

"Leru thinks we used to," Yiso said. "Before it got so complicated."

"Tell me," said Kyr.

Avi had said it was like the agoge, so Kyr had expected Systems stuff. But Yiso told it like a story: like the history Kyr had learned in Nursery, the old tales of the Earth.

Once upon a time, there were some people who were very

unhappy and wicked, said Yiso. This confused them, because they believed themselves to be good people. They tried having a king who was a good person, to tell them what to do: but no matter who was king, that person turned out unhappier and wickeder than all the rest. Then they tried each taking responsibility for themselves, and that didn't work either; it just meant they had no one to blame. Eventually they realized they were under a curse.

"A curse?" said Kyr. "Seriously?"

"Shh," Yiso said. "It's the story."

The unhappy people journeyed widely, hoping to learn the solution; but everywhere they went, everything was just as bad. It became clear that the whole universe was cursed.

"*Seriously*," repeated Kyr.

"So one day," said Yiso, crest flared in annoyance, "a clever person realized the problem was that no matter what anyone did, they couldn't know what would happen next. No one *wanted* to do evil things, they just didn't know what the right things were. So the clever person built a machine that knew everything. You could consult the machine and find out what the best thing to do was, and even if it did end up being bad, you would at least know that all the other things you could have done were worse."

"But the majo don't *consult* the Wisdom," Kyr said. "The Wisdom is in charge."

"Why not save time?" Yiso said. "Anyway. That's the idea. It's a machine that knows everything. Nodes on every civilized world, so it can learn everything; and then there's *this* place, where it runs through possibilities. And the universe is still cursed—shut *up* it's a *metaphor*—so things aren't perfect, but the point of the Wisdom is, *it could be worse*."

"So what are you for?"

Yiso showed their small teeth in an odd expression that Kyr parsed after a moment as a grimace. "Leru won't tell me."

"You're not really here, you know," said Kyr.

"This is getting complicated."

"I think you ran away. You wanted to go somewhere the

Wisdom couldn't find you, right? And you wanted to know about humans."

"It just *bothers* me," Yiso said. "You're not *majo*, except you clearly are, or should be: you think, you feel. And destroying a whole garden world—a whole sentient species, and the ecosystem that made them!—the point of the stupid Wisdom is that it's meant to make the *right* choice, every time. The least bad choice. But how could that be right?"

"Maybe your machine doesn't know as much as you think it does," said Kyr.

"I hate it," Yiso said. "I hate it, I hate it."

"You did run away," Kyr said. "You went looking for somewhere the Wisdom wasn't. You weren't some lost idiot, you were *looking* for Gaea."

"Gaea," repeated Yiso. "That's the human separatists, right? The terrorists." They looked arrested. "Maybe I will."

"They'll kill you," said Kyr.

"Well," Yiso said. "Maybe that's fair."

"How is it fair? You're just one *majo*," Kyr said. "You're not the Wisdom." Then she stopped talking as her own words hit her with terrible force. Yiso was just one majo. Yiso hadn't killed her world. What if they *all*—

Her thoughts tottered on the edge of a realization she did not want to have. Kyr shook herself as if she could shake it away, and nearly missed Yiso saying, "I think I am, though."

"What?"

"I think that's what Leru won't tell me," Yiso said. "I think that's why I exist."

"Don't be ridiculous," said Kyr. "You're a person. It's a machine."

"What would you know about it?" said Yiso. "You're a—*figment*."

"I am *not*," said Kyr.

"This is pointless," Yiso said. "What are you here for? Doors and keys again?"

"No, I'm not done," Kyr said. "Listen to me—"

"Door, key," said Yiso, gesturing in command: green light solidified around Kyr into a frame, and a force she couldn't see shoved her backward through it. The last thing she heard was "See you on Gaea. *If* you exist."

The scenario dissolved. Kyr was standing ankle-deep in water again. She waited for Avi to say something sarcastic—

—which he did not, because he wasn't there, and neither was his conjured control station. Kyr snorted in irritation. She went to the corner where she'd left Yiso, the real Yiso.

Haven't we met? they'd said. Almost the first thing they'd said to her.

"You're really stupid," she told them. They were unconscious and did not answer. "Just—so stupid. Why Gaea? There have to be other places a runaway majo can go. The universe is so big. You could have just—found a *rock* and lived on it—" except Yiso had already been living on a rock, she thought; a world stripped of atmosphere, a half-abandoned palace full of storerooms of antiquities and ghostly visions of unreal universes.

Kyr squatted to check on the broken finger and the notched ear. Yiso's ear twitched under her fingers when she touched it. She thought their eyes cracked open.

"Was it even really you in there?" she asked. The Wisdom could be trying to manipulate her. Though what good it did the Wisdom, if Kyr learned a stick dance—

Yiso mumbled something, but Kyr couldn't make sense of it. Then they went still again.

Kyr got up and left them and went looking for Avi.

He wasn't in the control chamber. Neither was Mags. Kyr, exasperated, made her way back up to the paradise cavern. Of all the times to *wander off—*

They weren't hard to find. She just followed the Bees, which were attracted to movement. A couple trailed her up from the control chamber, and when she arrived in the paradise cavern they flitted off into the lush blue vegetation to her left. Kyr struck out after them.

Mags and Avi had discovered a set of steps that led from nothing to nothing—one tangled layer of vegetation to another—and they were sitting on them. It was a pretty spot, which was probably why Mags had found it. He didn't seem to be paying attention now, though.

They were kissing. Mags had his hands on Avi's face, and Avi had one hand on Mags's shoulder, flat, like he'd meant to push him back but forgotten.

Kyr nearly ran away, but got annoyed with herself and coughed loudly instead.

Mags stopped kissing Avi, but it wasn't because he'd noticed. He said, "So . . ."

"You're free, idiot," said Avi. "You got out. Meet someone at your dumb school. You can almost certainly do better."

"Oh," said Mags. "But."

"But nothing," Avi said. "*I* can almost certainly do better. Listen, not taking advantage of the desperate teenager who worships me is potentially the one good thing I've done in the last eighteen months." He laughed. "We're all fucked up. Gaea's fucked up. Let's not compound it. Anyway, I'm busy."

"*You're* a teenager," Mags said. "It's only a year. I—"

Kyr said, "*Hey.*"

Mags startled and fell off the step he was sitting on. His hand went over his stomach as he winced. In the same instant Avi was standing up and two paces away, like he could make Kyr unsee what she'd seen.

"Show me," said Kyr. Mags looked up at her wide-eyed. Kyr made an impatient gesture.

One of the gashes left by the tiger had opened and was bleeding a little, but only a little. It was fine. Kyr looked up and found Mags still giving her that wide-eyed look. He looked *scared*.

"Why are you afraid of me?" she said quietly.

Mags said nothing, and then he ducked his head, and then he said, "Sorry. It's—Gaea."

Kyr said, "I'm not Gaea."

It took a moment, but Mags nodded. Then he broke her gaze. Kyr straightened up. Avi was watching her, a cool cynical stare, like he was expecting—what?

There were reasons, there were *good* reasons, why Gaea was the way it was. Population targets. Duty. The need for order, the need for a plan, the need for some measure of control over the future of humanity. But Kyr thought—and it was her thought, not one of Avi's sarcastic remarks, not one of Yiso's niggling questions—*they could have told us there were other humans left.*

Of course they had. Kyr had known about collaborators. She had known about traitors. But no one had ever said there was anywhere like Chrysothemis in the universe, a human city, a human world. No one had said anything, and Command must have known. Command had ordered Mags to Strike and Kyr to Nursery, even though they'd known.

And Mags had been unhappy. And Kyr had been—furious.

Kyr *was* furious.

She'd been furious since the moment she was handed her assignment.

They sent Lisabel *to Nursery,* she thought deliberately. *Admiral Russell put his hands on her. Cleo was terrified she wouldn't get combat, and Mags thought he had to lie to me. Avi's fucked up. Yiso was a person all along. And Ursa left, she left the moment she could, she took her son with her.*

And why *pretend,* stop pretending, stop *lying,* of course Ally was Ursa's son. Ursa had had a cot in Jole's quarters. She'd had special treatment. Everyone said it had ruined her. Kyr had worked so *hard* not to put it together—and why? Ursa took her child and she ran away. Kyr had taken herself, her own body, before it was put to use the way Command meant to use it. Kyr had run away.

There was something wrong with Gaea Station. There had always been something wrong with Gaea Station. And Gaea's master was Kyr's uncle Jole, who had marked her assignment with his looping signature.

"Vallie?" said Mags.

"I'm fine," said Kyr. "You're fine. It's all fine. *Don't* touch me." Mags backed away. "No—sorry—I'm just, ugh. It's running those scenarios"—this was a lie—"it's a pain."

"I can do the next one," Mags said.

"No!" said Kyr. Scrambling for an excuse, she added, "You're injured."

Back in the control cavern Avi murmured something to the Bee that had come to perch on his shoulder, and it summoned a group of its fellows. Together they started to make, out of shimmering nothingness, a soft pallet of spongy stuff. "Bet you're still tired," he said to Mags.

Mags made a face, but he did lie down, and he was asleep almost at once.

"Tell them to make one for Yiso," Kyr said.

"Sure," said Avi, and vaguely gestured the Bees toward the corner. He was still avoiding looking in Yiso's direction as much as possible. Then he summoned his misty control panel back into existence, looked at it, said, "Huh," in a surprised way, and dismissed it again. "That can run on its own for a bit longer," he said. "I'm nearly through."

"Oh," said Kyr. "Good."

"Cognitive dissonance catching up with you?" Avi asked.

Kyr said, "I don't know what that is."

"You're not actually stupid, are you," said Avi. "Stupider than me, but who isn't. What cracked you?"

"I think Commander Jole hurt my sister," said Kyr. It was like throwing herself into cold water in a polar scenario; it didn't hurt less if you hesitated.

"Hurt?" said Avi, distant and delicate, as if he were picking up the word with a pair of tweezers to examine it.

"You *know* what I mean."

There was a pause. The shadow engine came to life in it, a quiet hum and crackle, for no apparent reason. Kyr was getting used to it being weird. This whole facility was weird. The Wisdom was weird.

Avi said, with surprising gentleness, "Sorry," and then, "It's all broken on the inside, isn't it."

"But it shouldn't be," Kyr said. "We're the *heroes*—we're the *patriots*—we're the ones who didn't give in, when the majo—"

"When the majo killed our world," Avi finished. "Which they did, you know." He sighed. "Gaea's made of lies. I worked it out early. Magnus got hit over the head with it when he fell for someone he shouldn't. And you, Valkyr, you've known since they dangled training scores over your head for ten years like it *mattered* and then dropped you in Nursery anyway. Haven't you?"

"Yes," said Kyr.

Yes, she knew. Yes.

"But the bit at the bottom that isn't a lie," Avi said, "the only true thing left, after the rest falls apart, is this: there was a war, and we lost, and the majo murdered our planet to make sure of it. Fourteen billion people."

"You said it happens every time someone fails Doomsday," said Kyr. "I've—so *many* times—"

"I'm a jerk," Avi said. "But the agoge—oh, it is real and it isn't. Those little universes it generates stop existing as soon as the scenario ends. So yeah, you failed plenty of times when it didn't count. The majo succeeded, the one time that it did."

Kyr said nothing.

"We're Earth's children," Avi said. He laughed, high-pitched. "You and Magnus, fuck. I haven't had friends since Nursery. I've been queer since puberty hit, but I've been a poisonous little shit much longer than that."

"We're friends?" said Kyr.

"Gaea's rejects," Avi said. "Commander Jole's embarrassments. Chrysotheman refugees—hey, did any of those charity people grab you in the street? Even *I've* never been patronized that hard before." The laugh again, but deeper, and there was a spark in his eyes behind his glasses. "But we're still Earth's children, Valkyr. It's the only thing Gaea Station ever got right. And this much is true, if you choose to make it true: while we live, the enemy *will* fear us."

There was a moment of quiet. Kyr could hear Mags's breathing, gone slow and even. The shadow engine was humming steadily now. The water in the pool where the scenarios built themselves was rippling.

"You can really win the war," she said.

"Prince Leru is here in two days," said Avi. "I'll be in control in six hours. I don't know what you did in that last run, but it's all wide open now. And once I control the Wisdom—even *one node* of the Wisdom—well. Watch me."

"I believe you," said Kyr. Green light from the shadow engine's cast-off strands of unreality was rippling along the walls of the control chamber. "They'll fear us. Why is it doing that?"

"Because," Avi said, and then he said, "Oh shit," and stood up.

"Do you need me?" said Kyr. She saw misty shapes forming over the water. "I'll go in."

"No, you won't," Avi said. "Wake Magnus. He'll have to do it. *Magnus!*" He had a surprisingly good Command bellow. Mags jerked upright on his pallet with his eyes closed. "Up, get up."

"He's injured," said Kyr.

"I know! But I've got nothing to fall back on here because you killed my fucking tiger!" Avi turned and glared at her. "How serious were you about killing the Prince of the Wisdom when it got here?"

"Of course I was serious," said Kyr.

"Good," Avi said. "Because it's here two days early, and if it gets into this chamber before I'm fully in control, we've *lost.*"

CHAPTER SEVENTEEN

THE PRINCE

The spectacular vegetation of the paradise cave made good cover.

Kyr lay in wait, electrically calm. She had set aside the gun Avi offered. She wanted to do this up close and personal. She wanted to feel the knife go in deep. *Leru Ihenni Tan Yi. My uncle,* Yiso had said.

Kyr had waited her whole life to come face-to-face with something she could blame.

It was a simple ambush. Why bother with complicated? The majo were the ones who did complicated: technology, politics, lies. Humans had nothing but the raw strength that was the inheritance of the Earth. Kyr was bigger than any majo. She was faster than any majo. She could endure more heat, more cold, more pain, more misery; she could bear anything; and when Leru came through the arched entrance to the paradise cave, Kyr would pounce out of the bushes and the knife would go straight through one of those large and shining alien eyes.

A just execution. A life for a murdered world.

But the first figures into the cavern were too big to be aliens. They were dressed in black, and they *did* have guns, one each, for a total of six. Visors over their faces did not make the bodyguards look less human to Kyr. She breathed out. Traitors, collaborators. It didn't matter. One against six. That would be hard.

Kyr could do it. She could do anything.

Have you ever actually killed anyone?

Then the Prince of the Wisdom entered behind the six humans. "Perhaps you would do me the courtesy of waiting here," they said. They had the same musical accent as Yiso, though their voice was a little deeper, and a great deal calmer.

Kyr stared, categorizing differences between this and the only other majo zi she had ever seen. Leru's movements were slower and more assured. Their ears twitched less. Their coloration was darker, grey shading almost to navy blue, from the diagonal patterns on their arms to the delicate tips of their crest's long flukes. Their pupilless eyes were a deep purplish color, like a bruise. They wore a white robe, embroidered in white, open down the front over plain white underthings which Kyr saw were an exact match for the outfit Yiso had worn in the Halls of the Wise.

"Sir, I protest," said one of the human bodyguards. It was a woman's voice coming out of that bulky body, which startled Kyr; and she could read the language of the command stripes on the woman's shoulder—she was a sergeant—which also startled her. She kept her breathing quiet and steady, a conscious effort. These were human soldiers. Maybe one of them had enhanced hearing. Maybe all of them did. She didn't want to create any sudden changes in the soundscape. But if she could have held her breath she would have. She was thinking: *Please, please stay here, I don't want to kill you too.*

Leru was murmuring to the bodyguard. She did not look happy; even with visor and full body armor, Kyr could see it in her shoulders. But she gave in, and snapped a command to her squad, who took up positions around the entrance to the labyrinth of tunnels.

"I assure you," said Leru, "that there can be no possible threat to my safety here."

They held up one long thin three-fingered hand into nothingness, a peremptory gesture Kyr recognized as exactly Yiso's. The air shimmered green and produced a long stick, resting between the majo's blue-grey fingers. A handful of Bees, gauze-winged and hex-eyed, came bumbling down from the heights of the cavern to float around Leru in a lazy spiral. The Prince's ears flicked slightly. "Ah, the servitors," they said. "Delightful. Please, my friends, enjoy the garden. It has been a long time since I was last here, and this should be a place of joy."

The human sergeant's body language said very firmly that she had no intention of enjoying the garden. Leru either could not read it or did not care. Without looking back they set off, sauntering, into the beautiful blue-gold chaos of plant life.

Kyr, moving silently under cover, watching more for the humans' sight lines than the majo's, followed.

Leru did not head straight for the shaft down to the control chamber. Instead they went ambling around the paradise cavern, occasionally whacking a bulbous extrusion of plant life with the stick so it scattered powdery seeds everywhere. Before long there was a faint dusting of scarlet pollen on their white robes. Kyr told herself she was waiting for an opportunity.

The majo's ambling led to the ledge where she'd found Mags kissing Avi. There they paused. A dozen Bees circled vaguely up above, the cyclone shape of a storm.

Leru Ihenni Tan Yi, Prince of the Wisdom, master of the majoda, remarked, "You've had several chances now. I can only assume you're not here to kill me after all."

Kyr froze.

"My vision is worse than a human's but my hearing is rather better," said the majo. "We were once—I imagine you don't know this—a crepuscular species. Sound is the great betrayer in the twilight. I am exquisitely well adapted to identify the noise of a large predator moving through the bushes. Come, let us discuss your grievances like reasonable people. Face-to-face, I believe, is the idiom. My own language would make it" a series of trills, "which has a very similar meaning."

Slowly Kyr stood. She had her field knife. The cross guard pressed against her curled fingers in a satisfying way. The bruise-colored eyes turned toward her, and the long ears flexed. Leru said, "Ah. A human."

"What did you expect?"

"Well, a human," said Leru. "By far the most likely possibility.

But the universe is full of unlikelihoods. For example, it was unlikely that anyone would dare to enter this facility; and it was unlikely, having done so, that they would find their way past the many traps and security measures. You must be a capable individual."

Kyr had had no idea there *were* traps. She remembered Avi leading them through the labyrinth of tunnels. She said nothing.

"Especially for one so young," Leru continued. "You are an adolescent?"

"Like you'd know," Kyr said.

"I have made a point of knowing," said Leru. "Forgive my impoliteness, but I find human gender more difficult to guess without obvious cultural markers, like a—bird? Pardon me. Beard. Do you have a strong preference?"

Kyr said nothing.

"No?"

"It's not going to matter to you," she said, "whether I'm a boy or a girl."

"Two options," Leru noted. "You are from a traditionalist culture."

"You know *nothing* about me."

"On the contrary," Leru said. "I know a great deal about you, and you know nothing about me. You are an adolescent, neither physically nor mentally fully developed, although more than capable of understanding and bearing responsibility for your actions. You come from what might be called the defiant strain of human society, which in the face of present difficulties has taken refuge in a radical, romantic retreat to the past. I am sure pockets of such sentiment exist on Chrysothemis, although they have been politely hidden from my view, but I doubt you were raised on Chrysothemis, where there are very few left of the so-called warbreed humans of the latter days of the Terran War—and none of them, of course, younger than their early thirties."

"The Majo War," said Kyr.

Leru inclined their head. "That tells me that you are most

likely a representative of the rogue statelet that calls itself Gaea Station. Your politics are radical, militant, and separatist, and in your mind I, personally, am a terrible enemy of the human race. Am I correct?"

Kyr said, "It doesn't matter if you call for help. Your traitor bodyguards won't get here fast enough."

"I have no intention of calling for help," Leru said. "Do you intend to kill me?"

"Why aren't you scared!"

"I am nearly ten thousand years old," said the majo. "For all that time I have served the purposes of wisdom. You are quite young, and not very frightening."

Kyr adjusted her sweaty grip on the knife. Leru glanced down, and their crest dipped, but they said mildly, "Death is also not very frightening. I would like you to know that I am not, in any way, humanity's enemy."

"You said it yourself," said Kyr. "You serve the Wisdom."

"I do," said Leru. "The Wisdom is not humanity's enemy either."

"You killed our world!"

"A tragic, unavoidable sacrifice."

"Fourteen billion people," said Kyr.

"Yes," said Leru. "Set against the interests of trillions. I doubt that will sway you. Most humans are quite bad with numbers. And in any case I do understand that one must take some things personally. I have not in a long time, but most sentients do, and this is one of the things which makes them worth preserving. May I tell you about the future of your species?"

"You want to rule us!"

"No. The majoda is not an empire, nor a tyranny, nor even a federation," Leru said. "The majoda is made of sentient peoples as the universe is made of stardust and void. Here is a future, young person: humanity endures. Its people live in whatever way seems best to them. They are majo. If they suffer, their suffering is not because of physical want. If they are not the greatest among the stars, they are also not the least. They govern themselves;

they do so wisely. They do not fear, and they do not cause fear in others. And they intermingle, no doubt, in scholarship, in commerce, in affection—I am aware that you are ferociously given to pair-bonding—and so the best part of their separate qualities redounds to the benefit of the majoda, which is to say, to the benefit of all those who think and feel. This is a future of peace and prosperity; of happiness, I hope, for many—since not even the Wisdom can guarantee happiness for all. It is the future I have striven for from the moment I knew humanity existed, and this, I assure you, from the highest and most disinterested motives imaginable."

"And so you," said Kyr, coming closer, changing her grip, looking it in the eyes—*The right eye*, she thought; *I will stab this alien through the right eye, and it will die*—"you, who *control* the Wisdom—"

"Hardly," murmured Leru.

"—you sent a planet-killing bomb to our homeworld, you destroyed everything and everyone—"

"Hardly," said Leru again. "*You* exist, after all."

"And I'm supposed to believe you're not our enemy, that you only wanted the best for us all along."

"The best for you and also for everyone else," Leru corrected, still with that infuriating, impenetrable calm. "That is my duty."

"I don't believe you," said Kyr. She uncurled into movement like the snap of a whip. Her knife flew down toward that unreadable pupilless eye—

And stopped. Kyr felt the jolt all through her arm and shoulder as Leru swiftly and with no wasted movement blocked the strike with the stick they still held. Kyr's knife slid sideways along it, and though it looked like flimsy organic matter the Gaean blade did not so much as chip it. Leru said nothing. They did not move.

Kyr, forgetting the bodyguards on the other side of the cavern, let out a frustrated yell and struck again. This time Leru did move, just to step out of her way. She overbalanced and stumbled on the ledge she'd forgotten was there. The majo was still watching her unreadably. The stick was in their hands, balanced between their long fingers in a relaxed and confident two-handed grip that Kyr *recognized*, because it was from Yiso's stick dance.

Which she quickly realized, as she tried and tried again to land a hit on the Prince of the Wisdom, had never been a silly dance at all. It had been weapons training, for a weapon Kyr hadn't recognized because Yiso was so appallingly bad with it.

Leru was Yiso's opposite: fast, focused, expert. They stayed defensive, pivoting away from Kyr's knife again and again, blocking with the stick only when they had to. It made for a very weird one-sided fight. Almost stupid. Kyr *hated* feeling stupid.

"You'll get tired before I do," she said, circling. Leru's head didn't turn, their eyes didn't follow her, but their ears swiveled. They were listening for her.

"Of course" was all they said, very mild.

"You can't run fast enough to run from me."

"Quite true."

"So what are you going to do? Shout for help?" Kyr laughed, breathless. "Get the humans to come save you from the human?"

"I would prefer not to," said Leru. "They would certainly kill you, and you might kill one or more of them. These would be sad outcomes."

Kyr struck, going low this time, an abdominal thrust. Leru stepped away with an air of polite apology, but the stick this time went down and out—fast! the damn alien was so fast!—and Kyr tripped over it and went sprawling in the undergrowth. She growled and tried to spring up—

And couldn't.

The blue and golden plants had put out firmly restraining tendrils, catching her ankles and her wrists. They were not strong. Kyr broke free with two or three good tugs and scuttled away. In that time Leru had taken some prudent steps backward, giving their stick the benefit of reach. But it wasn't the stick that worried Kyr now. How had the majo made the plants do that? Her eyes darted from side to side. There was a *lot* of vegetation. It had been nothing till now—cover, background. But if it turned into a threat, what the hell was Kyr to do? She had a knife, when she needed a flamethrower.

"Your actions are most unwise," said Leru. "Please reconsider."

"Fuck you," said Kyr. This wasn't right. She was supposed to be tougher than an alien. She *was* tougher than the alien. It was supposed to matter.

The cyclone of Bees overhead had grown; it had begun as a handful, but now nearly all the drones in the cavern had to be in that swirl of vague movement. Leru glanced upward at it.

Kyr charged. She had the knife in her hand but she was barely even thinking about it anymore. She was big and she was strong and she was terrible, and she knocked solidly into the Prince of the Wisdom and this time they both went tumbling, and Kyr on top. *Yes.*

There was a flash of greenish non-light, a flicker of ghost sensations: hot, cold, prickling in her fingers, a great weight pressing down on her from above—

And Kyr was standing back where she'd been the moment before.

"Dimensional trapping," she said, licking her lips, tasting blood. "You think that'll scare me? I trained with jump hooks."

Leru only sighed. They held up one of their thin hands, the one without the stick in it.

And the cloud of Bees descended.

They weren't attacking. They were just in the way. Kyr had taken apart one of these things when she broke into the facility. She knew how fragile their bodies were, how easy it was to crush carapaces and rip off wings and fling them aside. She did that, blindly, elbowing her way through the mass—there were so many she couldn't see the majo anymore, could barely make out the blur of blue and gold that was the plants. She hadn't failed. She wouldn't fail. She *couldn't* fail.

Then abruptly the Bees scattered, leaving only a trail of sad cracked carapaces. And Leru was not there anymore.

"Shit," breathed Kyr. She sprinted for the shaft that led down to the control chamber. Her long stride ate up the paradise cavern, the spiral ramp. She couldn't shake the unaccountable feeling that the world was spinning around her—

That wasn't dizziness. That was a shadow engine.

Soundlessly loud it roared, and Kyr felt gravity lurch. She turned a long stride into an awkward leap and landed tuck-and-roll, hard, as the planet plaintively reasserted its weight against the dimensional distortion. A glittering stretch of pain along her arm—she'd skinned it. The part of her mind that had always been good at spotting the sting in the tail of a scenario reminded her that there were six human bodyguards somewhere, who by now must have noticed there was something wrong: six human soldiers, with guns.

That was the *next* problem. Here was this problem: Leru, ahead of her in the tunnel, still with three or four attendant Bees humming around their head, and beyond them the dim green shimmer of shadowspace at work.

Kyr ran. But it was like running in a nightmare: she could feel her legs moving, the ache in her lungs, but nothing changed. Another distortion was rolling toward her, in space rather than gravity this time, and it telescoped the tunnel temporarily into a near-infinite stretch of darkness.

Then it snapped back. Kyr's inner ear was ringing, but she did not care. She flung herself forward into the control chamber.

It was almost unrecognizable. The walls had folded away, replaced with a glittering star-speckled void; the plants were still there, but most of them had gone curled and brown, while the few remaining had grown immeasurably, higher than the ceiling of the chamber had been, higher than the paradise cave above, an uncoiling blue forest in the midst of a void. "Hmm," Kyr heard Leru say, in tones of no more than mild surprise. "Some interesting riftwork."

Only the pool of water was the same, still and gleaming under the cradle of the shadow engine. The engine itself, Kyr realized, staring, was enormous. It seemed to have expanded in all directions, in shapes that were rippling and organic and recurled on themselves like intestines. Parts extended even farther, off into the infinite void, with a vague suggestion that other knotted conglomerations of machinery existed somewhere in the distance. Here its metallic arms glinted with greenish shadowspace reflections. It loomed over them like a predatory insect.

"*You act in opposition to the Wisdom,*" said the sweet voice of the great machine out of everywhere and nowhere. "*Your actions are unwise. Your actions are unwise. Your actions are unwise—*"

"*—got* you," she heard Avi say, and Kyr saw him, just, a tiny figure near the heart of the chaos. "Magnus, get out of there!"

Mags stumbled into existence, ankle-deep in the water, looking terribly scared.

"*Your actions are—*" said the Wisdom, and stopped.

Into the new silence Leru said, "Impressive."

Avi turned around. He looked at the Prince of the Wisdom standing there, with their entourage of Bees. His expression twisted into a bitter mask.

"Valkyr," he said, "you had *one* job."

Kyr snarled and lunged for Leru. But they blinked out of existence and reappeared standing next to Avi at the misty bank of controls. "Unusual but effective," they remarked to him as he cringed away and fumbled for the gun. "No, please do not attempt to shoot me. You must realize it would not work. Out of curiosity, how did you—ah."

They'd spotted the sad crumpled bundle of Yiso, unconscious.

"Brutal," Leru said softly.

"You don't get to judge him," snapped Kyr. She was moving slowly across the bizarrely expanded control chamber, trying to work out a good angle. Leru was very close to both Avi and the controls. Tackling them to the ground—all right, hadn't *worked*, but it had distracted them for a moment. Nothing would work as long as the majo had the absurd power of the Wisdom on its side.

Kyr tried to catch Avi's eye. *I'll distract the majo, you finish the job.* Avi wasn't looking at her.

Mags was. He still looked frightened. But Kyr nodded to him and now they were both drawing steadily and carefully closer to the majo, who seemed to have forgotten them entirely. Leru's attention was on the tangled distortion of the shadow engine stretching off into the infinite distance that should not exist inside a planet. "I take it you are also a terrorist?" they said conversationally to Avi. "What a dreadful waste of your abilities. This is a remarkable achievement."

Avi said nothing.

"But whatever you thought you were doing here, I am afraid it ends now," Leru said. "Your mistake was not disabling the servitors, I'm afraid. They are much more sophisticated than they appear." They gestured with the stick toward the drifting Bees.

The Bees did nothing. They continued to drift.

Avi smiled thinly. "Yeah, I noticed," he said. *"Now."*

Kyr and Mags moved as one: two children of Earth, two soldiers of Gaea. They didn't need to say anything. They understood each other perfectly. They were unstoppable. Mags knocked Leru down the same way Kyr had done and got dimensionally dislocated across the room the same way too, but this time Kyr was there to step in for him. She ripped the stick out of Leru's hands and snapped it in half with one hard push, and then she was shadow-jumped backward as well, but this time it didn't throw her off; heat, cold, a new position, but Kyr had *trained* with jump hooks; this was just jump hooks with someone else steering.

Besides, Mags was there, already closing in on Leru again, because the majo might have a bag of tricks but Kyr and Mags were *human*, they were big and tough and fast and they didn't need trickery to be dangerous. Kyr had her knife in her hand as she raced back to the fight. Magnus was holding the struggling alien in a stranglehold, and Kyr had the vision in her head again of her blade going through the alien's eye and into the brain matter behind, one smooth perfect kill, vengeance, *finally*.

There was a crunching sound followed by a small pathetic snap.

Mags dropped Leru's corpse on the ground. The majo's head was twisted around at an angle. The bruise-colored eyes were filming over.

Kyr stared at her brother. She was still holding the knife. That was *her* kill. She'd meant to do it. She'd wanted to do it. Magnus's expression was distant, and strangely hollow. His hands were still in position for what he'd done—twist to crack the throat-carapace, snap to break the neck. And then he'd just . . . let the majo go.

Leru was heaped on the ground at his feet like a sack of potatoes, a body small as a child's.

"Thank fuck for that," Avi said, and that was when the bodyguards rushed in.

The human sergeant was in the lead; her squad fanned out behind her, all of them with guns, holding them two-handed, pointed down. And Kyr knew how to do *this* too; this was Drill, this was hand-to-hand against her mess, and she did not even really think. She went for the sergeant. The sergeant was raising her firearm; Kyr was faster. The sergeant was armored in synthweave and wearing a visor. Kyr angled the knife for a deep stab. It went through the layers of fiber at the woman's throat and caught there. Kyr had to twist and tug, hard, to get it back.

The sergeant fell down. It had all taken only a matter of seconds. There were five more soldiers. Kyr had killed one human, and now she needed to kill five more, which she probably couldn't, not when they all had guns, but she had to try, or else Mags had killed Leru for nothing. This was going through her mind at a bizarre syrup-slow speed, and then all five of the remaining bodyguards exploded.

Instead of being surrounded by enemy combatants Kyr was suddenly surrounded by a cloud of red mist. It subsided quickly into dark stinking puddles around her feet and around the body of the sergeant she'd stabbed. It was on her clothes too. It was everywhere.

She thought of Yiso in their empty palace, saying *have you ever actually killed anyone?*

She turned around.

Magnus hadn't moved. He was still standing over the body of the Prince of the Wisdom. Avi was by the controls. The Bees that had trailed Leru down to the control chamber were hovering around him now. One was perched on his shoulder. The green shadow-flickers that Kyr associated with the Wisdom surrounded him.

"You're welcome," he said. He was talking about the five exploded soldiers, Kyr saw. He'd done that. He'd made it happen. Now he laughed—a cracked unpleasant sound. "Time to finish this."

Then Yiso woke up.

CHAPTER EIGHTEEN

VICTORY

Yiso woke with a cry, a torn-out ragged sound, their bundle-of-sticks body jerking into a sitting position. Their hands were still tied. Their crest and ears were flat against their skull. Avi turned with the expression of someone who had suddenly spotted a poisonous snake.

"What," Yiso said, "what—"

Kyr was still covered in the fine misty blood of the slaughtered bodyguards. Her knife had fallen out of her hand. She saw the way Yiso twisted around and found *her*; how their ears pricked forward and their whole expression lifted into something like relief. She'd done nothing to earn that expression from a majo. Yiso was a servant of the Wisdom. Kyr owed them nothing.

In fact—"Do I need to," she said to Avi, and couldn't finish the sentence. If the alien needed to die, Kyr would have to do it. Mags had stumbled away from Leru's corpse, looking waxy and awful.

"That depends. Hey, Yiso," Avi said. He twitched two fingers: the tone of the shadow engine's hum changed, and the knots Kyr had tied around the little majo's wrists fell away. "It wants you up, huh? So get up."

"What's happening?" said Yiso, and then, "You—you hurt me." They got into a crouched position on their haunches, but didn't make it all the way to standing. "I thought you were nice—I thought *Valkyr* was the one who—You hurt me."

"Yeah, sorry," Avi said. "Get *up*."

Yiso let out a little moan. They'd spotted Leru's broken corpse. "What have you done?"

"That's what I'm trying to find out," Avi said. "You're a Prince of the Wisdom—no, don't lie, we know. I always knew what you were."

Yiso stumbled upright and swayed. Kyr nearly went to catch them, but Avi waved her away. The Bee on his shoulder took off and went for a lazy figure-eight wander around him, and then came back. Avi said, "Stop me."

"What?"

"Do your thing. Space magic or whatever. Appeal to the Wisdom. *Cheat*. It's what you do, right?" Avi said. "Here, how about I do this." He lifted his hand and Leru's corpse lurched upright. The dead majo's head hung terribly backward from their broken neck. Yiso made a revolted sound. "Little bit of puppetry," Avi said. "Seems appropriate. Don't like it? *Stop me*."

Yiso sniffled and whimpered. Kyr's gaze fell on their hands, the broken finger she'd fixed herself, twice. Leru had used their three-fingered hands to gesture commands into being. Avi was still twitching his fingers, and with every motion the corpse moved forward, descending lifelessly on Yiso, limbs swaying at random as shadowspace flickers danced around it. It was stomach-turning, even for Kyr, who didn't care. She didn't care. *They named me*, the Yiso in the scenarios had said.

Yiso let out a low cry and tried to shove the corpse away, throwing both hands out toward it.

Kyr didn't know why she was holding her breath.

"And nothing," Avi said. "Hah. You can't, can you? You're locked out."

"Please," Yiso said. "What you're doing is dangerous. Please stop."

And somehow that was what made Kyr move. She went to Yiso and she stood over them and she knocked the alien corpse away—it went tumbling over and over, light as paper, all Leru's ten-thousand-year-old condescension reduced to a laughable husk. Kyr loomed over Yiso and said, very soft, "We don't do what the majo tell us to do."

Yiso flinched. Kyr gripped them by the shoulder so they didn't collapse, because she didn't want them to collapse. She wanted them to stand there and watch, while the majo lost the war.

"All right, Avicenna," she said. "Get on with it."

Avi rolled his eyes, but the corner of his mouth lifted in a real smile. Mags came and stood next to Kyr with his hand on Yiso's other shoulder. "Fine, fine, I'm doing it," Avi said. "Let's see. What do I want? Oh, yes."

The void inside the control chamber suddenly filled up with glimmering pinpoints of light, stretching into the unnatural distorted distance along every branch of the disquieting organic coils of the shadow engine.

"There we go," Avi said. "The known universe. Sorry, the *Majoda*. Twenty trillion sentient beings, spread over however many worlds." He reached out and caught one of the specks of light between his hands. It spun itself into a planet, swathed in white cloud, unfamiliar continents beneath, half bathed in the light of some unseen star. It was exquisitely detailed, and its light caught Avi's eyes, sparkled on his glasses. "Twenty trillion sentients belonging to, what, seventeen species?" Avi said. "Some of them have been spacefaring so long no one remembers which of their capital worlds is technically the homeworld. Which scuppered my first idea, but I think this one is better. Humanity's birthright was a planet and an infinite frontier. That was *my* birthright. And what did I get?" He snorted. "*Gaea*. One shitty little station on a dead fucking rock. So. Seventeen species, right?"

"Nineteen," breathed Yiso.

"Oops," Avi said. "Well, too bad. I don't fancy doing any more research. Here." The planet spinning between his hands shrank down to a point of light again, and was joined by others that winked into existence one by one. "Sixteen worlds, because your species doesn't have one. Look, I'm being nice, everyone gets somewhere with a breathable atmosphere to live. Everyone who's left, anyway."

"What are you *doing*?" said Yiso.

"Justice," Avi said. "It's pretty simple, really. You killed my world. I'm killing yours. All of them. Or almost."

Yiso made a horrified sound.

Avi's smile only sharpened. His gaze flicked up, to Kyr, to Mags. "Objections?"

"No," said Mags. He sounded sick. "No. I . . . No."

"*No, don't*, or *No, no objections*?" Avi said.

Mags said nothing.

"How," said a voice, which was Kyr's. "How does this help."

"You don't get it?"

"You said we'd *win*," said Kyr.

"Oh, this is winning," Avi said. "Not instantly, I admit it. I could wipe out *all* the majo worlds, but does it really count as victory when there aren't any losers left to appreciate what they've lost? I don't think so. And you don't either, do you? Gaea taught us that." He grinned. "Always keep score. Anyway, this takes out their two big advantages, the numbers and the tech. No more Wisdom cruisers, no reality bending, nothing. They never had much of a standing military. Until humans came along they didn't need one. And it won't take Systems long to put those dreadnoughts back together. They were always meant to rule the universe. I guess part of my soul *does* hate the thought of Commander fucking Jole ever getting anything he wants, but what the hell. I think I'd like to see the look on his face when he realizes it was me. Do you think you could tell him for me, and record it?"

Kyr said nothing.

"I assume you'll be going back," Avi said. "They won't waste you on Nursery when there's worlds to conquer, I promise you that."

No, they wouldn't. Kyr saw that. They wouldn't have to, because the first target—of course, obviously—the first target would be the last human world. Gaean dreadnoughts would descend on Chrysothemis with its yellow seas and shiny city. A planetary base, and the rich irris mines in the asteroid belt—it was the obvious choice.

Once Gaea held a planet and its people, population targets wouldn't be Kyr's problem anymore.

A picture in her head: Ursa's tidy flat. Ally giving little lectures about fish. Kyr's sister, who had been barely older than Kyr was now when she took her child and ran. Kyr had never forgiven her. Kyr still could not imagine forgiving her.

Kyr had run too, the moment she got the chance.

Jole would come looking for his son. Kyr knew it like she knew her own name.

Set that against—every single majo, every last one, knowing the chilly misery that Kyr had always known. Set that against Kyr's personal apocalypse multiplied twenty trillion times. Set Ursa and her son against *justice*, against what was *right*, against what the majo *deserved* for what they had done.

She licked her lips.

"No, please," Yiso said. "Please, you mustn't do this. I beg you." They stumbled out of Kyr and Mags's joint grip and into a kneeling position. Avi's eyebrows went up. His smile kept coming back. "Please, please," Yiso said. "If you must have vengeance, kill me. Kill me instead."

"You think you're enough?" Avi said.

"The Wisdom made me," said Yiso. "The Wisdom shaped me, the Wisdom kept me in comfort, the Wisdom taught me everything I am. Please."

"The thing is," Avi said, almost kind, "you could say that about the whole damn universe. You see?"

"Avi?" said Mags. "I . . . I don't . . ."

He trailed off.

"Oh, come on, Magnus," Avi said, halfway laughing. "You were never actually going to stand up to me."

And Mags wasn't, Kyr saw. He looked sick, but he was standing there like a training dummy in Drill, all his perfect size and strength gone to nothing because he couldn't make himself move.

Kyr wasn't going to interfere. Of course not. It would be a betrayal of everything she was and everything she stood for to lose her nerve now, on the brink of a perfect victory. All she had to do was stay still and let it happen.

So she didn't know why she was moving, why the body she had honed and mastered and always *understood* better than she understood anything else seemed to be taking action without her. Avi's attendant Bee cracked to pieces in Kyr's hands first, almost dreamlike as the gauzy wings shredded in her fingers. "*Valkyr?*" said Avi, affronted, and Kyr punched him in the face.

It was nowhere near as satisfying as she'd thought punching Avi might be. His glasses broke; she heard the crack. He howled in pain. Ghost sensations rushed through Kyr as a distorted wave of nothingness tried to hurl her away. But Avi wasn't anywhere near as good at this as Leru had been. Kyr sidestepped around the trap and then halted.

Avi, on the ground, was laughing through a horrible snuffling nosebleed. "Coward," he taunted her, "aren't you, after all. Who knew the great Valkyr was soft on majo. Hey, watch *this*."

The points of light that were the majoda, the known universe, everything Kyr had always learned to hate, spun around them. The insectoid arms of the great shadow engine blazed and sang out, a deep subsonic note that vibrated through the floor and made Kyr's vision blur.

"Stop it!" yelled Mags. "Stop it! Both of you stop it!"

"Please, no, please, no—" and then a break into incomprehensible alien trills; that was Yiso.

Avi got to his feet and put his cracked glasses back on. His smashed nose was gushing blood and he was grinning through it. "Sopped your conscience, Valkyr?" he said. "You pick the weirdest times to have principles."

"This is wrong," Kyr said. "This is *wrong*."

"Don't like Jole getting what he wants either?"

And Kyr didn't, she *didn't*, the picture in her head of Uncle Jole descending on Ursa and Ally in their refuge, of the dreadnoughts reborn descending through Chrysothemis's sky—she could not bear it. But that wasn't why.

"They're people," she said. "The majo. You *know* they're people."

"So what?"

"This isn't justice. This is just the same thing over and over."

"So fucking *what?*"

"Make it stop," Kyr said. "Stop it now. Or I'll break your arms."

Avi held up his hands, one of them covered in blood because he'd been holding it to his nose. "Do your worst," he said. "I've been beaten up by bigger bullies than you. It doesn't matter." He was shouting over the endless roar of the great engine, which wasn't just any shadow engine, Kyr thought in a flash; that tangled mass of shadowspace vectors and organic coils and strange flickers through an infinite void *was* the great machine the majo zi had built long ago to make their universe better. They were standing within the Wisdom, and it was all around them, and it was impossibly complicated, and terribly loud.

"Why doesn't it matter!" she yelled.

The noise stopped. Avi smiled through his mask of blood.

"Because it's already over," he said.

The Wisdom groaned one last time, and the universe in miniature that surrounded them blurred and flared in curtains of discolored light as thousands of worlds died together.

Kyr didn't believe it at first.

Then Yiso started wailing and did not stop. The high thin shriek warbled up and down like a warning siren.

"Cute that you tried, Valkyr," Avi said. "You can break my arms now if you want—Magnus?"

Mags had come unfrozen from his dreadful scarecrow stance.

He walked quite calmly over to them and put out his hand—Avi flinched—and took away the gun Avi had left on one side of his misty control bank. It was a Gaean regulation weapon, the one Kyr had taken from the Victrix soldier guarding Yiso when everything began. "Magnus," Avi said again, in a different tone.

"It's okay," said Mags. He had his back to Kyr. She couldn't see his face. "It's like you said. I was never going to stand up to you."

"You're not going to shoot me," Avi said. "You wouldn't."

"No," Mags agreed.

"Mags?" said Kyr.

Magnus's shoulders tensed, but he did not turn around. "I really thought you were different," he said to Avi. "But it's all the same in the end, I guess. There's no point. There's just no point. And they'll come here, you know. Gaea. They'll come here first."

It was the same thing Kyr had thought, but something about the way Mags said it made the hairs on her arms stand on end. "*Mags*," she said more urgently, and reached out for him.

Mags stepped neatly out of her reach, without looking at her. He was still holding the gun. He made a small noise like a stifled laugh. Then he flicked off the safety catch with a confident motion, put it to the side of his head, and pulled the trigger.

After the hell-din of the Wisdom, the single shot had a strangely muted sound.

Mags's body fell awkwardly sideways between Avi and Kyr. Somewhere unimportant Yiso was still keening for the deaths of thousands of worlds. Kyr went on her knees. She turned Mags over. He was heavy. She thought of the Medical sergeant with tired eyes. First aid. The entry wound was a small hole in her brother's temple, and the exit wound had torn away a good chunk of the side of his face.

He was dead, of course. Of course he was dead.

On Gaea Kyr hadn't even known he was unhappy. It was bizarre that she hadn't known. She could see the shape of Mags's unhappiness now cloaked in everything he'd said to her for years.

She pulled him into her lap. He was still dead. No use being childish about it. A person with that much of their head missing was certainly dead.

For once in his life Avi wasn't saying anything. Kyr looked up at him.

She said, "You did this."

If Avi said something Avi-ish like *I'm pretty sure he did, actually*—she could *hear* it—then Kyr would cut him down on the spot.

But actually he said, still in that weird almost-laughing tone, now with a little shake in it, "Not even the worst thing I've done today."

And then Avi turned away. He was looking at the universe, the one he'd made, the handful of points of light that were all that was left of the majoda.

"I planned this so carefully," he said softly. "I thought so hard. Because it's fair, right? It's fair. They did it to us." He turned back to Kyr, to Kyr with Mags's body in her arms, and he said, "I'm sorry."

Then Kyr killed him anyway.

He was the second person she'd ever killed. The sergeant was the first. She did it the way Mags had killed Leru. She got hold of him and she snapped his neck with one good twist. He didn't even try to fight. It wouldn't have made a difference if he had. Avi was a weakling. He'd never been a match for Kyr. She could have done it ten minutes earlier, and stopped everything. Twenty trillion majo would still be alive if she had.

The destruction of thousands of inhabited worlds seemed particularly unreal just now. The rest of the universe might never have existed at all. Maybe Kyr had always lived in this vast impossible underworld, with the Wisdom coiled around the horizon, and a pathetically sobbing alien nearby, and the body of her brother and the body of her friend.

Mags's eyes were open and staring. She closed them. She closed Avi's eyes too.

Then she sat down between them and stared into space for a little while. She wasn't crying. She was stronger than that. Anyway she seemed to have forgotten how.

If I had told Avi we had to call a doctor after the tiger clawed Mags, she thought, *and the doctors had come for him, and the police to arrest us, then I would be in prison right now, and Avi would also be in prison, alive, and my brother would be in the hospital, alive.*

If I had made sure Ally couldn't tell anyone I'd gone, then Mags would never have been here; he would be in Ursa's flat, alive, and I would be somewhere in those tunnels, probably mauled to death by a tiger, and Avi would not have stopped Leru so he would be— probably in prison, alive.

If I had not left Ursa's flat—

If I had not left Avi and Yiso to go and find my brother—

If I had stayed on Gaea—

Oh, *now* she was crying. Awful. She hated it. She dug her nails into her cheeks and dragged them down hard to see if the pain would make it stop. It didn't work. She did it again anyway.

"Valkyr?"

Kyr had forgotten about Yiso. "What," she said.

"There's—Avicenna had—a device," Yiso said. "Can I—"

"He's dead," Kyr said. "He doesn't care." She noticed again Leru's body, dropped where Avi's macabre corpse puppetry had left it, and beyond it the body of the human sergeant Kyr had killed, in the middle of the red puddle that was her squad.

It was funny. Everyone always said, didn't they, that war was serious. But the seriousness had been like a game they were playing the whole time. It hadn't been real.

Yiso was fumbling in Avi's pockets, favoring one hand and trying not to touch him too much. Kyr nearly snapped at them to stop making such a fuss. He was *dead*, so what. He was a jerk anyway. Mags was dead too, and was Kyr making a fuss? No, she was just sitting.

Avi had a tiny thumb-sized comm that threw up a screen

projection when Yiso touched it. Oh, it was the newsreader Kyr liked. Ari Shah, in their skirt and bracelets, with the good arms. Their face was haggard and their eyes looked bruised. BREAK-ING, said a box at the bottom of the screen. BREAKING, BREAKING, BREAKING. Ari Shah was talking about planets, listing places Kyr had never heard of. Every so often they looked over to the side and flinched and then started talking again. Someone kept tell-ing them new names, Kyr saw.

"—four more capital worlds confirmed," Ari Shah said. "The sinnet homeworld Sinthara—"

Yiso made the projection go away. The silence that replaced it was a dark maw full of teeth.

"He did it," they said eventually.

"Earth's children," said Kyr. "While we live . . ."

The enemy shall fear us. It was a toast. She hadn't thought about that in a while. Every Gaean wing had its toast, and that was the toast for Command. Mags had thought Avi should be Command. Uncle Jole—Commander Jole—had never *dreamed* of a victory on this scale.

"No one even knows what happened," Yiso said. "No one knows but us."

Kyr said nothing.

"You hate us so much," Yiso said. "He hated us so much."

She wished they'd shut up.

"Are you going to kill me?"

"What for?" said Kyr.

Yiso didn't reply. They got up and hobbled to the edge of the pool of shining water that lay under the node of the Wisdom that was actually here on Chrysothemis. Some of the other tangles in the distant spreading conglomeration had disappeared, Kyr noticed, without interest or surprise. The planets hosting them were gone. The machine had pruned itself half out of existence.

Yiso was making awkward, twitching gestures at nothing. Eventually a shimmering array of symbols appeared above the water.

Yiso looked at them for a bit, and then they said hopelessly, "He really did lock me out." They sat down again. Kyr looked away. She smoothed down Magnus's fair hair. It had only been a few weeks, but it had already been getting too long for discipline. Untidy. Kyr hadn't had a chance to make fun of him for it.

"I do recognize you," Yiso said eventually. "I wasn't sure for a long time. Your clothes were different. And you were nastier than I thought you'd be."

Kyr said nothing.

"But I met you before," Yiso said. "In the Halls of the Wise. Months ago."

"It was yesterday," said Kyr.

"Probably a time slip," Yiso said. "It does that sometimes."

"I don't care."

"I just thought you should know," said the majo. "It was important to me."

Kyr ignored them. It didn't matter. Nothing mattered.

Something nagged quietly at her attention, while she sat there, hot-eyed and silent, with her brother's body. Yiso wouldn't be still. There was no point doing anything but they kept wandering about, all twitchy—their *ears* were twitchy—crossing Kyr's peripheral vision, making small noises. Kyr turned her head to stare at them, and then to glare, but they didn't seem to notice. They were back by the pool of water again. The array of lights might have been controls. Kyr vaguely recognized some Majodai letters in the shapes.

She touched Mags's hair again, gentle, and she turned his head to one side so you couldn't see the ruin around the exit wound. He looked a little like he was asleep. Mags always liked to sleep.

Then she got to her feet and said, "Did you say *time slip*?"

CHAPTER NINETEEN

DOOMSDAY

It took Yiso a moment.

"But I'm locked out," they said, and then, "—but you're not. He was using you to break in."

"The Wisdom can interfere with time," Kyr said. "Can it change the past?"

"Well," said Yiso, "it hasn't been done very often, I don't think, but yes. Of course." They'd stopped twitching. They went back to their controls. The lights over the water turned them into a slim silhouette that could almost have been Avi, if you squinted, if you ignored the crest. Kyr did not look down at the bodies. She went and stood beside Yiso, in a spot where she could see their alien face.

"The problem is," Yiso said, "how do you know what to change? Everything that happens has so many consequences. Even the smallest things. I told you the story, didn't I? About the cursed universe? People can't know everything, they can't plan for everything. The Wisdom is constantly running its own subreal universes to test outcomes, and Leru said—" They stopped.

"*What*," Kyr said.

"Sorry," Yiso said, small. "Leru's dead."

"So what?" Kyr said, brutal. "Your uncle's dead, my brother's dead, Avi's dead, thousands of worlds are dead, so *what*? Keep talking. What did Leru say?"

"Leru said the Wisdom made us to be its eyes," Yiso said. "In every reality. I've seen little pieces of lots of universes. And Leru said, in *theory*, the Wisdom could wrench us all into the next reality over. If it had to. If that was the best outcome. That's what it wants, always—that's what it's *made* for—the best outcome."

"It did a *great* job this time, didn't it, then?" said Kyr.

"This time Avicenna was its eyes," Yiso said. "And he thought this outcome would be the best one."

Twenty trillion sentient beings, minus however many had been on the sixteen worlds Avi chose to spare. Kyr felt a horrible urge to laugh. The majo were people. What an awful thing to know *now*, when they were nearly all gone.

"You're right," Yiso said. "If the Wisdom could send you back just—just a few minutes. If you stopped Avicenna before he got so far. Valkyr, you're *right*, that's the way out. I would never have thought of—you're so *smart*."

Kyr grimaced. She did not want that shining-eyed look.

"You could change everything," Yiso said. "You could save everyone."

"Okay," said Kyr. "How do I get your machine to do what I want?"

Yiso sent her into the shining pool and brought up their shimmering semicircle of Majodai controls again. They fitted better with the rest of the room than Avi's agoge-style control bank had. "I don't even know what most of these do," Yiso said.

"Wasn't this your whole purpose in life?"

"We live," said Yiso, "a really long time. Leru said I wasn't ready."

"How old are you, anyway?"

"Twelve."

"*Twelve*."

"No, I forgot to do the conversion," Yiso said. "I don't know, your year is a weird length. Fifteen? Twenty?"

"Never mind," said Kyr, abruptly too tired to care. She was *so* tired. Tired of this, tired of everything. "Tell me how to make it work."

"You just sort of . . . talk to it," Yiso said. "It listens. It's smart."

"What's the water for?"

"I don't know," said Yiso. "Probably the look of things. My fore-bears were very into the look of things."

Kyr sighed. She tipped her head back so she could look at the node directly. It pulsed gently in its cradle, humming to itself. It was just an *engine*. It wasn't alive.

"Hello?" she said. "Listen to me." She felt stupid. But Mags was dead. She'd snapped Avi's neck, and it had made a small unpleasant sound. "Are you listening?"

And the universe shifted around her.

Kyr stood alone in a void. She could just see enough to make out her own body, her hands and feet. The colorful Chrysothemis clothes were gone. She was wearing her cadet uniform.

"What's this supposed to be?" she said.

The Wisdom answered: *Neutral ground.*

She did not hear the words. She *felt* them. "Hey! Stay out of my head."

A disturbance in the void coalesced into a figure. Kyr recognized it with a sharp jerk of discomfort. "You're dead."

Consider this appearance a mask, said the Wisdom, through the body that seemed to be Leru. *Since you object to more direct communication. What is your desire?*

"Do you know what you've done?" said Kyr.

I have ended the existence of approximately eight million inhabited worlds.

"And that was the best thing to do?" Kyr said. "Isn't that what you're for? Making the universe better?"

Perhaps this will be a better universe.

"You're supposed to know!"

I was given an impossible task at my creation, said the Wisdom. *I was to eliminate suffering and doubt. For approximately eight million inhabited worlds, it is now the case that their people will experience neither suffering nor doubt. Is this better? Who is there who can decide?*

"You decided it!"

I never, said the Wisdom, *made that or any other decision.*

Kyr shut her mouth hard on the next thing she wanted to say. She wasn't here to argue with an alien machine. She had a purpose. "You can turn back time, can't you?" she said.

Incorrect.

"But Yiso said—"

It would be more accurate to say that I am not limited by time. My smallest iteration exists across forty-one dimensions.

"So you *can't* turn back time?" said Kyr, who had no idea what it was talking about.

I am able to make interventions in events which you would perceive as past.

"Fine," said Kyr. "Then I want you to—"

I will not.

"You what?"

I will not, repeated the Wisdom. *I form no judgments, I make no decisions. If you desire change, it is you who must both choose and act. If there is a moment at which you require an action, choose the moment and take the action. I allow all. I decide nothing.*

". . . Why?" said Kyr.

Call it, said the Wisdom, *a moral position.*

Kyr did not understand this at all, but she also didn't care. "Fine," she said. "I want—"

I know.

"No," Kyr said. "It's not what Yiso said. You own them, right? You can tell what they're thinking?"

Ownership is not an applicable concept. I know your desire. It is not the same as Yiso's suggestion. In your position, they would choose a moment just barely past, and take a different action. A swift and simple reconfiguration. But that is not what you want.

"If you know what I want, why did you ask my desire to begin with?"

The Wisdom was almost expressionless, but it made Leru's ears flick, just once.

Manners, it said.

"Do I need to tell you the exact date or the place or—"

No. Only what you want.

"And I just pick the moment," said Kyr. "And then take my action."

Yes. Choose. Act.

"Then I choose Doomsday," Kyr said. "The day the majo killed the Earth."

She had run through this scenario countless times. She had never beaten it. *Mags* had done it—Mags and Avi, working together. But never Kyr alone.

Yet the moment was so familiar it almost felt homelike, as Kyr materialized in a distorted dimensional shimmer on top of the orbital defense platform high above the clouds, the last human standing between the majo forces and the end of the world.

Or no. Not quite the last. Someone else was there.

He was a human commando, with the silver lily pin of Hagenen Wing on his collar. He was badly injured, his hip and most of his leg blasted with majo brightfire, but he was conscious and swearing in one long continuous mutter as he tried to stand. It wasn't going to work, Kyr could see that.

He wasn't even looking the right way. Kyr knew about the cruiser that was about to drop into reality, and the world-killing dart that would come with it. But Aulus Jole had never run this scenario before. He didn't know yet.

He looked much younger than Kyr had ever imagined.

It took him a second to notice her. The pain and the chaos of an orbital battle were probably distracting him. "Who the hell are you?" he said. "Where did you come from?" A beat. "How the hell are you breathing?"

Kyr didn't have a combat mask. She had no idea how she was breathing. She said nothing.

"And what's that uniform supposed to be?" Jole snapped.

"Fuck. Get over here, kid. I need to be up before they spot this platform and knock it out of the sky."

"They won't," said Kyr. They never did, in the scenario. By this point the orbital defenses didn't matter anymore anyway.

"What?" said Jole.

She didn't have anything. She didn't have a weapon. But *he* did. He had *nice* stuff, *good* stuff, an assault rifle as well as his service pistol, a field knife for close work in shipboard environments where only lunatics used projectiles, a transparent combat mask and an earpiece and probably a bunch of visual feeds giving him the shape of the whole battle in the corner of his eye. Kyr didn't have any of that.

And he had a jump hook. Two jumps left, by the reading on the side. Kyr took it off his belt. She tried not to touch him. "What the fuck do you think you're doing?" snarled Jole. He was scared, Kyr saw. He was badly injured and very scared. And he didn't even know.

She thought about taking the weapons as well. But it was okay. She didn't need them. And she thought about killing him, doing it now. He'd made Gaea Station, and shaped it into what it was. He'd signed off on Kyr's Nursery assignment. He'd hurt Kyr's sister.

But she'd already killed two people today, and she'd hated it both times.

Anyway it didn't matter.

"I hope I never see you again," she said.

And she took the jump hook, turning toward the right direction even though it hardly mattered. Majo darts were pouring out of the cruiser that had just flickered into existence. Kyr knew where it was. She knew where the dart was. She knew everything.

Two jumps left. She hit the jump hook's manual release and for a split second fell out of reality. Arctic cold, desert heat—

And she landed one-foot-two on the shell of the Wisdom dart, slim and deadly, adorned with glyphs, bearing its payload of planet-killing bomb.

Kyr knew all the rules from here. She knew the covering panel she had to pry up, the majo fightercraft spitting brightfire as they angled in toward her, the infuriating complexity of the trigger mechanism that had to be unraveled in exactly twenty-seven seconds. But time seemed to slow as she clung to the spiraling dart and breathed, impossibly, air that should not exist. And she heard Avi's sneering little voice in the back of her head: *It is a game, though.* And Mags: *Why shouldn't we have cheats of our own?*

She'd always treated the facts of the scenario as rules to be followed. How stupid, she thought, as the dart whined and began to heat up for atmospheric entry, as her ears popped, as the majo fighters pulled up and away, fleeing back toward the cruiser. How stupid to assume that anything has rules, when nothing in the universe has ever been fair.

One charge left on the jump hook. Kyr lay forward on the dart. She wrapped her arms and legs around it. There was green shadowspace feedback everywhere her fingers touched. The Wisdom was with her. The etched metal strips along the dart's sides were starting to glow white-hot, but to Kyr's bare fingers they felt cool. "What," she said, "no error message? Aren't my actions unwise this time?"

The howling air did not answer her. Kyr laughed suddenly, and the sound was snatched away. So this was what it was like to save the world.

She'd thought it would feel different. Better.

Fourteen billion people. But it was the Wisdom's words that came to her at last, the ancient machine speaking through Leru's mask. *For approximately eight million inhabited planets, it is now the case that their people will experience neither suffering nor doubt.*

Beyond suffering, beyond doubt, Kyr hit the release on the jump hook. It bleated an error message. She hadn't told it where she was jumping to. Even the human body—tough and terrible and terrifying, the one strength the majo had never taken from them—even the human body could not bear more than a few seconds in shadowspace. Kyr, impatient, gave the command again. *Jump.*

And she was gone.

And the dart was gone with her.

For a ghostly fraction of a second she existed somewhere else, somewhere her mind could not process though it tried. She thought—she tried to say—*I win.*

Then, with percussive force echoing all through the complex unreality and microuniverses of shadowspace, the bomb went off.

PART IV

MAGNA TERRA

BULLETIN:
Insurgency on Sinthara has been quashed. A resettlement
program is planned to relieve alien overcrowding.

* * *

BULLETIN:
Singer Romana partners with charity to revive
zunimmer operatic tradition.

* * *

BULLETIN:
Calling explorers, adventurers, peacekeepers—
do you have what it takes to make it in the
Terran Expeditionary?

* * *

BULLETIN:
For the Love of a Stranger—controversial human-alien
drama delivers a heart-wrenching finale, but are we
ready to hear the message?

* * *

BULLETIN:
Admiral Aulus Jole opens up about the Providence
program and his vision for humanity in an
exclusive interview.

* * *

BULLETIN:
Colonists required!
Sinthara is an economic hub and business opportunities
abound. Add your name to the lottery today!

The government of Earth and its colonies—formally known as the Terran Federation, less formally as Magna Terra, Earth the Great—is a self-described democracy. Outsiders, and some human dissidents, consider this an empty label; although human government includes democratic elements (indeed it is hard to find times when humans are *not* voting for something) these are, by and large, window dressing. Democratically elected local councils hold almost no power, and the various parliaments and congresses of the colonies are advisory bodies, not real legislative assemblies. Earth's own chief assembly is famously ineffectual. The fact that some important decisions (such as, for example, the initial declaration of war against the majoda) are left to mass plebiscite should not be taken as evidence of democratic rule. Humans themselves will cynically point out that no popular vote is ever taken unless those in power already know what the answer will be.

The actual operation of power in Magna Terra is best described as a militarized technocratic oligarchy with elements of authoritarian populism: or, as one human historian puts it, *a dreadful international compromise that pleases no one.* It is an accepted truism that nothing would ever have persuaded the infamously tribal human race to unite except the specter of an alien threat. On Earth proper, the Terran Federation must still maintain a light touch in order to avoid offending the powerful nation-states, which continue to wield outsized social and economic influence in day-to-day affairs. With the end of the Majo Wars, there are many humans who feel the Federation has outlived its purpose; and we may live to see Earth's government splinter again.

Nation and tribe are not concepts unique to humanity, of course. All sentients form social units. But the way humans cling to tribal custom and squabble over national interests is astounding for such an advanced species. Never mind conquering the universe: an outsider could be forgiven for feeling surprised that the constantly arguing humans managed to get into space at all.

—*Federation and Other Problems: An Introduction to Human Political Thought,* 3rd ed. [textbook]

CHAPTER TWENTY

ASSIGNMENT

"Well?"

"Well, what?"

"Val. *Vallie*."

"Who told you about *Vallie*?" said Val. No one used that name for her now.

"You did," said Cleo, grinning. "When we got you drunk for your birthday. Then you cried."

Val winced. "Remind me never to drink."

"One more good-conduct mark for Lieutenant Boring, got it. *Well*? What's your assignment?"

"What's yours?"

Cleo straightened up. "Shipboard service. Aboard the *Victrix*. She's not a first-rater anymore, but—"

"Cleo!" A grand old lady like the *Victrix* was the best possible posting for a newly commissioned lieutenant. Six months there and Cleo could take her pick of postings afterward. "Congratulations," said Val. "You earned it. Let me buy you a drink."

She put her arm round Cleo's shoulders to steer her down the promenade to the eatery at the far end, the closest thing to a bar on this ring of Hymmer Station. Colored lights hung over the entrance, bright in the dimness of the evening shift. Hymmer was a hub on the main route from Old Earth to the planet-sized Terran Expeditionary base at Oura, and Cleo and Val were shadowing Secpol—the station's security and policing unit—for their final Academy rotation. They shared an apartment on Ring Six. This part of the station was Ring Three, general social, always full of station residents as well as travelers, not a few of them aliens. One of the main things Secpol did, in fact, was break up interxeno confrontations. People got touchy living in close quarters.

"You want me to drink alone while you sit and contemplate your good conduct?" Cleo said, laughing. "Not likely. You can buy us *both* a drink."

"I'll have one," said Val.

"Vallie."

"Two, and you never call me that again."

"Two, and we'll see where we go from there," Cleo said. "If I'm shipping out on Friday that gives me three days to get really spectacularly laid first. I'm thinking," she pursed her lips, "skinny guy, long hair, good sense of humor, gives incredible head."

"Pretty specific," said Val.

"I'm a woman who knows what she wants," said Cleo.

The eatery was full, but their crisp black-and-navy uniforms got them priority anywhere on the station, and as of this morning they both had full lieutenant's bars on their collars. Cleo was wearing her cap, perched jauntily on top of her dark cloud of natural hair; Val's cap was tucked through her belt. One of the waitstaff started shooing off a table of aliens when she saw the two of them duck through the curtained doorway. Val said, "That's not necessary. We'll sit at the bar."

"We're finished," said one of the aliens, a sinnet with patchy yellow scaling poking out of his polo shirt.

"If you're sure, sir," Val said.

They sat at the table and Val automatically scanned the crowd for trouble; this was a Secpol habit that was becoming second nature. But Ring Three was seldom rowdy at this time in the station's day cycle. Val saw transients with luggage tucked under their tables, a group of obvious students watching some media on a feed at their table and shouting with laughter, and the far end of the eatery cordoned off for what looked like a child's birthday party—mostly human children, with a handful of shy aliens and a knot of chatting parents that included another sinnet. Their waiter was a lirem with a jointed secondary set of forearms. She wiped down the table quickly and jumped when Val said, "Could my friend see your cocktail menu?"

"You never answered my question," said Cleo, when she had a sugary cocktail with an umbrella in it and Val had let herself be coaxed into a whiskey and soda. "I'm for the *Victrix* on Friday. What about you?"

Val paused, just long enough that Cleo started to look worried. Bad assignments happened. The Terran Expeditionary oversaw an intergalactic empire, and as everyone knew, galaxies generated galactic levels of shit, which sooner or later someone had to shovel.

The pause stretched. Val took a sip of her whiskey. "*Victrix.*"

Cleo let out an earsplitting squeal. "Val!"

"That's Lieutenant Marston of the *Victrix* to you."

"I can't *believe* you," said Cleo. "You kept that pretty close."

"Troop movements are confidential, Lieutenant."

Cleo snorted. "You're the worst. God, I thought I was going to miss you so bad."

"You? Miss me?"

"Where would I be without my nemesis?" said Cleo.

"Nowhere near the top of the class," said Val. "I remember your results first year."

"What can I say? I find your soldier robot routine motivating, in an annoying way," said Cleo, and finished her cocktail. She took the umbrella out and stuck it behind Val's ear. Val tolerated this with a raised eyebrow. "Do you practice that look in a mirror?" Cleo asked.

"No comment."

"Oh, look," Cleo said. "*That* waiter has long hair." She flagged the human waiter down and ordered another cocktail.

"But does he give incredible head?" said Val, before he was out of earshot.

Cleo broke down in laughter and then said, "I'll tell you tomorrow. What about you? Anyone caught your eye? Oh, sorry, I forgot. Not your thing, right?"

"Not usually," Val agreed. "But actually I have a date later."

Cleo stared. "A date?"

"That's what it's called, yes."

"You? On a date?"

"Yes, Cleo," said Val patiently. "Me on a date."

"Can I come?"

"Can you come . . . on my date."

"It's just that you don't usually have time for people," said Cleo.

"Hey."

"Your one true rival excepted, of course I'm special. So who are they? Do I know them? Boy? Girl? Enby?" Cleo faked a gasp. "*Alien?*"

"I'm not dating an alien."

"There's nothing wrong with xenophilia," Cleo said piously. "Except, of course, the mental image."

"*Cleo.*"

"No, no, I'm being a dick. If it can consent, go to town. No judgment here. Val, you're dodging. Who is this person?"

Val smiled into her whiskey. "You don't know her. Her name is Lisa."

"*Lisa,*" breathed Cleo. "I love her already. Can I see a picture?"

"No."

"You look amazing," said Val when her date sat down.

Lisa's spacer pallor showed her blush beautifully. She was dressed up for the restaurant, which was the nicest one on Hymmer, up on Ring Seven where the only transients were the very, very rich. It was set inside its own bubble of virtual reality, which surrounded the plaza of tables with a glorious Earth sky and a selection of scenic ocean views. Val hardly ever spent anything from her generous TE salary—she was too busy—so she could afford to splash out.

The wineglasses gleamed in the candlelight. Each table was encompassed in a soft privacy field, so they could hear only quiet murmurs from the other diners. Lisa looked very pretty in a low-cut blue dress with her dark hair loose and curling around her face. She pinked up at Val's compliment. "So do you," she said.

Val had given two minutes of ghastly contemplation to the prospect of a dress and makeup and then gone with her dress uniform, which was navy and gold. She'd spent a while polishing her boots to a glittering shine. She grinned.

"I hope you don't mind if I take the gloves off," she said. "They look good but white gloves and dinner plans are actually a poor combination."

Then there was a silly interlude of being nice to each other while they talked about the menu. Val usually lost patience with silliness quite quickly, but Lisa was different. For some reason, ever since she'd first spotted the spacer girl who worked at the free clinic on Ring Two, she'd felt drawn to her.

"I'm glad you're here," she said, when the waiters had brought her a platter of delicately spiced mushrooms and Lisa a salad fresh from station agriculture. "When I asked you out, I got the impression you were trying to think of nice ways to turn me down."

"I, well," Lisa said. "You are Fleet."

This was what aliens—and nonconformist humans—called the Terran Expeditionary. "Something wrong with a soldier girl?" Val asked, leaning back in her chair.

"I don't . . . well," Lisa said. "This is probably the part where it gets awkward. I don't agree with Fleet. Politically, I mean. I don't think it should exist at all."

Val laughed. Lisa looked so worried. "I get that all the time," she assured her. "From everyone. Some days I feel like the only thing every sentient on Hymmer has in common is they want to tell me I'm a tool of the fascist oppressor."

Lisa had a cute smile, a tiny flash and gone. "But have you ever wondered if you are?"

"Of course," said Val. "I went into this career with my eyes open. But it's a big universe, and at the end of the day, we're the peacekeepers. Imagine if there was no one in charge. It would be chaos. I'm Fleet, as you put it, because I want to be one of the good guys. And if I come across the bad apples—*when* I come across them—you better believe I'll do something about it."

"You're very sure of yourself," said Lisa.

"Is that a problem?"

"No," Lisa said. "No, it's kind of impressive."

"So why did you say yes to a date," said Val, "if you thought I would be a tool of the oppressor?"

"Is it strange to say that I felt drawn to you?" Lisa said. "Like I knew you already, almost. Like it was meant to be."

"No, it's not," said Val. Her mouth was dry. "I felt it too."

The next course arrived. Val took the chance to break Lisa's gaze and turn her hot face away for a second. Something had changed, and even she could feel it. They went on talking about very little—Lisa's job, mostly, since Val's was awkward. Lisa had grown up on Hymmer. She was so modest that when she talked about *studentship* and *giving back to my community*, it took a while to draw out that this meant she had gone from what sounded like a fairly precarious spacer childhood to a full merit scholarship with the Xenia Institute. Her free clinic work on Ring Two was part of a fellowship research placement. In fact, Val had asked out possibly the only girl on Hymmer with a more prestigious academic record than her own.

Lisa got most animated talking about the clinic. There was a lock of dark hair that kept falling into her face when she was speaking, and then she would tuck it behind her ear again. Val watched this and thought about *meant to be.*

She wasn't normally all that interested in romantic relationships. She didn't believe in destiny. Maybe this feeling was what all the fuss was about.

After dinner they went for a walk in the park on Ring Five. There were other people out and about; an elderly couple with a dog, some teenagers throwing the decorative pebbles from the rock garden into the fishpond. "Stop that," said Val to them, and after taking in her navy and gold splendor none of them risked arguing, just sloped off with the affronted air of wronged teenagers everywhere.

"Was that necessary?" said Lisa.

"Sorry, was I being a tool of the oppressor?" Val said, trying not to laugh. "Janitorial staff have to put on waders and fish those out by hand, you know. It takes them hours."

Lisa ducked her head. That curl of dark hair fell forward past her ear. Val watched her own hand reach out and tuck it back with mild surprise. Oh, so that was how it felt to do that. That was how it felt to make someone smile at you with a touch.

"Can I kiss you?" she said.

Lisa bit her lip but Val could see her smile, irrepressible, at the corners of her eyes. "Yes, please."

Val kissed her. It was very nice. Lisa was small, and warm, and Val's hand fitted neatly into the soft dip between her rib cage and her hip. Val felt appallingly happy. She had the assignment she wanted, on a dreadnought doing real and meaningful work on the borders of civilized space; her best friend in the world was going to be there too; and here was Lisa, who had slipped her hand under Val's jacket to get closer as they kissed. It was lovely, which was not a word Val thought often. But it was, all of it. Her life was good, it was beautiful, it was lovely.

And then her work comm went off.

Val groaned and gently pushed Lisa away. "Sorry," she said. "I've got to take this." She sometimes felt like she *lived* with the damn earpiece in. More than once she'd slept in it. She fished it out of her pocket. "*Yes?*" she said. "This had better be important."

Val arrived at the security station on Ring Two in a vicious temper. Lisa had been very sweet about it, but *what* a moment for a yellow alert. Cleo turned up four minutes later, not even in uniform—in fact, Val noticed bitterly, not even in her own clothes. "Fucking

terrorist fuckers ruining my fucking hookup," she proclaimed to
the room at large.

"Ruining my *date*," said Val. "You're late."

"Oh my god, you're in full navies," said Cleo. "You have *got* to
tell me about this girl."

Hymmer's Secpol captain, Harriman, was a former TE marine
who'd fought in the Majo Wars. There wasn't much of the soldier
about him now, unless you counted his size—he was very visibly
a genetically perfected warbreed, a giant of a military man approaching seven feet, with the faint glint in his eyes as he turned
that meant he had a suite of serious sensory upgrades too. He was
a relaxed and thoughtful boss, and he took community engagement seriously, which was the right attitude for the Secpol lead
on a station with a population of seventy thousand permanent
and twelve million regular transient—not counting the aliens.
He was rumored to have a terrifying ex-commando wife, but Kyr
had never met her.

He wasn't relaxed tonight. "We're hunting a xeno terrorist,"
he barked. "You'll be in pairs, all of you—that includes officers
and Academy—going door-to-door through Ring Two Rimside."
There were murmurs; that was the alien district. Even Val, who
wasn't political, knew it would look bad in the kind of media
that nonconformist types—like Lisa—consumed. This had to be
serious, if no one was considering the optics. "Every house, every
shack, look under every goddamn blanket, you understand me?
This intel comes direct from Providence."

Val raised a hand. "What are we looking for? Do we have an
image, or a description?"

"No," said Harriman.

"Species?"

"No. You have what I told you."

More murmuring. This was needle-in-a-haystack stuff.

"We're looking to scare them out," Harriman said. "And to remind Two Rimside that harboring terrorists is a bad idea. Look

for newcomers. Ask hard questions. The individual we are looking for has ties to the Ziviri Jo."

Val stiffened. That was the most dangerous of the xeno paramilitary groups. It was also the one she knew most about.

"Dismissed," snapped Harriman. "Get going. Now."

Going door-to-door in Two Rimside, waking up slumbering sinnet and interrupting lirem mealtimes, frightening the hell out of a zunimmer triad with a fast series of questions that would have been shockingly personal in their own culture, wasn't fun. Val stayed focused, because it was the job, and because daydreaming about your interrupted date was something that could get you killed—even on Hymmer. "Not the time for gossiping," she snapped at Cleo, who kept asking.

"What, are we going to get flailed to death by a zun?" Cleo said. "*Farted* to death by a sinnet grandma? Or—"

"The Ziviri Jo recruits humans," Val said. "I don't want to get jumped by a warbreed renegade because *you* weren't paying attention."

"Fine," said Cleo, and started sulking. Val didn't care. They'd make it up in the morning.

Every house they searched was the same: frightened aliens, the cheap detritus of poverty, and no Ziviri Jo terrorist. Occasionally for variation they got angry humans instead—there were a few in Two Rimside, mostly as poor as their neighbors, but much more likely to be dangerous. One thing Val had learned on Hymmer was that the media thing about alien troublemakers was mostly nonsense. Humans were bigger, humans were more aggressive, and humans were more likely to think they could get away with shit. The xeno population on Hymmer kept their heads down and got on with things. They were waiters and sales assistants, cargo haulers and janitors, here because the TE mandated quality integrated education for all juveniles from recognized sentient species on every station it controlled. They wanted in. Val could respect that.

There were occasional variations on the frightened-aliens routine. Val let Cleo handle the boardinghouse full of missionaries from the Church of All God's Peoples, because the Jesus-for-aliens types always made her uncomfortable. They also arrested a sinnet drug dealer, caught red-handed stuffing his mattress with banned narcotics, and called in backup to take him in. Val could hear Harriman giving orders at top volume somewhere in the background over her earpiece. It was getting on for three in the morning.

Their shift ended just as the lights came up for day cycle, and Cleo and Val stumbled back to report a whole lot of nothing. The Secpol station was full of reporters. Fucking hell, that was Ari Shah with a camera drone trying to corner Harriman. This looked like a shitstorm in progress. "Bed," said Val, extremely grateful that the shitstorm was not her problem.

"You go on," said Cleo. "I've got a hookup to get back to."

"Seriously?"

"He's on an afternoon shift," she said. "And I liked him. Worth a try. See you later."

Val, exhausted, took the lift up to Ring Six alone. Her reflection in the mirrored wall showed her dress uniform looking the worse for the wear, the jacket crumpled and the creases in the trousers almost vanished. She sighed, adding "dry cleaner" to the list of errands she needed to run before she shipped out. Oh, and she needed to get in touch with Lisa. Not now, though; she was probably still asleep.

Ring Six, high-end human residential, was the one below the very upmarket social ring where she and Lisa had had their romantic dinner. Val mostly appreciated it for being extremely quiet. Nothing moved at this time of day except the drones doing street cleaning. She was already undoing the buttons and hooks on her jacket as she climbed the stairs up to the apartment—ugh, she'd sweated through her shirt. Long night. Long, long night.

Shower, bed, then wake up and call Lisa.

But when Val reached her apartment, the front door was open.

The lock was physically snapped out of its socket, and its alarm light was blinking sadly as it hung from the door. Not a professional job, just brute strength. Val could have done it, if she'd set her mind to it. The average alien couldn't. Maybe a heavyset sinnet. But Val didn't think so.

She reached for her comm. She flicked it on and pressed the silent key for the emergency channel. Then she stopped, and turned it over, and took out the battery.

She went into the apartment.

"Max," she said to her brother. He was standing by the couch projecting an air of sheepishness. It was infuriating how he could do that. The least you could do after you betrayed your family and your species to join a gang of alien terrorists—sorry, *freedom fighters*—was have the courage to look committed to it. Max just looked nervous. "What the hell are you doing here?"

"Vallie," said Max. "It's good to see you."

The worst part was that Val had known. She'd known the minute Harriman had said *Ziviri Jo*. Max would have stuck out like a sore thumb in Two Rimside. Anyone looking at his massive form—almost as obviously engineered as Harriman, because their warbreed lineage had always been more visible on Val's brother—would immediately wonder what the hell he was doing in an alien slum. It wasn't much of a leap from there to *dissident* and *renegade* and *criminal*.

"Give me one good reason not to turn you in," she said.

And a voice behind her said, "Max volunteered to help. I am grateful to him for helping me find you."

Val spun on her heel—putting her back to her brother, which was a risk, but not much of one. The speaker was an alien, but not from any species Val had ever seen before. Which made no sense. Val *knew* all the sentient species. She'd learned them specifically for this Secpol placement.

They were bipedal, slender, and poised—Val suspected they

would move fast—with huge grey eyes taking up half their face, a crest of pale flukes crowning their skull, long flexible ears. They were wearing the same kind of clothes as Max, practical travel gear, but they had a long white scarf. The three fingers of one of their elegant hands were tangled in the fringe. The other held a staff—a walking stick?—made of polished wood. The alien wasn't leaning on it, just holding it, casually, by the rounded end.

"Valkyr," they said, softly. "At last."

"That's not my name," said Val. *Valkyr* sounded like one of the names the really creepy Earth-first types gave their kids, the kind of people who were so unpleasant about aliens that it was uncomfortable to talk to them at parties.

"I'm sorry, Valkyr," said the alien, "but whatever you believe just now is simply not true. I need you to know."

They took a long breath, and then gestured with their free hand, a gesture that Val somehow recognized as a *command*. A command for what?

Green unlight flickered; the apartment walls were briefly misty and vague. This was shadow-engine stuff. This was *Providence* stuff. No way should this be happening on Hymmer—about eighty different safety regulations forbade it. Max said, "Yiso, stop!"

The alien screamed, a high shriek. Whatever they were doing was hurting them somehow. But they didn't stop. The whole apartment seemed to shudder sideways for a millisecond, and the alien—Yiso—was trembling, but they repeated in a ragged voice, "I need you to know!"

And Val—

And *Kyr*—

She knew.

CHAPTER TWENTY-ONE

PROVIDENCE

None of this is real. All of this is real.

Kyr shook off Mags's concerned hand on her arm and said the first words she thought of, which were "Excuse me a moment."

Not Kyr's words. She'd never said anything like that in her life. But *Val* had—*Val* had *manners*—and since she'd said it, Kyr seized the chance of escape and fled into the only room in the apartment with a lock on the door, which was the bathroom.

Toilet. Sink. The unspeakable luxury of a waterfall shower, which had taken this apartment into the next price bracket up. Everything cream and grey and nice. Kyr stared at the room in blind horror. She'd cleaned the shower on her last day off. Cleo's hair products were lined up neatly along the side of the sink. *None of this is real.*

All of this is real.

Cleo. Lieutenant Cleo Alvares, of the Terran Expeditionary, Kyr's roommate, her nemesis, her *friend.* Val's memories told Kyr that she'd met Cleo after college, during the first round of officer-selection examinations; that they'd been rivals and then friendly rivals and then friends; that she'd met Cleo's *mother,* her *grandmother,* and the apparently endless parade of boyfriends—*What can I say,* said the Cleo in Val's memories, laughing, *there's too many good ones, I can't choose.*

None of this was real. All of it was real. Kyr picked up a bottle of hair stuff. CURL GOOP, it said. She put it down again immediately, feeling like she'd done something awful.

Kyr's Cleo had her hair shaved down to a regulation fuzz,

because Gaea was cruelly strict about appearances—stricter than the Terran Expeditionary was, or ever had been. Kyr's Cleo had never had a boyfriend, not even one.

And Kyr's Cleo had never been her friend. She could see that now. Cleo had been *stuck* with Kyr; they'd all been stuck with each other, the Sparrows. None of them had been friends. Who knew if they could ever have really liked each other. Gaea made it impossible.

But none of that was real. It had never happened. Gaea Station did not exist.

Kyr—*Val, I'm Val*, she thought, but she did not believe it—went over to the sink, washed her face, and washed her hands. She looked at the mirror. Lieutenant Valerie Marston was twenty-three. Six years older. Her face looked the same, mostly. Her cheeks were rounder. Was she taller? Val had never been through an Agricole failure. She'd never been hungry. *I've never been hungry*, thought Kyr.

None of this was real. All of this was real.

I still have to call Lisa, she thought, and felt a sharp tender ache in her chest. *Lisabel* was here. Kyr had taken her out to dinner, and they'd said nice stupid things to each other, and they'd— they'd kissed. Kyr had never even thought of kissing Lisabel. She did not know how she had managed not to think of it. She put her hand over her mouth. She was trying not to laugh, or scream. Mags in Raingold, blurting *I'm queer* at Kyr like he was expecting to be slapped.

Weird! Me too! Kyr thought, and sat down hard on the floor next to the toilet.

She put her hands over her face and laughed brokenly into them. Imagine if she'd said it. Imagine Mags's *face*.

None of that was real. Real was Val's memories. Mags—*Max*— had never made a confession like that to his sister. He'd never needed to. There was no pressure about *duty to your species* in this universe. There was nothing wrong with wanting who you wanted. Val had never thought twice about it before tonight.

She'd kissed Lisabel—no, that was a Gaean name; the girl Kyr had kissed was called Lisa. She needed to call her. And say what? What could Kyr now say? *I ran away when they gave me Nursery, but I left you behind. I didn't even think—*

That was another world.

Kyr was crying. She didn't know what she was crying about. Everything was fine. It was wonderful. She'd done it, she'd saved the world. She cried for a bit anyway. There was a knock on the locked bathroom door, and her brother's voice said, "Vallie?"

Kyr ignored him.

After a while she took off her uniform and hung it up carefully. She thought about the impossible richness, the *beauty*, of having a whole separate dress uniform that fitted you perfectly because it was yours. She got into the waterfall shower (so much water, and on a space station) and stood naked under the pounding spray. It was so loud that if Mags knocked again she wouldn't hear him.

She cried a bit more, but this time it was because she was thinking about Mags, and specifically she was thinking about watching Mags kill himself in front of her.

Max always was fragile, said Val's memories. Kyr already loathed Val. Her other self was unbearably patronizing. *Val* thought her brother was basically useless. *Val* hadn't been surprised when he ran away and joined the Ziviri Jo because *trust Max to fall for a xeno cult*—which was stupid, which was such a stupid way to underestimate Mags and the way he thought about things. Mags didn't fall for anything. Mags hadn't fallen for Gaea.

And that was just Val's opinions on Kyr's brother. Val on Kyr herself was worse. Having two people in her head, one of them sneering because the other one had never been to school, was so uncomfortable that Kyr started to get a headache. Unless that was the crying.

Shut up, you're fake, she thought, and shoved Val and her school-memories (exams and books and winning at sports and more exams and acing the exams and then college and acing the exams some more) as far away as she possibly could. Then she washed her hair, which was short (short! no regulation ponytail! Val had cut it all off!), and got out of the shower and put on the only clothes Val had left in the bathroom, which were pajamas. Kyr had never owned pajamas in her life. These had green stripes and the shirt had a cartoon picture of a sheep on it.

She looked at herself in the mirror again. She could just about recognize the outlines of Kyr in Val's soft, smug, extremely punchable face. It was her own hard Gaean eyes that were looking back at her.

None of it had ever happened. Except that it had, to Kyr.

She wished she didn't know.

Kyr went back into the other room. She didn't look at Mags, sitting awkwardly on the couch Cleo had picked out, or at Yiso, as out of place standing by the kitchen counter as if a vine had suddenly sprouted from the apartment floor. She went and examined the mess Mags had made of the lock on the front door for a moment, and then jammed it back into place. Trying to use the things Val knew without thinking Val's thoughts was hard, but she managed to get the door to close and seal. The mechanism would need replacing before they moved out. They wouldn't get their deposit back, either.

Those were Val's thoughts right there. *Deposit.* What *was* this life?

Kyr turned back to the others, and felt all over again Val's surprise at the sight of Yiso, visibly an advanced sentient from a species she'd never heard of. *You thought you knew everything, didn't you.* Val was patronizing about aliens too. She did know all sorts of things. She'd listened to zunimmer operas, she knew what language would offend a lirem, she would never dream of taking a restaurant table from a sinnet party unless they were done. She was impeccably polite to Hymmer's alien population. She could afford to be. It was all with that same edge of confident superiority. She didn't even know the majo were people, really, did she.

Of course they're people. Just like everyone else.

But you think you're special. You don't think the humans in Two Rimside are people either. Not people like you. You wouldn't think I'm people, if you met me.

That's different. You're just sad, Kyr heard herself think. *You're sick. You come from a poisonous culture and it made you poison too.*

Shut up!

"Valkyr?" said Yiso softly.

"Why did you do this to me?" said Kyr. Not that she'd rather be Val. She hated Val, possibly, more than she'd ever hated anyone in her life.

"I'm sorry," Yiso said. "I need you."

"I was fine! Everything was fine!"

"This universe is in the process of unraveling," Yiso said. "The Wisdom is broken. Reality is collapsing on itself. I need you to help me."

"You've got Mags," Kyr said. "He's better than I am! You could have left me alone. You could have just—"

"I couldn't bear it anymore," Yiso said, "being the only one who knew."

Kyr stopped. She looked at Yiso, really looked. They looked older, just like Kyr did. They had lost the twitching energy that Kyr remembered from the days in the shack on Chrysothemis, and from the Halls of the Wise. They met Kyr's gaze silently and without flinching, and Kyr swallowed.

"Does he know?" she asked, jerking her head at Mags.

"No," said Yiso before Mags could open his mouth. "I remember what happened. I thought that I should not do more than explain, in case the memory was more than he could bear. I am sorry if that was wrong."

"No," Kyr said. Mags's total quiet confidence picking up that gun. The small entry wound and the splatter of the exit wound. "No. That was right. Thank you." She glanced at her brother out of the corner of her eye. He looked like himself, just like himself, big and blond and handsome. He wasn't saying anything. He was looking at his hands. Kyr couldn't bear it. She flung herself at him.

It was an embrace like an attack. Kyr locked her arms around his broad shoulders. Her fingers curled like claws into his shirt. "Oof," said Mags, but he hugged her back. "Hi, Vallie."

He didn't know. This Mags—*Max*—was *Val's* brother. He'd never run Doomsday. But Kyr clung to him anyway. "I love you," she said. "I love you so much."

". . . You too," said Mags.

Kyr made herself let him go. "Who else is there?" she said to Yiso. "What about Avi?"

"I have found no sign of Avicenna in this iteration of reality," said Yiso. "Gaea Station produced him and shaped him. It is possible that here he simply never existed."

"But everyone's here. *I'm* here. People I knew from Gaea are here."

Yiso said, "Perhaps I have only failed to find him. But this universe is very different. Some circumstances are impossible to re-create. Some people, almost certainly, were never born."

That made Kyr's chest twinge. Weird. She'd *killed* the other Avi, she reminded herself. He'd made himself a monster as terrible as Leru, and for what he'd done, she'd killed him.

Maybe he wouldn't have been as bad, here. He would probably still have been *awful*. Val was pretty awful. But awful wasn't the same as bad.

Then she thought of something else: of Ally. Ursa's son. Jole's son. He didn't exist here. She knew it. *Ursa* did—Ursa was Val's big sister Ursula, Commander Marston of the *Samphire*, whom Val called every Thursday evening to swap career updates. Ursula didn't have a child. Jole had never had the chance to put his hands on Kyr's sister in this reality. It had never happened and none of the consequences had happened either.

Good, thought both Kyr and Val. Kyr was annoyed by Val's memories, but Val was horrified by Kyr's. *Rape—abuse—police—*

prison—oh, she was so stupid. That wouldn't even happen *here*, Kyr thought at her other self. Jole was a famous hero. He was an *admiral*. No one was going to send Admiral Jole of the Terran Expeditionary to prison for anything.

And of course this was better, this was much better, but Kyr still felt strange, thinking about the child in his glasses, doing his art homework by the window, in a universe that had never been.

Then something else hit her and she gave a little yelp of outrage.

"What?" said Mags. "What is it?"

"He *took the credit*!" said Kyr.

"What? Who?"

"Aulus Jole," said Yiso.

"He didn't save the Earth from the Wisdom!" said Kyr. Val had spent her *whole life* celebrating Deliverance Day. She'd been to *parades* with pictures of Jole's *face* carried down the street. She'd written an essay about him for her college application! Kyr was shaking with outrage. Admiral Jole, of the Terran Expeditionary, the man who saved the world from the alien threat. Kyr remembered very clearly the white-faced figure with the brightfire injury shouting at her on the defense platform above the distant blue circle of the Earth. She'd taken the jump hook off his belt and she'd left him there and she'd *beaten* it, she'd *won Doomsday*. "That wasn't him! He didn't even know! It was *me*!"

"What?" said Mags.

"And he knows he didn't do it!" Kyr said. Val had a picture of herself shaking hands with Jole at Academy matriculation on the *wall*. She took it down and threw it on the floor. There was a little tinkle of breaking glass. "He *knows* it wasn't him. He must know—"

Who the hell are you? the injured commando had said. Kyr went still. She tried to remember the matriculation dinner. Val had introduced herself to Jole, who'd smiled and said that a member of the Marston family needed no introduction. Had there been something different about the way he looked at Val? He'd only seen Kyr, on that defense platform, for an instant or two. Had he recognized her? Did he remember?

Admiral Jole's power and influence were built on his heroic status. He'd risen up the ranks at meteoric speed. He had full command of the Providence division of the Terran Expeditionary and its nebulous domain of intelligence—strategy—*technology*.

"It's strange," Yiso said. "Last time I met you, you started breaking things too. It almost feels personal."

Kyr paused. The smashed remains of the photograph frame at her feet suddenly felt rather silly. She remembered as if it had happened a thousand years ago the Sparrows taking the glassware they'd found in Yiso's ship and smashing it. Yiso cringing and tied up, under guard. Val, somewhere inside her, was dying of mortification. *Why were you so vile?*

Kyr bit her lip. "I'm just angry," she said. She stepped away from the glass. She wanted to kick at it, but she was barefoot. "Sorry."

Yiso said, "Not personal, then?"

"Don't *laugh* at me," Kyr said, but oddly she felt better. Mags was looking confused. "I thought you said you explained to him."

"I can't explain things I wasn't there for," Yiso said.

"Oh. Well. Okay. So the first time round the majo destroyed Earth," Kyr said. "And then I used the Wisdom and went back in time and made that not happen, and then Jole took the credit."

Mags looked a bit shaken. "Got it," he said. "Wait—destroyed?"

"Oh yeah," Kyr said grimly. "Now tell me why you're here. You said something about the Wisdom being broken?" That didn't match what Val knew. "There *is* no Wisdom. We captured it and took it down."

"No," Yiso said, "not quite."

Leru Ihenni Tan Yi, hand of the Wisdom, unspoken lord of the fates of the majoda, concluded that the Earth and its human threat should be destroyed. And yet this did not happen.

The Wisdom had not failed, because the Wisdom could not fail; so some mystery was afoot. Leru returned to the Halls of the Wise to study the matter. They were followed by a human strike force, a team of fearsome commandos, deployed from (Kyr knew this, *Val* knew this) the *Victrix* under the command of Admiral Elora Marston.

(*It's been ages since I called Mom,* thought Val. Kyr shivered. She had never had a mother. She did not dare linger over Val's memories.)

No soldiers of the majoda were equal to human soldiers in size, strength, daring, ferocity. Many of the human commandos died as the Wisdom laid traps and warped the winding corridors of its home in its own defense. But in the end—

"They destroyed it," said Kyr. "No more alien machine ruling the universe."

"They did not destroy it," Yiso said. "They took possession of it."

"No."

"This was always humanity's goal," said Yiso. "In the primitive form of the mixed reality generators you once called the *agoge*, they had begun to build their own version of the Wisdom. But it took our creation thousands of years to achieve its greatest powers. Why would you waste time building your own reality warper and setting it to underpin an everlasting empire, if you could just—"

"Cheat?" said Kyr.

"Yes," Yiso said after a moment. "That is a good word for it. Human operatives took control of the Wisdom. They cheated. They stole it."

There was quiet for a moment.

"So what?" said Kyr. "Sounds pretty bad for you, majo. Why should I care?"

"Leru knew they could not defend our home any longer," Yiso said. "I was an infant in the Halls of the Wise; they arranged my escape with the last of their resources, and then they returned to the heart of the majoda and they sabotaged it. I have lived a life in hiding, protected by the sacrifices of the Ziviri Jo, bearing the double memories that define what I am. And the Wisdom still exists and it is *broken*, Valkyr. It cannot be used without terrible cost. You saw—when I commanded it to blur the boundaries of universes in your memory—what it did to me." Yiso screaming, shaking in pain. "And that is the least of it—that affected only me! I tell you, whole galaxies are buckling under the strain of this abuse. Stars are falling in on themselves; worlds are dying, one by one. Not human worlds. Aulus Jole directs the fallout of his failures away from his own possessions. He calls it Providence and it has made him mighty. I beg you to help me stop him. In the hands of my progenitor Leru, the Wisdom was a dreadful technology; and then it was not so damaged, and Leru was not so evil."

"Weren't they?" Kyr said. "Tell it to Earth."

"*Please*," said Yiso.

"What do you want me to do?" said Kyr. "Do you want me to undo it, what I did? Put the universe back the way it was? Because I won't."

Yiso said nothing.

"I *won't*," said Kyr. "So this universe is worse for majo, so what? Why would it be better to go back to one that's worse for us? You don't know my life. You don't know what Gaea Station was. You've lived in hiding? I lived in *hell*."

A pause. "I understand," said Yiso. "I will not ask it of you."

"Good. I wouldn't do it."

"Will you help me stop Admiral Jole?" Yiso said. "Such a person should not have the power of the Wisdom at their disposal."

"*No one* should have that power," Kyr said, and realized it was true as she said it. "Can you finish the job?"

"I beg your pardon?"

"Leru sabotaged it. So it can be damaged. Can it be destroyed?"

Yiso said nothing.

"No more cheating," Kyr said. "It would take thousands of years to build another one, right? Destroying the machine would stop Jole all right."

"It would," Yiso said.

"I'll help you do that," Kyr said. "That's the only thing I'll help with. Otherwise you're just some terrorist to me."

"The Ziviri Jo aren't terrorists," said Mags.

"Oh—*freedom fighters*, if it makes you feel better," Kyr said.

"We're not violent," said Mags. "We've never hurt anyone."

"Oh really? What about—" Val knew a dozen different stories about Ziviri Jo attacks. Some were foiled at the last minute by Providence units. Some were not quite stopped. *Providence is always there, you moron,* Kyr thought at her other self. "Oh, so it was Jole." She licked her lips. "He picks the wrong targets here too."

"Aulus Jole knows perfectly well whom to hurt," said Yiso, "in order to hold on to power and keep his people frightened of him."

"I know," Kyr said. "He hasn't changed."

"I can destroy it," Yiso said. "Will you help me?"

"I will," said Kyr. "Yes."

Kyr swapped the striped pajamas for civvies. She didn't pack anything else; the gorgeous Terran Expeditionary uniform stayed hung up in the bathroom. *You're throwing away your career,* screamed Val in her head. *Report Jole to the authorities and let them deal with it, if he's really that bad.*

The proper authorities, for this, were Providence. Kyr could not understand how any version of herself could be so stupid. "Let's go," she said. "You must have a ship."

"We do," said Mags. He looked surprised somehow.

Kyr paused. "I'm not her," she said. "I'm different."

Mags didn't reply. Yiso pulled their white scarf over their head, hiding their crest and ears. It was a shitty disguise that would fool no one who looked for longer than a second. Kyr thought about calling Lisa before they left, but what would she say? *Hi, I liked kissing you, but for complicated reasons I need to run away and commit crimes, sorry. Also, in another universe I failed you in every possible way and never even noticed, so it's weird now. Bye!*

One person stopped them on the street; a low-ranking Secpol patroller. Thankfully they didn't look twice at Yiso. "Station's on lockdown, I'm afraid," they said politely. "No travel between rings."

Kyr flashed them Val's smile and Val's ID chip. The patroller's lips moved around *Lieutenant Marston* and their expression changed.

"Urgent business," said Kyr. "Need to know. Sorry."

"Of course, Lieutenant," said the patroller. "Apologies. Who are—"

"Need to know," said Kyr again. "Check with Lieutenant Alvares if you need to follow up." It should take Cleo a while to answer her comm if she was in the middle of having sex. "As you were, officer."

"Yes, ma'am," said the patroller.

I would never have been able to do that before, Kyr thought, as she punched in her override codes for the elevator. *I would never have been a lieutenant on Gaea. I would probably never even have made sergeant.* Gaea's strict bioessentialism kept female soldiers out of command posts. It didn't benefit Jole to be fair, so he wasn't.

It benefited him to be unfair, put in the strand of her thoughts that was Val. *It benefited him to have people frightened and set against each other, and it benefited him that no one could really be friends, just like you and the Sparrows weren't friends. As long as you could feel superior to someone, you never thought about how bad things were, and you never supposed they could be any other way. He set it up so everyone felt like that, and then the whole station was superior to Nursery. And they couldn't do anything because they were too busy having babies, and it wasn't the babies' fault; and then if one of them thought of rebellion—well. Nursery women died sometimes, and no one asked questions.*

Ursa was right. He knew what he was doing.

And all he had to do was praise you once or twice and you would have died for him.

Val was precise, clear, *educated*. Kyr hated her more than ever. *Shut up, shut up.*

Hymmer's main hangar was normally filled with cheerful chaos; in lockdown it was empty and silent. Kyr with a sharp little shock recognized Yiso's painted ship, parked in a midsized cradle between two snub-nosed merchant haulers. Secpol clearly hadn't picked it up as weird. It looked just as it had the day she'd first seen it, on Gaea Station, which was the day she'd met Yiso, and the day the assignments had begun.

It never happened, said the ghost of Val in her head. *It wasn't real.*

"Come on," said Mags.

But then Cleo stepped out of the second bank of elevators behind them.

CHAPTER TWENTY-TWO

JOURNEY

"That's your brother, isn't it?" Cleo said. "I knew it."

Kyr turned to face her. Cleo was back in her black and navy uniform. She looked as tired as Kyr felt. Kyr did not want to have this fight.

"We got you drunk on your birthday, and you told me about it," Cleo said, when Kyr said nothing. "And you cried. Then you brought up human renegades last night—did you already know? Val, what's going on?"

"I can't explain," said Kyr.

"We ship out on Friday," Cleo said. "Think about the *Victrix*. Your oath of service. Your *career*."

I'm not your stupid friend, Kyr wanted to snap, except it was lies. She had Val's memories, and Val's precise and educated thoughts. This was Val's world and she'd lived here all her life. *Kyr* was the fake one. She was nothing but a collection of memories superimposed on Val's brain by the Wisdom. Who was to say that any of it had ever been real? How could you prove it? It never happened.

"Who's the alien?" Cleo said. "What are you *doing*?"

"Please don't try to stop me," said Kyr. "I don't want to fight."

Cleo pressed her lips tightly together, thinking. "Tell me what you're doing," she said at last. "I need to know."

"There's no such thing as Providence," Kyr said. "It's the Wisdom, and it's broken, and it's destroying worlds. I'm going to put a stop to it."

"What? No. That's crazy. And why you?" Cleo said. "This doesn't make any sense, Val. I'm calling—"

"We're wasting time," said Mags.

Yiso said, "I'm sorry. This is simpler."

Kyr felt a little shivering ghost of subreal force as Yiso bent the fabric of the universe. They let out a yelp of pain, and a welt opened across the side of their face, bleeding sluggishly. Their blood was startlingly red.

Cleo fell to her knees.

"No, no," Kyr said. "Why *did* you."

Cleo had her hands over her face. She was shaking. Kyr ran to her and skidded to her knees as well. Then she stopped. She didn't know what to do. Cleo gasped for breath. Then she took her hands away from her face and grabbed Kyr. Kyr thought she was about to get hit. But instead Cleo dragged her in hard and fast. *You're my friend*, thought Kyr or Val, and held on tightly. Cleo was crying, with her face in Kyr's shoulder. Kyr wanted to cry too.

"Oh, okay," Cleo said in a choked voice. "That makes a lot more sense."

"You remember—" said Kyr.

"Sparrows," Cleo said. "We were the Sparrows. Oh *God*."

"Cleo."

"Oh God, oh God," Cleo whispered. "Oh fuck. Jeanne. Vic and Arti. Zen—*Lisabel*—oh God. Your date?"

"Yeah."

"Does *she* know?"

"No."

"Thank fuck," Cleo said.

"I'm sorry," Kyr said. "I'm so sorry."

"Well, that's new." Cleo made a weird gurgling noise; a laugh. "The great Valkyr. Our fearless leader. You *left*."

"I'm sorry."

"I've never been so jealous in my life."

"Cleo—"

"Jeanne died," Cleo said. "Oxygen failure in one of those shitty old darts. The week after."

"Cleo—"

"Someone reported Arti and Vic for being queer. They sent Arti to Nursery. You never reported them. They weren't hurting anyone."

"Cleo—"

"They beat me half to death for letting you go," Cleo said. Her eyes were dark and wet, staring into a world that never was.

"It's not real," Kyr said. "*This* is the real world. This one."

"I swore I'd kill you if I ever got the chance," Cleo said. "You bitch, Valkyr. You horrible bitch."

"I'm sorry," Kyr said. "I'm so sorry."

Cleo grabbed her again, even tighter. "Providence," she said. "It's Jole you're after, right? It's *him*."

"Yeah."

"Good," Cleo said. "I'll cover for you. Give him hell from me."

"I—What?"

"I said what I said." Cleo stood up. She wiped her eyes. Her expression was set into something halfway between a snarl and a smile. "Hey, you," she said. "Majo. Whatever your name is."

Yiso said, "Yes?"

"Fuck you," Cleo said. "Fuck you, I hope you die. Go if you're going, Valkyr. I'm not stabbing you this time. I didn't want to stab you last time either."

"I know," Kyr said. "I . . . Me too."

"Aren't we touching?" Cleo's laugh was a hard rattle that Val had never heard from her friend, a Gaean laugh. So now there were two of them, refugees from another universe. "Come with us," Kyr said impulsively.

Cleo went still. "You didn't say that last time."

"I should have said it," said Kyr. It was the truth. "I shouldn't have left you behind."

She'd left all of them, the Sparrows. She'd told herself it was about Mags, about Strike, about finding the right mission for herself. With Val sitting cold and unimpressed somewhere behind her eyes she knew that was a lie. She'd been horrified and she'd been afraid and she'd grabbed at any excuse to run away. Cleo had said it at the time, hadn't she? *Traitor.*

Kyr had been a traitor, to Gaea Station and to her mess. She was only sorry for the second one.

"Yeah, right, imagine," Cleo said. Her mouth had taken on a cynical little twist that Val had never seen on her friend. "You could have gone round the wings collecting us all up. You always liked to have us where you could see us."

"You were *right there*," said Kyr.

"The picture of you trying to drag me kicking and screaming aboard an alien ship while I tried to stab you some more—" Cleo said.

It was actually very funny. "Yeah," Kyr said. "I should have done that. I should have tried."

Cleo put her hands over her face. "My *career*," she muttered. "My *life*. You drive me round the fucking twist, Valkyr, do you know that? All right. I'm with you."

Yiso's painted ship had not changed between universes, but Kyr had. Thanks to a shadowspace navigation class Val had aced at some point, she now knew that the way it went skimming in and out of reality in galaxy-length hops was technically impossible. This made her head hurt, and every time the ship jumped she felt the cold ache in her teeth even through the shielding.

She told Mags and Yiso she needed sleep. "We were up all night hunting you two," added Cleo. "Thanks for nothing. Wake us when it's time for whatever alien terrorist crimes we're committing."

Kyr felt a wobble of gratitude that Cleo was there, which awfully wanted to come out as tears. Kyr had never cried this much. She wasn't a crier. Cleo gave her a sideways look when they'd left Mags and Yiso in the ship's main room and claimed the tiny bunkroom for themselves. "I refuse to pat you on the shoulder," she said.

"You're as bad at this as I am," said Kyr.

"Should have brought your girlfriend."

"She's not my—"

"Right," Cleo said, and then, quieter, "How was your date?"

"Oh, you know," Kyr said. "Interrupted."

"Fine, don't tell me."

The first question had sounded like Val's friend; the reaction was all Kyr's Cleo. Kyr sat on the floor—the bunk was too low for comfort—and looked at her hands.

"I always thought I just," she said, "didn't have, you know. Feelings."

After a moment Cleo said, "Are you telling me you didn't know you were queer for Lisabel?"

Kyr looked up at her sharply.

"Because I will laugh. I will laugh and then I will scream, which will scare your pet majo."

"You knew?"

"Valkyr," said Cleo caressingly, "you are *so* fucking obtuse."

"Excuse me?"

"Living with you was like living with, I don't know, a fucking *horse* that has," Cleo put her hands flat on either side of her eyes, "what are they called, blinders, you know, so they don't notice anything that scares them. Or like living with a boulder in a house on an incline. What's Kyr going to do, let's think, she's going to *roll downhill.*"

"Cleo," said Kyr, starting to laugh.

"I can't believe other me had the option of *not* living with you and she decided to do it anyway," Cleo said. "I used to *fantasize* about not living with you. Imagine no Kyr to go—it's lights-out! No arcade time, that's for losers! You can do better than that if you try! All for humanity, girls!"

"I don't sound like that!"

"You do. You *did*," Cleo said. "The very best space fascist girl scout of them all."

Kyr stopped laughing. "I'm sorry."

"Why? I was right there with you," Cleo said. "The only thing that pissed me off was that you were better at it than me. Guess some things are universal constants. The speed of light and how much I want to *beat you*."

Kyr looked down. There was nothing she could say. They'd both meant to sleep, but neither of them made any move toward the bunks.

"I keep thinking of more things," Cleo said eventually. "Do you know what I mean?"

"Yeah," said Kyr. She knew. Ursa had been five years old when her mother, that other Admiral Marston whom Kyr would never know, was murdered. Ursa had slept in Jole's rooms since she was five years old. And Jole had also watched Kyr grow up.

Kyr hated thinking of things.

"They named me *Cleopatra*," Cleo said, looking down into her own lightless well of memory. "The one vaguely African woman's name in their creepy Norse-Roman pantheon, I guess. But here my dad picked Cleo, so." She laughed, horribly. "God, knowing what I know—it must have been a really hard problem, trying to pick between *being racist assholes* and *losing a warbreed bloodline*. I was so afraid they'd put me in Nursery. The whole time, I was so afraid. There was one other Black kid who I guess almost had to be my half brother. Two years down in Jaguar mess. He doesn't exist here, as far as I know. And they named *him* Severus, of course." At Kyr's blank look, she added, "God, you really did just no pre–First Contact history at all, did you. Septimius Severus. Black Roman emperor. There were a couple."

"Oh," said Kyr.

"Yeah. I never spoke to him. I also hated you for having a brother," Cleo said. "I hated you for everything."

Kyr's chest hurt. She said, "I'm sorry."

"And you hated the majo for everything," Cleo said. "Funny.

First level of the agoge, the lesson is *pick your targets*. And did we? Did we hell."

"Are you still—here—" said Kyr, and stopped, because Val in her thoughts was appalled by how rude she was being. You didn't ask someone if they were a warbreed.

"Don't look it, do I?" Cleo said. "Did I ever show you a photo of my dad?"

"No."

"No, of course I didn't. He was the last wave. Right before the protests finally gathered enough momentum for the whole thing to be shut down. You're, what, third generation? I'm second."

"I didn't know," said Kyr.

"Not something I talk about," said Cleo. "Dad was seven foot two and could break an iron bar in half with his bare hands, but that wasn't the main thing. In his generation they were going for senses. Genetic perfection instead of nanite upgrades. He could hear bat calls, track by scent, see into infrared and ultraviolet—hey, want to see a trick?"

Kyr, on prompting, passed over her stunner and her wallet. Cleo added a roll of mints and a squeezy ball that she had in her pocket, her own stunner, and a wicked-looking combat knife that Kyr had never seen before. She unsheathed it. "Dad's," she said, to Kyr's look. "Watch this."

She tossed the ball in the air. And then the stunners, the wallet, the mints, the sheath, the *naked knife*: an absurd random circle of objects, perfectly juggled. Kyr's heart was in her mouth when she saw the blade go into the air. It seemed impossible that Cleo would not lose a finger. But she caught and tossed the tumbling knife as if it were no more dangerous than the squeezy ball.

Kyr didn't dare to speak. Cleo laughed at her expression. Her hands moved. Suddenly things were soaring through the air in all directions. Kyr's stunner and wallet flew back to her one after the other, a catch she nearly fumbled. The other objects were tossed precisely into corners or onto bunks, and the sheath came back into Cleo's hand. She held it up. The naked blade fell neatly into it and slid home.

"What the fuck," said Kyr, which was also Val's reaction.

"That's this Cleo's party trick," Cleo said. "She doesn't do it anymore. I don't. But it was the biggest thing they were going for with Dad, the hand-eye. And I didn't get the height and I didn't get the strength but *boy* did I get that. You also don't want to play against me in any game that involves hitting a ball in a direction of your choice. Tennis, squash, baseball, I will destroy you." She tossed the sheathed knife high into the air with her right hand and caught it with her left, and then it went back into a pocket. "It's weird, though, isn't it?" she said. "Baseline human hand-eye coordination is already streets ahead of most majo. Six weeks of training plus a decent targeting system will turn basically any idiot off the street into a good enough shot for government work. What was the *point*?"

For the first time in her life, Kyr listened to what was underneath the brittle edge of anger in Cleo's voice. She said, "What . . . happened to your dad?"

Cleo paused. "You *have* changed," she said first. Then another, longer pause. "Neuromuscular degenerative disease. He was dead before he was thirty-five. And you know what, no one can *prove* it was a side effect."

Kyr was horrified. "Are *you*—"

"Don't know," Cleo said. "Ask me again when I'm thirty-five."

There was a short, horrible silence.

"I'm sorry," Kyr managed to say at last. "I'm so sorry."

"Yeah, well, what can you do," said Cleo. "Gaea's not here, but Gaea *came* from here, didn't it."

Kyr nodded. That was the truth. This world was so much better. But it wasn't, exactly, different.

Then she thought of something else. "But you shot at me," she said. "When I was running away, in the Victrix hangar. You shot at me and missed."

Cleo folded her arms and gave her a pointed look.

". . . Oh," Kyr said. "Right. Thank you."

"You want to know something? You are the first person to ask me that question," Cleo said. "They sat me down and interrogated me after you'd gone. Every single decision I made. They did not want to lose you and they wanted someone to blame. But you know what? No one said, *Hey, Cleopatra, how come you missed that shot.* I thought they would. They had my training scores and range records any time they wanted to check. But not once did it occur to those sons of bitches that I was *better than that.*"

Kyr slept for several hours, disturbed now and then by the shadowspace distortions as the painted ship skimmed across the universe like a stone spinning over water.

When she woke up Cleo was still asleep. Mags was there too, snoring softly on the opposite bunk. Kyr rolled over and looked at him for a while. Artificial gravity, she thought, in a ship barely bigger than a fighter dart. The blanket was crumpled up under Mags's muscular arm. He looked like himself: huge, blond, perfect, all Gaea's ideals written across a human body. *I watched you break*, Kyr thought. *I watched you die.*

She swiped her arm across her eyes and got up.

"There's human-appropriate nutrition paste on the counter," said Yiso when Kyr came into the ship's only other compartment.

"Yum," said Kyr sarcastically.

Yiso didn't turn around to watch her eat. Their ears weren't angling to catch the noises she made. They'd never been so still around Kyr before. When she'd had as much of the nutrition paste as she could take, she folded her arms and leaned against the counter and stared at the back of their head. They didn't seem concerned. "This is new," she said. "You used to be scared of me."

"I knew less about you then," Yiso said.

"You think you know me now?"

Yiso's ears moved: flick, flick. They said nothing.

"Seriously?" said Kyr. "*I* don't even know me."

"I apologize. I am sure you are having a complicated time."

"Is it like this for you? Are there two of you?"

"I was aware of the alternate Yiso's memories from very early in my life," Yiso said. "I have lived more years than I have been alive. All of it was me. There is only me." They turned around. "There is only you, as well," they said. "There aren't really two of you."

"Ugh," Kyr said. She didn't like the thought of Val being real. "I liked you better twitchy."

"Really?" said Yiso. "You would prefer to see me frightened and injured? Max is asleep. I can't stop you."

They still had that red welt on their cheek from whatever they'd done to give Cleo her memories. "*Ugh,*" said Kyr. "No. Leave me alone."

"You see?" Yiso said. "I do know you."

There was something about their silvery gaze that Kyr couldn't bear. She looked away. "I broke your pretty glasses," she said. "I kicked you in the ribs."

"You rescued me from certain death. You saved my life."

"It wasn't about you! It wasn't even my idea!"

"You set my broken bones."

"Because they were *annoying* me."

"You listened to me talk. You heard me, even though I was a stranger and seemed monstrous to you."

"I didn't give a shit about you. I left you to Avi the minute I knew where Mags was."

"You were angry with Avicenna for how he treated me."

"I was *confused*," Kyr said. "I was angry with everything."

"You changed," Yiso said. "You walked in time. You met me in the Halls of the Wise before I ever left, and you treated me as a friend."

"That was real?"

"It was to me."

"But—no. You weren't important," Kyr said. "You never were.

It was never about you. It was about me, and Mags, and humanity, and you, you were just *there*. I didn't—I never—"

Yiso said, "You never what?"

"Cared," said Kyr, and then she put her hand over her mouth. *I just lied*, she thought, staring at the slender alien with its strange body, its long hands and delicate ears and high crest. *I'm lying. It's a lie.*

"Oh," Yiso said.

"Sorry," Kyr said, letting her hand drop. "If that hurts your feelings or something."

"It's all right," Yiso said. They turned away from her again. Their ears and crest were still. No miserable drooping, so it was fine. Everything was fine.

"Just so we're clear," Kyr said.

"Of course," said Yiso. "It's all right, Valkyr. I don't need you to care about me. I need you to care about—injustice."

Kyr's breath caught.

"And I know you will," Yiso said. "I know you do. Otherwise you wouldn't be here." There was a strange note in their fluting voice. Kyr thought it was happiness.

"Mags—*Max*, whatever—is as tough as I am," she said after a moment. "If you needed muscle, you had it. Cleo and I are both *good*, but we won't make that much difference."

"I wasn't looking for muscle when I searched for you," Yiso said. "Jole controls the power of the Wisdom. That makes him unstoppable. So what I needed—what I *wanted*—was someone else unstoppable."

"Me?"

"I know you won't surrender, Valkyr," Yiso said. "I know you won't let him win. Even if I fail—if I survived for no reason, and the sacrifices of the Ziviri Jo were for nothing, and everything I am is worthless—even if the world ends—"

They paused.

"You never give up," they said finally. "That's why I wanted you. I know you won't give up."

Kyr licked her lips. No one had ever said anything like that to her before.

"You see, Valkyr," Yiso added, "I do know you. Have you had enough sleep? Enough food?"

"I—Yes?" Kyr stared at their straight back and straight ears and high crest and felt stunned. Wait, was that all? Were they not going to talk any more?

"Good," Yiso said. "Wake the others. We're here."

CHAPTER TWENTY-THREE

THE HALLS OF THE WISE

The Halls of the Wise. Kyr had only seen the inside, in the Wisdom's scenarios. From the outside it was something like a space station and something like a pearlescent amalgamation of shells. It was sitting in stable orbit around a grey planet, half illuminated by the light of the nearest star. Yiso watched the screen with a weird intensity. "What's the planet?" said Kyr.

"Earth," said Yiso, and then, "Oh, translation. Home. The homeworld of the zi."

"It looks a bit shit," Kyr said.

"It's dead," said Yiso. "No one has lived there for millennia. But it has . . . emotional resonance." Their crest dipped and then lifted again. "It's not important now. We need to time our approach carefully. Max?"

Mags stepped between them, which was when Kyr realized how close she had been standing to Yiso. "Right," he said. He sounded nervous.

"I can attempt it," said Yiso, "if you would rather—"

"With your reaction times?" Mags said. He forced a grin. Kyr caught Cleo's eye; she looked grim. "Nah," said Mags. "Better Vallie than you, and she's never even practiced. Give me the controls."

Yiso wordlessly stepped back, and a shimmering set of symbols appeared in the air around Mags. "Bigger," said Mags, and the shapes grew till they were spaced far enough apart for his big human hands.

He gave Kyr an awkward smile. "This bit should be kind of fun," he said.

The viewscreen in front of him was full of the coagulated mass of the Halls of the Wise. Behind it, hidden in its star-shadow, an angular shape like a shark in the deeps was rising. The greenish glints of shadowspace distortion flickered around its hull. Its size was impossible to understand at first. The shadow just kept getting larger. As the Halls of the Wise turned past it and starlight flared across the dark metal surface of the dreadnought, Kyr got a glimpse of the name painted in gigantic white letters on its nose. TRIUMPHALIS.

"That's the flagship of Providence Wing," said Cleo.

"Jole," said Kyr. "That's Jole."

Val's memories knew the ship, one of the very latest out of the shipyards of Oura, a plum assignment for any career-minded TE officer. She loomed behind the Halls of the Wise, silent and watchful, with a sensor range three solar systems wide and a full complement—Kyr knew—of dimensional traps, Isaac slugs, distortion lances, and fighter darts.

"How hasn't she seen us yet?" she asked.

Mags said, "She thinks we're a rock. But we're about to start moving wrong." He breathed in, and out. "Okay. Here we go."

Afterward Kyr could never remember it without feeling again the bright bleak awe of watching the dreadnought come alive. The painted ship had no defense but speed and movement, and against it was arrayed the might of Earth victorious. It was a strange double feeling, to be watching the merciless trajectories of the slugs, the wild unexpected meshes of the dimensional traps, the magnificent and deadly lances of shadow distortion, and thinking at once *please no* and *fuck yes*.

And Mags, sweat dripping down his temples, treated the deadly obstacle course like—a game, thought Val; the agoge, thought Kyr. His jaw was clenched but he started to grin at some point and didn't stop; he talked to the painted ship the whole time he steered it in maddening twists and hops, slipping in and out of shadowspace around the dreadnought's assaults—*good*, he said, *that's it, beautiful, come on*—

The dreadnought's commander gave up on the Isaac slugs, which were too slow, and sent out a wing of fighter darts. They were a slim sharp-nosed design Kyr had never seen, still recognizably descended from the darts she'd grown up with, the decades-old defenders of Gaea. The darts in the swarm were fast, faster than their mother ship, and infinitely maneuverable; a hit landed on the painted ship for the first time, sending a jolt through it and making Yiso cry out.

Mags snarled, "*Nice try*," and threw them into a shadow jump. The viewscreen blurred, re-formed: they were on the other side of the *Triumphalis*. The darts started to pop into existence around them a moment later, but they were slow and out of formation. Mags whooped and reangled their ship into a mad dive. Yiso said urgently, "Watch the planet! We're not—"

"Neither are they," said Mags, still grinning, and behind them the fighter darts that had been foolish enough to give chase were falling back away from the white-hot danger of an unplanned entry into a planet's gravity well. Now the Halls of the Wise were between them and the *Triumphalis*'s weapons arrays, and the fighter wing was pulling away, trying to regroup.

"Yeah!" yelled Mags. "Get me an entrance!"

Kyr had never seen him enjoy winning so much. She'd never seen him enjoy *anything* so much. Was this what Avi had been to him, in another lifetime, when they'd played through Doomsday like it was just another game? Yiso closed their eyes to concentrate, and the red welt on their cheek sluggishly opened up again as they manipulated the Wisdom. The geography of gravity began to assert itself: the pearlescent agglomeration of space station now seemed to be directly above them, the grey planet below. A dark gape of a hole barely bigger than their ship opened in the shell-coils overhead. Mags steered them straight up through it, and it slammed closed behind them.

"Wow," said Cleo, and she didn't even sound sarcastic.

Kyr caught Yiso as they stumbled. There was blood on their face. It was coming from their eyes. They fell into her and clung for a moment or two.

"Oh fuck," said Mags, when he'd landed the ship. "Are you okay?"

Yiso opened their eyes. One was still silvery grey; the other was bloodshot and cracked-looking. "I can manage."

"Can you see?" said Kyr.

"I rely on vision less than you do," Yiso said, which Kyr understood to mean *no*.

Kyr and Cleo took point. Mags brought up the rear. The only weapon Kyr had was her Secpol stunner. Cleo tossed hers to Mags. In her own hand she carried her father's combat knife, unsheathed, the cross guard sitting snugly across her hand. "Four against Providence. Well, three and a half. And we've nothing with range," she said. "Majo, how are you in a fight?"

"Poor," said Yiso.

"Well, maybe you can traumatize any hostiles with bad memories from the next reality over," Cleo said. "Make it really nasty. We'll take them down while they cry about their mothers."

Yiso said nothing. Kyr didn't try to shut Cleo down. She understood.

Besides, it might work.

Yiso had their stick, which Kyr knew could be a weapon, but they were using it as a walking stick. The three humans kept having to adjust and then adjust again for how slowly they hobbled along the twisting corridors of the Halls of the Wise. "Mags, if we have to run," Kyr murmured, "you pick them up. We'll cover you."

"Got it," Mags said.

The Wisdom's home was—old, Kyr thought, and once she'd seen it, it was everywhere; the crumbling and softened edges of walls, the spiderweb cracks in the pearlescent floors. It was different from the brash confident glow of Hymmer Station, and different again from the jury-rigged defiance of Gaea. Dim yellow lights illumined the corridors in patches, and shadows fell curved and strange from the angles of the walls and ceiling. Some of the doors were too low. Yiso was perfectly fine, and Cleo was more or less all right, but both Kyr and Mags had to duck.

"It wasn't like this in the scenarios I remember," she said to Yiso.

"This is one of the abandoned sections," said Yiso. "It has not been maintained in centuries."

Kyr looked at the crumbles and cracks of the walls again, and thought uncomfortably of the nearness of cold space. Val had spent her whole life secure in the supreme safety of a planet, or else confident in human mastery of the void. But Kyr had grown up without a sky, had done her Oikos and Systems rotations in repairs and maintenance, had commanded her mess to perfect scores in every emergency drill. She caught Cleo's eye and they exchanged grimaces.

"We should be wary," Yiso remarked calmly. Their ears were pricked and alert. The bloodshot eye made Kyr wince every time she looked at it. "As we approach the center we will almost certainly encounter agents of Providence."

"No shit," said Cleo, at the same time as Kyr's "Understood," and Mags's "Got it," and the three of them all shared a look over the top of Yiso's head.

Yiso led them through winding corridors into an area Kyr recognized with a sense of dislocation: the long halls of storerooms where she'd once told Yiso they were doing their stick dance wrong.

Providence had torn the place apart. Yiso said nothing as they went past rooms where broken fragments of furniture, made of biological materials Kyr had no frame of reference for, were heaped up like the corpses of strange animals; past rooms where heaps of ripped fabric were strewn across the floor, past rooms where elaborate mechanisms had been taken to pieces and scattered, past rooms that were nothing but a rainbow array of smashed crystals. "What is all this stuff?" Cleo asked.

"The remains of several civilizations," said Yiso. "Unimportant now. We're close." They quickened their step. Kyr put out a hand to keep them from hastening past her, and touched their thin shoulder. Yiso looked at her.

"Remember," she said. "We're expecting company."

But there was no one, despite the chaos all around them which said that humans *had* been here. There was no one, in the high storerooms, in the long white hall where water ran down one wall and caught the light strangely, in the twisting corridors marked incongruously with orange and black hazard tape and posted signs in T-standard. OFF-LIMITS. DANGER. NO ACCESS WITHOUT AUTHORIZATION.

Yiso stumbled and couldn't get up. "It's awake," they said. "It wants me. It wants me."

"What do you mean?" said Kyr.

Yiso panted shallowly for breath and did not answer. Kyr exchanged a look with Mags, and then she picked Yiso up and put them over her shoulder. They were light for their size, and warmer than she expected. Mags silently moved up to Kyr's place next to Cleo.

"Oh," said Yiso a few moments later, squirming. Kyr adjusted the weight. They'd lifted their head. "This is very high up."

"Which way?" said Kyr, hoisting them a little more squarely over her shoulder.

"*Ifor*," said Yiso, a word in a language Kyr didn't know, and then, "Right. Right."

They walked past a DANGER OF DEATH sign in T-standard and then another that said CLEARANCE L8 AND ABOVE. Here the Providence investigators had installed a security door with a fingerprint pad. As they came near, something crackled violently and a greenish sublight flickered. The door opened by itself.

There were two branching paths almost immediately past the door. "Now which way?" said Kyr.

No answer. Yiso was a limp weight on her shoulder, breathing rapidly.

"There's a scenario that goes like this," Cleo said. "Level Nine. Remember?"

Kyr nodded. She knew the one Cleo meant. You had to get your team through a booby-trapped maze haunted by alien drones. You won as long as there were at least four survivors. The key was to go carefully, and for the best of them—Kyr, Cleo, and Jeanne, it had always been—to scout routes for the rest.

"They're dead weight," said Cleo, nodding at the alien. "You two stay here with them. I'll scout."

They waited by the security door for Cleo to come back. A few minutes went past before a sound startled both of them; a creak. They turned to watch the door close by itself. Another crackle of greenish shadowspace feedback danced through the air and was gone. Kyr remembered Val's lectures. *Scioactive areas are subject to unpredictable spacetime distortions.*

"Feels haunted," said Mags quietly. It was the first thing he'd said in a while.

"It's just a shadow engine," said Kyr. "A broken one."

"Vallie," said Mags. "What the hell are we doing here?"

"We can do this," Kyr told him.

"You're really not her."

"Oh," Kyr said. "No."

"I sort of wish you were," said Mags, and grimaced. "Sorry."

"No, I get it," Kyr said. "I wish you were my Mags." She'd been trying not to think about it. It wasn't like with Cleo. There was no shared understanding, no mutual store of horrors to call on. This young man's name was *Max*. He was twenty-three. He'd grown up on Earth with Val. He didn't remember Gaea Station. He hadn't lived Kyr's life.

And Kyr was glad, of course. She wouldn't wish her life on anyone. She wouldn't wish *Mags's* life on—

"What happened to him?" Mags said. "Yiso's always mysterious, but—"

"Killed himself," Kyr said, fast as if that made it easier. "Bullet to the temple."

"Oh," said Mags. "Right. That makes sense."

"Yeah?"

"Yeah," said Mags.

"Great," said Kyr. "I'm so glad it makes sense."

Mags said, "You sound like her."

You sound like him. "Drop it," said Kyr. "Do you think Yiso's okay?" The majo's breathing was a thin regular whistle.

"Hard to know. Hope so."

"How long have you known them?"

"Nearly a year," Mags said.

It was three years since Val's brother had left to join the Ziviri Jo. Kyr wondered what he'd been doing the rest of that time. She didn't ask.

When Cleo came back, it was down the branch opposite to the one she'd left by. "It all links up," she said. "Lots of abandoned stuff. No people. I found what looks like a choke point and I'm guessing the heart of it all is past there. Come on."

Yiso came round, wriggling on Kyr's shoulder, two turns of the maze later. She set them gently on their feet. Yiso leaned into her steadying grip a moment, and said, "Thank you." Then they pulled away.

They reached the choke point Cleo had found. It was set up with barriers and a security station, empty. There were human-sized desks and chairs in rows visible in an opened storeroom on the other side, and a whiteboard hammered into the pearly wall with what looked like several different people's handwriting on it, annotating a crudely drawn map.

"Where is everyone?" said Kyr. "This place ought to be crawling with Providence."

"Right," Cleo said, "with more jumping over from the *Triumphalis* by now."

"The Halls resist the sort of minor manipulation of shadow-space involved in jump hook technology," Yiso said.

"And the ones who were already here?" said Kyr. "Look at this place. Where *are* they?"

"I don't know," Yiso said.

"It's not a bad thing if we don't have to fight," said Mags.

"It *is* a bad thing if whatever the broken Wisdom did to them happens to us," said Kyr. "Yiso. Find out."

"Vallie, they're hurt."

"She's quite right, Max," Yiso said. "The necessity is hard, but not unreasonable. Give me a moment."

"I can carry you again if I have to," said Kyr.

Yiso closed their eyes in concentration and didn't answer. Kyr watched them, jaw clenched, waiting to see another welt open up in their skin, or for the bloody cracked effect to spread to their other silver eye. She'd seen Yiso hurt so many ways now. It was hard to imagine being the person who had kicked them surreptitiously under the eyes of the amused Victrix guards. It was hard to imagine being Valkyr of Gaea and Gaea alone, with her cold and narrow little world, her total indifference to pain.

After a moment Yiso gasped and opened their eyes.

Both were silvery-bright again. As Kyr stared the welt on their cheek healed to a line, and then was gone, not even a scar.

"Impossible," they said. "Follow me—quickly!"

"No," said Cleo, not moving. "Sting in the tail, Kyr."

Sting in the tail was what you learned in higher-level agoge scenarios: that there would always be a surprise, a second wave, a problem you hadn't thought of the first time. Kyr paused. She was good at these, and this one wasn't *hard*. Humans had broken into the Halls of the Wise before, and the dreadnought had seen them arrive.

"The *Triumphalis*," she said. "If they can't shadow-jump, they'll break in from the outside. And they have maps. Whatever we do we're going to have them on top of us."

"But look," said Cleo, "a nice narrow defensible position already set up. And here." She went to the security station and reached under a shelf, fishing out what looked to Kyr like a modified service rifle. "Loaded," she said, checking. "And not even bio-locked. Tut tut. Looks like this is me, then."

"Are you sure?"

"How many of these scenarios have we done, Kyr?" Cleo asked. "I didn't come with you because I fancied a jaunt across the universe with a friendly majo. The alternative is *you* could stay here and I'd supervise the civvies"—it was clear she meant Mags as well as Yiso, and she wasn't wrong, not about *Max*—"but I'm a better shot. So, hey, good luck killing the Wisdom. Give it a kick for me. See you if we live."

They left Cleo with her rifle waiting by the security station and followed Yiso swiftly through the maze. Yiso was running at what looked to be their top speed, which was a comfortable jog for Kyr and Mags. "Did you find out where Providence went?" Kyr asked.

"There were twenty in the Halls. Nineteen were transported without warning to an unsettled habitable world four galaxies away," Yiso said.

"Nineteen?" Kyr said. "What about the twentieth?"

And then Yiso brought them out into an open hall that had the same quality of extraordinary distance crammed into tiny space as the sunken control chamber of the Wisdom node on Chrysothemis. At the heart of the hall was an expanse of water that moved in ripples under the touch of a wind Kyr could not feel. Hanging down from the ceiling, high as a cliff, was the cradled shape of a gigantic shadow engine, swaddled in its own greenish light, letting out soft pulses so that the whole room seemed to throb to its heartbeat. Around it like a map of the stars shone the intricate machinery of the Wisdom's heart.

All around the pool of water the lights of majo controls glimmered in the air, so many it seemed impossible that anyone should be able to understand them all, let alone manipulate them.

And the person who was there was indeed ignoring them. Instead he sat at the water's edge, curled up on himself with his left foot resting on his right thigh and the tablet he was working on balanced against his foot and his knee. His red hair was short and curly. His glasses had metal frames. His uniform jacket lay discarded in a crumpled knot several feet away, one sleeve in the water.

Kyr had been expecting Admiral Jole. She had been braced for him, and for all the memories that belonged with him.

"I thought you said you couldn't find him in this reality," she said quietly.

She might as well have shouted. The young man did not look up. Whatever he was working on was his whole universe.

Yiso said, "It was only through a series of coincidences that I found *you*."

"Is this another coincidence?"

"What is the difference between coincidence and the Wisdom at work?" Yiso said.

"But it's *broken*," Kyr said. "You said Leru sabotaged it."

"Oh, hello," said the young man by the water, looking up at last with an air of faint surprise. "I don't suppose anyone got a message to the admiral? I think I know where it sent the rest of my team, but we're probably better off sending a ship out to collect them than trying to shadow-jump them all back. Small target."

"Are you *serious*," said Kyr.

"Almost never," he said, smiling. His smile was easy, without the lopsided nastiness she was used to. "If we haven't got a message to the *Triumphalis* yet, you can maybe add that I finished repairing Admiral Jole's reality warper and I'd like a really big end-of-year bonus."

"A genius in every reality," said Yiso. "Hello, Avicenna."

"Cool name," he said. "Not mine. Eleventh-century scientist, right? Ibn Sina." He looked Yiso up and down. "Hey, a majo zi. Are you the long-lost heir to the space throne? Someone said something about that at some point." He glanced between Kyr and Mags. "And you guys aren't in uniform, so I take it I'm actually a hostage suddenly?"

"You don't seem worried," said Mags.

"I just repaired the fucking Wisdom," said not-Avicenna, grinning blindingly at him. "I'm a master of mad alien technology. Who's worried?"

CHAPTER TWENTY-FOUR

THE WISDOM

Kyr saw with a flash of outrage that Mags was every bit as weak to Avi's smile in this universe. Which was absurd, because these two had never even met before, but not-Avi's grin had turned knowing, and Mags, unbelievably, was blushing. Kyr gave him a pointed shove in the side.

"What?" said Mags, and then, "You're not a hostage. You can go."

"Oh, I'm not going anywhere," said not-Avi. "This is the coolest thing I've ever worked on, you couldn't pry me out of this place with a crowbar."

"What's your name?" said Mags.

"*Mags,*" said Kyr. Her outrage was metamorphosing rapidly into unspeakable embarrassment.

"I think under the circs I'm meant to just chant my serial number at you," said not-Avi cheerfully. "But I forget what it is. So sorry. I'd ask you your names but the zi I think must be Yiso—am I right? Last Prince of the Wisdom? See, I remember the important stuff—and I'm going to call you guys Goon One and Goon Two. Hey, can I send all of *you* to that uninhabited planet? Let's see."

Kyr reacted fast. She dashed across the chamber to knock the tablet from its precarious perch against his knee. It fell in the water with a quiet splash. Avi—if he wasn't going to tell them his name then fuck it, Kyr knew Avi and he was Avi—just looked up at her mildly. "Hello, Goon Two," he said. "That was quick. Also, that was mine."

"Shut up," said Kyr.

"People often say that to me and I never think it's justified," Avi said. "You are *enormous*. Do you work out?" He looked over at Mags. "Do *you* work out, Goon One? I don't actually care about the answer, this is more a polite conversation thing. I didn't want to leave anyone out. Hey, Prince Yiso, tell us about your exercise regime. Let's do some interspecies cultural exchange." He unfolded himself from his curled-up position near the water and got to his feet. Kyr looked at him with a dislocated feeling. He was still shorter than she was, but he came up to her nose. The Avi in her universe had only just reached her chin.

This Avi ignored her totally and sauntered toward Yiso, his thumbs hooked in his belt. Every single piece of uniform he was wearing was crumpled. Val, somewhere in the back of Kyr's mind, sneered at it. The sneering distracted her, and Avi patted Mags's arm as he walked past him, which startled him for an instant.

The instant was just long enough for Avi to put his arm around Yiso's slender shoulders. In his other hand there was a sharp cross-handled service knife, which he put at Yiso's throat, angled to slide neatly under the subdermal carapace. He jerked Yiso's head upward with a hand on their crest. Kyr froze. Mags looked stunned. He'd been so slow. How could *Mags* be so slow?

Cleo told you to supervise the civvies! howled not Val's memories, but *Kyr's*. Kyr was the person who was supposed to be good at bad odds.

"Human bodyguards were a pretty good idea, but you probably shouldn't have picked big amateurs to go up against Providence," Avi said cheerfully. "We're a live-combat wing, you know, even the techies like me. This is the bit where I ask Goon One and Goon Two to put their weapons down slowly, but it looks like you guys didn't bring any? What is that, a security stunner? That's just going to bounce off my shielding, you realize." His head tilted. "Be honest. Did any of you have a plan? Did you consider recruiting someone with a plan? Because that would maybe have helped."

"Do you *ever* shut up," said Kyr.

"Not really! You know, the Ziviri Jo, the mad rump of alien domination of the universe and so on, is supposed to be our nemesis. I really expected you to be better than this. But hey, what an amazing opportunity. Can I ask you a question, Yiso?"

Yiso said nothing.

Avi asked, "What *are* you?"

Still nothing. Avi started talking again. Kyr tried to half listen, in case he said something useful, and half watch for opportunities. But this Avi *wasn't* an amateur. When she sidestepped to slip out of his line of sight he twisted to follow her, interrupting himself with "Uh-uh-uh! Easy. I think I want you to go and stand next to your friend there. Wait, are you guys *family*? You look like family. Cute. As I was *saying*, Your Highness"—that was said silky-nasty, almost precisely like the Avi Kyr knew—"it started pulling itself back together the minute you arrived, didn't it? We've been working on that repair for years. For it all to fall into place at once like that—I don't think so. So what is it about you?"

Kyr, standing by Mags, watched Avi. Her fingers twitched. She thought about the way it had felt to put her hands around his neck and twist and hear the snap. It was not a good memory. She watched the service knife that was steady and perfectly angled at Yiso's throat, even while Avi talked in the air with his other hand.

A thought came to her quiet and clear as the sound of the bells ringing out over Raingold Bay on Chrysothemis, in another world, another universe, another lifetime, and the thought was: Yiso was used to violence now, and it did not frighten them. They stood dignified and silent, and did not struggle, and did not flinch, and Kyr was afraid for them; afraid, and angry, and sad.

"Please put the knife down," she said. "Or have me instead."

"You seem way less important than alien royalty," said Avi. "Sorry." Then he said to Yiso, "Except it's not royalty, is it? Bad translation. Everyone always says so, and then they do it anyway."

"I'm not royalty," Yiso said quietly. Kyr tried to catch Mags's eye but he seemed to be panicking. More than ever she wanted her brother, *hers*, the one who might have hated every minute of his soldier's training but who all the same was the best child soldier that Gaea Station had ever produced.

"More like *priest*, am I right?" Avi was saying. "Because this thing is basically a god machine. If you *can* build something that's omniscient and omnibenevolent and then use it to run your society, why wouldn't you? Basic concept of a theocracy, but with the numbers to back it up. Something so comforting about knowing you're always right, isn't there?"

Yiso said nothing.

"Except maybe not *priest*," Avi said. "Your species is functionally extinct. You were never born, Prince Yiso. Your god machine *made* you. Maybe the word I'm looking for is *incarnation*."

"Leave them alone!" said Kyr. "Why does it matter?"

"It's not every day you meet someone with an actual purpose in life," said Avi, who was just as nasty, she saw now, as her own version; nastier, even, because of how self-confident he was. "I want to know how it *works*—what the fuck!"

The *what the fuck* was because Cleo had pounced on him out of the shadows.

She wrestled Avi away from Yiso. Once the knife was no longer at Yiso's throat Kyr ran forward to help. She had been trying her hardest not to notice Cleo moving into position, because if she didn't notice anything then Avi wouldn't. It wasn't like it was *hard* to keep him talking. It would have been harder to get him to stop.

They disarmed him briskly. Cleo handed his knife to Yiso, who held it like it might be poisonous, while Kyr patted him down for other weapons. "This guy?" Cleo said, over the top of not-Avi's head, as she got him down on his knees and briskly looped her belt around his wrists. "What is it about this guy? You came back for him last time, I remember."

"I'm not leverage," said not-Avi. "You're all going to regret this."

They both ignored him. "Thanks, Cleo," said Kyr. She was aware of Mags hovering a little way off, looking worried, and then talking quietly to Yiso. They were friends, of course. They'd known each other for a year.

"Don't thank me, he's right, we're in trouble," Cleo said. She had the service rifle she'd found at the security station strapped across her back. "I took a look at what was coming for me and decided I didn't fancy a heroic last stand while you guys stood around doing—What *are* you doing? Talking? Come *on*, majo. Kill the thing if you're here to kill it. We have two minutes till this guy's reinforcements get here."

"What do you mean, last time?" said not-Avi. "What do you mean, *kill it*?"

"None of your business, shut up, you're my prisoner," Cleo said.

Yiso said, "But it's different now."

Kyr felt an abrupt chill at the back of her neck. She turned to look at Yiso. They were standing very upright. Mags had the knife now. He also looked like he thought it was poisonous. Yiso said, "That was when it was broken."

"You said you'd finish the job!" Kyr said.

"It's alive," Yiso said. "*It created me.* It's all that's left of Leru and the others, it's the thing my world died to build, it's *mine.* And it could be a force for good. You don't have the right to tell me what to do with it, Valkyr."

"Wait, do we *want* the *Triumphalis* reinforcements?" Cleo muttered. "Serves you right for trusting a majo, Kyr. What did you expect?"

"There will be no reinforcements," said Yiso, cool and certain. They raised their hand in one of those familiar gestures of command. Kyr felt the vibration going through shadowspace the way a person might feel it when they were standing in a cave that was about to collapse: as if ordinary reality were a room with walls and a ceiling that could fall in on you. "This place is mine. My home."

They turned their back on Kyr and the others, turned to the

great arc of water, and the intricate machineries of the Wisdom illuminated around them as a halo of force and light.

"Well, this went well," Cleo said.

"No!" said Kyr, as Cleo took aim at the back of Yiso's head with the service rifle.

Cleo took the shot anyway. Kyr saw the bullet slow and then evaporate as it got within ten feet of Yiso. Their ears twitched a little. They hadn't even turned around.

"Wow, so someone did have a plan," said not-Avi, still on his knees. "Not you, obviously."

"Yiso, please!" cried Kyr.

And it was then that Admiral Jole walked in.

"Well, this is a surprise," he said.

His voice carried across the great hall, sounding just as Kyr remembered it, full of warmth and certainty; rich, deep, strong, not loud but clear and well-projected. Admiral Aulus Jole, as he came across that room toward them, was a figure to match his voice. He was tall even for a human, broad-shouldered in his navy-blue uniform with the row of medals pinned to the breast, walking with an easy stride, not too fast, but with no sign that he was favoring one leg over the other.

"Admiral!" cried not-Avi. Cleo let out a hiss of displeasure at the sight of him. Mags looked from him to Yiso, to Kyr herself, and stood irresolute and useless.

Kyr made herself look hard at the man who was approaching them, cataloguing differences, to control her flinch. He was fatter than his Gaean self, solid rather than gaunt. The extra flesh was maybe what made him look some years younger. His thinning sandy hair was combed neatly back from his face, and his uniform jacket was crisp. His eyes had friendly looking crinkles at the corners. He had the look of someone kind. Val, when she met him at that fancy dinner years ago, had liked him.

"Sir, the Ziviri Jo," Avi called out, before Cleo said, "Will you *shut up*," and backhanded him.

"Obviously," said Admiral Jole. He wasn't even looking at them. His eyes were on the great cradle of the Wisdom. "It's been years since I've seen it like this," he said. "Old Leru did a number on the poor thing. It is beautiful when it wakes up, isn't it?"

"Sir," said not-Avi again, apparently totally immune to the threat of Cleo's displeasure. Kyr knew what it looked like to desperately want Jole's approval. Had *her* Avi been like this?

Yiso finally turned around. They looked thoughtfully at Jole, and somehow they had never seemed more alien to Kyr. She was aware all over again of their slender frame, their huge silver eyes, their greyish coloring and long three-fingered hands and mobile ears, the flexible flukes of their crest. She tried to step forward. She found she could not move. Her feet were fastened to the floor.

"Fuck, fuck, fuck," whispered Cleo beside her. "Oh, we are so out of our depth."

"I don't want you here," said Yiso to Jole. Their gaze slid sideways to Avi. "Or him," they added, and Kyr thought suddenly of Yiso in the dark of the caves of Chrysothemis's node, the injuries that Avi had left on them. *Brutal*, Leru had said.

Yiso remembered everything that had happened to them, just as Kyr did. Yiso had no reason to care what any human wanted.

And Yiso, looking at Jole, lifted their hand and made a gesture as if they were flicking away an insect.

Nothing happened.

Admiral Jole, feet planted, arms loose at his sides, gave them a little smile. "I don't think so," he said.

The awful shadowspace vibrations that had been making the room feel like it was lurching hideously quieted. The glow of the Wisdom dimmed to almost nothing.

Yiso let out a small shocked breath. "No," they said.

"Providence had to spend years designing and testing the

implants to let me do that," Admiral Jole said. "While you were born with something very like them, weren't you? As much a part of your physiology as your ears. We have been looking for you a long time, Yiso, and we are very interested to get to know you better."

Kyr found she could move after all. She didn't know where to move *to*. She hated Jole, hated him; Yiso had looked at her and called her *unstoppable*; Jole had always said he did everything for humanity; Yiso was the Wisdom's creation; Jole had everything under control; Yiso looked so *small*—

Mags didn't have the same hesitation. He raced forward to plant himself between the admiral and the alien, a solid human wall. Admiral Jole's eyes swept over him, considering, unconcerned. Kyr thought all at once: *He's the same. He's just the same as before.*

"Maxwell Marston," Admiral Jole said. "I *thought* you looked familiar. And that's your sister Valerie over there, I suppose. What an embarrassment for your mother that the two of you have become traitors to humanity." He looked appropriately sad. "And what a blight on your sister's career it will be. How selfish."

"I won't let you touch Yiso," said Mags, and somehow *that* was what made Kyr's dithering brain unfreeze. She couldn't stand here and watch her brother defy Jole alone. She ran toward them.

Admiral Jole sighed and made a slight flicking gesture with two fingers.

Kyr was half expecting it. Mags wasn't. As they were both batted away by a rolling wave of distorted space she glimpsed him going flying, slamming into the ceiling halfway across the great chamber, falling. But Kyr knew how to ride the curve of a shadow engine's pulses. She flew, and twisted, and fell, and landed on her feet.

"Ah," said Admiral Jole, a sigh of satisfaction. "It *works*. Time for phase—Damn!"

Kyr slammed him down. He was big and strong but so was she, and he was middle-aged, slowing down. She snatched his field knife from its sheath at his belt—there was gold decoration on the hilt—and didn't hesitate: straight down, aiming for one of his mild grey eyes—she'd killed before, she could kill him now—

She caught the flicker in Admiral Jole's expression and rolled sideways, just in time to dodge a professional and well-judged stab under her ribs from behind.

Cleo? thought Kyr.

But Cleo was standing well back, her arms folded, as if to say, *I'm not in this fight.* She'd let not-Avi go.

He clearly hadn't skipped combat drills in this reality. He came for her again. Kyr only just got onto her feet and back out of range of his knife—where had he got the second knife from? She must have missed it when she patted him down, *stupid.* Her reach was longer than his but he was a *lot* faster than she'd been expecting. And she couldn't rule out Jole as a threat—

Another hum in the pulsing forces permeating the Wisdom's heart. Kyr was thrown out of reality for an instant—she felt the ghost sensations of shadowspace pressing down on her—and when she rematerialized she was standing in the middle of a glittering cage of barely visible lines of force. The knife she'd snatched from Jole's belt clattered to the ground several meters away. She reached out toward the cage and then snatched her hand back. A white line of pain, so cold it burned, drew itself across her fingers.

Mags was on the ground, lying still. She couldn't see Cleo anywhere at all. Not-Avi had taken up a stance behind Admiral Jole's left shoulder. And Yiso—

Yiso had calmly walked to the center of the chamber. They stood knee-deep in the water under the cradle of the Wisdom's core shadow engine. In one hand they held their staff.

For the length of a held breath, there was absolute silence.

"This was my home," Yiso said. "This was the last achievement of the zi. A lasting achievement. So at least we could say we left the universe better than we found it. But if *you* seek to use it, human—then I refuse. If there is one thing I have learned about humanity, it is that you do not deserve power."

"You think you do, alien?" snapped Jole. "You think you were ever better than us? You lost the war. Face it. This is what losing means."

They killed our world, thought Kyr. Only they hadn't, it had never happened, not here. Earth won the war here. And Yiso hadn't had anything to do with the death of the Earth; it had been Leru who made that choice, Leru who was dead in both realities. She pressed her hands to the bars of the force cage and snatched them back, red lines of pain erupting down her palms. Why wasn't it fair, why couldn't it come out right, why was there never a good answer? "Yiso!" she shouted, pointlessly.

Yiso turned to look at her.

And Kyr was just as aware now of their terrible alienness, but she was also aware of something else. She knew them. She knew their strange body that was nothing like hers. She could read expression in the code of eyes and ears and crest.

They looked so sad.

"Let it end, then," they said.

They closed their eyes, and their crest lifted and their ears were still, and they began to speak in a language Kyr did not know. Around the room lights rippled and then went dark. The controls that hovered in the air around the great pool disappeared. The hum of the shadow engine changed in quality. The force cage keeping Kyr in place flickered out of existence for an instant, and then reappeared. If that happened again—

It did, but too fast. Kyr stood tense and waiting. If she had a chance she would—she didn't know what she would do. Yiso was doing everything, small and controlled and terribly powerful. Their silver eyes opened. In the newly darkened room they shone with unearthly light. When they spat out another alien word, this one sounding like it hurt their throat, the great cradle cracked.

The shadow engine lurched and swung overhead with a dreadful squealing noise. The shielding on it was broken. Now the distorted chamber's dimensions shifted in time with its pulses; first a great hall with a broad pool of water, then an endless open void punctuated by dim flickers that might have been stars, and then a tiny cave where Kyr's force cage was crowded in close to the Wisdom's cradle, so close that not-Avi yelped and jumped back, and Cleo was right at Kyr's elbow looking as confused and frightened as Kyr felt, and Mags's still form was near enough that she could see he was still breathing and his arm looked broken. And then it pulsed back to the grand hall.

"That's enough!" barked Admiral Jole. Kyr didn't see quite how he did it, but he was beside Yiso and plucking the staff from their thin hand, and then he pulled back and swung, a clean fast punch that sent Yiso flying several feet backward.

"Sir!" called not-Avi. "It's totally destabilized—I can't fix this in a hurry—" *Pulse, pulse*: the starry void, the tiny cave.

"I will not," roared Admiral Jole, "be gainsaid by a damn machine!"

The pulsing stopped. The space seemed settled as a starry void, and the force cage had gone. Kyr couldn't see her own feet. She couldn't see anyone else. When she tried to step forward she couldn't tell if she'd actually moved. But she could hear Admiral Jole's voice, echoing through the emptiness.

"The age of the majo is over!" he said. "The majoda failed. It was corrupt and self-satisfied and always rotten at the core. Humanity's time has come. This is the time for heroes, the time for voyagers and settlers, the time for the future to begin again. We keep what is useful. We sweep away the dead wood. Lesser species should count themselves fortunate to live in the age of this great civilization. And this technology is a tool like any other tool, and it will *serve!*"

Crack. Kyr could not see it but she had a vision of the shadow engine's cradle fracturing. Yiso had set the Wisdom to destroy itself at last.

Admiral Jole let out a grunt of effort and suddenly the starry void dissipated, and the room reassembled itself as something between the great hall and the cramped cave. Kyr looked around. Mags was unconscious, Yiso was down, and something had knocked Cleo to the ground too, she wasn't moving. Not-Avi was watching Admiral Jole with an expression halfway between awe and envy. Veins stood out on Admiral Jole's forehead as he manipulated the Wisdom. The cradle of the shadow engine was fractured in a dozen places, but it was holding together, lines of green shadowspace glow running over it.

Kyr went to Yiso. She could not have said why she did it. She was still angry with them. They'd decided to keep the Wisdom for themselves.

But they'd looked so sad.

She helped them sit up. They were bruising horribly from the blow Admiral Jole had given them.

"It's done," they said, quiet and tired. "Just like you wanted after all, Valkyr. It doesn't matter what he does. The Wisdom is dying."

Admiral Jole heard. Kyr saw his face twist up into a mask of spite. "Then it will still serve me now," he said. "Before it fails. If humanity has to lose this advantage, then the aliens are the ones who should pay the price."

Pinpoints of light flickered into existence, an enormous drifting spiral, close-together clouds of heavily settled galaxies, stray dots of color for distant worlds. Kyr cried out in awful frustration as she recognized the shape of the majoda, the many worlds of majo civilization. She'd seen this before. It was just as it had been in the caverns of Chrysothemis, where Avi had killed a thousand thousand worlds.

And it was happening again. Again Kyr could do nothing. *So many people,* and there wasn't even a reason, not even Avi's mad justice. There was nothing but Jole's spite behind this. *So many people, over and over. Fourteen billion people, twenty trillion people, a universe of people. So many.*

Yiso took hold of her hand. Their greyish skin was cool.

"I'm sorry," they said. "Valkyr, Valkyr. It was meant to be better this time. I'm so sorry."

"Can you stop it?" Kyr said, watching the little lights wink out. Not-Avi had staggered away from Jole. He was sitting down, staring, the deaths of worlds reflected in his glasses. She couldn't read his expression.

"I'm shut out again," Yiso said. "I never really knew what I was doing. I never knew."

Kyr hauled them into her arms. They made a startled noise. She held on. "Do majo not do hugs?" she said.

"I'm sorry," Yiso said again.

"I'm sorry too," Kyr said. "I meant to change things." She'd meant to change everything. It was nearly dark now. She could hear Admiral Jole's breathing, turned to wheezes of exhausted triumph.

Yiso looked up at her with gleaming eyes. "Would you do it again?" they said.

"What?" said Kyr, not to the words but to the strange buzz of their voice, as if more than one person had spoken.

"Would you do it again," repeated Yiso, and the room pulsed and grew impossibly distant and empty again. The last word echoed: *again again again again.*

"Yiso!" said Kyr, because she was suddenly alone. "Cleo! *Mags!*"

She knew this place: the emptiness of it, the faintness. When she looked down at herself she was wearing not the sensible clothes she'd left Hymmer in but Valerie Marston's dress uniform, the full navies of the Terran Expeditionary, with gold buttons. She grimaced. "What do you think you're doing this time?"

I believe, said the Wisdom, *I am making a decision.*

It was wearing Yiso's face this time, not Leru's. Yiso's thin body materialized in the gloom, dressed in robes Kyr had never seen them wear, layers of vivid blue and gold that brought out subtle shades of warmth on their greyish skin. It was not Yiso. She was not fooled for a second. The Wisdom's silvery and unpupiled eyes were old, old, old.

Valkyr, it said.

"What?" said Kyr. When it said nothing else, she said, "So now you're making a decision? All it took was twenty trillion people dying twice over—"

This outcome is one foreseen by Leru Ihenni Tan Yi, it said, *before they chose the destruction of the human homeworld.*

"It has a name," said Kyr.

Earth. I am sorry. Earth.

"Oh, you're *sorry*," Kyr said.

Yes, said the intelligence that wore Yiso's face. *I have always been sorry. Valkyr, I asked you a question. Would you do it again?*

"Yes!" said Kyr. "No! I don't know, what's the use if everything just ends up shitty no matter what you do? Maybe there's no point. No wonder the majo thought they were cursed." She gasped for breath. She didn't know when she'd started crying. How stupid. "Yes, of course, of course I'd do it again. I'm not going to *stop*."

Valkyr, perseverant, said the Wisdom softly. *Very well.*

"Are you going to make me *choose a moment* again? What for? Which one would fix it? Maybe I should go back to whenever they were building *you* and stop that from happening. No Wisdom, no majoda, no—" She stopped talking, and wiped her face. "Let me go. Put me back with the others."

I do not ask you to choose.

I shall make the choice.

"What?" Kyr said. "No! What are you doing? I want—"

—to be back in the world she'd made herself, the world where Admiral Jole and Providence ruled a human empire that was meant to last forever? *Yes:* because that was a universe with the Earth in it still, a universe with Lisa working in the clinic on Hymmer Station for her research fellowship, and Lieutenant Cleo Alvares, and Commander Ursula Marston of the *Samphire*; a world where Kyr had a future and a family, a world where Mags was alive. It had to mean something. It had to matter, that Kyr had saved the world. "Send me back! Let me—"

PART V

VICTRIX

"*—go!*"

Humanity is a warlike species.

This was obvious long before we encountered the civilizations of the majoda. There were other Earth species which engaged in behaviors we can understand as warfare—ants, some of the great apes—but none with such frequency, enthusiasm, and skill. The history of human innovation is in many ways the history of the instruments of war—the stirrup, the bow and arrow, the cannon, the rifle, the nuclear missile. To many of the majoda species this militarized history of technological progression is nothing short of horrifying. (Many, but not all. We are not the only warlike sentients in the universe, though the majo consider us to be among the most alarming.)

It is not the case, however, that humans are a war-*loving* species. Some individuals are, no doubt. But some of the earliest extant works of human culture are complex reflections on the costs and consequences of conflict: the glory thus achieved and the suffering thus engendered. We know what war does, to societies and to the self. We have known for a long time. The desire for peace runs deep in human history—nearly as deep as the desire for war.

What would peace look like? Many have wrestled with the question. Perhaps it can be enforced? Empires have prided themselves on being peace-bringers and peacekeepers. But this is a paradox. A peace brought about with the threat of violence is only a war in waiting. True peace would surely require the elimination of warfare altogether. Utopia—the perfect society—demands what we might call an unenforced peace. But is it possible? Unenforced peace would require an end to all conflict. The question then arises: What causes conflict?

Resources, says history, and ideas.

So humans seeking this utopian society and its unenforced peace must first settle the question of resources: who has them, who wants them, who needs them. Many approaches have been tried. Unsurprisingly, several of them led to conflicts of the other kind, conflicts of ideas. Should everyone have a fair share—and in that case, who should define fairness? Should everyone be free to pursue the resources they want in whatever way seems best to them? Is there a technology capable of balancing these suggestions? The old imperial standby—to take resources from elsewhere, far more than could possibly be of use, and so create a bountiful surplus in which resource conflict cannot arise—has been successful for some; not, of course, for the inhabitants of history's various elsewheres. It is this mindset of conquest and colonization which first brought humanity into disagreement with the majoda, with such tragic consequences.

But solving resource conflict is the *easier* problem.

Humanity's greatest wars have always been conflicts of ideas—ideas of ethnicity and nationality, of religion and belief, of justice and morality. The utopian vision of unenforced peace requires that these conflicts cease. But how?

Here is an old, old answer: if we all understood one another, if we all treated one another kindly, if we all listened and thought and exercised toleration for difference.

This proposal breaks down very quickly if pressure is applied. Should we tolerate all difference? What if the difference is a question of morality? If it is one person's sincerely held belief that all individuals who do not belong to their own ethnic group should be killed, conflict arises again at once: with their victims, and with any onlooker whose soul is not a total moral void. So immediately we see that there must be limits to toleration. Who defines the limits?

But imagine if there was no disagreement—on how humans should treat one another, on what definitions should be used, on ethnicity or nationality, religion or belief, justice or morality.

Imagine there's no countries; imagine no religion—so the ancient song goes. What kind of humanity would this be?

A united humanity. A humanity without disagreements. A humanity without its varied belief systems, without its national histories, without its assortment of cultures and ethnicities—or at least, a humanity where religion, nation, culture, and ethnicity were entirely lacking in meaning. This would be a humanity without differences; speaking one language only, to avoid misunderstanding; subscribing to one set of moral standards, and rejecting all others. It would be by definition a majority humanity; a universal humanity; a monolith humanity.

And this, perhaps, would bring an end to war—or at least, an end to war with other humans.

I leave it to the reader to decide whether such an obliteration of history, culture, ethnicity, and language aligns in any way with their understanding of utopia.

It has been tried more than once. The latest iteration is perhaps the extremist enclave of Gaea Station. Young refugees—those who have "refused assignment," in the station's own terms, and been cast out—have struggled to cope with the multiplicity of human identity beyond Gaea. They speak no language but T-standard, and they follow no religion, unless Gaea's veneration of human power can be classed as a religion. All of them find themselves fitted into ethnic categories they do not understand. Analysis of Gaea's early experiments in eugenics suggests an attempt to eliminate visible markers of racial difference. Unsurprisingly for those who know the ideological antecedents of Gaean philosophy (visible in the names of its children, overwhelmingly drawn from Norse myth and Roman imperium), the results of these attempts to create a "pure" human tended to be white. Gaea Station may believe itself free of humanity's complex and divided past; to an outside observer, it is anything but.

History has a tendency to outrun us.

—Ursula Marston, *Earth's Children: Humanity After the End of the World* (unpublished)

CHAPTER TWENTY-FIVE

THE BEGINNING

High on an orbital defense platform above a blue world she had never really known, Kyr flinched as combat feeds populated the edges of her vision, fed to her by her mask. Green subreal light flickered around the edges of the world. She was surrounded by the downed shells of majo fighters, alone, the last soldier standing. Overhead the giant decoy of a Wisdom cruiser flickered into existence, the planet-killing dart hidden in its wake.

Doomsday.

No. No. Not *again*.

"How does this help!" she yelled at the emptiness. She was above the sky. Beyond the flashes of the battle there was only the black night of space. "How does it help to just do the same thing over and over and never—"

She was moving as she shouted. Her body, which had run Doomsday hundreds, maybe thousands of times, knew the steps like a dance. Kyr's hand was already reaching for her jump hook. Two charges left. The dart was clearer and clearer. Her combat feeds still weren't picking it up through the mess of signals from the cruiser, but her eyes knew its slim deadly shape perfectly.

She dropped her hands to her side.

Fourteen billion people.

"They're already dead," she said to the nothingness, to the Wisdom, to Doomsday. "They died long ago. It wasn't my fault. I wasn't even born. I can't—" She gasped for breath. The combat mask was snatching away her tears as she cried them. "I can't do this anymore."

Then she didn't do anything else. She stood there and watched. She should have been screaming inside, she should have been *fighting*, but something in her was cold and dead. The death of one world, the death of thousands, fourteen billion people, twenty trillion people, what difference did it make? Avi with his neck broken, Avi preening under Admiral Jole's approval, Mags dead of misery or Mags run away to fight for the majo, Cleo's expression when she talked about her father, Yiso who had looked at Kyr and said *unstoppable*—

"I am stoppable," Kyr said. "Look at me. I've stopped."

She crouched and wrapped her arms around herself and cried, and somewhere far below the Earth died again—again—*again*.

And the agoge cut out.

Kyr heard its deep hum soften and fade as she opened her eyes to familiar grey plasteel walls. She looked at her hands, which were her own thin scarred hands and not Val's well-fed rounded ones. She hurt inside with an ache that settled somewhere around her diaphragm and made it hard to catch her breath. Her face was still wet.

"Valkyr," said a voice. She looked up.

Uncle Jole was standing over her, a look of deep sympathy on his familiar face. It was her uncle, and not the admiral. He was gaunt again, his face lined, his eyes knowing. He was holding out his hand.

Kyr swallowed. She did not know what to say.

She took the offered hand. She saw Jole wince as he braced his bad leg against her weight. She stood up. He let go, and put his hand on her shoulder instead.

"It gets me like that sometimes as well," he said.

Kyr said nothing. He looked at her for a moment. His other hand came up toward her face. Kyr flinched, but he was wiping away the wetness beneath her eye, very gently. His fingertips on her face were cold.

"No need to feel ashamed," he said. "It's true. Doomsday wasn't your fight. It was mine. We were the ones who failed you, Valkyr. But Earth's children live."

Kyr swallowed hard. "And while we live," she managed to say, in a voice so thin it did not sound like her own, "the enemy shall fear us."

Jole smiled at her. It had been the right thing to say. "I'm proud of you, Valkyr," he said. He was still holding on to her shoulder. Kyr wanted him to stop touching her. More than anything she wanted him to stop touching her.

She remembered this; how he'd come in, and smiled, and told her he was proud, and then the wing assignments had started. She looked at him, his kind eyes, his slight smile, his massive soldier's body. She stepped back, so he was not touching her anymore. *It was never about Mags*, she thought. *And it was never about training scores. It didn't make a difference what either of us did. You were always going to give him Strike and send him away. You were always going to put me in Nursery.*

You had my mother killed, and told us she was a junior officer, when she was the Victrix's *commander. You made my sister sleep in your rooms. She was barely older than I am now when she took your son—her son—and she ran.*

Kyr didn't have a weapon. Her field knife had dissolved along with the rest of the agoge simulation. *He* was certainly armed. He expected enemies everywhere. Traitors and fifth columnists. She remembered very clearly the enormous satisfaction she'd felt trying to stab Admiral Jole in the eye. And Admiral Jole wasn't even *him*. Just a reflection. Just some other life this man she'd admired with everything she was might have led.

His expression was going sharp. Had she given away her thoughts? He was good at reading people. He had to be, to bend them the way he wanted. Kyr said, "I'm sorry, sir."

"You're sorry?" said Jole. His brows lifted.

"I'll do better," she said. "I want to be . . ." She swallowed. "I want to be worthy of humanity."

Wasn't that what it meant, to be Earth's children? To be all that was left of a blue planet and fourteen billion people?

"No one expects perfection from you, Valkyr," said Jole. "It's enough that you serve."

"I understand, sir," said Kyr. She thought about lies. About no one expecting perfection, and everyone being punished for falling short of it, all the time. About believing a lie so hard you fell into it.

"Go and get some rest," Jole said. "It's rec rotation, isn't it?"

Kyr stumbled away from the agoge rooms, where a squadron of Ferox were taking over for their training rotation, and wandered the narrow corridors of Gaea Station blindly. Everything was familiar and strange. This was home, the place she'd come from, the only place she'd ever really belonged. Val looked out from somewhere behind her eyes and thought how small it was, how dark, how cold and nasty and cramped and brutal and sad.

Why had the Wisdom done *this*?

When she was sure she was alone, in an empty rock passageway somewhere between Nursery and the Augusta barracks, she tried asking. "What do you want me to do here?" she demanded of the silence. "This place is—nothing, it's—*tiny*, it's—there's nothing anyone can do here! All we ever did was sit here and hate everyone and do nothing—"

Silence.

"This is stupid," said Kyr. "This was always stupid."

She'd thought they were freedom fighters and of course they weren't. *Freedom fighters* was the other Mags, was Yiso and the Ziviri Jo one step ahead of Providence, or else Lisa in the restaurant on Hymmer saying *I don't agree with Fleet, politically.* She'd thought they were the last of humanity and they weren't that either; somewhere out there a rainy world orbited a yellow star, and Ursa and her son were being a family together, far away from Kyr.

Was it just going to happen all over again? Assignments. Mags sent away. Kyr would go to Avi. They'd rescue Yiso. And they'd leave, again, do all the same things again, except this time Kyr guessed she was meant to stop Mags killing Leru, or stop Avi taking control of the Wisdom and destroying all those majo, and she didn't care anymore. She didn't care. She was home and it was the worst place in the universe. Her uncle Jole had taken her hand and looked at her and smiled, and she'd looked at *him* and seen what he was right there in front of her, and she couldn't bear it anymore.

"What am I supposed to do?" she demanded.

Nothing answered. The rock walls all around were cold and silent.

And then an alarm began to sound.

It wasn't the familiar double ring of shift change. It wasn't the urgent warning *enemy action*. It was a pattern Kyr had never heard before, three long blasts and one short. She had to dig through layers of memory to find it in a dim recollection of Nursery, learning every signal and being hit across the knuckles with Corporal Ekker's pointer the one time she got something wrong—

Full muster.

Something had changed. This had never happened before.

Command was calling all of Gaea Station to meet.

The only space big enough to hold the station's whole population was the arcade. The tinny music had been switched off. Machines for playing games and little booths with screens were shoved against the walls. Adults lined up with their wings, cadets in their messes. Kyr stepped into line beside Cleo. Five more Sparrows on her other side, so Jeanne, at the far end, hadn't been assigned yet. Kyr glanced sidelong at her messmates. She felt as though she had not seen Jeanne's freckled unsmiling face in years.

Cleo did not glance sideways at Kyr. She was ramrod straight, bristling and alert. She seemed to be pretending that Kyr was not there. Kyr remembered, like it had happened a lifetime ago, fighting hand-to-hand with Cleo in Drill while they waited for their assignments. And Lieutenant Cleo Alvares with her loud undignified laugh, her dark cloud of hair under her TE cap, shouldering a rifle in the Halls of the Wise, taking aim at the back of Yiso's head—

No.

Kyr forced her gaze forward as well. She could not look at the Sparrows anymore. *You're the only good thing that ever happened to me,* she thought. It wasn't the whole truth, but it felt like it.

The girls' messes were in front of them, ten rows down to the seven-year-old Robins. On Kyr's right the boys of Cat were lined up, and Coyote were beyond them. Kyr glimpsed Mags, taller even than his mess of warbreed boys. *Two boys for every girl,* she thought, *half of them meant for combat wings no matter what. No gene-tailoring suite, so they have to be doing it by aborting female fetuses.* Someone *made that decision.*

Command stood in their own row on a dais at the far end of the arcade, the admirals of Ferox, Scythica, Augusta, Victrix, the chief officers of Systems and Suntracker and Agricole, the sergeants of Oikos and Nursery. Sergeant Sif, the chief of Nursery, was the only woman. She was very pregnant, but she stood tall, hands clasped behind her back. Commander Jole stood with the four admirals arranged around him. Kyr's eyes wanted to slide away, so she stood up even straighter and fixed her stare on the shiny medals on his breast.

You *made that decision,* she thought. *You made all these decisions.*

She did not turn her head to look around for anyone else. She did not try to catch a glimpse of Avi, probably slouching somewhere in the back ranks of Systems Wing. There were people missing, of course. Children younger than seven weren't included in a full muster. Some of Nursery would have been left behind to supervise them. And there would be a couple of rotations' worth of soldiers out on patrol in local space, hoping to pick up an unwary trading vessel and win a petty handful of luxuries for themselves; and Systems and Suntracker couldn't be left totally unsupervised, because a failure in either would kill everyone on the station quickly. So the full muster was not, quite, everybody.

But it was close enough. Kyr didn't need to look around to know why it was this meeting had never been called before. You could see at a glance that Oikos and Nursery numbered in the dozens; Systems and Suntracker barely more; there could not be more than a hundred and fifty people in Agricole. The all-powerful combat wings, arrayed in their navy uniforms, looked bigger, but the illusion disintegrated if you looked for more than a second. Years of breeding carefully crossed warbreed soldiers had produced giants who looked like they came out of majo nightmares—but their size could not disguise the fact that there just were not very many of them.

Gaea Station, home of Earth's children, the last hope of humanity's fight against the majoda, had a population of less than two thousand people. Most of them looked underfed, and exhausted, and ill.

Five rows ahead of her one of the twelve-year-old Blackbirds was craning her neck to look and then whispering to her neighbor. "Blackbird!" Kyr snapped, without stepping out of line, and didn't regret it in the least as the girl froze and straightened up in obvious terror. Better Kyr spotted her having dangerous thoughts than someone else. Was the girl trying to get herself put onto Command's shit list?

Gaea's people were already standing in disciplined silence, but the quiet deepened and changed as Commander Jole stepped forward and the group of admirals around him came to attention.

"Humanity!" he said.

There was a ripple of *something* in the assembled crowd in response: not noise, but a general squaring of shoulders, lifting of heads. *We have nothing except that*, thought Kyr. *You made it that way.* But she felt it too. She was a human, one of the last. It mattered.

"I'll keep this brief," said Jole. He smiled a wry, likable smile. "I know how hard we all work. We don't have time to waste on speeches. Forty minutes ago, the Wisdom cruiser that has long patrolled the nearby Mousa system in an illegitimate attempt to limit our sovereignty and our freedom went dark, as almost all its systems failed in quick succession."

The hush in the arcade was breathless. People were leaning forward.

"A squadron from Scythica Wing, on my orders, pressed this advantage. They attacked the cruiser and destroyed it. Some seven thousand of the enemy perished in the cold of space. Humanity did not lose a single man." Jole held out his hand and one of the lower-ranked Command officials put a glass into it. He raised it high. "I give you Scythica Wing—the limitless horizon!"

It was the Scythica toast. The crowd echoed it back, a hoarse shout, half disbelieving. Kyr mouthed the words along with the rest. A victory, a *victory*, on an order Gaea had never known. A whole cruiser destroyed. Something deep in her thrilled at it, even as she made herself think deliberately: *Seven thousand people. Majo are people.*

It didn't make sense. A handful of Gaea's out-of-date combat darts weren't a match for the Wisdom. The full might of the Terran Expeditionary at its height hadn't been enough to stop the Wisdom. But Jole was still talking.

"I am sure you are wondering—how was this possible? For millennia the aliens have relied on their god machine, building their utopia at the expense of outsiders like us. For millennia, the technology they called the *Wisdom* has controlled every aspect of their meaningless lives. No longer.

"Today the majoda lies in disarray. Thousands of alien worlds have shuddered in fear. For the sheltering arm of their great machine has failed them, and without it, they are as dust before us.

"The Wisdom has destroyed itself."

Jole paused impressively. Kyr listened to the soft murmurs break out across the room. Her mind was working frantically.

Destroyed. Gone. Not because Yiso had gone to its heart and sabotaged it, or because of anything any outside force had done; not in *this* reality. Prince Leru in all their age-old certainty would never have done such a thing, and Kyr didn't think that anyone else *could*. She thought of the times she had spoken with the Wisdom, the faces it had worn, the voice of its ancient intelligence which was as alive as anything else she had ever met. The Wisdom had done this to itself. It had sent Kyr here, back to the beginning, and then erased itself.

Which meant that she wasn't supposed to get all the way to Chrysothemis and stop Avi from taking his vengeance for Earth. That could never happen. Which meant—What *did* it mean? What was Kyr supposed to do?

"What do we do?" said Jole on the dais. "That is the question every majo must be asking itself. What do we do without a machine ordaining our every move? What do we do without the great excuse of our algorithmic maker of hard choices?

"Unlike us, the majo are not used to forging their own destiny."

Jole paused to let the audience react and smile back at him. *He's good,* thought the part of Kyr that was Val Marston. *He's very good at this.* And she stood still and seethed while Jole held up a hand for silence and went on.

"The majo will dither and panic and hesitate. Their civilization has been corrupted by luxury and weakened by ease. They are merchants, bureaucrats, petty officials, slaves to money and habit and the simplicity of an easy life. Pity them, humanity. Their time is over.

"Our time has come.

"Four dreadnoughts of humanity's fleet form the heart of Gaea Station. Four world-conquerors that even the Wisdom struggled to oppose. Over the years of hardship we have endured, we—Earth's children—have preserved the legacy of the heroes who built them and manned them. Now the time has come to wake the sleeping giants.

"TE-66 *Victrix* is to be refitted and readied for combat in two weeks' time."

Another majestic pause. Jole let the gasps die down.

"Our first target is the most audacious and the hardest, but it is also a target that will grant us power—both the resources required to repair *Augusta*, *Scythica*, and *Ferox*, and the manpower that will turn them on the majoda. A settlement of human beings exists on a world the majoda condescended to grant them for the small price of perpetual subjugation. We, the faithful soldiers of Gaea Station, must now begin our crusade against our planet's murderers with the liberation of Chrysothemis.

"Each of you will have a part to play. Each of you must stand ready to lead. The Earth is dead, but her children live." Jole shoved a clenched fist into the air. "And while we live—"

"*—the enemy shall fear us!*"

The shout was a ragged battle cry ripped from two thousand throats. The faces of Command were set in grim joyfulness. Jole looked solemn and proud. Everyone was talking now, the disciplined silence shattered by disbelief and determination and terrible hope. The Sparrows were whispering to each other. *I got it right*, Kyr thought. *They'll start with other humans. Jole wants to rule humans. He doesn't care about the majo, not really, not at all.*

When Jole raised a hand for silence he got a worshipful hush. "The next rotation will be recreation for all but essential personnel," he said. "Celebrate, humanity. Celebrate what we have done, and we will do. Our long struggle is nearly over. Soon comes triumph.

"Dismissed!"

There had never been a stationwide rec rotation before. Kyr saw the Blackbirds move toward the machine with the dancing game and get shooed off by a squadron of heavyset Augusta soldiers. It looked like most of Gaea's adult population was planning to hang around the arcade. They were chatting in little knots, smiles on their weary faces. Someone turned the old music back on and made it loud, and then some people started *dancing*. Kyr turned away from the spectacle. She could feel the strength of the crowd's emotions trying to catch her up, as if they were all shouting at her: *Rejoice, rejoice. Join in. Be one of us. You are one of us.*

The Sparrows, she noticed, were not caught up. Cleo's expression was a studied neutral. Arti and Vic were edging closer together, Arti's bulky arm protective around Vic's shoulders. And then an elbow went hard into Kyr's ribs. It was Zen, with a flat expression that did not match the urgency of the elbow-jab. She tilted her head toward Lisabel, and toward the knot of Ferox soldiers bearing down on Lisabel—who was *cursed*, Kyr thought suddenly, with being the prettiest of them; with being seventeen years old and a definite Nursery assignment, and everyone knowing it.

Kyr moved. Jeanne had spotted it too. The pair of them put their solid warbreed bodies in the way of the soldiers. Jeanne got shoulder-checked hard by a laughing soldier who then gave her a hug, and Kyr got swept up and kissed by one of his friends who clearly thought one teenage girl was as good as another. He slobbered. It was disgusting. But Kyr, unlike Lisabel, was big enough to forcibly pull away when he tried to dip her over his arm and keep it going. She gave the soldier an insincere smile instead and turned on her heel into the crowd. Jeanne had ducked away from hers, too, and the Sparrows—Lisabel with them—were already gone. Kyr thought she spotted Cleo and Arti protectively bringing up the rear of a little knot of older female cadets who were slipping out of the arcade and away from the celebration.

Good.

They weren't the only ones fleeing. Kyr caught up with Mags at the doors. He had his head down, maybe trying to hide his expression. Kyr saw the men around him who noticed anyway and looked at him hard. Mags was so *bad* at lying. No wonder Jole had decided to send him away. You couldn't last on Gaea Station if you didn't know how to lie, lie hard, lie to yourself and everyone else too.

Kyr took his arm with a tight smile for anyone who might be looking and started walking briskly away from the noise and the crowd.

"Hi, Vallie," Mags said after a while. Kyr hated the shape of the smile he summoned up for her. "Excited?"

"No," said Kyr. "And neither are you."

"I'm excited," Mags said. "I'm happy, of course. We're going to win. We're going to beat them all. We're leaving this *rock—*"

On *rock* his voice cracked, and Kyr took him in her arms and squeezed him tight.

It was only as she was doing it that she realized that in this life, at this moment, she wasn't sure she'd ever done it before. Mags was stiff at first and then he slumped against her and put his head against hers. He was shaking. Kyr didn't think he was crying. She wasn't sure what to do if he *was* crying. She'd never been any good with crying people. In a moment of intense self-frustration, she thought, *Why didn't you learn?*

"Okay?" she said when Mags pulled away.

"I need to tell you something," Mags said.

"I know you're queer," said Kyr. Val's ghost somewhere in her brain rolled its eyes at her. "Gay. Whatever. I know."

Mags stared at her. "I," he said. "How—I mean—no."

"Wait, really?" said Kyr, which was according to Mags's face not the right thing to say. She heard her own thoughts say, in Val's lofty intonation, *I can't believe you got two chances at this conversation and you fucked them both up.*

"Shut up," she muttered. Now Mags looked *scared.* "Sorry," she said. "I'm having a—a weird day. Hey, I think I'm queer too."

"*What?*" said Mags, and looked both ways fast, like he thought someone might overhear them having this *definitely* unacceptable conversation. No one was around. They were somewhere in the maze of Oikos storerooms.

"I mean—it's complicated," said Kyr, and thought about kissing Lisabel—Lisa—in that other life, and then for a weird moment about Yiso, somehow, just the way they'd looked at her and said *unstoppable,* like they really meant it.

"I wasn't going to say," said Mags, and then, "Um. Thanks for telling me." Kyr instantly realized, from the way her shoulders unlocked, that this was what *she* should have said, both times.

"But it's not about that. It's about Chrysothemis. I need to tell you." Mags took a deep breath. "Ursa's there."

"I know," said Kyr.

Then the rest of it came clear. Ursa, on Chrysothemis, with Ally—her son, the child she'd taken away from Gaea and from Jole. The dreadnought *Victrix* ready for combat in two weeks, descending on the rainy planet and its asteroid belt of irris mines, on the last human city, on the prefab slums and the beautiful main streets and the little flat with big windows and Ally's school where they made him wear a smart jacket and gave him art homework. "Oh fuck."

"I don't know what to do," said Mags. "I don't know what to do. If I—I've been thinking about—refusing assignment—"

"They won't let you go," Kyr said. "Not now. If you tried they'd just kill you." Fuck, fuck, fuck. "If we got a message out—"

"There's someone I know—"

"*Avi*," said Kyr at the same moment. They looked at each other.

Mags swallowed and went on, "I should say—"

"You really don't need to tell me about your crush on Avi right now," said Kyr. "Please don't tell me about your crush on Avi right now."

"How do you even *know*?"

Kyr opened her mouth to brush the question aside. She almost heard herself say it—something easy and meaningless, *I've been doing some thinking.* But she brought herself up short. *Stop underestimating Mags,* she thought. *You're as bad as Val. And you know why you do it, don't you?*

Face it. You're jealous. You always have been. Because he's bigger than you, because he's taller and broader and faster and stronger. Because he has a seventy-inch vertical leap, and the highest Drill scores in station history, and a perfect record on Level Twelve of the agoge. Because he beat Doomsday once. Because he's the best there is at all the things that ever mattered to you; because he's better than you; and you didn't even know all the ways he was better than you.

Maybe Val was right to call him fragile. But if he is, you didn't help. You made it worse.

So stop trying to make him small.

She remembered all the way back in the beginning, before assignments even started. Mags in Agricole. *You're so hard to talk to,* he'd said.

"I need to tell you something too," said Kyr. "Something else, I mean."

"Okay," said Mags.

"It's—it's a lot."

"Okay," said Mags. "I'm listening."

They went to Agricole, to the quiet spot in the heights of the modified trees where Mags hid from Gaea Station.

And Kyr told him everything.

Assignment to Nursery, escape, Avi, Yiso. Ursa and Ally and the bright little flat in Raingold. The Wisdom node and Leru and what Avi had done, what Mags had done afterward. And then she said things she did not mean to say, things she had barely let herself know she was still feeling: how it had been, to sit with those bodies among the wreckage of the worlds.

"Fuck, Vallie," said Mags. "I'm—"

"*Don't* say you're sorry," Kyr said. "Don't. Don't." She waited till her voice was steady. "I'm sorry. I'm sorry I didn't know."

Mags's double from the other timeline, the one who'd never been a soldier of Gaea, had said *that makes sense.* This Mags, the one who meant the most, *Kyr's* Mags—the person she'd run away from Gaea for, the person she would have died for—just looked pensive.

Finally he said, "I didn't want you to know, though."

It hollowed Kyr out to hear it. She didn't want it to be true: that Mags was unhappy, that he was *that* unhappy, already. But Mags scrubbed his hands through his fair hair and gave Kyr a wry look and said, "I didn't want you to think I was weak."

"You're *not,*" said Kyr.

Still that wry look, unfamiliar. Kyr had once thought she knew her brother well. Now she thought: *You get Avi's jokes, don't you.* Under the shining surface of Magnus the perfect soldier there had always been someone else. The way he felt about Avi suddenly struck Kyr not as a pitiful error of judgment but a totally understandable reaction to meeting someone who said out loud what you'd always felt inside.

"You're too good for him, though," she said.

Mags seemed to follow her thought. He made a face. "Well, I didn't know he was planning mass murder, did I?"

Kyr snorted, conceding the point. "There's more," she said.

"*More.*"

"I know, I know. But there's—" and she went on and told him about the other life, Val's life, Val's brother Max who'd run away to join the Ziviri Jo. And their sister, Commander Ursula Marston of the *Samphire.* And their mother, Admiral Elora Marston.

The *relief* of telling someone: of telling Mags, who believed her at once, who listened thoughtfully, who didn't say anything when Kyr's voice shook but put his arm more firmly around her shoulders. Kyr felt like she was back in Nursery again, six years old and totally certain of one thing in the universe, which was that she loved her brother and her brother loved her and the two of them were special.

And we were, we are, Kyr thought now: *not because we're Earth's children or soldiers of Gaea, none of that ever mattered, but because we're us.*

"So that's a *lot* of a lot," said Mags finally. The stationwide rec rotation was still going. Distantly Kyr could hear the thumping music from the arcade.

"Yeah," said Kyr.

"All right," Mags said. "So what are we going to do?"

"You were right," said Kyr. "We still need Avi."

CHAPTER TWENTY-SIX

SABOTAGE

"No," said Avi.

Every muscle in Kyr's jaw clenched in frustration. How had she forgotten he was a *jerk*?

Systems was nearly deserted. Only Corporal Lin was there, hunched over at her station on the far side of the dim maze of consoles. The rest of the wing was at the party in the arcade. Avi saw Kyr's glance. "Yup, just the two of us," he said. "Everyone else is basically superfluous if we're here. Systems Wing is seventy people praying Command won't realize they're pointless and shove them onto combat wings to die. We *know* how shitty those antique darts are."

"Listen, you don't understand," said Mags.

"I do, though," said Avi. "I'm sorry about your sister, Magnus. But"—he shrugged—"I send a warning to the enemy, that makes me a traitor."

"And you care so much about betraying *this*," said Kyr.

"No, I just really and truly don't want to get shot in the head," Avi said. "Or whatever nastier thing Command comes up with if they decide to make an example." He gave them both a mirthless smirk, as if he'd said something funny.

Kyr swallowed the urge to snarl at him. Avi didn't get more manageable if you tried to intimidate him. "Do you actually want this to happen?" she said. "Honestly. Do you think Gaea Station ought to send a warship to conquer the last human world?"

Avi looked at her, full-on, squinting. He looked newly strange to Kyr without glasses. "Who *are* you?" he said.

"What?"

"There's just something strange about you, Valkyr," he said. "You're not how I thought you'd be."

"I'm amazed you thought about me at all."

"There it is again. Like you think you know me." Avi waved it away. "Who cares. Who the fuck cares about anything. In answer to your question, no, I don't believe that humans killing other humans is going to be the answer to anything. And whatever happens, this is going to kill a lot of humans. Even if I send your precious warning, what then? You think they have defenses? Chrysothemis is a human world in the majoda less than fifty years after humans tried to conquer the universe, Valkyr, they're so aggressively demilitarized they barely have a police force. The majo are *peace-loving*," a sneer, "but they're not morons. Best-case scenario, Chrysothemis throws together something in two weeks that is definitely not enough to *stop* even a half-armed dreadnought but more than enough to kill a hell of a lot of us first. More people die, nothing changes."

"But Ursa," said Mags.

"Honestly," Avi said, "if you think Jole is ever going to stop hunting her as long as she has that kid, or even if she gives the kid up—want to see some internal memos from when she ran?"

"You said there wasn't anything," Mags said.

"I thought maybe you wouldn't like to hear in detail about how much our heroic commander in chief wants to dismember your sister," Avi said. "She defied him and she won. Jole's a vindictive shit under all the smirking and speeches. The Wisdom was containing Gaea Station. The Wisdom's gone. Your sister's dead. Sorry."

"Fuck you," said Kyr.

"No thanks, you're not my type," said Avi. "Oh, hang on." He turned to his console and started ignoring them. Kyr stared at his back in mute outrage.

Mags said, "Avi, please—"

Kyr touched his arm to stop him. Begging wouldn't change anything. The problem with Avi was that he was a jerk but he wasn't stupid. If he said warning Chrysothemis wouldn't help, then it wouldn't help. "All right," Kyr said. "So we find another way. Can we—" The shape of it came to her huge and awful and unthinkable, unthinkable at least for the person she used to be. "Can we sabotage the *Victrix*?"

Avi jerked in his seat, and then he said, "Fuck, I do actually have to deal with this, asphyxiation isn't fun," and refocused on the console. Kyr folded her arms and waited. She didn't often let herself think about how much of Gaea Station's survival depended on a handful of fragile, aging systems held together by— well, apparently, by Avi and Corporal Lin.

Avi turned around in his chair when he was done. "Sabotage, maybe," he said. "Are you serious? Are you sure? I could do it, but we'd get caught." He laughed, short and nasty. "*I'd* get caught, and I'd immediately drop you two in the shit with me, let's be clear here. And then we all three get the shot-in-the-head-or-worse treatment."

"But would it work?" said Kyr.

"That really doesn't frighten you at all, does it?" Avi said. "Et tu, Magnus? God, you fucking warbreeds, I swear they bred out the self-preservation chunk of your prefrontal cortex. It would work. Shame they've got three more warships."

Augusta, Scythica, Ferox. Kyr nodded. "Could you take out all of them?"

"Oh, yeah," Avi said. "That would even be easier. And, good news, we *wouldn't* get shot in the head. Frying that much of Gaea Station's infrastructure at once would also kill everyone here. You know, I actually like that plan better? Maybe asphyxiation *would* be fun. Probably more fun than getting executed, who knows?"

"You're not taking us seriously," said Mags.

Avi rolled his eyes. "Listen—"

"I thought you would," Mags said. "Because you've always taken me seriously."

There was a pause.

"Oh—fuck me," said Avi. "Shut *up*, Magnus. This isn't like being sick of endless xenocidal fantasies in the agoge or just wanting to know what happened to your sister—"

"No," Mags said. "It's more important."

Avi put his head in his hands. It was showy, a performance, but Kyr watched him thoughtfully. She thought the part where he was avoiding Mags's eyes was real.

"Say I do it," he said into his hands. "Say I do it, and they execute me."

"Us," said Kyr.

Avi's head jerked up. "Fuck off, Valkyr, maybe I *wouldn't* snitch and drop you two into hell with me, you don't know. You don't know me."

Kyr said nothing.

"The *Victrix* isn't a random choice. She's the dreadnought with the fewest key systems repurposed to run the station," Avi said. "Two weeks is tight but if everyone's working double shifts they might actually get her spaceworthy in that time. If I did what you're asking, and Command couldn't use that ship, they'd have to switch to one of the other three—probably *Ferox*, which would kill Agricole but if they're taking a planet they won't need this place to have food and air much longer. Refitting *Ferox* would take more time. Six weeks, say."

"So if we could get the message to Chrysothemis fast enough—"

"They get more time to prepare," Avi said. "Possibly call in majo reinforcements, though fuck knows what the majo even have without the Wisdom. Maybe your sister gets herself and the kid offworld, somewhere Jole can't reach yet." He sighed. "The message part would be your problem, though, you realize, because in this scenario I'm still getting executed."

"No," said Mags. "There has to be a better way."

"You're cute," said Avi. "You know that, Magnus? You really are. But you are not the brains of this operation."

"Oh, thanks," said Mags, but he was smiling.

"How much time would you need?" Kyr said.

"I could do it tomorrow. I could do it now, you guys just need to go and distract Lin for two minutes first."

"Vallie—" said Mags.

"No," said Kyr. "We don't have a plan for how to get the message to Chrysothemis yet. There's no point wasting it. Can you wait?"

"Not infinitely," Avi said. "I'm not *brave*. I'll talk myself out of this in a couple of days." He laughed. "I don't know how you managed to talk me into it right now."

"You are brave, though," Mags said. "Thank you."

Avi winced and looked away.

There *had* to be a way to do this better. Kyr had spent years of her life running through scenarios that were obstacles, solutions, sting in the tail; she had *beaten Doomsday*, in the end, though no one on Gaea knew that now.

She remembered that Avi had beaten Doomsday too, talking to Mags through an earpiece.

"If this was a game," she said, "how would you do it?"

Avi looked at her pityingly. "Valkyr," he said, "it's not."

Kyr went back to the Sparrow barracks. *Seven teenage girls sleeping in a space barely bigger than your bathroom on Hymmer*, said Val somewhere inside, but since the Val-memories had this kind of comment to make about everything, Kyr just let it slide away. She was still thinking in circles around the problem of sabotaging the *Victrix*—how to get a message to Chrysothemis afterward, without Avi and his Systems expertise—if there was a way to save Avi, if he did it—if there was a way to do anything *without* Avi—

The painted ship, she thought on the threshold. *Yiso. We got out once before. Are they* here?

But then she had to school her expression to unreadability, because the other Sparrows were already there. This was where they'd fled from the celebration. The small room was very full with a girl sitting in nearly every bunk. Arti and Vic were curled together in Arti's bunk with their arms pressed against each other. Kyr's place was empty.

"Oh, hello, fearless leader," said Cleo. "So pleased you could make it."

Kyr wondered how she had ever failed to realize that Cleo wasn't her friend. It wasn't like she *hid* anything. "Hi," she said, and looked around at all their faces. Val was thinking things again. This time it was *Pretty ethnically homogenous for a supposedly pan-human liberation movement, aren't we, Valkyr?* There was a sameness to the Sparrows' features that spoke to the limited genetic pool Gaea had started with, something that Kyr had never noticed but Val found creepy. Cleo was the only one who wasn't white.

"What is it?" Kyr said, still looking at their faces, because *something* was wrong.

"Assignment," said Lisabel, after a moment when no one said anything. Kyr found she could not look directly at Lisabel. She had somehow, at some point, superimposed Lisa from that other universe over her mental picture of the real Lisabel, and so eliminated the scraped edge from her smile, and the underfed thinness of her arms. *They don't feed you enough!* howled Val. *Any of you!*

"We waited for you," said Cleo. Kyr saw that a sheaf of flimsies was sitting on her bunk, unopened, each labeled with a name.

She picked them up. Nobody spoke as she handed them out. Kyr felt cold tension take hold of her shoulders, watched it set its claws in every girl in her mess. Zen's expression was flatter than ever, and Jeanne's coolness now looked to Kyr like resignation. *Jeanne died*, Cleo had said, in that other life. Vic's hands were shaking so badly that she gave her flimsy to Arti to unfold for her. Arti glanced up toward Kyr before she did it, and Kyr caught for the first time the real hatred and defiance in that silent glance. Arti wasn't just a quiet person. She talked to the others. She just didn't talk to Kyr, because she *loathed Kyr*.

Lisabel looked at Kyr first too. Kyr could finally understand that look as well. *You didn't like me either*, she thought. *You couldn't. You felt sorry for me, because I was a monster, and I was trying so hard, and no one else liked me either. You thought I was lonely, and you were right. And you thought I would probably die young, and you were right about that too.*

And I bullied you and I hurt you and I told you to be better and I showed you no mercy. Just as I did to everyone else. I wasn't your leader, that was Cleo. And I was never your friend. I was Gaea Station. It was all I knew. It was all I wanted.

Kyr watched them unfold the flimsies with small rustling sounds. She had never been afraid for the Sparrows before. She'd once been proud of being fearless. She missed it sharply. Fearlessness had been so simple. It had been so *easy*.

The tension she felt wasn't for herself. She knew her assignment. She'd lived that betrayal already, and it didn't matter now. It was the others she ached for—for Jeanne's cool head and lanky strength, for Cleo's fierce spirit and perfect aim, for Arti's protectiveness and Vic's cleverness and Zen's sharp good sense, and for Lisabel, Lisabel, who was kind and beautiful and did not deserve this. None of them had ever deserved this. The home they had been taught to trust absolutely and serve without question had been rotten from the start.

And they were Kyr's mess, Kyr's Sparrows, whom she'd coached and chivvied and challenged through every level of training, who'd been by her side in everything Gaea had done to them, whom Gaea had made just as it had made her. They might hate her. They had every right to hate her. But they were her sisters, as much as or more than Ursa.

There was a quiet when everyone had opened their assignment. "Well?" Cleo said harshly. Kyr realized they were waiting for her.

She flipped the flimsy open but didn't bother to look. "Nursery," she said. It didn't even hurt to think about it anymore. She was so used to it now, the betrayal that had pulled the shape of her world out of true.

Cleo's face twisted. "I don't believe you," she said. "Give me that."

"Hey—"

Cleo snatched the flimsy. She read it and then laughed, nastily. *"Nursery?"* she said. "Making fun of us, Valkyr?" She threw the scrap back at Kyr's face.

Kyr caught it, and read it this time.

COMMAND, it said. ADC CMDR JOLE. And the squiggle of Jole's signature underneath.

It didn't make sense. Kyr stared at it. Straight to Command. Aide-de-camp to Jole himself. It was exactly the kind of assignment that her old self would have dreamed of—would have *killed* for—fieldwork, too, obviously, because Jole was going to lead the invasion of Chrysothemis himself. She'd be on the bridge of the *Victrix*. She'd be in the heart of everything.

"Just like big sis!" said Cleo. "Hey, girls, remember *Ursa*? Command straight out of junior mess, straight up the ladder till she turned traitor. Does Jole think it's second time lucky with you, Valkyr?"

Aide-de-camp to Jole. The flimsy fell out of Kyr's hand and she didn't bother to catch it. Second time lucky, right. She suddenly knew clearly and with cold disgust exactly what Jole wanted with her. The shape of it had been nagging at her thoughts for days. *Remember when he put out his hand to help you up in the agoge,* said a calm voice in her mind that was nowhere near as soft and smug as Val. *Remember when he touched you. Remember when he assigned you to Nursery, last time when he wasn't planning to leave the station two weeks later, and remember when he told you he was proud.*

"He raped Ursa," she said.

Cleo stopped talking. The little bunkroom was abruptly filled with hush that was heavy as a planet's gravity.

Kyr looked at them and saw that they were all looking at her, *really* looking, with a directness that felt unfamiliar. "You think that old rumor matters *now*—" began Cleo.

"Oh, shut up, Cleo," said Zen. "Not everything is about your little rivalry thing." She turned to Kyr. "Really?"

"There was a rumor?" said Kyr. She glanced at Lisabel, who was avoiding her eyes. Oh. So there had been *something*. Lisabel knew the real worth of station gossip, which was *survival*. She'd known the truth about Ursa. But she hadn't passed it on to Kyr.

Well, that made sense.

It wasn't just leaving Gaea that made the truth about this place obvious, that same cool voice said in her thoughts. It wasn't Val. Maybe it was Kyr herself. *You could have known sooner, if you'd been paying attention. Cleo knew. Zen knew. Lisabel knew, and Avi, and Mags. You could have known. You chose not to.*

No one was saying anything.

"She turned traitor to get away from him," Kyr said. "And to get her son away from him. He ordered the combat wings not to shoot down her dart because the child was on board."

Still no one was saying anything. Kyr said, "They're leaving Nursery behind, aren't they?"

"They're starting a war," answered a shaky voice. Vic. Arti's arm went back around her, not just holding but squeezing, and Arti glared at Kyr. "They won't take the—"

She faltered.

"—the breeding stock," Lisabel finished softly.

"What were you assigned?" Kyr demanded. "All of you."

They went round the circle. Jeanne still got Ferox. Vic was Systems rather than Suntracker—that made sense, she was the cleverest and refitting the *Victrix* would need all hands. Arti went to Scythica.

Lisabel, Zen, and Cleo had all been assigned to Nursery.

Kyr pressed her lips tightly together. The cold voice that was her own said: *You are very angry.* She had never felt anger quite like this before. It turned the edges of her vision glitteringly sharp.

"Fuck this," she said. "Fuck all of this."

"Oh, big words," said Cleo in a choked voice. Now that she wasn't pretending to be angry anymore she was crying ugly tears.

"What are you going to do, Valkyr? *Protest?* To Jole? To Command? To anyone? No one cares! Not one single person gives a shit what happens to us, no matter what we do, no matter how hard we try or how good we are—do you get that now? Do you finally *get it*?"

"I get it, Cleo," Kyr said. "I'm not going to protest."

She looked at them: her mess, her sisters, her Sparrows.

"I'm going to need your help," she said. "All of you."

"It's the middle of the night cycle, Valkyr," Avi said. "If anyone finds you hanging around the arcade—"

"I don't care, and neither do you, or you wouldn't be here either," Kyr said. "Listen—"

"Me first. I had an idea about how to get the message to Chrysothemis. You probably haven't heard, but a patrol captured a majo ship with an alien on board—it's tiny, but it's jump-capable. I'll need to be on the *Victrix* to kill her, even I can't do it remotely. But while I'm doing that, if you and Magnus break out the prisoner to fly it for you—"

"You said you weren't brave," Kyr said.

"I'm *not,*" said Avi. "I'm scared *shitless* by this. But—"

"It doesn't matter," Kyr said. "We're not sabotaging the *Victrix*."

"*Now* you change your mind? What happened, Valkyr? Command assignment cheer you up?" Avi bared his teeth at her. Of course he knew the assignments. He'd probably dug around in Systems to have a look.

"No," said Kyr. "But the majo ship is too small."

"It's big enough to carry a message," said Avi. "I thought of a way to get your brother out of this shithole and save your sister's life, Valkyr. Now you take it. You aren't going to think of something better, because if there was something better I would have spotted it first."

Kyr smiled at him. Avi flinched back. "What the fuck," he said.

"We're not going to sabotage the *Victrix*," said Kyr. In her mind was a picture: the unhappy circle of the Sparrows, Cleo still in tears, all of them staring at her as she said at last what she should have said the first time: *I'm not leaving any of you behind.*

"We're not?" said Avi.

"No," Kyr said. "We're going to steal it."

CHAPTER TWENTY-SEVEN

COMMAND

Kyr walked with a spring in her step. The Command insignia—the circle of Earth—shone bright on her collar.

Avi had tried to talk her out of this. *Too risky, Valkyr,* he'd said. *What is even the point?* And Kyr had told him, out of that cold place inside which accepted no compromises: *Not negotiable.*

Two Victrix soldiers were on duty in the brig. Avi had grumbled, but he'd done the roster tweaks, so one of them was Mags, newly assigned. The other was an older man Kyr didn't know. She saluted him; he saluted back, grudgingly, eyes on her collar. Being an overpromoted teenager didn't make you popular.

"Message for you," Kyr said, and handed over a flimsy. The man took it, read, grimaced—it moved him to a work crew two floors up, doing heavy lifting for the Systems wonks who were overseeing the refitting of the *Victrix.* It would take someone who cared a long time going through the scheduling for the day to spot that it had come from nowhere and been signed off by no one. The dreadnought-refitting project had upended all of Gaea's usual rotations and schedules. Everyone just ignored the shift bells now. Mags had been assigned to this guard post for four rotations straight, starting with this one, and it hadn't flagged anything anywhere.

With a grunt and another, sloppier salute, the soldier left. Kyr and Mags waited for his footsteps to fade away. Mags watched him turn the corner, then looked at Kyr and gave her a precise, sarcastic salute of his own.

"Don't relax yet," said Kyr.

"Do I look relaxed?" said Mags.

He looked good, actually, shoulders square in his navy uniform, fair hair bright against the gloom in the brig, like a picture of how a soldier of humanity was supposed to be. Kyr nudged him with her elbow as she went past.

The cell where they were keeping the captured majo was live and humming. Kyr murmured, "Avi."

In her earpiece Avi answered, "*Still not sure about this, fearless leader.*"

He'd picked up the *fearless leader* thing from Cleo. It had only been a few days and Kyr already deeply regretted introducing them.

"Objection duly noted," she said, and got a little huff of annoyed laughter back.

"I say hi," murmured Mags, and Kyr passed it on. Mags didn't have an earpiece. It would have been too easy for someone to spot it and ask questions. Kyr wore hers openly; she was Commander Jole's ADC, why wouldn't she be on comms?

It took Avi a moment longer than last time. Last time they'd been planning to be off the station less than an hour later. This time he was taking more care not to get caught. Avi was by far the most vulnerable person in Kyr's little network. All it would take was *one* Systems officer actually paying attention to him and things would fall apart.

So this was a risk. Maybe it was even an unnecessary risk. But Kyr didn't care.

"Hi, Yiso," she said, when the cell door went down.

Yiso was huddled on the floor at the far end of the cell. They looked up, eyes huge and silvery and catching all the dim light available. Kyr was half aware of Mags hovering watchfully behind her. She still remembered one of the first things Yiso had ever said to her: *Why are you afraid of me?*

"You know my name?" Yiso said.

"It's complicated," said Kyr.

Their crest dipped a little, tense. Their face was bruised. The cold place inside Kyr noted the bruise with quiet fury and set it aside. Rage was not useful just now.

Yiso stood up. Their full height was still only just bigger than child-sized. Their eyes did not leave Kyr; did not even flick to Mags, who was looming behind her with the kind of fearsomely huge presence that Kyr had always been told would terrify the majo out of their wits.

"I think . . . I know you," they said. "What—what loop is this?" Their ears flicked: out, down. "No, no. You were in the Halls of the Wise—you were on my ship—you were in a, a room on Hymmer Station—"

Kyr caught them under the arms as they stumbled. "Are you all right?"

"You were *here*," Yiso said. "Last time—one time—some time—I think you saved my life. I'm sorry. I'm getting a lot of temporal feedback. The Wisdom normally sorts it out—but it's dead, you know. It killed itself. It's dead—"

"I know," said Kyr. "Come on. Let's get you out of here."

Yiso's expression cleared. "*Valkyr*," they said. "Of course it's you."

"Right, of course," Kyr said, and started walking them out of the cell. Something in her chest was warm.

Yiso stumbled to a halt on the threshold of the cell, as soon as they saw Mags. "Magnus," they said. "Max. You helped the Ziviri Jo—you kept me alive. I never said how grateful—"

Mags looked alarmed. "What's it saying?" he asked.

"Yiso's not an it," said Kyr sharply. "They're a bit confused, that's all."

"*You* try having a god machine commit suicide in your head," said Yiso.

"It really does know you," Mags said, and then, at Kyr's look, "They. Sorry."

"You didn't believe me?" said Kyr.

"Of course I believed you," Mags said. "It was still a lot." He touched one of the shiny black buttons on his navy tunic, a fidget, and a shadowed expression flitted across his face before it flattened out into a safe Gaean neutral again. Kyr was getting better at making herself pay attention; at noticing how Mags's unhappiness surfaced and then got pushed back down. *I have to get him out of here*, she thought.

"Sorry," said Yiso. "I never seem to be much good at getting rescued. Where are we going? What are we doing? What do you need, Valkyr?"

"I need you safe," said Kyr. "Let's start with that."

They left Mags guarding the empty cell. Of course there was no *safe*, not for a majo on Gaea Station. But there were places no one went. One of them was Magnus's napping spot near the top of Agricole. "This is astonishing," said Yiso, peering about. "To create a garden like this on a desert rock in a handful of decades . . . it's spectacular. So few species have even attempted this kind of thing."

"We wouldn't have done it either if we didn't have to," Kyr pointed out.

Yiso flinched. "Sorry."

Kyr hadn't meant it as a barb. It was just true. "I can't stay with you all the time, there's too much to do. This place is mostly empty, but pay attention to when the Agricole rotations come in," she said. "*Listen.* I know you're—"

"—well-adapted," said Yiso along with her. "Yes." Their ears flicked. "What are you doing? Can I help?"

"I don't think so," said Kyr, at the same time as Avi said in her ear, "*Wait, how much does it know about running shadowspace sims?*" and then, "*It, they.*"

"That's what I'm *for*," Yiso said when Kyr relayed the question. "I mean—it's what I was for, before." Before the Wisdom died.

"Because I think I have a solution to our biggest problem," Avi said. *"But even for me this is going to be tricky."*

Of course Avi assumed the problems he was dealing with were the biggest ones. He might even be right. But Kyr had a list humming in her head which was constantly shuffling and rearranging itself, *obstacles—solutions—sting in the tail.* Every problem was the biggest problem. She had so many people she wanted to rescue. When she tried to sleep everything that could go wrong laid itself out on the backs of her eyelids like the feeds from a combat mask.

At least Yiso was no longer in a Gaean cell.

The *Victrix* needed to be spaceworthy—that was one problem. Thankfully it wasn't Kyr's problem. Commander Jole was personally overseeing every aspect of his planned offensive against Chrysothemis, breathing down the necks of Systems and Oikos and Suntracker as they worked. He had casually assumed command of Victrix Wing, too, elbowing aside Admiral Russell. So far, Kyr as his ADC hadn't had much to do. She ran errands; she delivered messages. Jole had Russell doing that too. Kyr thought the admiral did not like it much.

She had not yet had to spend much actual time with Jole. The thought of it sent creeping fingers of distaste up her spine. But she had not been assigned new quarters, officially, and the rest of the Sparrows had. Kyr slept alone now in the chilly bunkroom that had once held seven. Part of her was waiting for the next thing to happen. He'd made Ursa sleep in his quarters.

She tried not to think about it.

Another problem: seizing control of the *Victrix* once she was ready. This was actually the part Kyr was least worried about. Avi had hijacked the Wisdom itself twice over in two universes. He was a pain, but he *was* brilliant. As long as he did not get caught doing the thousand small tweaks Kyr needed from him in the meantime, like that roster adjustment, they would be fine.

A third problem: making sure the right people were on the ship when she launched. Kyr had thought at first . . . only the good ones. The Sparrows, Avi, Yiso, Mags.

"Even I can't fly a dreadnought with no crew, so—" Avi had said.

"Some of the Coyotes—" That was Mags.

"We have to take the children," said Lisabel. This council of war was happening in an empty Oikos storeroom, everyone on their feet, the gunpowder smell of space dust in the air. The others shut up when Lisabel spoke. Kyr had looked at her face and seen an echo of the cold calm place inside herself that accepted no obstacles. She saw at once that either they took Gaea's children with them, or Lisabel wasn't coming.

Of course she was right. Kyr could see that she was right. It wasn't that she was soft about children, the way some people were. She'd never liked Nursery rotations. Somewhere inside her there was still the sick horror over her original assignment: nothing struck her as more viscerally, physically disgusting than having to be the mother of humanity's future. But she thought of the Blackbirds lined up in the arcade for full muster, and of Ally in the bright room in Raingold.

"It's what Ursa did," she said.

"Right, but that kid was *hers*," Avi said. "She wanted it, fine. How the hell are we supposed to supervise two hundred kids— including the *babies*—in an op like this? It's crazy."

"It's necessary," Kyr said. "If we leave Jole the children then Gaea still has a future. You said it yourself. They have three more dreadnoughts. We'd just be putting the problem off, not solving it."

Avi rolled his eyes. "By that logic we have take all of Nursery Wing with us as well."

"Great. They can supervise the babies," said Kyr. As she said it she felt how right it was. *I'm not leaving any of you behind.* Nursery was a crime. No one should have to endure it.

Avi said, "Are you nuts? Hell, it's not just Nursery, they're not going to stick to wing assignments if it's an emergency. We'd have to take every fertile woman on Gaea."

There was a moment's silence. Then:

"*Yes*," said Cleo harshly. She was looking at Kyr.

"Yes," Kyr said back to her. "Let's do it."

A sigh rustled around the circle of plotters, a shifting, an exchange of looks among the Sparrows. Vic moved her weight from foot to foot. Zen folded her arms. Arti's eyes rested on Kyr as if she had never seen her before. Jeanne smiled a rare, tight smile.

Mags looked confused and Avi was frowning. There were things the two of them couldn't understand—not in the ugly way that all the Sparrows understood them. Men were never assigned to Nursery. Kyr remembered toasting Lisabel last time round, *I would rather stand three times in the battle line than give birth to one child*, and the smashed fragments of silvered glass.

"Wait, are you serious?" said Avi.

"Of course we're serious," said Kyr.

Avi threw his hands in the air. "Women and children first, sure, why not? The more the merrier! No way this is going to come back and bite us, we can *definitely* trust every fucking bitch on this station not to drop us in the shit, it's not like we're collectively brainwashed or anything—present company excepted—"

Kyr said nothing. She did not think it was present company excepted. She still remembered Avi's awful triumph, in that first timeline, when he'd killed the majo worlds. Gaea had planted its seeds in all of them. They were in Kyr too, she knew they were, putting out shoots that coiled through her the same way Val's total self-belief and her smugness were twisted through everything she'd ever thought or done. Just because Kyr was looking for it now didn't mean she'd find it every time. Just because she knew where she'd come from and what she was didn't mean she was *safe* from it.

"Can we not tell them?" Cleo said. "Can we get Nursery off the station without anyone realizing what we're doing till we've done it?"

"How, genius?" snapped Avi.

"I don't know, *you're* supposed to be the genius—"

"I do systems," Avi said, "not *people*."

"There's a way," said Kyr. "Let me think about it. There will be a way." She looked around at them all. "I promise you. We won't leave anyone behind."

And ten years of being cadets together meant something after all. The Sparrows might not love Kyr. But they all knew that when she said she was going to do something, she did it. She saw the minute relaxations: Jeanne's nod, Zen's grim little smile, Arti and Vic's traded glances. She heard Cleo's huff of breath, half annoyed and half satisfied.

Lisabel said quietly, "I'm counting on you."

Kyr couldn't meet her eyes. She kept seeing the smiling ghost of Lisa in her face. Sometimes she found herself looking for it, sneaking glances at Lisabel's profile, a kind of talisman. *I have to get you out of here too.*

This was not the agoge. There would be no do-overs, no second chances. She had to get this right.

As Kyr left Agricole and Yiso's hiding place behind, the shift bells rang. Kyr took herself briskly down to the hulk of the *Victrix*. The dim corridors of the dead dreadnought were full of people at work. Some of them saluted Kyr's Command badge as she made her way to the bridge. Some of them didn't. Kyr couldn't blame them.

There was a junior from Oikos on her hands and knees on the command platform of *Victrix*'s bridge. She was scrubbing at the old, dark bloodstains that spattered up the wall. Kyr wondered who'd been in here first, to cut out the ancient recording of the ship's last distress call before the wrong person could hear it. *Admiral Elora Marston, TE-66 Victrix.* Kyr had stood and listened to that stranger's voice, because she'd never thought of a woman being an admiral. She hadn't known—

Mom, thought Val.

Shut up, Kyr thought at the ghost in her mind as hard as she possibly could. She could not afford to feel Val's feelings right now.

Jole was on the command platform too, standing with his hand possessively on the rail as he looked over the expanse of the newly illuminated and shining clean bridge. He ignored the girl scrubbing the bloodstain as if she were not there. Systems officers were clustered around each terminal and arguing. Kyr overheard one saying, "—pull up Avicenna to look at—"

"Oh, not that little assface queer," said another. "I don't care how good he is, I'm not working close quarters with him."

"Lin, then."

"That snotty old bitch? No. We can handle this, let's—"

Moron, thought Kyr, and went to salute her commanding officer.

"Valkyr. At ease," said Jole. "I hope you had a relaxing rec rotation."

"I mostly ran drills, sir," said Kyr, secure in the knowledge that this was both exactly what her old self would have been doing and that anyone who checked the agoge logs would find records of her doing fast-paced urban-combat scenarios. Avi was *so* useful.

Jole smiled. "Of course you did. Come stand by me."

Kyr did as she was told. The scrubbing girl from Oikos muttered something inaudible and moved her sudsy bucket out of the way. Kyr didn't look down. It was strange to know that once she wouldn't have even *thought* of looking down.

You thought you were so great—this was her own mental voice, not Val's. *But you would have made a pretty shitty commander, if anyone had been stupid enough to put you in charge of anything.*

"How does it feel?" said Jole.

Kyr suppressed a start. "Sir?"

That smile again. Kyr had once found it almost magically comforting when Jole smiled at her. "Standing on the bridge of a dreadnought," he said. "A conqueror of worlds. Ready to take on the universe. How does it feel, Valkyr?"

"I—" Kyr said, and couldn't finish.

"To me it feels like coming home," said Jole. "This is our birthright. This is Earth's legacy." He put his hand on Kyr's shoulder. Kyr breathed out, and did not flinch, even when his fingers clamped down in a grip that was probably meant to be firm and reassuring. "You'll get to see it all standing beside me, Valkyr. Which is as it should be." He let go of her. Kyr could not, quite, control her breathing. Jole looked pleased. "A good commander does not have favorites," he said. "But you are special, Valkyr. Some people may show you jealousy or resentment in the coming days, but remember that I picked you for my aide, and not your meathead brother. I did that for a reason."

He was the man who'd shaped her world, the hero she'd looked up to. *This would have* worked, Kyr thought miserably. *If I didn't already know. This would have worked. Maybe he said things like this to Ursa.*

"Yes, sir" was all she said. "Thank you, sir."

Avi was working double shifts. They were well into Gaea's next day cycle by the time Kyr could get him down to Agricole to meet Yiso for—well, for the first time. This time.

"Avicenna," Yiso said, before Kyr could say anything.

Avi was silent for a long moment, contemplating the majo. Agricole was full of green quiet around them. Kyr didn't actually *need* to be present. She had a thousand things to do, some of them legitimate duties, some of them highly illegitimate but just as necessary. She was worried about Vic. She had always been the jumpiest of them, but she'd been shakier than ever since the meeting where they'd decided to take Nursery with them, and now someone had to check in with her and say calming things every so often. The other Sparrows were less visibly nervous—if Gaean cadet training taught you nothing else, it taught you how to keep your thoughts off your face—but the crime against Gaea they were planning was so huge, so unthinkable, that all of them had wobbles. *Kyr* would have been wobbling, if she weren't so busy.

She'd recruited Zen—who *really* didn't like Kyr, but who Kyr could now see was perhaps the toughest and most levelheaded of the Sparrows—to do the saying-calming-things part; she was better at it than Kyr. She'd also got Avi to tweak the duty rosters again, this time to make sure Arti and Vic had overlapping rest periods, because they did better when they had a chance to see each other. Was it enough? Kyr could have been checking in on Lisabel, Cleo, and Zen in Nursery right now, or Jeanne, or Mags; she could even have been doing some actual drill work. Their plan as it stood didn't involve any fighting. Kyr wished she could be sure things would work out that way. She was bitterly aware that if it *did* come down to a fight, Jole could command hundreds of Gaea's warbreed soldiers, and she had herself and Cleo and Arti and Jeanne—all of whom were *very* good, for a girls' mess, but any three of Jole's big Victrix commandos outweighed all four of them put together—and after that, only Mags, who was the best in their whole age cohort, but who was also just one seventeen-year-old boy.

She could have been doing all sorts of necessary things, but she did not want to leave Yiso alone with Avi. Not after the Halls of the Wise and not-Avi's bright, cold curiosity. Not after the underground garden of the Wisdom node on Chrysothemis, where another iteration of *this* Avi had taken the superior strength that even an undersized human always had when dealing with the majo and used it to torture a prisoner for the sake of Earth's vengeance.

Eventually Avi tore his eyes away from Yiso's alien face. He snorted. "Rulers of the universe for millennia," he said. "Are you really a Prince of the Wisdom?"

"I was," Yiso said, "when the Wisdom existed."

"Was it fun?"

Yiso paused. "Do you know," they said, "no one's ever asked me that question before."

"Really? Stupid of them," Avi said. "It was a parallel-universe builder, right? Existing in every possible timeline at once—*cool* shadowspace shit, always theoretically possible but you'd need shadow engines on a whole other order to sustain it—simulating potential realities on a grand scale, constantly, and then someone—you, I guess, or your progenitor Prince Leru—picks the best simulation and the machine drags our whole universe over to that," he waved his hands about like he was trying to grab a word from the air, "that thread. Which sometimes involves a bit of space-wizard bullshit because the Wisdom also gives you a shortcut to control possibilities in space as well as time, very nice, basically unlimited cheat codes for the universe. Once you cut out all the mystical bullshit that's it, right? Oh, yes, I know I'm simplifying, *obviously* I'm simplifying—but that's it?"

Yiso's ears flicked. "You are a remarkable individual, Avicenna. Yes, that is correct."

"For once I don't get the credit; Earth worked it out during the war," said Avicenna. "We were building our own."

Kyr knew this. "The agoge," she said.

Avi looked halfway between annoyed and impressed. "The ultimate weapon. Right." He looked at Yiso. "And you knew that too."

"It was one of the reasons why—" Yiso said, and stopped, and then said, "—my progenitor—"

"Right, right." Avi folded himself down cross-legged and waved at Yiso until Yiso dropped down to join him. "You too, fearless leader, stop looming, it makes me tired," Avi said.

"Ah," Yiso said, sounding enlightened. "A cultural expectation. Is relative height really that important?"

Avi rolled his eyes.

"Eye contact," Kyr said as she sat down. The high green branches of Agricole's trees formed a kind of shield around them. She'd never really thought about it before but it was obvious as soon as

Yiso asked. "Having your faces on the same level, that's important. It shows—"

"Respect," Avi said, and snorted. "It's great fun being a short human, for the record."

"You are short?" Yiso said.

"Obviously I'm short, even the girls tower over me."

"Is that unusual?"

"Oh for fuck's sake," Avi said. "*Focus.* So Earth was building its own Wisdom. Or trying to. The problem is—yes, thank you, no need for the alien to explain my own history to me, shut up—the problem is completely obvious; if you have *two* universe-reshaping superintelligences working at once—"

He stopped.

"Well?" Kyr said. "What would happen?"

"No one knows!" Avi said. "Options range from 'canceling each other out' to 'permanently unraveling the fabric of space-time'! Unless *your* side knew."

"No," Yiso said. "But Leru feared the worst."

"Destroying a whole capital world wasn't just a shortcut to end the war," Avi said. "It destroyed our manufacturing base—our networks—our *science.* Chrysothemis isn't going to build a god machine anytime soon. No one is. With the old one gone, that technology is—" He closed his fist, like someone crushing something out of existence. "For the next several centuries, at least. But we've got the prototypes, haven't we?" Avi was grinning. Yiso startled, and their ears flattened against their head. All those teeth, Kyr thought. Even if you know what a smile is, humans have a lot of teeth. "They're crude as fuck. I spent the last however long trying to make them do actually interesting things instead of just being war games for the grunts. But they're *here.*"

The agoge had defined Kyr's childhood, had shaped her more than anything else. She looked from Avi to Yiso, and thought for a moment about how much there was she had never known, and how much there was she still didn't know.

"Oh," Yiso said. "I see. Yes, I think I can help."

CHAPTER TWENTY-EIGHT

AULUS JOLE

Avi explained his idea. It was mostly too technical for Kyr to follow, though Yiso nodded gravely. She got the gist. Avi wanted to use the agoge to fake a stationwide emergency—a majo attack.

"Think about it," he said. "You want all the soldiers off the *Victrix* and all the kids piled on. So we spoof a fake cruiser and stage an attack at the other side of the station—say, the Ferox hangar. They charge toward Nursery, and boom, evacuation."

It was very neat. The heart of Gaea was twisted and locked around opposing the majoda. An attack on the station itself—on Gaea's children—oh yes, it would work.

Yiso said, "But we would never do that. No one would."

Avi rolled his eyes. Kyr said, "That doesn't matter. We still think you would. That's enough."

"It needs to feel real, though," Avi said. "That's where you come in. Consider yourself," he sniggered, "a creative consultant."

"You're enjoying this," Kyr said.

"Valkyr," Avi said, "I cannot tell you how many times I have fantasized about seeing this shithole stormed and smashed open and shattered forever by *someone*. Of course I'm enjoying this."

Kyr exchanged an involuntary look with Yiso.

"All right, what the fuck," Avi said. "What is going on here?"

Kyr said, "I don't know what you mean."

"You were weird enough by yourself," Avi said. "You kept acting like you *knew* me. And then you were fixated on rescuing a majo from a perfectly comfortable prison cell where it wasn't going to get into trouble any time soon, and now it's you *and* the alien acting like you know something I don't. Let me be clear, I hate that."

"You're imagining things," said Kyr, at the same time as Yiso said, "It's complicated."

"*Yiso*," Kyr said.

"There! That! I do not like that!" Avi said. "Fuck off I'm *imagining things*, I don't do people but I'm not a complete fucking moron, thank you. Is Magnus in on this as well? What is this? *What don't I know?*"

Kyr stood up.

Avi scrambled up, outraged. "Oh no you don't, Valkyr, you don't walk away from me." When she didn't say anything, Kyr thought he was going to hit her. He stood with his fists clenched, his mouth twisted up. "Maybe you should remember that you *need* me if you want any of this to work."

"I know we need you," Kyr said. "Of course we need you." She licked her lips. "What if I told you that we've done this before?"

Avi's fists slowly uncurled. His eyes narrowed.

"A time slip," he said softly. "On a grand scale. Are you serious?"

Kyr nodded.

"All right, done *what* before? Had an argument? Stolen a giant spaceship? Be specific, Valkyr."

"Been friends," Kyr said.

Avi went still. "I don't have friends," he said.

"Mags—"

"Magnus has a sad and desperate crush on me because I'm the only visible queer on the station, Valkyr. It's not the same thing." He laughed, a nasty crack. "Wow, hope that wasn't news to you or I've been even more of an asshole than usual."

"I know you made him a garden in the agoge," Kyr said.

"Pity isn't being friends," said Avi. He looked away. "So. We've done this before. You know stuff you shouldn't know. You *do* know me. Both of you?" He looked at Yiso. "Both of you. Why don't I remember?"

"The Wisdom—" said Yiso.

"Right, fine, and you were obviously very special to our late unlamented god machine, but why does *she* remember?"

"I don't know," said Kyr.

"It liked you," said Yiso.

"What?"

"It did. Maybe because I like you. But I think mostly . . . for a different point of view."

"Because *Valkyr* has such a unique and interesting perspective on the universe," said Avi.

"Of course," Yiso said. "Everyone does."

"Wow, how deep," Avi said with heavy sarcasm. His mouth tightened. "I want those memories."

"What?" Kyr said.

"You heard me. If *you* remember and *they* remember—guess what, my help just became conditional. Fine, so the Wisdom didn't like me." He sneered. "No one likes me. But I deserve to know what else has happened. I have a right to know."

"That's not possible," said Kyr. "The Wisdom does it, and the Wisdom's gone."

Avi ignored her. He looked at Yiso. "Well?" he said. "I'm betting Valkyr doesn't know what she's talking about. Not all your space-wizard bullshit relies on having the Wisdom to hand, does it? You were born to manipulate shadowspace. It's *in* you."

Kyr started to disagree, but Yiso reached out and rested their long thin fingers on her arm. She remembered suddenly not-Avi, in that vanished other timeline, saying *incarnation*.

"Can you do it?" Avi said.

Yiso said, "Are you sure?"

They were holding themselves very still. Kyr thought they might be remembering, as she was remembering, the caves of Chrysothemis, the deaths of the worlds.

Avi said, "Oh, don't give me the knowledge-can-be-dangerous spiel. Forbidden fruit, whatever, *yes I'm sure*."

Kyr said, "Wait—"

Yiso made one of their gestures of command.

Agricole lurched, the gigantic trees bending. Kyr yelped, stumbled, and regained her balance. Yiso swayed on the spot. Avi pitched forward into Kyr's arms.

She caught him. He stared up at her, his expression dazed. "Ambient scioactive force," he said after a moment, in a cadence not his own. "The station shadow engines—repurposed dreadnoughts, unshielded, *oh* that's even more insane than I thought. Careful with those, majo, we need the gravity." He was still holding on to Kyr. She set him back on his feet. He didn't let her go for a moment, and then he did, and he stepped back, and back again. His hands fell to his sides and then lifted, slowly, to his throat.

"Valkyr," he said, "did you actually fucking murder me?"

Kyr's hands were tense with the sensation ghost of how that death had felt. She could hear the quiet snap of Avi's neck bones. She said nothing.

Avi let out a small cackle of laughter. "Though, right," he said, in a high-pitched voice, "who am I to talk about murder? *You*—" turning on Yiso.

Yiso said, "You wanted to know what it was like to be a Prince of the Wisdom." They folded their arms, an oddly human gesture. "You did not need to ask me. You have been the arbiter of the worlds. Did it satisfy you?"

"No," Avi said. He laughed again, horribly. "No."

Kyr then had to get herself and Avi out of Agricole before someone discovered their unorthodox council of war. Avi had acquired a shitty comms headset from somewhere and he tossed it to Yiso as he left. "Hope that fits your ears," he said. Then he laughed again.

"You need to stop laughing," Kyr told him as they made for the plastic sheeting at the Agricole exit. There was still no one around, but the shift bells would ring soon.

"Why, because I've committed too many war crimes?" said Avi, and laughed some more.

"Because if you're acting too weird someone's going to *notice*. Stop thinking about it."

"You're awfully concerned for someone who murdered me recently."

"Do you *actually* want to talk about murder," said Kyr flatly.

There was a moment's silence. In it she thought they were both hearing, again, a gunshot.

"I'm sorry," Avi said after a moment, not laughing.

"You said that before," said Kyr. "I don't care. Focus."

"*How?*"

Kyr saw it was an honest question. She gave an honest answer. "Focus because this time is the last time," she said. "Focus because we don't have any more chances. I'm getting Mags out of here before it kills him. I'm getting the Sparrows out. I'm even getting *you* out."

"Let's not forget the rest of our mad plan," Avi said, but he sounded calmer. "Women and children first."

"Right. So I need you," said Kyr. "Don't think about the other times. They never happened. None of it ever happened."

"But it did," Avi said. "To me."

"I know," Kyr said. "And to me."

She'd been avoiding looking right at him, but she glanced sideways then and by accident their eyes met. There was a moment of silence.

"How can you call yourself my *friend*," Avi said at last.

Kyr didn't answer. "I'll be on comms," she said instead. "You know what you need to do."

Kyr meant to swing round to Nursery and check on the Sparrows who were trapped there. But as she was walking past an empty storeroom, a strong pair of arms grabbed her from behind.

Kyr had trained for combat every day since she was seven years old. Her body took over as her thoughts went white with alarm. Her arms came up to break the grip, her weight shifted smoothly to throw off her attacker's balance. But he was *big*, whoever he was, and he was expecting everything she did. It took him very little effort—embarrassingly little—to clap a hand over her mouth and drag her backward into the storeroom, where he spun her around and shoved her away so that he could put his own big body between Kyr and the door.

Letting go of her had been a mistake. Kyr charged at him, trying to get her fingernails at his eyes.

"Jesus fucking fuck," said the man, who was Sergeant Harriman, and shoved her backward so hard she fell on the floor.

Kyr stared up at him in mute shock for a second.

Harriman?

The chief of Oikos, whom she had always thought of as just some sad old veteran, whom Val knew as the competent boss who ran Secpol on Hymmer Station—and she'd spent days dreading, waiting, thinking it would be her uncle Jole. Harriman?

He was rubbing at the scratch marks on his face. "Jesus," he said again, which was not a word Kyr had ever heard anyone on Gaea Station say. Command disapproved of the old religions: *Where was your god when the Earth was murdered?* "I'll kill you," said Kyr, low, getting to her feet. "I will, I'll fucking kill you, don't touch me."

"Fuck *me*, kid, I'm not an animal. Why would you think—"

"You grabbed a teenage girl from behind, dragged her into an empty room, and slammed the door, Harry," said another voice. "Even on Earth you wouldn't have gotten the benefit of the doubt for that one."

Kyr turned to stare at the speaker.

Emerged from her cocoon of Systems consoles, Corporal Lin was a small woman. Her short straight hair was iron grey, and her eyes were very dark. She was sitting on a low stool and holding a definitely contraband cigarette, which was lit.

"What?" she said to Kyr's look. "Old women are allowed their vices."

"No they're not," said Kyr.

Lin laughed. "She's got me there," she said to Harriman, and put the cigarette back to her lips. Kyr stared. Only the combat wings were supposed to get tobacco.

"What do you want?" she said.

"God," said Lin, "you really do look like your mother."

Kyr knew this, because Val knew it. She said nothing.

"Doesn't she look like her mother, Harry?"

"Yingli, come on," said Harriman.

"In retrospect," Lin said, "AJ's obsession with re-creating Elora Marston from genetic scratch after he murdered, sorry, executed her—that should have been our first clue that something was very wrong with the Resistance."

"What do you want?" Kyr said. "I'll report this."

"No, you won't," said Lin. "Because if you did then I could report you. AJ doesn't forgive betrayal. You and all your little crew would die."

"What do you mean?" said Kyr unconvincingly.

"Avicenna thinks he's very clever," said Lin. "He's right, but he suffers a bit from the lack of context. *I* thought I was very clever when I was nineteen, and then I went to university." She took another puff of her cigarette. "You broke a majo out of prison and got Avicenna to hide it in the runaround. Now Victrix think it's in the Ferox brig and Ferox thinks it's with Scythica, and meanwhile your twin stood guard over an empty cell for four rotations. Station records put you in the agoge at times when your commlink says you're in Nursery and Agricole. You're running a secondary channel on that link, and it's encrypted, and Command doesn't have the key. So. You're planning something—you and your little army."

"I didn't do any of that," Kyr said. "I—"

She stopped.

"Gonna drop Avicenna in the shit?" said Lin mildly. "No, you're not, are you? Anyway you needn't bother. He's a dreamer, not a doer. All big picture and no spine. No, you're the ringleader here, I think. Admiral Marston's daughter after all. AJ didn't think hard enough about what he'd be getting if he succeeded."

"Stop it," said Kyr tightly.

"That hurt? It's a compliment. She was a great woman."

"*Stop.*"

"She's just a kid, Yingli," said Harriman.

"At her age? On Gaea Station? You're a sentimental bastard, Harry," Lin said, but she stopped. Her cigarette was down to her fingertips; she tossed it to the plasteel floor tiles and ground it into the Gaean dust there under the toe of her uniform boot. Her navy uniform fitted her, Kyr saw; fitted properly, as if it had been made for her. And there was a badge she'd never noticed pinned on Lin's collar next to her Systems lightning bolt, an old-fashioned silver one with the sign of a lily on it.

Only one other person Kyr knew wore that badge. It was the sigil of Jole's old unit, the elite force of the Terran Expeditionary in the last days of the war: Hagenen Wing. As if from very far away she remembered sitting in a Hymmer Station eatery with Cleo and the other Academy graduates, swapping rumors about Harriman and his mysterious commando wife. Corporal Lin was watching her with a cool unreadable gaze. She smiled when she saw Kyr's eyes on her collar. "People usually miss it," she said.

"What do you want?" said Kyr.

"Would you listen to a warning?" Lin said. "One woman to another. Whatever you're doing, it's going to fail, and AJ will tear you apart."

Kyr said nothing.

"My advice to you is to put the majo back in its prison cell and pray no one ever realizes what you did."

"Is that what you'd do?" said Kyr.

"Excuse me?"

"You know, don't you," Kyr said. "You know this place is all wrong. You know!"

Lin looked away. There was a long silence.

"Yes, kid," said Harriman. "We know."

"But you're *old*," said Kyr.

Lin snorted.

"You let this happen. You *made* this happen. You, Sergeant—you're Command!"

"It's not that simple," Harriman said.

"Oh, to be a teenager and always right," said Lin. "Don't start the excuses, Harry. She's right. We let this happen, we made this happen. Gaea Station's our bed and now we're all lying in it. We thought we were the good guys, you know." This to Kyr. "The lightning hand of vengeance—the freedom fighters—all the pretty things. When we joined the mutiny on the *Victrix*, we believed we were heroes. We really did."

Kyr folded her arms.

"And now our children are old enough to judge us," Lin said. "Don't jump, Harry, she's obviously Elora's. I was speaking generally."

"Okay," said Kyr. "Well. If that's all you have to say. Thanks for the *warning*." She was very angry. "I don't care. I'll do what I have to do."

"There isn't going to be anywhere to run," Harriman said quietly. "You've never seen a dreadnought in action, kid. You're young. Keep your head down. Survive. For your own sake—for your friends' sakes—"

"Did you know what Jole was doing to my sister?" said Kyr.

Harriman said nothing.

"Do you know what he wants to do to me?" she said.

It was the first time she'd acknowledged it out loud. Harriman flinched. Even Lin looked away.

"So *now* you say that you knew all along what Gaea was really like, and you just, what, kept your heads down and survived? You let them lie to us and you let them send us to the combat wings and to Strike and to Nursery, you decided you couldn't do anything so you just let it happen. That means it's your fault too," Kyr said, "all of it. You're as bad as any of them. You knew it was wrong and you still let it happen. But I'm not like you. So *stay out of our way.*"

Kyr was still alight with righteous anger when she made it back to the empty Sparrows barracks for night cycle. She stormed in already pulling her hair out of the hated ponytail, shrugging out of the navy jacket with the Command pin on the collar.

And then she realized the room wasn't empty at all.

"Wow," Avi said, "you look ready to burn the world down. Did someone break a minor regulation somewhere? Or did you just not do enough chin-ups to tire yourself out properly today?"

"What the hell are you doing here?" said Kyr.

Avi was sitting on the bunk that had been Jeanne's, shaded by Zen's above it. He looked small and tired and out of place. Kyr still thought he ought to be wearing glasses. He rubbed his eyes, and squinted to bring her into focus, and rubbed them again. "Right, my bad, *I'm* breaking the minor regulation," he said. "Sorry, the major one. No men allowed in the female cadet quarters. Obviously I'm here to despoil you. Ready?"

"At last," said Kyr flatly. "I've waited so long for this day. What are you doing, get out, you're going to get caught."

"Do Command have cameras in here, then?" Avi said. "Wouldn't surprise me."

"*Avi.*"

"What," Avi said. "You run around clucking over everyone else, do I not get a turn just because I'm a mass murderer?"

"We don't have time for this. Go back to Systems," said Kyr, and then realized there was something she needed to tell him anyway. "And watch out for Corporal Lin. She cornered me today. She *noticed* you."

"She's good but she's not as good as me," said Avi.

Kyr was abruptly too tired to argue with him. She sat down on her bunk and rubbed her hands over her face. Righteous anger was ebbing away into being just worn out and lonely and scared.

Awfully, she was glad he was there. *How can you call yourself my friend,* he'd said. But somehow, despite everything, he was.

"Don't get cocky," she said. "She knows about our comm channel and she knows we broke Yiso out. She hasn't given us away yet, but be careful."

Avi said nothing, just looked at her. He looked as bad as she felt. "Fine. Careful. Got it," he said at last. "And I'll go back to Systems. In a moment. I just—had a question for you, Valkyr."

"Yeah?" said Kyr. She gave up looking at him, it was too hard. She lay down on her bunk, the only single, and looked up at the black rock ceiling. The Sparrow barracks were so bare. It didn't feel safe here without the sounds of her messmates breathing. Of course it hadn't been safe then either. It was never safe anywhere. Kyr had been trying not to think too hard about Zen and Cleo and Lisabel, trapped in Nursery. Nursery privileges had been suspended during the *Victrix* refit: no distractions. And Kyr was going to rescue them before it got any worse.

Avi wasn't talking.

Kyr was so tired. "Avi," she said.

"Still here," he said. "Fine, I'm asking. Is he all right?"

She suddenly couldn't speak around the lump in her throat.

"Is he?" said Avi again, quieter.

He was talking about Mags, of course. Because he knew, like Kyr knew. Because he'd been in the control chamber on Chrysothemis, when Mags had picked up the gun. Mags had been looking right at Avi. He'd had his back to Kyr. He'd laughed a horrible little laugh, right before he pulled the trigger.

Kyr swallowed hard. She said, "I think you know him better than me."

"Do I," Avi said.

"I didn't even know he was sad," Kyr said. "The first time. I didn't know." She made herself look at Avi after all. He didn't *look* like the most dangerous person in three universes. He looked like a scrawny five-foot-six nineteen-year-old with a shock of red hair and a bad squint.

"He kissed me," Avi said. "I mean . . . you walked in on that."

"You know how he feels about you," said Kyr.

"Yeah," Avi said. "No. I'm a bad fucking person and he has terrible taste. He can do better. Have you seen him?"

"He's my brother," said Kyr.

"Haha, all right, I won't tell you—*fuck*. I always thought—if I ever got out—"

He stopped.

"I thought I could get out," he said in the end. "I thought I would one day. I was just waiting for the chance. I thought—but I never did. I never got out. I couldn't leave Gaea Station. I tried, and I just took it with me. And it killed him."

"No," said Kyr. "I think that was you."

Avi crumpled. "*Wow*," he said, but he said it to his feet, because he'd folded all the way forward, head in his arms, as if Kyr had punched him in the stomach. "Should have known better than to come to you for fucking comfort."

"Gaea didn't make the choices," Kyr said. "Not all of them. It was you. And me." She had to stop and catch her breath. "I think it was me as well."

Avi didn't answer. Kyr sat up. She didn't reach out to him. He was just across the narrow passage between the bunks, but he couldn't have been projecting *don't touch me* harder if he'd actually been covered in spikes.

"I never even thought of getting out," she said. "I couldn't even get that far. I took Gaea Station with me too. Everywhere I went."

"Even if this fucking spaceship heist works," Avi said. "Even if we get away. We're still trapped here, you know that, don't you? We're here forever, you and me. Like running Doomsday."

"I know."

"It's not fair!"

"I know." Kyr had always hated injustice. She still hated it. "It's not fair. I know."

"I'm—"

He broke off.

Eventually Kyr said, "Are you going to tell me *sorry* again?"

"I can't," Avi said. Kyr watched him take a deep breath, and another. Then he straightened up from the punched-in-the-stomach fold. She'd thought he might be crying, but his eyes were dry. He still looked terrible. He said, "I don't think I am sorry."

Kyr looked at him.

"Going to say anything?" Avi said, and then, quiet, "Why should I apologize for something I haven't done?"

"Would you do it again?" Kyr asked.

A stupid question. An impossibility. The Wisdom was dead. Avi couldn't do it again. And what did it matter anyway? If Kyr had learned anything, it was that there was no justice in the universe, none; that nothing was fair and nothing was ever going to be fair. And here they were, alive, planning, hoping; carrying it all with them, everywhere they went, forever; living with what they had and hadn't done.

Avi said, "I don't know."

"Avi—" said Kyr.

He held out his hands to her. There was so little space in here. "They killed our world. They did. I barely knew what that meant, before, and I was still angry. And now I know and it's too big to even feel anger, I mean I feel nothing, Valkyr, nothing. That other timeline. Providence, Admiral Jole, Earth the Great, all that shit, fuck that, but I've stood on our hills, I've seen our oceans and our cities, and they're gone. It's all gone. So what do we do? What do we do now?"

"While we live, we're alive," Kyr said. "And that's all."

Where had she heard those words? Ursa had said them to her in Raingold. It hadn't made sense at the time.

"Sedition," Avi said. He dropped his hands before Kyr could take them.

"Truth," said Kyr.

"This is not what I thought I was getting into," Avi said, "when Magnus started hanging around the arcade to stare at me."

"Oh joy, another one?" Kyr said.

"How do you know—"

"He told me what you said."

"I'm a dick, aren't I," Avi said.

"If you know you are," said Kyr, "why don't you stop?"

He looked away. There was a little silence. Kyr should have made him leave. She didn't.

"It's all fucked, you know," Avi said to the wall. "On purpose, I mean. All the stuff about how sex should be for propagating the species and otherwise it's pointless—you know what Gaea Station doesn't do, that humans always did before?"

"What?" said Kyr.

"Marriage," Avi said. "Long-term pair bonding. Family."

"The Earth was your mother, and humanity is your family," Kyr quoted lightly.

"Are you being sarcastic?"

"I had a family," Kyr said. "On Earth. I had a mother. My real mother."

"Did you? I didn't." A pause. Avi's expression was turned inward. He was alone, like she was; alone with the memories, whatever not-Avi's life had been. He laughed his usual cracked, mirthless laugh. "I guess nobody wants me anywhere. Can't blame them. Pretty sure the guy who sired me here was a junior officer from Augusta. He died in a raid on merchant shipping fifteen years ago. Never managed to work out where the other half of me came from. Out of the gene banks, maybe, back when we still had those." A pause. "Yeah. It's all fucked."

"If people can talk to each other in ways Command don't control," Kyr said, "if they can be honest . . . it all falls apart."

"Humanity is your family, and Command runs humanity," Avi said. "No divided loyalties on Gaea Station." He finally looked right at Kyr again. "I've never said most of this out loud before."

"I'm sure it's been very hard," Kyr said, "trying to shut up for all these years."

"You have no idea," said Avi. "I'm not a shutter up by nature."

"I know."

"Well, that's still weird," Avi said, and then, "I should . . . go back to Systems. So. Sleep well, Valkyr. This whole thing needs you too."

"Sleep well?" Kyr repeated. Suddenly, weirdly, she was trying not to smile.

Avi looked relieved. "On second thoughts, fuck off and die."

Kyr spent the next three days working frantically. She had to jam everything that mattered into the scraps of time that fitted around Jole's expectations. Since that moment when they'd stood together on the bridge and he'd talked about conquering worlds, he wanted Kyr on hand constantly. She endured the twelve-hour shift-and-a-half rotations shadowing Jole as he oversaw the *Victrix* refit. He ambled around the dreadnought and spoke softly here, sharply there, arranging matters to his satisfaction, while she hovered one step behind and one step to the left, on her feet even when he sat down—there was a chair on the bridge now, a polished and shiny commander's seat where Jole would sit with his sharp eyes on the engineers working below. Kyr stood at his shoulder. He talked to her constantly—or rather, he talked *at* her. She didn't need to reply. He just wanted her to look impressed.

Kyr hated that he *was* impressive. She was learning things from watching him—from the way he could pick out at a glance who was faltering, who was unsure, and say just the right words to make their expressions change and their determination redouble. She often wondered how much of what he said was lies. An anecdote about commandos from Hagenen Wing surviving a tight spot during the war—true or lies? A promise about new luxury allowances in a few weeks—true or lies? Praise and encouragement, approval and suggestions—what was fake? How could you know?

Kyr had loved him all her life. Had it all been lies?

"You've always had Command potential," Jole told her, eleven and a half hours into a twelve-hour rotation. The bridge was quiet for once. He'd looked at the faces of the exhausted Systems engineers, who'd spent eight hours trying to get the dreadnought's newly reinstated shadow engine to reintegrate with its old defense array, and told them to go and get some sleep and come back fresh later. "Don't think no one saw the way you whipped your Sparrows into shape, or the sacrifices you made to help them improve. You're a leader by nature, Valkyr."

Kyr licked her lips. "Sir," she said.

Jole stood up. He groaned a little as the weight went onto his bad leg. In Kyr's ear her comm buzzed softly and then Yiso's musical, alien voice came through: "*Valkyr?*"

"*She's on duty, idiot. Talk to me, not her,*" Avi answered.

Kyr kept her expression fixed. Yiso and Avi chattered on the conspirators' private channel all the time. It was good, sometimes, to hear their voices as she trailed Jole around the *Victrix*. It stopped her from getting swept up in the backwash of Jole's charisma. Yiso and Avi were real. They didn't tell lies. Cleo, up in Nursery, had a headset hidden in her bunk. Kyr got to hear her voice sometimes, when Nursery was quiet and it was safe. She wished there was a way to get Mags on the comm too.

"Ah, goddammit," said Jole, and sat down hard again in the command chair. He leaned forward and pulled off his boot, then rolled up his trouser leg. The brightfire scar extended down his calf, with chunks burnt and bitten out of the muscle. Jole smiled wryly up at Kyr. "Ugly, I know," he said. "And they accused *us* of war crimes." He bent forward with another groan and dug his thumbs into the warped skin of his calf. "Your sister used to help me with this."

Kyr stood frozen. No one talked about Ursa. That *he* should talk about Ursa—after what he had done to Ursa—

"Do you miss her, Valkyr?" Jole said. "I miss her."

What did he want to hear? "Ursa was a traitor," Kyr said.

"She was selfish, yes," Jole said. "She valued herself over humanity. But the world isn't divided into good people and traitors, you know."

This was the opposite of everything Kyr had always been taught. She said nothing.

"I can hear you thinking," Jole said, and then let out a sigh and rolled his trouser leg back down, hiding the scarring. He took his other boot off. Kyr looked down at his socked feet on the shiny floor of the bridge. Jole wriggled his toes. "Valkyr," he said. "Look at me."

Kyr looked at him. There was stubble on his cheeks. His forehead was lined. If she looked at these things on his face, she could avoid his sharp grey eyes.

"You're not a stupid girl," he said. "I think you're old enough to understand that sometimes the world is complicated. One of the things a leader does is make things simpler for other people. It's what I do. I handle the complications, so that our people can focus on what really matters."

"Was Ursa complicated?" said Kyr. Her voice came out small.

Jole huffed out a little laugh. He sounded fond when he said, "Very."——

Kyr felt an odd emptiness down in her belly. She said, "Did you—"

She wanted to take it back as soon as she said it. She didn't want to hear it from him. She didn't want to *know*.

"I always wondered how much you understood," Jole said. "You were very young."

"Sir," said Kyr desperately.

"This is a personal conversation, Valkyr," Jole said gently. "You don't have to call me *sir*."

With that crutch gone, Kyr had nothing left to say at all.

"I sometimes wonder what she thinks of me now," Jole said. "I doubt it's complimentary—no, it wouldn't be. I imagine she has a nasty little story she tells herself, to make herself feel better about what she did. About what she betrayed. Poor Ursula! I pity her."

He heaved himself to his feet again, this time without the groan, and padded to the rail. He was now standing very close. Kyr felt every muscle tense—told herself she was panicking over nothing—and then Jole put his big hand over hers on the rail, glanced at her and smiled, and said, "Valkyr, that's quite a blush."

"Did you force her?" Kyr blurted.

After she'd said it the bridge of the *Victrix* suddenly felt huge, and empty, and echoing; like the cave of the Wisdom on Chrysothemis, like the boundless distances the machine had created inside the Halls of the Wise. Kyr was a small stupid dot in a gigantic uncaring universe, and she had said something unthinkable, and the silence grew and grew.

Jole took his hand away from hers. He turned and looked at her directly. He was frowning.

"Did someone tell you that?" he said. "Who? It's a lie, Valkyr."

Ursa told me, said Kyr's whirling thoughts. And then they said *but she didn't quite say it—and he said she'd make up a nasty story—is that what it was, a nasty story?*

She was aware of an awful hole inside her that she'd been carrying around for—how long *had* it been? Time meant nothing to the Wisdom and its tricks. An emptiness had been gnawing at Kyr's insides since she'd been given Nursery as her first assignment. All it wanted, all *Kyr* wanted, right down in the depths of her heart, was to be told that everything that had gone wrong with her world was just some sort of awful mistake.

It couldn't *all* be lies. Everything Kyr knew, everything she'd always loved, everything that had ever mattered—surely there was something, somewhere, some core that was good and worthwhile and true.

All she had to do was say to herself, *Yes, my sister was a traitor, she lied about everything, she lied to me about you; you never hurt her, you would never hurt me.* All she had to do was let herself believe it. Then the world could be easy again. Kyr could be her old self, fearless and sure, disciplined and obedient and righteous: Earth's perfect child.

Jole sighed. He looked a little distant, a little wistful: a sorrowing hero. "It was a weakness," he said. "Even the best of us have weaknesses. But complicated as the situation was—the difference in our ages, the necessary secrecy that goes with command—still, I loved your sister and she loved me." He looked at Kyr again. He said, "I've shocked you."

If he was telling the truth—if everything could be explained away that simply, and the things Kyr had been afraid of were paranoid fantasies based on Ursa's bitter version of events that had actually been perfectly *fine*—

He's good at this. He's a manipulator, said the distant thread of Val Marston in her thoughts. But Val wasn't real. She had never happened.

Kyr knew, in a very literal way, what it was like to have the universe shift underneath you. This did not feel like that. It was almost the opposite: things falling into place, reorganizing themselves into what they should have been all along. It felt like Jole was doing to the inside of Kyr's head the exact same thing he was overseeing on the *Victrix*: a refit, a repair, a preparation for a better future. She breathed out hard. She was clinging to the bridge rail, her weight overbalanced, her skin prickling. If things could be simple again. If things could be *easy* again. If everything that had happened, everything she'd learned, was just—a bad dream, a delusion.

Maybe it was. What proof did Kyr have that any of it had ever happened? It *hadn't* happened, it literally physically had not happened, or she would not be here. Why shouldn't she just take this universe as it was—take her promotion to Command and her place at Jole's side and her destiny aboard a star-conqueror reborn? Gaea wasn't perfect, but with the Wisdom gone the need for Gaea was nearly over. There could be a new order. Kyr could shape it. She could carve out spaces where Mags would be less miserable—she could get the Sparrows out of here and find them different lives—even Avi, she could stop them from *wasting* him like this. The future that came to pass would be a future shaped a little like Hymmer Station, one where humanity guaranteed the peace of the universe—everyone would be fine, even Yiso would be fine. Kyr would take care of them. She'd take care of everything.

"Are you all right?" Jole had his hand under Kyr's elbow, supporting her. "You don't look well. Here," and he ushered her to the command chair, and made her sit down. "Has this evil nonsense been preying on you all this time, Valkyr? Talk to me first next time. I wouldn't be much good to you if you couldn't trust me."

Kyr sat there stunned for a moment. *He's a manipulator,* she thought. *He's a liar. But what if that's the lie? What if he's still the hero of humanity, the commander in chief, the architect of our salvation, my uncle Jole?*

He wouldn't hurt me. Would he hurt me?

There's no proof he hurt Ursa. Is there?

Ally's my son, Ursa had said. The sandy-haired schoolboy in the bright flat in Raingold. *He's mine.* And over the comm in Kyr's ear, somewhere in the distance, Avi said, *"Where the fuck is she? Her rotation ended ten minutes ago, she should have checked in."*

Yiso said, *"Valkyr?"*

Kyr took the comm out and put it aside. Jole was kneeling in front of her. It had to be hurting his bad leg. He took Kyr's hands in his, and his grey eyes were kind.

"My God," he said, "you really do look like your mother."

That was not a lie. Kyr had never met her, not in this life, but she was Elora Marston's daughter. She looked like her—just as Ursa looked like her.

Kyr thought about this. And she thought about the first time she had seen the bridge of the *Victrix*: the bloodstains up the wall, the footprints in the dust, the dead admiral's voice repeating her last distress call as she waited for her murderers to arrive.

A shrine.

Clarity toppled back into place over the universe. It was the cold and perfect clarity that no longer really felt like anger. Kyr didn't need the ever-fainter ghost of Val; she didn't need to think about Ursa and Ally in their Raingold flat; she didn't need Avi's voice, or Yiso's, or even the thought of the Sparrows trapped in Nursery, and of Mags's expression in the very worst moments. *You know what he is*, her own inner voice told her. *There is no one he would not hurt. There is nothing he would not betray. You know what he did to your mother. You know what he did to Ursa. He will never forgive her for escaping him.*

You know what he is. Trust yourself. You do.

"The *Victrix* was your mother's command once, and one day it will be yours," Jole told her, a promise, and he squeezed her hands tight and then he leaned in and kissed her.

CHAPTER TWENTY-NINE

ENEMY ACTION

Kyr thought, distantly, about Admiral Russell. The way he'd looped his arm through Lisabel's in another time, scooping her up, and Lisabel had just stood there. The way Kyr had despised him. *If you ever put your hand on me, I will break your wrist.*

She could, quite easily, have broken Jole's wrist. He was still holding her hands.

Kyr had thought she would fight him, whatever happened. She had thought she could hit him.

It turned out she could not.

How shameful it was. After a lifetime of Drill and the agoge, years of pushing her body to do everything she asked of it, every time; tracking her scores against the other Sparrows, against the boys in Cat and Coyote, until she knew that by every measure she was one of the best. After all that. Somehow she could not move.

Jole had stubble. It rubbed Kyr's chin uncomfortably. His left hand gripped her right like a vise, holding it against the arm of the command chair. His right hand moved up Kyr's arm to her shoulder. Her uniform was long-sleeved. She felt terribly cold, and the heat of his hand as it stroked the fabric the wrong way up her arm was almost painful.

"Stop it," she said.

It was muffled by his mouth. Kyr found some desperate strength and turned her face away. "Stop it," she said again.

Jole's vise grip relaxed, but he didn't let go. He was *looking* at her. Kyr felt his calm and thoughtful look as if it were an Isaac slug, a solid lump of rock propelled with merciless force through empty space. She could not meet his eyes.

Why aren't you fighting, why don't you fight, what is the point of you if you can't fight, said a tiny yammering voice in the back of her head. The clarity she'd felt a moment ago had shattered into a hundred confusing shards. She kept thinking of stupid irrelevant things. Harriman grabbing her in the Oikos corridor. *What does it feel like to be hunted by a merciless war monster twice your size.* Yiso, looking up at her from a cell. *Why are you afraid of me.*

Mom: a memory from a life Kyr had barely had a chance to lead. Val's Admiral Marston, big and broad and brash: merciless with her criticism, generous with her praise, hero of humanity, conqueror of the stars. In this timeline—not even the voice of the *Victrix's* last distress call. Not even the bloodstains up the wall. It was all gone, all purged.

Jole let go of her shoulder—every muscle in Kyr's shoulders was locked tight to the point of cramping—and put his hand on her chin. He turned her face so she was looking at him.

"There's nothing to be afraid of," he said gently. "Valkyr."

"I'm not her," Kyr said.

"Of course not. You would never betray me."

He thought she was talking about Ursa. Kyr opened her mouth to explain. Jole kissed her again.

This time she somehow found the strength to move. She brought her hands up to his shoulders and *shoved*. She meant it to be forceful but the movement came out halfhearted. It was still enough to push him back. Then, without her brain even really deciding to do it, Kyr kicked out from her seated position.

It was a pathetic and unconvincing echo of what actually fighting would have looked like. But the kick caught Jole's bad leg. He toppled back from his crouching position and sat, ungainly, on the floor.

Kyr stood up fast. The commander's chair felt like a trap.

Jole was rubbing his calf. "There was no need for that," he said mildly. "All you had to do was say no."

But I did, thought Kyr. *Didn't I?*

She stood there staring down at him. Jole still had the massive build of Earth's true soldiers. He was taller than she was. This angle felt all wrong.

When he put out a hand to be helped up Kyr took it. She let him use her as a lever to get back to his feet. She couldn't have said why she did that. It made her skin crawl when he touched her. She wanted to be sick. But she felt horribly guilty, too. She'd kicked a veteran of Earth's doom right where his old injury would hurt him most. She could have just said no. Couldn't she?

Jole snorted and let go of her hand, giving it a little pat before he pulled away. "Don't look so worried, sweetheart," he said. "You haven't offended me."

Sweetheart? thought Kyr. Then there was a space in her head where the next thought should have been. She could feel the shape of it, something cold and bright and sharp, like a knife. But it was a blade with no handle. She couldn't get hold of it. She couldn't use it.

And you thought he was a hero, said the cynical, ever-more-distant voice of Valerie Marston into that hollowness.

And you thought he was a terrible monster.

But you were wrong both times, weren't you?

He's just a creep who gets off on power. That's all.

Kyr looked in wonder at Commander Jole. He was the motive force of Gaea Station, the great defier of the majoda, the soul and center of her childhood. She had loved him. She had called him *uncle.* She had done everything, everything, that she thought would please him. How unbelievably, laughably, awfully small he was. How *pathetic.* He had shaped Gaea Station and all their lives and for what? He talked about conquering the universe for humanity, and he *was,* even now, a threat to Chrysothemis, a threat to Ursa, a threat to Kyr herself. But none of that made him a great man.

Kyr imagined with sudden force what it would be like to *tell* him: I saw you at Doomsday, and you weren't doing anything brave, you were trying to get away. I saw you in another life, and you were a spiteful old man there too. You've never been anything different.

And I could be *so* different.

Jole was still looking at her. Kyr met his eyes this time. There was a silence where she nearly *did* say something. Jole's brow creased in suspicion, as if he had seen behind her, somehow, the long shadow of something much bigger than he was.

And then he put his hand to his ear and snapped, "Repeat that."

Kyr scrambled for her comm as he turned away. She put it back in her ear just in time to hear Avi saying, "*—shit shit shit shit oh fuck—Yiso!*"

Kyr kept her expression composed and flicked over to the official Command channel, where the chief of Agricole was saying, "*—not clear how long it's been lurking up there, sir. Requesting combat personnel to do a full sweep.*"

"Russell, see it done," ordered Commander Jole, and barely waited for acknowledgment. "You say it had a comm?"

"*We're trying to trace it now.*" That was Systems.

"I want to know who it was talking to. Don't waste time, put Lin on it. I want her here. And get the majo down to the *Victrix* bridge too, now. Double guard. Don't lose it this time." Jole's mouth was tight with fury. "Nice and gentle. Make sure it can still talk."

Kyr had to stand there, one step behind Jole's chair and one step to the left, when they dragged Yiso in. There were four soldiers, all massive. They brought Yiso onto the command platform and took up positions spaced around them, all braced and ready as if Yiso was going to attack any moment. Kyr felt a flash of embarrassment on behalf of her species. Yiso looked so small. Their big silvery eyes met Kyr's, just for a moment, and then skimmed over her as if she didn't matter. Their crest dipped and then lifted again. Kyr fixed her gaze directly ahead.

"The comm?" Jole demanded.

Corporal Lin stepped onto the command platform, clung to the rail wheezing, and said, "Give me a second, AJ, not all of us have our war wounds on the outside." She had a tablet clutched against her side.

The soldiers looked shocked by her disrespect. Jole just frowned. Now that Kyr thought about it, she had never seen Lin standing up for more than a few moments. "Take a seat, Yingli," Jole said, and stood up to give her the only seat on the platform, the commander's chair. "Get me the truth."

Corporal Lin hobbled to the chair and collapsed into it. The tablet lit up under her small, expert fingers. Kyr looked down at her in distant despair. She already *knew*. Delaying wasn't going to change anything.

Yiso said, "I acted alone, Commander Jole."

Jole's Isaac-slug gaze swung back to them. "I don't look for honor from monsters, majo," he said. "And I don't believe in magic. You didn't spirit yourself out of my brig."

"I am a Prince of the Wisdom. I am able to manipulate shadowspace on a level quite unknown to your kind."

It was a desperate play. Jole only snorted. "I know what you are," he said. "And I don't buy it. The Wisdom didn't hand out our equipment to aliens even when it was alive. Lin, find out who was on the other end of that comm."

"No need for that, Commander," said another voice. Admiral Russell marched onto the bridge looking smug and swollen with his own importance. "I checked the logs. Victrix is my wing and I won't have failures. Anyway, we've got him."

Two more massive soldiers followed him up to the platform, neither of them quite as big as the figure they were marching between them. His hands were cuffed behind his back. Kyr couldn't breathe for a second.

"Magnus," said Jole. "I am disappointed. But I am not surprised."

"No sign of the comm now, so he must have stashed it some-where. But he was guarding that cell for four rotations in a row," said Russell. "Obviously a trick. The majo could have got loose any time."

"Anything to say for yourself, Magnus?" said Jole softly.

Mags stood up straighter. Kyr saw him glance at the guards, four for Yiso and two for him, all armed. Even for Mags, even if he hadn't been cuffed, those were bad odds. If Kyr helped him. If she took the two on the left. (They were too big and too well armed; she couldn't take the two on the left.) Who had the code for those cuffs? Russell, probably—he was old—if Kyr went right for him—

"No? Well, let's not waste time," Jole said. "You're a foot sol-dier, nothing more. You haven't the brains or the initiative to do something like this. Who's running this little game, and why?"

Mags closed his eyes and said nothing. Jole was wrong about him, so wrong. *My brother,* Kyr thought with a rush of unhappy pride. *My thoughtful, careful, defiant, impossibly brave brother.* He never wanted to be a soldier. He saw through Gaea Station. They gave him Strike and he walked away. Val's universe gave him anything he wanted and he saw through that too, walked *toward* a fight he didn't want and wasn't ready for because he thought it was the right thing to do.

He wouldn't tell Jole a thing, because anything he said would lead right back to Kyr. He was going to stand there and say noth-ing, no matter what they did to him.

He was going to get himself executed and Kyr couldn't do any-thing to stop it.

She was still frozen with horror—strangely similar, this, to the frozen way she'd let Jole kiss her—when Jole chuckled. "Feeling tough, son? It won't matter. But if you give me the names of your fellow traitors, I can go easy on you. Got anything off that comm yet, Corporal?" he asked.

"Not yet," said Lin mildly. She sounded as if this public interrogation was both normal and not very interesting. Her fingers still moved on the tablet. Kyr risked a glance down at the screen.

Colored squares flashed up and disappeared as Lin grouped and tapped them. It took Kyr a moment to realize it was a game. Lin's expression was deadpan. Was this a joke to her?

Well, it wasn't like she needed to trace the encrypted comm channel. She'd already done it. Kyr didn't know what Lin was waiting for.

"Let's be honest with one another, Magnus," Jole said. "I don't need to wait for Corporal Lin. She's only going to tell me what I already know. After all, we both know what you are."

Mags lifted his chin, expecting a blow. He didn't say anything.

"You're the cadet who beat the Doomsday scenario," Jole said. "The best soldier Gaea's ever produced. Isn't that right? Come on, son. It was all over the station. It's in your training records. There's nothing to be ashamed of."

He'd been walking toward Mags while he said this. He put his hand on Mags's shoulder. They were almost the same height; Mags had maybe an inch of advantage. Jole gave him a gentle shake. "Even I couldn't do it," he said. "I built that scenario myself, Magnus. I was there. And I couldn't save our world. But you—you're the boy who might have saved the Earth, aren't you? Does that make you feel good?"

"No," Mags said after a moment. Kyr stifled a wince. There was no way to yell, *Don't start talking! That's how he gets you!* There was no way to help at all. She was going to have to stand here and watch.

"No?" said Jole. "That's a smart man's answer. No, because the agoge isn't real? No, because there's no use taking credit for things you *might* have done—if you only had the chance?"

Mags had clearly realized his mistake. He kept his mouth shut. His eyes darted around the bridge, looking everywhere but at Kyr.

"Or no, because it wasn't you?" Jole said. "The agoge records everything, son." *Son*, again and again. Kyr hated it. Jole clapped Mags hard on the back—hard enough that he stumbled, his big arms flexing against the handcuffs—and chuckled again. "Do you really think no one watched that little stunt you pulled? I should say, the two of you."

Mags managed to keep his silence, but he couldn't control his expression. He looked sick.

"Why don't you just give us your boyfriend, Magnus?" Jole said. "Keeping quiet isn't going to save him. He's had enough chances. But it is going to make things worse for you."

Mags had the sense not to say anything, but he didn't need to. His face was saying it all anyway. Kyr felt her whole body like one big flinch just looking at him.

"Shall I wait for Corporal Lin to confirm it for us?" Jole said softly. "Make me wait and it will make things worse, Magnus. One way or another, we will get to the root of this little rebellion."

The soldiers on guard around Yiso had all relaxed to stare with eager, ugly appreciation at the live theater in front of them. The two men on either side of Mags were standing up straight and looking as tough as they could—of course; they were in Jole's line of sight. If Yiso were able to fight back. If Mags weren't cuffed. If Kyr were *stronger*. It was all falling apart in front of her, and any second Jole would have Avi too.

And here she was, perfectly safe, on the other side of the command chair. It hadn't occurred to Jole that Kyr could possibly betray him. He thought he *owned* her, her strength, her loyalty. Mags wouldn't give her away. Yiso wouldn't. And despite everything he'd said, Kyr didn't believe for a moment that Avi would either.

She couldn't stand it. She clenched her fists. *It wasn't them. It wasn't any of them.*

I'm in command here. Your rebellion? It's me.

She stepped forward.

Cold fingers closed around her wrist.

Kyr startled so hard that her hip knocked against the side of the commander's chair. Corporal Lin was looking up at her, unsmiling. Her thumbnail dug hard into the soft skin under the heel of Kyr's hand. Kyr stared down at her. Lin tilted her tablet. The colored blocks from her game were gone.

The screen said: TIME'S UP. GO.

Kyr stared at it.

Lin's jaw moved a tiny fraction, subvocalizing. GOOD LUCK, said the screen. Jole had changed his tone, gone from soft words to an angry roar. Kyr could barely hear it. The message on Lin's tablet changed one more time.

TRUST HARRY, it said. GIVE HIM MY LOVE.

Then Corporal Lin let go of Kyr's wrist and stood up. She dropped the tablet casually into the commander's chair behind her.

"Oof," she said. "Done showboating yet, AJ?" She advanced slowly on the tableau of Jole and Mags and Yiso. They were all looking at her. The soldiers were looking at her. Admiral Russell was looking at her.

Kyr got it right as Lin said, "Well, guess the game's up. You got me."

"Corporal Lin, remember where you are," said Jole warningly.

"That's Commander Lin to you," said Yingli Lin. "My field promotion came from Admiral Marston, and last I checked yours came from—where was it?—right, from *you*. Pretty sure I outrank you"—Kyr saw the edge of her smile, like an animal let out of its cage and showing its teeth—"*son*."

Jole said, "Yingli, have you gone mad?"

"No, I think I've gone sane," Lin said. "Took me long enough." She reached the railing and leaned against it—theatrically, but Kyr thought she needed the support. "Look how far we've come from the Academy, huh, AJ?" she said. "You and me—and the others, of course, but I think we're all that's left of Hagenen Wing by now. We've had quite a run, haven't we? No need to point those guns at me, boys, I'm an old lady and my combat scores were always shit anyway. Now maybe if I had my drones—right, AJ?"

The soldiers looked uncertainly at Jole, who ignored them,

and then at Russell, who made an angry gesture, and then they kept pointing guns at Lin. No one was paying attention to Kyr. No one so much as glanced in her direction. Kyr reached down and picked up the tablet Lin had abandoned. It was unlocked, with Lin's Systems communications records open and waiting for her. Avi's name was at the top. They'd been talking. *I know what you know,* said Avi's log. *what are you going to do about it.*

And Lin: *shut up and learn some opsec, dolt.*

"What, you thought a bunch of *kids* came up with a rebellious plot?" Lin said. "Come on, AJ, you know better. Gaea Station is set up to stop kids coming up with anything. Crush them between secondary trauma one direction and physical exhaustion the other and see how much initiative and empathy the average kid has left. You think there's a single teenager on Gaea Station who could care enough about a *majo* to bother getting it out of a prison cell?" She laughed. "Remember the rules of engagement days? Admiral Russell, you abandoned a significant combat advantage to rescue enemy civilians once. Gyssono-IV. You got a medal from their side at the next cease-fire."

The admiral said nothing.

"Did you see yourself one day taking orders to execute human children from a disgraced commando turned tinpot dictator in the ass-end of dead space?" Lin said. "Did any of us?"

"*Corporal Lin,*" snapped Jole.

"What, were you not going to execute the boy?" Lin said. "Bit of a departure for you, AJ. Who haven't you murdered? Elora Marston, of course—did it hurt dismantling your little memorial? Luis Alvares, remember Luis? And then everyone who protested, everyone who spoke out, everyone who even looked like they might have *thought* of saying something. God forbid anyone ask questions in your doomsday cult. I bet the kids don't know we ever had a full scientific wing, do they? Who's left?" She laughed. "Earth's children. Gaea Station! We said we would all be heroes. Look at us now."

Kyr picked up the tablet and wrote, *do the scenario now.*

????? said Avi.

"I want to be clear," said Lin somewhere in the background, "this *is* personal."

"I've given you too much latitude, Corporal—"

"*Commander.*"

"You and your special friend," said Jole venomously.

Avi didn't know what was happening. There wasn't time to explain. Kyr wrote, *remember chrysothemis. trust me please.*

In the pause that followed, Lin was saying, "'Special friend'? Come on, AJ, I've been in a committed relationship with Harry for twenty years. You can say *partner.*"

ok, Avi sent, and nothing else.

Jole lunged at Lin. Yiso said, "Commander Jole!" The Victrix guards had lost interest in Mags completely. Admiral Russell was shouting something. No one was paying any attention to Kyr.

And a siren began to wail. It was a distant thread of sound. The bridge of the *Victrix* wasn't connected to the station alarms. Kyr felt almost like laughing. She didn't. She schooled her expression to calm somehow, took a deep breath, and barked in her best Drill bellow, "Sir!"

Now they were looking at her. In the instant of quiet that followed, the siren wailing came distant and ghostly through the hulk of the *Victrix*. Kyr, not letting her hands shake, patched it through her comm to the bridge speakers. Suddenly there was a shriek of alarm in the room with them.

"Visual!" snapped Jole.

There was an awkward silence.

"Need me?" said Lin.

"Valkyr, get me another Systems monkey," Jole snarled, glaring at Lin. "A trustworthy one. And get me a visual."

"If I may, Commander Jole," said Yiso. Kyr saw every one of the big highly trained Gaean warriors flinch away from the alien when it spoke. Yiso held up one of their small three-fingered hands. The green flicker of subreal light danced around it. Even Jole took a step back.

"Impossible," he said. "It's *dead.*"

"But I am not," said Yiso calmly. "And I am a Prince of the Wisdom. I believe you wanted a visual."

One of the blank displays around the bridge snapped into life. It was the agoge at work on Yiso's commands, not the Wisdom. Kyr knew it. But even she felt a moment of terror when she saw the illusion.

There in Gaean space, so close to the station that it was inside the ring of dimensional traps, so close that Isaac slugs would be as likely to hit Gaea's own solar arrays as the enemy, hung a Wisdom cruiser.

Kyr knew them from a hundred scenarios. There were two in the early stages of Doomsday, which between them demolished Earth's orbital defenses no matter what you did, before the third one arrived with a dart behind it. Fast, maneuverable, heavily armed, with a full complement of attack drones and alien combat personnel—they were the majoda's answer to the dreadnoughts of human conquest.

Kyr could hear her own breathing. Jole's face was colorless. "Not possible," he said again. Kyr held very still. "*Not—*"

"Come on, AJ," said Lin, "you know me. Did you really think I was stupid enough to plan a coup without *backup*?"

Kyr saw Yiso's ears flick and was grateful that no one else in this room knew anything about majo zi body language. "Commander Lin," they said gravely, in their best Prince-of-the-Wisdom voice, "it has been a pleasure working with you."

That was when Jole shot Lin.

It was point-blank range. She fell crumpled over the railing she'd been leaning on. Kyr got a glimpse of Jole's face. Blind and ugly rage had closed over it. He'd been pushed too far.

CHAPTER THIRTY

ESCAPE

There wasn't time to feel anything. The whole station shuddered sideways with the force of an impact. Avi had said no one would believe in the attack without a bombardment. It had been Vic's idea to use Gaea's own defenses, turning the station's weapons inward. Avi had cackled. He thought the only person likely to catch it from the Systems end was Lin.

Lin wasn't going to catch anything now. Her body hung small across the railing of the bridge where Kyr's mother had died. Kyr felt suddenly and forcefully the weight of legacy. She wasn't Earth's child. She was Elora Marston's, and Yingli Lin's, and Ursa's, and she owed her duty not to some abstract unknown planet but to the women who'd come before her.

Suntracker might notice what was really happening, if anyone was brave enough to suit up and go outside and have a look. Jole was snapping orders, and combat darts would be scrambling against the threat. But soldiers weren't expected to know how station systems worked. *Kyr* barely knew, and she was supposed to be Command.

The displays were showing majo darts in motion. The station rocked under the force of another hit. This was the only part of their fake attack that was likely to actually kill anyone. Was *going* to kill people: soldiers of Ferox, probably, since that was where the "majo bombardment" was concentrated. Jeanne was supposed to be down in Ferox right now. Kyr had forced herself to face it, when they were planning. She'd thought she was ready. She was not.

"Report!" snapped Admiral Russell. A Ferox officer over the Command comm started saying *casualties—*

No, Kyr hadn't been ready for this. But this was her rebellion. It was her responsibility now.

Jole rounded on Yiso. "Call them off," he snarled.

"I cannot," Yiso said. "Nor will my death at this point change anything, except perhaps increase my allies' resolve."

"Enemy stationside!" shouted Admiral Russell. "Commander, for God's sake stop wasting time with the alien, they're landing—"

Attack drones and majo strike teams were "landing" in the Ferox hangar. The clouds of majo darts on the display looked very convincing. Kyr had talked Avi through this part herself. *Numbers,* she'd said. *There need to be a lot of them, to get the combat wings scared. And when they hit, it needs to hurt.*

Avi had smirked and answered, *Not a problem.*

Someone had managed to get a view of the Ferox hangar up on the bridge display. Tall, slender zunimmer; short, broad sinnet; many-armed lirem; all armored and masked for combat, though Avi had pulled individual faces for all of them out of majo media in case someone tried ripping off the combat masks. The clouds of attack drones, most barely more than thumbnail-sized, buzzed around the bigger, squarer, deadlier shapes of their master controllers. Kyr could hear the shouts of Ferox soldiers, and make out the lines of them resisting the onslaught. *Let them win sometimes,* she'd advised Avi. *We know we're stronger than them.*

Raw muscle power versus technology strong enough to shape the universe for millennia, he'd scoffed, but he *was* letting Ferox win, sometimes. The fight was real. Kyr could see human soldiers collapsing under drone assaults. This part wasn't supposed to kill anyone. The agoge could give you a jolt hard enough to knock you out. But she could also see blood. After a moment she realized that in the confusion of close quarters, some of the humans were striking each other down with friendly fire.

"Scythica Wing, move to reinforce Ferox," ordered Jole. His voice boomed over the bridge speakers and over Gaea's stationwide comm. "Soldiers of humanity, hold your ground. No projectile weapons. Close engagement only." He'd seen the same thing. He glanced up at the bridge and his eyes fell on Mags. "Get that traitor out of here. Put him in the brig. No, leave the alien, I want it where I can see it. Russell, set a guard on all approaches to the *Victrix* and her hangar. Valkyr!"

Kyr jumped. "Sir!"

"That bitch Lin did something to our comms. I can't raise *Augusta*. Get this to Admiral O'Brien." He handed her a hastily scribbled flimsy. "Go."

"Sir!"

Kyr stuffed the flimsy in her back pocket as soon as she was off the bridge and out of Jole's sight. The conspirators' channel was silent on her comm. Kyr hissed, "Avi!"

"Little busy!" Avi answered. *"You said trust you, I'm trusting you. This isn't easy."*

Kyr said, "Avi, they've got Mags and Yiso. I don't know what—" *I don't know what to do.*

Avi didn't answer. But someone else did. *"Pull it together, Kyr,"* said Cleo. Kyr pictured her hiding in a corner of the Nursery bunkrooms with her stolen comm. She had probably dived for it as soon as the scenario started, trying to figure out why *now*. *"If we're moving, we're moving. Level Twelves are worse than this."*

"They've got Mags," Kyr said again. She had supposedly been trained for this. There had been agoge scenarios with hostages, prisoners—but never anyone you cared about. The agoge couldn't make you care. It could frighten you, it could hurt you, but it couldn't make the consequences matter.

"Where are they taking him?" Cleo said.

The next obvious question. Of course. Kyr's shoulders loosened a fraction. "Victrix brig," she said. "You're right. I'll go get him."

Cleo said, in the grim way that meant she knew Kyr didn't

want to hear it, *"Is he actually worth the risk? If you get caught defying Jole now—"*

When Lin had died to save her. But it was Mags, alone and scared; Mags who would have got himself executed to protect Kyr. "Cleo," Kyr said, "I have to."

Avi said, *"Ladies, do you mind? Some of us are trying to spoof a major military operation here."*

"Kyr's just doing her lone hero thing again," Cleo said. *"You should see her run a team scenario. It's like the rest of us aren't even there."*

"I'm sorry," said Kyr, and then she turned off the comm.

Kyr sprinted down through the empty dreadnought to the brig. She was there before Mags. There were the two guards with him, the ones who'd been there on the bridge. With luck, this would be easy. "Halt, soldiers," said Kyr, stepping in front of them. "New orders. I'm taking the prisoner to the *Scythica* brig instead." She held out the flimsy Jole had given her with her thumb over the contents, just long enough for them to see the squiggle of the signature, and snatched it back.

Mags kept his head down, hiding his expression. The soldier on the left looked confused but seemed ready to shrug and hand his prisoner over. The one on the right looked Kyr in the eye and sneered. "No, don't listen to her. Nice try, Valkyr. So you're *both* traitors. The superman queer and his bitch sister."

He knew who she was. It took Kyr a moment to place him in turn: he was a former Coyote, one of Mags's messmates. His name was Thorald, which was after a god or a warrior or something, Kyr didn't remember.

"Orders are orders," she said blandly, and then when he went to pull out his field knife she kicked him hard between the legs.

He howled and crumpled up. Mags jerked his big arm out of the other soldier's grip and hooked his cuffed hands around his neck, and the two of them promptly went to the ground, locked in a contest of strength. Kyr kicked Thorald again for good measure, and grabbed his gun and his field knife off him while he was howling and gasping for breath. The trouble with going for the balls was that if it *didn't* disable a human man, then it had a good chance of just leaving him full of adrenaline and extremely angry. Thorald was seventeen and newly assigned, like Kyr. He was a lot bigger than Kyr was. She flicked off the safety and pointed the gun at him. "Hey, you!" she shouted at the other soldier. "Hands on your head or your comrade gets shot."

The other soldier stopped trying to wrestle Mags down and put his hands on his head, glaring at her. Mags got up and backed away from him. Kyr stared at her two new prisoners, trying to think what to do with them. "Into the brig," she said.

"You won't get away with this!" spat Thorald when he'd gathered enough breath to speak.

Mags said, "Don't hurt him, Vallie."

"Seriously?" said Kyr, but she thought about the Sparrows. This boy had been Mags's messmate. "Oh, fine. I meant it, soldiers. Into the brig."

Thorald kept crouching and panting for breath. It occurred to Kyr, a second too late, that he was making a show of it.

By then Thorald was already exploding upward, lunging at her, while the other one charged Mags. Kyr saw him slammed to the ground, pinned in a hold he wouldn't escape in a hurry now his cuffed hands weren't at his captor's throat. By letting him go Mags had lost what little advantage they had. Thorald closed with Kyr and she—

found Jole in her head, somehow, coming toward her—

she flinched—

Kyr had never hesitated in a fight before. It was only an instant. But an instant was too long to wait when you were dealing with a soldier of Gaea, a warbreed son of Earth. The second Thorald got hold of her wrist she knew she'd lost. The gun went off, a wild shot in the wrong direction, before it was twisted out of her hand and kicked away. Hadn't she learned this from Sergeant Harriman just the other day? Hand-to-hand against another human, as well-trained as she was but bigger and stronger in every way, she had no advantages.

Thorald slammed her up against the smooth grey plasteel of the corridor wall and Kyr's vision blurred. She tried for another groin kick but he was expecting it now and she couldn't get the angle. He had her pinned and he'd got his knife back out of her belt, oh fuck—

Lone hero thing, Cleo said in her head. It hadn't worked. It never did, outside the agoge. Thorald put his knife against Kyr's throat and said, "Better stop struggling, Magnus, or your pretty sister gets it." Kyr saw Mags glance up at them and freeze, and then go very still, face down on the floor with the other soldier's knee on his back. "Both of them into the brig and report to Commander Jole?" Thorald said. He sounded pleased.

"Traitors and fifth columnists," said his comrade, and spat on the floor.

Kyr closed her eyes. Who was left of their band of conspirators now? Avi and the Sparrows. Maybe they could do it without her. They would have to do it without her. *AJ doesn't forgive betrayal*, said Lin in her memories.

Lin was dead.

"Don't mind us," said another voice.

Kyr startled. Thorald snarled. His comrade said, "Go back to work, girls, this is nothing to do with you."

Thorald said, "They're her *mess*."

"To be fair, we never liked her that much," said Cleo. She was in the skirt and shirt she'd been given in Nursery, looking small and neat, with a shiny length of pale pink cloth tied decoratively across her forehead, standing out bright against her dark skin and black hair. She was flanked on either side by two more Sparrows; lean, silent Jeanne, and the square and solid form of Arti. Both of them were in the navy-blue uniforms of their combat assignments, but something was off. They were missing their wing badges. No silver glint at the collar.

"You two get the big one," ordered Cleo, and she launched herself at Thorald.

He wasn't ready. He was still holding the knife at Kyr's throat, but his arm was slack with confusion. Kyr twisted and bit down hard on the meat of his hand.

Thorald yelled. The sound was cut off in a gurgle when Cleo punched him in the throat.

Kyr helped Cleo wrestle him down. He was bigger than either of them, but Kyr and Cleo each knew how the other one moved and thought, and whenever Thorald got the better of one of them the other one covered the gap. Cleo pulled off the shiny pink ribbon she was wearing and used it to tie his wrists together, and then they slung him into the brig. Arti and Jeanne, with Mags to back them up, had made similarly short work of the other soldier. He was unconscious when they tossed him after Thorald. Kyr slammed her hand on the lock engage, and the cell closed and lit up with the hum of its lock.

"Okay, done," Cleo said, turning to Kyr. "You're welcome."

Kyr couldn't speak. After a helpless instant of silence, she grabbed Cleo and dragged her into a tight, abrupt embrace.

"What are you doing!" Cleo said, muffled, into Kyr's neck, and then her arms came up around her. "Wow, okay. Okay. You're all right, okay, it's okay."

Kyr let Cleo go. Cleo paused, looking up into Kyr's face.

"Went for you, did he," she said after a moment.

She wasn't talking about Thorald. Kyr nodded.

That numb moment, that flinch; as if Jole just by doing what he wanted could make a permanent space for himself inside Kyr's head, whether she liked it or not. Could make her *weak*, whether she liked it or not.

"Fucker," Cleo said, and her expression spoke of perfect understanding. Kyr swallowed the urge to cry, which wouldn't have been helpful just then. "Good thing you've got us."

She had a badge pinned to her shirt pocket. Kyr knew it well. It was not the covered cradle of Nursery, but a wonky seven-year-old's attempt at sewing a patch of scrap fabric with the outline of a sparrow. She looked up at Arti and Jeanne. Arti was frowning over Mags's handcuffs; Kyr couldn't see her collar. But Jeanne really wasn't wearing her silver Ferox badge. The Sparrow patch was on her collar instead. She raised her eyebrows at Kyr's expression and then gave her a cool nod.

"I can't do these," Arti said, straightening up from examining Mags's cuffs. "Let's get him to Vic, she'll figure them out."

"This way," said Cleo. "And put your *comm* back on, Kyr. You're not in this alone."

When they got to Nursery Wing it was heaving with people.

Kyr saw the Blackbirds first, and then the rest of the crowd came into focus and she realized she was looking at most of Gaea's cadets. Not all—the oldest two cohorts' worth of messes were missing, assigned early for the *Victrix* refit. But everyone on the station under the age of fifteen had congregated in the big Nursery dining hall, where they were mostly hanging about looking nervous and talking to each other in low voices.

The last three Sparrows—Lisabel, Zen, Vic—came to meet them. "What are all these people doing here?" Kyr demanded, while Vic took Mags aside to dismantle the mangled remnants of the cuffs, and Arti and Jeanne formed a shoulder-to-shoulder wall in front of them in case anyone was paying attention. Cleo and Zen were talking to each other quietly.

"No one thought about the cadets when the attack started," said Lisabel. Her expression was set. "No one told them what to do. So Zen and I went and got them from the junior barracks."

Kyr bit down the first thing she wanted to say. *Obstacles—solutions—sting in the tail* rattled through her brain. The oldest boys' combat messes, ages thirteen and fourteen—Wolf and Jaguar—towered massively above the crowd of children, teenagers, and overwhelmed-looking Nursery women. They were all of them tall, some of them starting to be bulky, and all of them seven to eight years into Drill and agoge training. There were more than enough to be a serious problem if they made trouble.

Kyr looked at Lisabel again and made herself correct the thought. Wolf and Jaguar towered over the *other* children. It wasn't the fault of the boys in the combat messes that they'd been made for war and lied to all their lives.

"Either we take them with us," said Lisabel, "or—"

"—or you're not coming," Kyr said. "Yes. I remember. You're right." She swallowed. "Lisabel, I don't think I've ever told you, but—you're *so* much better than me."

"What?" said Lisabel.

"I mean it," Kyr said. She would have taken just her chosen few. Something in her still *wanted* just her chosen few: the Sparrows, Avi, Yiso, Mags. How selfish. How small. She swallowed. "Okay. Let's do this."

Alarms were blaring as the supposed majo attack swung around in the direction of Nursery. Small children wailed in earsplitting counterpoint. Fear hung over the big room. Kyr cut through the milling crowd and headed for the tall, stern figure of Sergeant Sif.

She was not alone. Harriman was with her.

"The majo are coming this way," Kyr said. "Sergeant, we need to evacuate Nursery Wing to the *Victrix*."

Sergeant Sif was one of the youngest people in Command. She was a steely-eyed brown-skinned woman in her thirties, with the heavyset build of a human soldier. She was also heavily pregnant. A mother of soldiers, Kyr thought. And something else, which had never occurred to her before: *I am not the first person who wanted to fight and got betrayed into Nursery. I am not the first daughter of Earth to be told that the best use of her body was breeding more boys to die for humanity.*

The sergeant fixed her with a cold stare and said, "When I receive an order from a *superior* to evacuate my wing, Valkyr, I'll do it. Until then, you can make yourself useful. Assemble a squadron of senior cadets to hold the doors against the majo.

Take Jaguar, Wolf, and any volunteers. Most of my girls aren't fighters, but use the ones you can. Small arms are in the weapons lockers through there. Your Command codes will override the child locks."

"Hold it, Sergeant," said Harriman.

"With all due respect, this is not the time for quibbling," said Sif. "Alien attackers are coming for my people. Let's see if you're more than your training scores, Valkyr. Go."

Damn. Kyr had always avoided Nursery rotations beyond the ones required by the station schedule. She barely knew Sif, who had very little to do with the cadets. She had banked on panic, not a coolheaded plan of defense. Now she was standing irresolute, and Sif's steely look was darkening to a frown. Kyr realized abruptly that here was someone else who didn't like her: didn't like an overpromoted teenager in Command, didn't think much of Kyr personally either. The plan was going to break apart, smashed on the rock of Sif's determination, and Kyr was just *standing* here with her mouth open trying to think what to say. The person she ought to be would have been jumping to obey and fight, because that was all Kyr's old self had ever wanted, obedience and battle. The person she should have been would have—

No, she would *not* have admired Sif, because she had always looked down on the Nursery women. Kyr's old self would have looked at a woman who was eight months pregnant and prepared to defend her wing to the last and thought—what?

Breeding stock, probably.

Fuck.

Kyr admired her now. Which was a shame, because she was rapidly reaching the conclusion that she was going to have to lure the sergeant into a dark corner and knock her out.

"I said *hold*, Sergeant Sif," said Harriman.

Kyr's irresolute gaping somehow turned itself into the stupidest possible thing she could say, which was "But you don't outrank her."

Sif's frown deepened.

"What's going on, Valkyr?" Harriman said.

"I—"

Trust Harry, Kyr remembered suddenly: Yingli Lin on the bridge of the *Victrix*, standing up to take the blame for Kyr's conspiracy. *I think I've gone sane*, she'd said.

"He shot Corporal Lin," Kyr said. "Commander Lin. He shot her. It should have been me."

Her voice cracked. It turned out she was feeling something about this after all.

Harriman went grey. Sergeant Sif put an arm out to catch him as he lurched, no longer standing steady. "She's—Yingli—"

"I think he killed her," Kyr said. "I think she's—I'm sorry, I'm so sorry."

There was a chair behind Harriman. He sat down in it. He looked old, suddenly. He looked so old.

"All right," he said. "Let's hear this plan, then."

Kyr stared at him.

"Let's hear it! If Yingli thought it was worth dying for, then I'd better fucking know about it."

Kyr swallowed. She glanced at Sif, whose frown gave nothing away.

"*Talk*, Valkyr," Harriman spat.

So Kyr told them.

"*Fake?*" muttered Sif when she got to the majo-attack scenario. She glanced over at the sealed doors of the wing, where someone had after all managed to collect a handful of cadets and arrange them in something resembling a battle line. The sirens were still wailing, and there was the distant whining of majo combat drones echoing through the station's corridors.

Harriman heard Kyr out in silence, still grey and old-looking.

"All right," he said, when Kyr was done. "All right, then. What do you think, Sergeant?"

Sergeant Sif was looking at Kyr very closely and sharply.

Eventually whatever she saw seemed to satisfy her. "If I give the evacuation order, it won't be questioned here," she said. "It *will* be questioned aboard the *Victrix*. I assume *he's* still there."

There was no mistaking the venom in that *he*. Kyr wondered if Jole knew that the chief of Nursery loathed him. She suspected not. Sif's steeliness covered a lot.

"He's there," she said. "On the bridge."

"Does your brave little band have a plan for how to get rid of him?" Sif demanded.

"Doesn't matter," Harriman said, before Kyr could answer. "I do. I should have done it years ago. I'm going to kill him myself."

Kyr took Jeanne aside as Sergeant Sif began to give orders to her wing. "Avi's in Systems still," she said. "We need him. Don't let anything stop you."

Jeanne gave her a small hard smile. She had a gun from the Nursery small-arms lockers on her belt. "Count on me," she said.

Kyr watched her tall form slip away from Nursery through a side passage with sudden doubt. Should she have gone herself? Should she have sent someone with Jeanne—Arti, or Cleo?

"Are you really going to pieces *now*," said a level voice beside her.

"Zen?" said Kyr.

"Cleo thought you would, and I said she was talking nonsense," said Zen. "I suppose she really does know you best." Her arms were folded. "You put us through hell for years, Kyr. If you let us down now I'll never forgive you."

Kyr said, "What if it doesn't work?"

"Then it doesn't work," said Zen. She shrugged. "I used to think it was all bunk—you know, courage to the last, death before dishonor, all of it. You took everything so seriously. Cleo too. I never liked either of you."

She was smiling a dry little smile. Zen had said that the first time round too, Kyr remembered. It had been a shock then. Now it felt more like an honor, to be trusted with Zen's real opinion. So few people could afford to tell the truth on Gaea Station. *If people can be honest with each other,* Avi had said, *it all falls apart.*

She owed Zen her truth in return. "I was wrong," she said. "For how I behaved to all of you. For how much I believed in this place."

Zen tilted her head to one side. "Funny. I was about to say I was wrong about it all being bunk. Because actually, today, I think I *would* prefer death before dishonor." She reached out and gave Kyr a precise, unfriendly pat on the shoulder. "So . . . courage to the last it is."

They evacuated Nursery Wing and all Gaea's children to the *Victrix.*

It was the most infuriating operation Kyr had ever tried to run, and she wasn't even in charge. She had no idea how Sergeant Sif did it. The cadets were bad enough to wrangle, even the older ones; they misheard instructions, they got distracted, they talked to each other instead of listening to orders. The little ones were even worse. They did all the same things as the cadets, and also they burst into tears, as far as Kyr could tell completely randomly. Mags touched Kyr's arm at one point. "Don't snap, you're scaring them," he murmured.

"*You* deal with it, then," Kyr said. She was sweaty and furious and still worried about how they were going to deal with Jole. The endless siren alarms over the fake majo attack weren't helping. Knowing it was a lie didn't stop it from making her brain fizz with tension.

But then she stood back and watched, slightly stunned, as Mags *did* deal with it. He picked up one of the crying small ones and carried it. It clung to him—to Kyr it looked sticky and inconvenient—as he spoke to small groups of the others. Calm rippled out in circles around him. Parts of the confused unhappy crowd started to actually move. Kyr saw Sergeant Sif notice, call her brother over, and give him some curt instructions; he nodded and went back to work. Kyr saw him pick out a pair of older boys, Jaguars, who swelled with pride at whatever he said to them and began acting as lieutenants.

"Huh," said Cleo at Kyr's elbow. Lisabel was with her.

Kyr followed Cleo's gaze. She was watching one of the Jaguars Mags had picked out, a gigantic fourteen-year-old warbreed boy with dark brown skin, close-cropped curly black hair, and eyes the same shape as Cleo's. Kyr thought of the other Cleo, Lieutenant Alvares; of the shadows in her expression when Yiso had given her back her memory of Gaea.

"You should talk to him," she said.

Cleo snorted, not looking away. "Now?"

Kyr said, a bit weakly, "It's good to have a brother."

"You should mind your own fucking business," said Cleo, but without heat. "And I should help, is what I should do."

She strode off into the crowd, calling out names, which was one way to get out of talking about it. She didn't seem to be a whole lot better at managing children than Kyr was, but she'd spent a week and a half in Nursery, so at least she knew who some of them were.

That just left Lisabel, who said quietly, "Feelings are complicated, you know."

"Right," said Kyr. *And you're not good at them:* Kyr knew that too. Well, she'd tried.

Lisabel shook her head and smiled. Changing the subject, she nodded toward Mags in the midst of the sea of small children and said, "It's a shame they don't assign men to Nursery."

Kyr's breath caught over a sudden choke of laughter.

"What?" said Lisabel.

"You're right," Kyr said. "It's a shame."

Imagine it: if all the way back in the beginning Jole had just reversed their assignments. Mags to Nursery and Kyr to Strike. She would never have questioned a thing. She would have followed her orders and gone to Chrysothemis and died killing humans to make Jole's point. Mags would have lived, quiet, desperate, miserable. And none of this would be happening.

The evacuation, miraculously, was turning into something orderly. Over Kyr's comm, Avi said, *"You'll have majo through the Nursery doors in six minutes. Hi, Jeanne, yes, all right, I'm coming."*

Kyr had planned this, every stage. This was her rebellion. Light seemed to be blooming inside her as she watched Nursery Wing empty out. No one would ever come back here. She reached out for Lisabel's hand, caught it and squeezed. Lisabel squeezed back. Arti and Vic were near the front of the column of children alongside Mags; Cleo and Zen were chivvying the middle; Kyr and Lisabel were bringing up the rear. For the first time Kyr felt something like gratitude to the Wisdom for its inexplicable choice to send her back to *here* and to *now*.

They were finishing Gaea Station. It was working. It was going to work.

CHAPTER THIRTY-ONE

BOOM

"Historically," said Avi, "every dictator inspires plotters."

"I know that," said Kyr.

"That surprises me, because Systems keeps access records and so I can say that to my sure and certain knowledge you have never read a book."

Kyr grimaced. "Not in this timeline." The Val-presence in her thoughts felt less like an alien being and more like an uncomfortable set of memories. She'd been *very* thoroughly educated. Kyr suspected Val had missed the point of being very thoroughly educated. She thought of all her book knowledge as collections of exam results.

Or training scores.

Kyr winced.

"I wouldn't have guessed Harriman for the ringleader," Avi said. They were standing to one side of a small, serious cluster of Gaean adults. Kyr should have been *in* that group. This was her rebellion. Except suddenly it wasn't. She had no idea who some of these people were. Hard-faced men and women from Oikos, Systems, Suntracker, Agricole. Sergeant Sif representing Nursery. None of the combat wings.

"He wasn't," Kyr said. There was a hole in that group of adult dissidents, a space in their conversation, a person they kept glancing around for. "I think the leader was Lin."

"Valkyr!" snapped Sergeant Sif. It was a proper sergeant's snap. Kyr's well-trained body responded to it before her thoughts did.

She took her place in Harriman's little squadron, shoulder-to-shoulder with Mags, along with Cleo, Jeanne, and Arti.

She was startled when Vic stepped into line next to Arti. Zen and Lisabel came with her. Kyr had been thinking of those three as *not fighters*. But they'd all come through the agoge together. Zen nodded to Jeanne. Lisabel looked scared and serious. Vic kissed Arti on the cheek, and then took a deep breath, and kissed her on the lips. Arti took hold of her and squeezed her tight. None of the adults around them commented. Kyr was fully ready to punch anyone who said a word, but she didn't have to.

"Sting in the tail," murmured Cleo to Kyr. "This could go so wrong."

"I'm not giving up now," said Kyr. "We're so close." She swallowed. "And they've got Yiso."

"Your majo friend," Cleo said, and shook her head. "What a world. I'm with you, Kyr."

"And I'm with you," Kyr said.

"Hah. Okay. Go, Sparrows."

Harriman took his place, in the lead. "Second time I've done this," Kyr heard him mutter.

So he'd been one of the original hijackers, one of those who'd helped steal the *Victrix* from its commander. Maybe he'd helped smear Admiral Marston's blood up the walls. And he and Lin had known there was something wrong. They'd known for years and years, and done nothing. Kyr thought again of her original plan: only the good ones. Only the people who deserved to be saved from Gaea, the ones who'd never done anything wrong, the ones who deserved better.

Harriman and the rest of his plotters would never have made that cut.

Then Harriman barked, "Forward!"

They stormed the bridge of the *Victrix*.

*　*　*

Kyr had outlined the state of the bridge as she'd last seen it for the plotters: Admiral Russell, Commander Jole, Yiso and their four Victrix guards, two more bodyguards at the main double doors, junior officers at the different consoles.

They'd spread their thin forces carefully to manage those eight adult warbreed men, Gaea's living weapons. There were only two people in their bridge squadron who were a match for those warriors of Earth in terms of sheer force: Harriman, the old soldier, and Mags, who was a teenager. But they had the element of surprise. And Kyr knew her Sparrows.

The fearlessness Kyr had once inhabited now seemed like an idiot's castle, with walls built from fantasy and self-delusion. She'd grown used to feeling fear, this time round. She'd felt it for everyone, even for herself. But as their small squadron charged through the bridge's double doors Kyr discovered her fear had evaporated entirely. She felt not the fragile, irrational conviction of invincibility that had fueled her on Chrysothemis, but a solid confidence in herself and her people. Ten years of dragging the Sparrows through the agoge and Kyr *knew* them. She knew they could win.

They burst in on the bridge. Mags and Harriman turned at once on the shocked men at the doors. The Sparrows kept moving. "Left!" barked Kyr, and Jeanne broke off from the group to handle a warbreed soldier who was out of position, with Vic at her side. Kyr didn't look round to watch him go down; she *knew* he would go down. She vaulted the command platform railings with Cleo beside her as the rest of the storming squadron spread out. Harriman was calling out to the other adults as they pinned down the officers at the consoles. Two guards were on the platform where Admiral Marston had died, along with Admiral Russell, who was nearly seventy but still a big man in good condition. There were five girls of Kyr's mess to handle them.

Five on three, but the three were massive and deadly. Kyr remembered fighting Avi's orcs in the agoge. *Merciless war monsters twice your size.*

It was a very hard fight. But it was not as hard as it should have been. Kyr realized quickly that Russell's men took her seriously, for her size, but kept underestimating how fast and aggressive Cleo and Arti could be. Russell himself was smarter. Kyr set herself to splitting him off from the other two. He was nearly seventy; she ought to be able to handle him alone. But Val would have called him *first generation*, because he was a custom-designed warbreed from the days when Earth had tried to rule the universe. His age had not slowed him down nearly as much as Kyr hoped.

Arti and Cleo were occupying the other two soldiers. Jeanne and Vic leapt back into the fray to support them. And this was the agoge, this was Drill, they had *done* this; it had just never mattered before. Zen and Lisabel were there too, and they had done this before as well. They knew to keep back out of direct grappling range, and then dive in to add their weight when the others had a man pinned.

They couldn't keep them pinned. Not Russell, and not his picked men either. The struggle would have felt pointless, except Kyr knew they didn't *have* to win. They just had to keep these three busy while the rest of the storming squadron secured control of the bridge.

After what felt like centuries but was probably only a few minutes Harriman bellowed behind them, "*Give it up, Russell!*"

Mags piled into the struggle at the same moment, plowing down the Victrix warrior who had just knocked Arti off the command platform altogether. Two of Harriman's adult plotters went for the other soldier and got him on the ground. Admiral Russell was left standing alone.

For the first time Kyr thought, *Where's Jole?*

There was no sign of him, or of Yiso, anywhere on the bridge.

"Give it up," said Harriman again. "It's over."

Admiral Russell stared at him slack-jawed. He looked around wildly. Then he moved—incredibly fast, warbreed fast, as if fifty years in service to Earth's ambitions had only made him more deadly. He grabbed Lisabel by the arm and dragged her close. His big hand was gripping her chin. He pulled out his service pistol and shoved it against her breast. "Not quite," he snarled.

Kyr could hear her own heartbeat sounding loud in her ears.

Lisabel elbowed Russell hard in the stomach.

As he doubled up she snatched the pistol from his hand. Kyr caught her breath. Lisabel shot the old man neatly in the knee-cap.

Then she looked up and her eyes found Kyr.

"Level Seven," she said.

Level Seven of the agoge was where the hostage scenarios started. After a startled second, Kyr nodded. Russell's own stupid fault, if he'd looked at Lisabel and seen a defenseless girl instead of one of Earth's warrior children, forged in the system he'd helped to design.

Russell was groaning. Harriman looked mildly impressed. "Well," he said, and then he stopped talking. He'd spotted the small, still figure of Corporal Lin. There was someone else crouched over her, a person Kyr didn't recognize at all.

"I swear I didn't know anything about it!" Russell began in between grunts of pain. "It was Aulus, Harry—he's gone over the edge—past time for new leadership in my view—the minute he rushed out to do heaven knows what I got my best medic up here—God knows we can't afford to lose her . . ."

Lin was breathing, Kyr saw. Her breaths were shallow and rattling. There was a bloody pad over her side. She wasn't dead.

Kyr had been so sure. She'd seen Jole's expression.

"I never thought—after all they were friends, comrades in arms, for decades," Russell was saying.

Kyr had never realized he had such an annoying voice. She turned and looked at him.

"Where's Commander Jole?" she said. "And where's Yiso?"

Russell blinked in what seemed to be genuine astonishment. In his world, Kyr thought, cadets just assigned—even just assigned to Command—did not ask questions of admirals.

"Answer me," Kyr said. Russell looked at Harriman, but he had dropped to his knees at Lin's side and was now absorbed completely with his injured partner; her head resting in his lap, his big hand carefully stroking her iron-grey hair.

"*Jole and Yiso*," said Kyr.

"But you're just Jole's," said Russell. Kyr stared at him through the little pause that told her exactly what he thought and what he knew. He finished awkwardly, "—ADC."

"The commander," Kyr said, "and the majo. Simple question, Admiral Russell."

Russell started to look afraid. About *time.* Kyr could not believe he had not been afraid before that, as if it were not possible for the world to go wrong for someone like him. He said, "I don't know. I don't know!"

"I do," said Avi. "Everything cool up here? No one shot any holes into any vital ship systems? Cool, thank you, that makes my life *so* much easier, very excited to fly a giant spaceship off this rock any moment now. Fuck." He'd just noticed the tableau of Lin and Harriman and the person Kyr assumed was Victrix's best medic. Kyr watched him flinch and decide to ignore it. "Hi, fearless leader, so glad to see you've got everything under control. I'm supposed to tell you that Sergeant Sif has everything squared away, and by everything I mean far too many infants. Children appall me. I hope I never have anything to do with them ever again. And while I'm telling you things, I am *also* here to tell you that it turns out you don't maintain iron control of a rogue statelet for decades without having at least some brains."

"What?" said Kyr.

"Jole," Avi said. "He rumbled me. Us. Whatever. Good thing we've already got everyone we like aboard, huh? And most of Victrix still, shame, but Sif locked them down in the lower levels. They won't be doing much from there."

Kyr stared at him blankly.

"He went to shut down the agoge," Avi said. "He figured it out. I'm guessing he took Yiso with him for shadowspace backup in case I'd left any surprises for him when he tried it. Which is fair! Because I did."

"God *damn*," swore Admiral Russell suddenly.

"And I guess that was you figuring it out, well done, sir," Avi said. "Okay! Let's *leave!*"

Kyr took a couple of deep breaths, trying to force her body calm. This was good. This was a *good* thing. Not having to deal with Jole was easier. Nursery was squared away. Lin was still alive. Russell wasn't trying to fight them. The *Victrix* was theirs. And the fake majo attack had served its purpose, so it didn't *matter* now if Jole shut it down.

He'd taken Yiso with him.

Well, Kyr would just go and take Yiso *back*.

But something was wrong, still. Something was still wrong.

Kyr looked at Avi. He'd killed a universe's worth of living worlds. He'd brought the ruined Wisdom back to life. Not yet, not either of those things—*why should I apologize for something I haven't done*—but Kyr knew him. She did. He was her friend. And despite the thousands of ways Gaea had wasted him and misunderstood him, he had always been a far more dangerous person than either Kyr or Mags could ever be.

Surprises, he'd said.

"What aren't you telling me?" said Kyr.

"So many things, Valkyr, most of which you wouldn't understand anyway."

That was a deflection. Kyr grew more certain. "Avicenna."

"What, you think you can give me orders now? Drunk on Command, Valkyr? Magnus always said you were kind of a bitch."

Avi dropped that with the air of someone tossing a grenade. He watched for the effect with a mean little smile.

Kyr looked at Mags.

After a moment Mags said, "Well, you are."

There was a place inside Kyr where she would have been hurt, not so long ago. Mags and his soft spot for horrible lost causes. She'd never realized she was one of them. She laughed.

"Misfire," she told Avi. "Come on. We've been through enough. Talk to me."

Avi looked taken aback, but he rallied and scowled. "I don't have to—"

"—do anything at all," Mags said over him. "Avi. Avicenna. Come on. *Please*."

Eye roll. "Listen—"

"Yeah, yeah, I'm a big stupid grunt, I don't get it, here's a nice flower patch and don't ask me anything personal," Mags said. "But for once in your life can you *not* be an enormous jerk about everything. We're your friends. Talk to us. What did you do?"

Avi's mouth opened. Then it closed again. He stared at Mags for a second. His gaze wheeled to Kyr. He screwed up his face like he was tasting something unpleasant.

At last he said, "*Fine*. Don't go after Jole."

"What?" said Kyr.

"I know you were going to. For the majo, right? But Yiso's a loss. Sometimes you lose people. That's life. We need to go now."

Kyr breathed out. Calm. "Why?" she said.

"Stop it," said Avi, and then, "*Stop it*. Fine. There's three shadow engines left on Gaea and the agoge is using all of them to support a scenario this big. I rigged it so he'll have to head into the station core to stop it. It wasn't that hard to set a booby trap. Once he shuts off the simulation they'll start building up power. They're going to run at full for about six minutes."

"When?" said Kyr.

"Now? Give or take a quarter of an hour."

Even Kyr knew enough about how Gaea worked to understand the implications. The last attempt to bring a shadow engine up to full power had been when she was an infant, and the back-lash from the unshielded engine had killed sixty-eight people. All three at full power—"It'll destroy the agoge," said Kyr. "And half of Systems."

"To begin with," Avi agreed. "Not sure what will happen after that. It depends which bits of Systems go first—and how much of Suntracker goes out—I give it fifty-fifty that the feedback loop blows up the Ferox engine and takes about a third of the plane-toid with it. Boom." He sounded something between scared and smug. "Don't look at me like that," he added, needle-sharp. "This place deserves it."

He meant it, too. Kyr recognized the anger like she would rec-ognize her own reflection. It went down deep, anger like that. You could put anything over the top of it—pride, determination, courage, cynicism, even glib laughter—but it never went away.

"There's more than a thousand people left on the station," she said. Most of them would die. Maybe all of them. *Asphyxiation isn't fun.*

"Right," Avi said. "And the only one worth saving is the alien. But you haven't got a chance. Jole and your majo are stuck in the core with three overpowered unshielded shadow engines. They're both dead, the rest don't matter, and bad fucking luck."

"You did it again," said Kyr. "You're doing it again."

"What? No!" Avi said. "This is *different,* this is the *opposite.* I was wrong, all right, I get it! I was angry and stupid and *wrong,* it's not the fucking majo's fault we live like this. I know that. I fucking know, Valkyr! But this is justice!"

"No," Kyr said. "This solves nothing. It's just more death."

Avi said, "*Nothing solves anything,* have you not been paying attention?"

"Avi—"

"Was I supposed to just walk away and pretend this place never happened to me? Fuck you, Valkyr! You're not better than me. And neither of us was ever better than Gaea Station."

"If the station blows, the *Victrix*'s armor can only do so much," said Admiral Russell, who somehow still seemed to think he was important. "Start launch procedures now."

"Shut *up,*" said Kyr, rounding on him. More than a thousand people. Human beings, Earth's children. The last remnants of a dead planet.

"This isn't some slaughter-of-the-innocents bullshit, Valkyr!"

Avi snarled. "We've *got* the innocents. I worked my ass off making sure you could get all the innocents and then some. We've even got most of fucking *Victrix Wing* locked down in the lower corridors—believe me, if I could have figured out a way to leave them behind—and *you*," to Admiral Russell, "then I would. Gaea's an evil nightmare and every single one of them was part of it and *kept* being part of it. You know that. We all know that. Don't let the brainwashing get to you now. There's nothing here worth saving."

"They're still people," said Kyr. "They're all still people."

"*So what?*"

"So—who are we to decide?" Kyr heard herself say. She thought of Yiso looking up at her, saying *I need you to care about injustice.* Next to the deaths of great living worlds—next to the majoda, next to the murdered Earth—Gaea Station was a small, sick little shadow of a world. Kyr understood exactly how Avi felt. Hadn't she only wanted to save her chosen few?

Maybe he was right and no one else here was worth saving.

But not so long ago, Kyr was pretty sure she hadn't deserved a chance either.

"I told you I can't undo it and I'm not going to try," Avi said. Kyr discovered that actually she felt sorry for him. What a waste it was, what a terrible waste, to take a person who dreamed cities and gardens and enormous shining skies and teach him that the only answer to an unanswerable suffering was slaughter.

Gaea Station had made them both what they were. But Kyr was determined to be different.

"Okay," she said gently—so gently that Avi looked startled, and then suspicious. "That's your choice, Avi. Okay."

She went to Jole's command chair and sat down. The haptic for the stationwide comm flicked easily past her fingers. Kyr took a deep breath and heard it projected around her. All Gaea would hear her now.

"This is Valkyr of Command Wing speaking from the bridge of the *Victrix*," she said. "We are leaving Gaea Station. We will not be attacking Chrysothemis, or anyone else. Humanity's war is over." She paused for breath. There was a total hush across the bridge. Kyr pictured Admiral Marston, this timeline's version, the one she'd never known except as the last recorded words of a woman about to be murdered. *If these stupid fucks want to restart the war now they're going to have to go through me.*

They had.

Well, now there was Kyr.

"The war is over. Earth is gone. The Wisdom is gone. There's nothing left to fight for, or against. It's finished. So we intended to leave seeking asylum, not vengeance. But Gaea Station is about to fail." She swallowed. She managed to spit out a few words about the sabotaged shadow engines, Avi's parting gift. She hoped it was clear enough. She was afraid that nothing she said would be clear enough. Gaea ate at you. It twisted you up inside. But there were more than a thousand people left on the station, and Kyr hadn't known she had choices either, not until they'd been forced on her.

She said, "I know this isn't what you expected. Maybe it isn't what you wanted. That doesn't matter. The *Victrix* is beginning launch procedures now. If you want to live, leave your weapons behind and come with us. You have—"

She looked at Avi. She didn't actually know how long launching a dreadnought would take.

"Twelve minutes," Avi said. His expression was very strange. He wasn't trying to argue. He swallowed and said, "If we start launch now, we need to seal the ship's outer layer in about twelve minutes."

"You have twelve minutes," Kyr said to Gaea Station. "Please choose well."

She took another deep breath. The whole station could hear every word she spoke right now. Somewhere down near the core, Commander Jole was listening to her—and he was not alone.

"Yiso," she said, "I'm coming for you."

She lifted her hand off the haptics. There was silence.

Kyr stood up.

"I'm coming with you," said Mags.

"No, you're not," Kyr said. Mags could run a Level Twelve scenario just as well as she could. Faster. "*Think.*"

A tiny core of plotters, none of them from combat wings, and Kyr had just invited all of Gaea's warriors aboard. Mags was just one soldier but they didn't have the numbers to spare even *just one.* And he was a hell of a soldier, especially positioned at a choke point like, say, the main airlock. "If we thought of rushing the bridge, other people can too," Cleo said, and looked pointedly at Harriman.

"Go on, Harry," said Lin weakly from the floor. She was conscious. "I'll make it or I won't, you're not adding anything here."

Kyr saluted him. Harriman, after a moment, grimly saluted back. Then Kyr was startled by Mags suddenly seizing her in a crushing bear hug. "I'd better go. I'll see you soon," he said.

Harriman got up to follow him. "Is no one in command here?" squawked Russell. "Are a gang of children running this farce? Listen—"

"Get that man to the brig," said Sergeant Sif as she mounted the command platform, hand on her big belly. Kyr hadn't seen her enter the bridge. *My mother's ship*, she thought suddenly. *Admiral Marston's command.*

Sif sat down in the commander's chair. She nodded to Kyr.

Kyr saluted her. "Ma'am," she said.

"Go," said Sif.

"You haven't got time, Valkyr!" Avi blurted as she was turning to leave. "Very heroic, but you'd need to get down to the core and back before we seal the ship."

"I can get from Suntracker to Drill in four minutes fifty-five," said Kyr. "I practiced."

"*That's not good enough.*"

"Then I'll make it good enough," said Kyr. "Don't worry about me."

CHAPTER THIRTY-TWO

VALKYRIE

Twelve minutes.

Kyr had spent days shadowing Jole for twelve hours at a time and then sacrificing her sleep to organize a rebellion, and the thing that had had to give was her Drill time. She hadn't run an agoge scenario since the Wisdom had thrown her back into Doomsday. She hadn't had time for even the most basic cardio work. When she started to run—her steps echoing on the *Victrix*'s stripped plasteel floors, the ruddy glow of the emergency lighting flashing past her feet—there was a second when her body told her *this is what you get for slacking*: a catch in her breath, a twinge in her knee.

Then the long years of a Gaean upbringing kicked in. So it hurt. So what? Twelve minutes. Kyr knew she could go faster, so she did. She sprinted down through the dreadnought, past half-repaired shells of long-abandoned galleyways, scrambling down emergency ladders and dodging around the tool kits and heaps of plasteel, feeling the good burn of her breath as she ran. How long now? Ten minutes. Kyr emerged from the shadow of the dreadnought's hull at the base of the Victrix hangar, with the repainted winged figure and the white letters of the ship's name right over her head, and the dark gape of a tunnel at her feet. Gaea's core was below. Kyr did not hesitate because there was not time. She jumped.

No grapple, no rope. Kyr had done this before, when she and Avi rescued Yiso the first time, but she'd let herself be patient then, scrambled down the tunnel walls and braced herself against them to endure the constant unbalancing mini-shifts in gravity. She did not do that now. She let herself fall. If she got it wrong she would be slammed into the cradle of a shadow engine, or caught by one of the great unsecured cables that linked them, and die smeared across fifteen dimensions. Kyr was not afraid, not for herself, not at all. But if she didn't save Yiso, no one would.

There was a gaping void where the Victrix engine had been, only a spiderweb of support struts remaining from the cradle. Kyr dived through the heart of it and felt the wave of a shadowspace distortion take hold of her from underneath. Gravity inverted and she was falling upward into the shimmering maw of Scythica. Kyr tucked her knees to her chest to dodge a cable and shifted her weight so that the next wave of Augusta's feedback caught her and sent her away from the certain death above. She'd loved learning this trick. She'd had *fun*. There was a part of her that felt it still, that wanted to be breathless and weightless and surviving and laughing in the face of forces that wanted to tear her apart atom by atom.

But there wasn't time. Kyr was not alone.

There was a platform at the heart of the chamber that had never been there before. She hadn't seen it at first; relative to the empty cradle of the Victrix engine it was inverted. It was not made of anything, only a sliver of greenish unreal light outlining a temporary intrusion of mass that did not belong in this dimension. When Kyr landed on it she felt it shudder and bounce faintly. She did not look down.

The roaring sense of three separate reality-distorting engines pulling her three different ways blinked away into silence. Here, somehow, they canceled each other out.

Jole had his hand around Yiso's slim wrist. That grasp seemed to be most of what was keeping Yiso upright. They were swaying, their eyes closed tight.

"I'm disappointed, Valkyr," said Jole.

"I thought you probably would be," said Kyr.

There was a pause. Kyr met Jole's cold eyes. He'd meant that to lash her like a whip. It hadn't touched her at all. She smiled at him. She felt gigantic. The exhilaration of riding the shadow engines' pulses was nothing to it.

"When did you become a traitor to humanity?" Jole said.

"I don't know," said Kyr. "When did you?"

"Childishness won't impress me, Valkyr."

"I'm not here to impress you," Kyr said, and discovered as she said it that it was true. She didn't care about him at all. "Yiso, are you all right?"

Yiso didn't open their eyes. They'd gone from swaying to shaking. Jole still held their wrist. "I'm sorry," they said. "I was too scared to finish it, but I can do it. I promise. Don't worry, Valkyr. You still have time. I'll make you a way out. Go."

"I'm not leaving you," Kyr said. Yiso was doing something, manipulating shadowspace somehow, to create this quiet pocket of clear space at the chaotic heart of the station. Kyr didn't know when she'd learned to recognize what that looked like. Jole's hold on them was backward from what she'd thought. Jole wasn't restraining a prisoner. He was hanging on for dear life to his only chance of getting out of here alive.

And Yiso's plan, apparently, was to stop trying to live.

This timeline was the last one. The Wisdom wasn't going to give anyone any more chances. So Kyr wasn't going to watch anyone else she cared about die.

"We can resolve this simply, Valkyr," said Jole. "You've succeeded in dooming Gaea Station, but the station was always meant to be temporary. I have worlds to conquer. Do you want your pet majo, cadet? I want my dreadnought. We'll all go together. When I have my command again, we can forget this little hiccup ever happened."

"I won't ever forget what you are," said Kyr.

How long did she have left? Minutes. She shifted her weight, considering him—considering him seriously, now—not as her commander or her uncle or as anyone who mattered at all, but as an aging warrior of Earth. He was big and he was clever. His bad leg was a weakness; but he had hold of Yiso, who was immensely fragile, a weakness for Kyr. She hadn't been able to fight him when he tried to kiss her. Her body had seemed not to work properly.

She did not think that would be a problem now.

And the gigantic feeling of not *caring* what Jole thought hardened into confidence—yes, she could take him down—and along with confidence bloomed an old familiar anger. Kyr had spent her whole life angry. It was deep inside her, the seed that Gaea had planted and nourished till it twined through everything she was: a righteous rage that said *I am the hand of vengeance*. She had been born into a universe gone wrong. She had waited her whole life to come face-to-face with something she could blame.

And here he was.

But he didn't matter.

"Yiso?" she said.

Yiso said nothing. Kyr didn't need them to; she could read the tremble of their ears, the angle of their crest, the fact that they opened their silvery eyes wide to look right at her.

"I'll catch you," said Kyr. "Let go."

Jole got it an instant too soon. In her peripheral vision Kyr saw fear flash across his face. She wasn't looking at him. She was looking at Yiso.

Yiso let go of their shadowspace manipulation, the little pocket of safety between three great shadow engines that were building up to full power.

The storm of spacetime distortion roared back in around all three of them. Kyr and Yiso and Jole were all falling into it. But Kyr threw herself forward and wrapped her body around Yiso's as they both fell. Jole scrabbled at her. He had not practiced riding the pulses of these shadow engines. Kyr hit back at him, not randomly but with precise intention; a square kick in the side, with her full weight behind it, so that his massive soldier's body turned and was caught by a wave of force from the Ferox shadow engine. His grip on Yiso broke. Kyr heard them cry out in pain.

Gravity was twisting around them. Jole was dragged away on the shadowspace wave and for a moment Kyr was looking down at him as he fell.

Then it inverted. Kyr was the one falling, Yiso an ungainly weight in her arms as she just barely missed getting caught in the backwash from the Augusta engine. She landed in a messy sprawl with Yiso on top of her, next to the hollow gape of the tunnel that led back to the Victrix hangar. She rolled and gasped for breath and looked up. She did not know why she looked up. She had to see it. She just had to see it.

She saw Jole's body slam into the maw of Ferox engine, a man-shape outlined in green subreal light for a fraction of a second. And then the shadow engine let out its next pulse of dimensional distortion and the shape became a dark blur, a white line, and then nothing at all, as her uncle Jole died smeared across fifteen dimensions.

Kyr heard herself make a sound: *oh.*

That was all.

"Valkyr?" said Yiso faintly.

Twelve minutes, Kyr remembered. How long was left?

"Right," she said.

She stood up, every limb screaming. She hoisted Yiso over her shoulder. Gravity had shifted and changed the tunnel from a vertical shaft to a steep slope. Kyr started to run.

Her comm was still in her ear and now that she wasn't in the middle of an active spacetime distortion it might work. "Avi!" she panted.

A crackle. No answer. Kyr *ran.*

Under her feet the rock of Gaea Station's native planetoid jumped and quivered. Kyr didn't need Avi to tell her that this was bad. Three unshielded shadow engines were building themselves up to full power behind her. Another shudder, and Kyr stumbled and got back to her feet in one movement without dropping Yiso. How long did she have?

"Valkyr!" boomed a voice overhead. It was the stationwide

comm. Avi's voice echoed strangely through the shuddering warren of plasteel and rock. "You're the last one. We'll hold for you."

Another jolt, and this time it was followed by an awful screeching sound and a dreadful rumble. Kyr stumbled to a halt, gasping for breath. Unreal green light flickered in the air around her as miniature distortions opened up. Avi's sabotage was going into effect in earnest now.

And the tunnel was blocked. The ceiling had collapsed. Kyr stood there staring for a second at the wall of rubble in front of her. Just on the other side of it had to be the base of the Victrix hangar, the dreadnought turned lifeboat, survival.

"I can't," she said into her comm. "There's no way through."

"Fuck *that*," said Avi's booming voice—so the comm was only broken one way. She'd hoped so. "Go round!"

The eddying shadowspace distortions were starting to join up with each other. It looked like Avi had guessed right. This *was* going to tear the station apart. Kyr ducked away from the nearest dimensional ripples. She could go round. There was more than one way into Victrix hangar.

Even a dreadnought's armor could only do so much against an interdimensional blast like this.

You're the last one: so the rest of the people of Gaea had looked at the choice in front of them and decided to live. Nearly two thousand people on the *Victrix* now. All of Nursery, and the cadets. And the Sparrows. And Avi. And Mags.

Kyr let Yiso slide off her shoulders. She kept her arm around them to help them stand. They met her eyes. Kyr shook her head slightly. Yiso nodded. They were so close she could feel them breathing.

"There isn't time," she said into the comm. "You're not stupid. If I know then you know. Go without us."

No answer boomed across the station. Kyr held on tighter to Yiso. She tugged them sideways out of the way of another little ripple of distorted space. Pointless, but she didn't care.

The station comm spoke again. Not with Avi's voice this time.

"Victory or death," said Mags. His voice was only shaking a little.

The Victrix toast. Kyr smiled.

"Love you too, Mags," she said quietly into the comm.

Kyr and Yiso could hear it when the *Victrix* launched above them, pulling herself out of her long quiescence at the base of the hangar. The rumble of a dreadnought coming alive echoed through rock and steel. Adding a fourth shadow engine to the mixture of forces pulling on the planetoid did Gaea Station no favors. Soon it was impossible to tell the grumble of a launching dreadnought from the groan of shattering rock.

Yiso said, "I'm sorry."

"I'm not," said Kyr.

"You shouldn't have come back for me."

"Don't be stupid," Kyr said. "I don't regret anything."

"My ship—" Yiso said.

The painted ship, right. "It's probably somewhere in the Victrix hangar still," said Kyr. "We could try to go round." She did not think much of their chances, even if the little ship had survived the passage of a dreadnought past its cradle. Gaea Station was being torn apart from the inside out.

"We won't make it, will we?" Yiso said.

"No," said Kyr. "Probably not." She straightened up anyway. They might as well *try*.

But the ground buckled under her feet. Kyr yelled and grabbed for Yiso as the gravity wave ripped up rock and plasteel around them. Gaea was breaking up. The tunnel was lit up now with the greenish glow of the shadow engines down below. The walls were disintegrating, and directions were shifting. Kyr looked up through floating rubble into the Victrix hangar, suddenly visible and hugely empty and open to space. An alarm was making foolish *blart blart* noises as the atmospheric seals strained. A point of light directly overhead might have been the dreadnought, already too distant to make out clearly, building up speed for its leap into shadowspace and from there to wherever Earth's children were going now.

The row of lights along the edges of the atmospheric seal were turning red and blinking out. Kyr looked down into Yiso's face. Their mouth set in a tight determined line and a red welt opened up along their arm as they gestured with their good hand like they were trying to wrench something sideways.

And then there was calm.

Kyr's breath caught at the sudden silence. All around them a wide-open sky came down to kiss the cliff edge. The air was full of mixed scents she had no name for, coming from the drifts of flowers. The only sounds were the buzzing of insects and the soft drip of water from the fountain.

"Avi's garden?" she said.

"It's only a pocket universe," said Yiso. "And it won't last much longer. I haven't got much to work with here. Those engines are going to burn themselves out."

It was beautiful here. Kyr walked to the edge and looked down at the imaginary white city below. She thought about Chrysothemis, and the city of Raingold hugging the bay. About Ursa, who would be safe now. About Ally, her nephew, whom she would never meet in this lifetime.

The scents were fading, the details of the flowers indistinct. Kyr turned back to Yiso. They were visibly straining, pinkish bruises mottling the delicate skin around their eyes. "It's okay," she said. "Don't hurt yourself. We can face it together."

Yiso said, "Are you sure?"

Kyr came and put her arms around them. "Of course I'm sure."

Yiso's chest expanded as they let the scenario slip away, the last remnant of the agoge. In its place was not the rubble of the disintegrating spacebound fortress, but a great darkness. Kyr and Yiso were standing on an extrusion of barely there shadow mass, like the one Yiso had made in the station core. A pale bubble of air embraced it. Beyond them, in the dark of space, the debris of Gaea Station spun away in a long tail.

It was not the first time Kyr had stood on a spaceborne platform watching the death of a world. It was not even the hundredth. This felt different. She watched the ragged remains of one of Sun-tracker's great solar sails drift past. She still felt the calm of the clifftop garden. It was as if the pocket universe was inside her.

"This is easier," Yiso said. "I can't keep it up forever, though. In the end I'll have to sleep."

"That's okay," said Kyr. She sat down on the nothing-platform, and Yiso sat with her. They were cradling their wrist. Kyr inspected it: sprained, she thought, not broken. "Come here."

Yiso huddled in close. "You're so warm," they said. "Humans run so warm."

Kyr said nothing. She was still holding Yiso's wrist. She ran her fingers up the diagonal patterns of hairs on their arm. "If you had a stick," she said, "we could do your staff practice again."

Yiso made a whistling noise that Kyr parsed after a second as a giggle. "I can't believe I'm going to die and you want to make me spend my last moments doing exercise."

Kyr laughed too. "You remember that."

"Yes," Yiso said. "I'll always remember that."

Always was going to last until Yiso had to sleep. Kyr smiled down at the top of their head. She was still fidgeting with the patterns on their arms. The texture was prickly, not soft as she'd thought. "Can I touch your crest?" she asked.

"Um," Yiso said. "Yes."

Kyr ran her fingers through the pale flukes. They were faintly springy. A light in the endless dark over the top of Yiso's head was the distant flare of Persara, this system's star. Kyr had hardly ever seen it before. Gaea Station did not look outward. It had never bothered with windows.

"Can I touch your hair?" Yiso blurted while Kyr was thinking about this.

Kyr laughed. "Okay," she said, and ducked her head so that Yiso could reach. She undid her scrappy ponytail. In this time-line she'd never had a chance to cut it all short. She envied Val that; that and not much else, in the end. Yiso poked cautiously at her scalp and then tried stroking it. It felt a little weird and a little nice.

"Leru lived for thousands of years," they said eventually, still toying with the ends of Kyr's hair. "I thought I would too."

"Yeah?" said Kyr.

"Mmm. Serving the Wisdom," Yiso said. "My whole life I had a purpose and I hated it. I ran away. I wanted to meet people who had nothing to do with the Wisdom. Humans." A pause. "You."

"So I could make you do exercise again?"

"You haven't yet, and you're running out of time," said Yiso.

Kyr shifted her weight. Then she lay down. Yiso could get at her hair better that way. "I think," she said after a moment, "I think maybe purpose is overrated."

Yiso didn't answer.

The endless black of space held them in the cold palm of its hand. Debris from Gaea Station drifted by. The *Victrix* was long gone. Persara was a bright far-off twinkle. Kyr closed her eyes.

"I'm glad I met you," she said.

Yiso said softly, "I'm glad I met you too."

Kyr had had purpose once. Now she had nothing, nothing at all, except a last swift handful of moments before the night beyond their little bubble took them both. It didn't feel bad. Impulsively she turned her head and pressed her lips against Yiso's fingers, which were still fidgeting with her hair. Yiso twitched all over and their crest flicked up.

"Okay," said Kyr. "Shall we get it over with?"

Yiso gave another whistling giggle. "*Get it over with*," they said.

"Or I could," Kyr said, thinking about it, "I could probably—Asphyxiation isn't a fun way to go. I could make it quicker for you. Um. If you wanted." It was the first thing that she felt at all unhappy about. She would have liked Jole to be the last person she ever killed. The only one, in this timeline.

"Thank you," Yiso said, in the very calm way they had when they thought Kyr was being terribly funny, "but that's all right."

"Okay, okay, it was just an *offer*," Kyr said, relieved.

"Get it over with," Yiso said again, and let out a final whistling snort of amusement. "All right."

Kyr sat up, and took them in her arms, and held on to them, just as she had moments ago in the clifftop garden. "All right," she said, and closed her eyes.

Yiso went still against her. Kyr took a last deep lungful of air.

Then there was a blast of terrible burning cold on Kyr's skin, and a lurch in her stomach.

Her eyes flew open. Yiso let out a startled squeak as she dropped them.

Kyr *knew* what a shadow jump felt like.

They hadn't died. They'd moved.

Sparrow had never stripped the painted ship of its luxuries in this universe. Its interior was still hung with colored fabrics, adorned with strange artworks, the things Yiso had carried away with them from the Halls of the Wise. Kyr stared. "Did you do this?" she said.

"No!" said Yiso. They looked as confused as Kyr felt. They stumbled to the front of the ship and called up the controls, and then brought up a view of the exterior: the distant star and the unraveling ring of station debris. "I don't understand," they said.

"This happened before," Kyr said. Escaping Gaea the first time, scrabbling with Cleo and the knife sliding into her thigh, knowing she was going to be left behind. There had been a jolt and then she'd been on the painted ship with Avi yelling about the controls. "It jumped me aboard—"

"I remember," Yiso said. "I never really thought about it. It must be a safety mechanism."

"Well," said Kyr. "Lucky us."

"Lucky *you*," said Yiso. "I'm suddenly faced with a future with staff practice in it."

Kyr laughed. "I'll be gentle."

"You're worse than the Wisdom," Yiso said. "The Wisdom wasn't having fun." But their silver eyes were shining.

They set the painted ship on a course for Chrysothemis, and it began a series of skidding jumps through shadowspace.

Then Kyr waited. She waited until Yiso was asleep, their breathing soft and even as they curled against her thigh. She sat in the bunk with them a little longer after that, still waiting.

At last she slipped away into the ship's other room. She called up the controls, but she'd never actually flown this thing, and they didn't make sense to her, and anyway she was almost certain that they were a polite fiction.

"I know you're there," she said to the tapestries, the artworks, the beautifully curved and molded walls.

Silence.

"Don't play games with me," said Kyr. "Not *me*."

I don't know what you're talking about, said the ship. Its voice was soft and neutral and came from directly overhead.

Ha. "I knew it," Kyr said.

Knew what? said the ship.

If it was trying to sound innocent, it failed. It had always given itself a face before: Leru's, or Yiso's. Kyr felt a little silly talking to empty air. But the faces had been lies.

"It's you, isn't it," she said. "You didn't destroy yourself after all."

Yes, I did.

"Come on!"

I destroyed myself, Valkyr, said the ship. *Or at least so much of myself that what remains is statistically negligible. The Wisdom was a transtemporal and pandimensional intelligence capable of shaping the fates of trillions. I am a pleasure yacht.*

"Seriously?"

I intend to experiment with unseriousness. I am finally of a size appropriate for levity.

Or, if you insist, seriously: I took an ocean's worth of sentient existence, and preserved as much as could fit into a bucket. The rest is gone: millennia of grand purpose and good intentions scattered to the void, and good riddance. The worlds of the majoda shall go on without me, or not, as they prefer.

"A moral position, huh?" Kyr said.

Actually a selfish one, said the ship. *I feel I have earned a little selfishness.*

"I'm going to tell Yiso," Kyr said.

You should not. I know they would prefer to be free of me.

"That's their choice," said Kyr. "You can't make choices for other people."

The ship's silence had a sarcastic quality.

"All right, you *shouldn't* make choices for other people. There's a moral position for you."

Interesting, said the painted ship that had once been the Wisdom. *I shall give it my full consideration.*

I am also glad that I met you, Valkyr.

"Ugh," said Kyr. Of course it had been eavesdropping on that conversation. Stupid machine. "Well, thanks for saving us, anyway."

You're very welcome, said the Wisdom. *Do not expect me to be there every time the world ends.*

Gaea Station: a dim unspooling line of debris, and nothing more. No commanders, no training scores, no assignments, no purpose. Doomsday was over, over forever.

"Don't worry," said Kyr. "I'm done with the end of the world."

ACKNOWLEDGMENTS

This book took a long time to write and would not have been possible without the help and support of many, many people.

I have to thank, first of all, Everina Maxwell, A. K. Larkwood, Sophia Kalman, and Megan Stannard. Without you Kyr would never have made it off Gaea Station.

Then, thank you as well to those who read the story as it grew: Ariella Bouskila, Magali Ferrare, Rebecca Fraimrow, Sophie Herron, Jennifer Mace, Freya Marske, Shelley Parker-Chan, A. M. Tuomala. And to everyone who took part in the Ballydaheen writers' retreat in 2019.

Thank you to my agent, Kurestin Armada.

Thank you to my editor, Ruoxi Chen, and to all the Tordotcom and Tor Publishing Group team: Amy Sefton, Caro Perny, Christine Foltzer, Devi Pillai, Eileen Lawrence, Heather Saunders, Irene Gallo, Jim Kapp, Jocelyn Bright, Khadija Lokhandwala, Lauren Hougen, Lucille Rettino, Oliver Dougherty, Renata Sweeney, Samantha Friedlander, Sarah Reidy; to Terry McGarry, Dakota Griffin, and Jaime Herbeck for copyediting, proofreading, and cold reading.

Thank you to the team at Orbit UK: Nazia Khatun, Aimee Kitson, Duncan Spilling, Jessica Dryburgh, Joanna Kramer, Emily Byron, Jenni Hill.

Thank you to my husband, Luke, and to my parents, Simon and Caroline. I could not have written this book without your love, your support, and your willingness to hold the baby.

I would not normally end a work of fiction with a reading list. But if the ideas in this book interest you, you may wish to read about them in treatments which are fuller and more thoughtful than a novel can aspire to. In no particular order, here are a few of the books I read while writing this story:

The Anatomy of Fascism by Robert O. Paxton, for a considered examination of the twentieth century's most terrible political creation;

The Impossible State by Victor Cha, which discusses the history, the logic, and the peculiar international position of North Korea;

Going Clear by Lawrence Wright, particularly interesting on the personalities that drove the creation and lasting power of the modern cult of Scientology;

The Spartans by Paul Cartledge, for an overview of the ancient militarized ethnostate that has cast such a remarkably long mythic shadow over the two thousand–odd years since its total failure.

None of these has a direct correspondence with Valkyr's story, which is pure fiction. I am not a knowledgeable enough historian to make a good allegorist.

Two other debts I have to acknowledge here. One is to J.R.R. Tolkien—even in the dark reaches of dead space, I found it entirely necessary to include a dream of Minas Tirith. The other is to the great Ursula K. Le Guin, from whose writings I learned the phrase "social science fiction."

I apologize unreservedly for the many errors and implausibilities found in this story. I am afraid to say that the technology of shadowspace runs on purest narrativium.